Love Thy Neighbor

WINDMERE series – *book thirteen*

D1738671

Michelle Tschantré

Dedicated to:

… unexpected rewards from a kind gesture.

Preface

In Windmere Series, Book 1, "Laura's Big Win", the reader meets Laura Nessing and Ryan Williams; they are two people with deep emotional voids in their hearts caused by very different conditions, his loss of his wife and her absconded husband. The common thread is the place called WINDMERE, a former private estate, maybe with some magic included, but certainly with dynamic relationships as things evolve between Laura and Ryan; each is filling the void in the other's life, unsure about many things but sure in the growing love each has for the other. Some of the characters one meets in Book 1 also play parts in subsequent releases, such as Love Unexpected and Love Unlimited. As the series unfolds each book is a bit different from the circumstances of book 1, sometimes in how the main characters meet, quite often in their personalities and situations. Many times there is a secondary couple involved with each other and perhaps shading how the main characters react to each other. These are stories of how people meet and grow in their relationship with each other through a series of events. The characters vary from the stranded Laura with children to the dynamic Marti, from the wounded veteran Zach to his counterpart, the oppressed Katherine. There is the reclusive Margaret being thawed by a caring Kevin, and many more. The characters are different yet exist with every possibility of being as realistic as those situations which life presents all of us.

CONTENTS

Chapter One

New Neighbors

Slowly sinking, yet with no feeling of panic; breathing in spite of sensing he was somehow stifled, replete with the knowledge this was not real yet seemed very real, and then there was Maddie, the very Maddie he knew had died and left him alone as he once again reached out for her, knowing within himself he could not touch her. His eyes would open slowly and another day without her would begin. The girls would be up soon, seven year old twins Ally and Anna, lighting up his day as they did each day of this altered life. There was a history in Maddie's family of brain tumors, every second or third generation or so one would rear its ugly head and claim another victim. This time they really believed it could be stopped with one of the ultra cures out there somewhere, and the doctors did manage to slow it down, but trying to treat something with a long head start and hiding in an impervious lining is difficult at very best; the side effects of the "cure" take the final toll as much as the original problem. So it went with his beloved Maddie; she knew in spite of his denials of what was taking place within her, and consoled him as much as he tried to console her. In the end the only positive thing was speed; the end came quickly for her, two years ago now, two years in which he was both father and mother to his beloved daughters who very much reminded him of his loss with their copy cat looks of their beautiful mother. His thoughts often drifted back to the wonderful years he and Maddie had enjoyed together, the silly things enacted between them at times, playing like kids when they could, loving their daughters. He missed Maddie very much but did not dwell on the fact moment after moment, realizing that also was not to be done if he was to raise his daughters in some semblance of "normal" in a one parent home. He knew at times they also missed their mother, times when they sought and needed a woman's counsel but had to trust in their fathers male tinged wisdom instead.

Alan Behr rolled out of bed, fit and trim in his mid-thirties, standing just over six-two in his bare feet, and began this new day as he heard the music start up in the girls room. At times it seemed almost strange to him that they had opted to remain in one room when there was that spare bedroom one of them could have used to assert her independence. It would have worked out well had there been more children born to them, but that also was not to be; the bedroom remained vacant. They did the due diligence into the issue a few years after the girls were born, while the tumor was still in hiding but already having an effect on her body; Maddie was no longer fertile, reasons unknown at that point, but that was the reality and they accepted it, didn't like it, but accepted it. After a year or two other means were considered, but by then the tumor was started to exert its damage and the inevitable was before them. The girls were it, but it was not to their detriment; they were given room to run but knew their limits, maybe pushed the boundaries a bit from time to time as kids are known and somewhat expected to do, but were gently restrained with explanations and love for them. They were growing up into the beings their parents, now only dad Alan, had hoped for and guided toward.

As always, the first hour of the day bordered on being a bit chaotic, breakfast to be consumed, the right clothes to be found for school during that season or the right clothes for a summers day activities, all the things that make life an adventure to be assembled, not a travail to be feared. By the end of that first hour each of the three in the house would have some recognized plan for the day. The girls were out of school for the summer but had swim, ballet, and gymnastic lessons, piano lessons for one and French horn lessons for the other, plus play parties with their friends, church camp some summers, maybe a trip to the nearby theme park, and wearing the tires off their bikes. The theme park, Big Flags, held a special place for them; it was on one of those days they were with their father doing errands of some sort around town when they got to meet the three girls who were in that TV commercial for the park; even the car from the commercial was there, the little yellow roadster, and the girls talked to them like they were real people, not seven year old pests. The girls learned the three in the commercial really were sisters, but not as young as they appeared to be, the oldest being already in her twenties. All that didn't really matter much; the contact was what mattered and Ally and Anna were thrilled.

Their neighborhood had some years on it compared to assorted other areas of town, but had well maintained dwellings on decent sized lots, not all squished together or separated so far they looked like separate enclaves. There was a small play park nearby kept in good condition by the city parks department, intact sidewalks, even access to a walking and riding trail in what would have been an alley in older cities. The actual houses were of an assorted variety, no vast strips of tract homes all looking mostly the same; the majority were two story frame of different variations plus some ranch on basement types and even a handful of "starter" homes, small two bedroom units with a low price range for new families and maybe no attached garage or just a single car garage; the older places had single car garages because back in the day they were built people didn't own more than one car, if they owned a car at all. There was one of the smaller houses on one side of the Behr residence and a two story with a room addition and extra garage in the back yard on the other side. The Behr residence was a combination of things, a ranch on basement but with a slab on grade room extension off the kitchen toward the back of the house, plus the single car garage toward the back of the property in addition to the two car house garage; the addition wasn't readily visible from the front of the house, but the important fact was that it was where Alan Behr earned a living for his family.

When they were first married, with Maddie barely a year out of college, he was employed by a local manufacturing plant in their developmental lab area. Mostly his task was to find ways to reduce the cost of making their products and perhaps as a byproduct to that task finding a better way to do things or improve the product itself, at no additional cost to manufacture of course. Then the plant closed without warning, abandoned their staff and physical location, and moved off shore, leaving hundreds in the town unemployed, many with few skills beyond assembly line repetition to tide them over. Alan was one of the fortunate few who already had a sideline of sorts. He had always been the inquisitive type of person, and with an engineering background could quickly grasp how things were made or how they functioned, or maybe didn't function or could function better. They lived in an apartment for a couple of years, but as soon as they knew they were about to become parents started looking for a more permanent location; the house met their requirements for space, floor plan, and mostly price, plus there was that room addition in back. The owner explained the room had been added to house their hobby activities that had outgrown the original house, a large model railroad for him and a quilting area for her. By that time Alan had a bit of a reputation as a design problem solver and had built a sideline as a resource to be tapped by other companies; he always ensured his outside work didn't interfere with his "day job", but came to realize his employer could not have cared less about anybody or anything when they bailed out and ran. The added "back room" worked well to house the tools of his trade, that being whatever he needed at the time to resolve some problem he had been handed. Often times it was just how a problem was seen by the original designer, or perhaps some anomaly that popped up in daily use by the end user, a residential consumer perhaps, a fault that had to be remediated quickly to staunch the flow of complaints or even the frightening prospect of an expensive general recall. Like many professional trades, word of mouth was important to gaining new business and Alan Behr enjoyed being "the word" often used by others as a problem solver. He was comfortably well off in most respects with a plan in place for the inevitable college tuition bills he could see in his future; although he often told the girls they would have to get jobs in a few years to support him, they had every reason to believe their father would support them in their own future efforts. Today, this morning, he headed for his shop as an idea for solving a problem with a piece of equipment that had been shipped to him came into mind; it was not at all unusual for such an idea to be in his mind when he awakened; in fact, he was a true believer in the "sleep on it" method of problem solving as it had so often served him well. Five minutes in the shop, coffee powered, and he was already fully engaged.

Dressed, fed, and reminded to neaten up their room, the girls ran the vacuum once lightly around the house, threw a load in the washer using those skills their father had patiently taught them, then went bike riding in the neighborhood, stopping at the play park to visit some friends; the common recognized practice in the neighborhood said they would not stop at the park if there was an adult there they didn't recognize. Back home by lunch time, they had PB&J sandwiches with their dad and related their limited adventures of the morning. Ally did remember something out of the ordinary.

"Dad, the house next door, where the Millers used to live, there's a moving truck there and men taking stuff into the house. Who's moving in? Do you know?" Ally had voiced the question first; she was usually first to take action while Anna was a bit more methodical, slower to react, and slightly less volatile.

"No, I sure don't but I did see the SOLD marker on the yard sign a couple days ago. Anyway, moving day can be a real chore, so we are going to leave them alone the rest of this afternoon; besides, you two have music lessons and that twirly stuff to do." Anna couldn't let that pass.

"Daddy, it's not twirly stuff; it's ballet; we do ballet."

"Which has a lot of swirly twirly stuff in it, right? Anyway, get your selves ready so we can go; we'll go introduce ourselves to the new neighbors when we get back. Now, off with the two of you; get your stuff and let's go to music lessons."

Later that afternoon the three had returned home, better educated for their efforts, and still curious about the new neighbors. The moving van was long gone. Time to go visit and Alan, with a daughter on each hand, made the short walk and pressed the bell button. In only a few seconds the door came open and they saw the woman and her two children. She spoke first, with a voice that sounded a bit frazzled at best.

"Can I help you?" He noted she looked tired, a bit the worse for the wear.

"Hi, I'm Alan Behr and these two vagrants are Ally and Anna. We're your next door neighbors just come to say hi and welcome you to the neighborhood. I'm fairly handy so if there's anything I can do, just yell. Okay? My apologies I don't have a pie or something to give you in welcome; not one of my strengths." It was a good place to stop talking, and he did so.

"Sorry, I must look a mess and I don't mean to sound tense with people; I'm Lynnette, Lynn for short, and these two are Brad and Ben. It's just been a long day; I can't find anything for dinner even though it has to be in here somewhere. Sorry, don't mean to complain, not your fault."

Alan knew in a flash there was indeed something he could do to help. "Been there done that, although it's been a while. But, look: I didn't bring any sort of welcoming gift and I know that sets a bad example for starting off on the right foot. How about we take you for pizza at a really great place, treats on us of course? Should be room enough in our van. Okay? Good to go? Boys look hungry and I know these two can always eat pizza."

She was unsure, feeling hungry but unsettled, nervous. "Please, we don't mean to impose; you don't have to do that. Just knowing there are friendly neighbors here feels good. Anyway, thanks for the kind offer; I'm sure I can find the food we brought."

Alan, ever the reality based engineer, was unmoved. "Nope, not acceptable. What if you can't find it in a timely manner and get all weak and stuff, then what? No sense starting things out that way in your new adventure. Anyway, we don't have much in our house and I'm no culinary artist, so come with us; okay? If we have to wait on someone or you need to let someone else know where we're going, fine with me. I don't really want to ask if...um...you know...someone else, husband, someone, trying to not be nosy."

Lynn recognized his unease at that difficult point of conversation and knew she had to help him out. "No, no one else here...and won't be. I didn't want to ask either, but you?"

He understood. "No, not for some time now. We'll talk. Into the van?" and they did walk to his driveway, filling up the van sitting there. "Mama Leoni's Pizza Palace, absolute best there is."

The conversation lagged as the group of six ate heartily. He expected as much from his daughters but was equally impressed by her sons. Filled to capacity, the four kids headed for the play area, leaving the parents to their own devices. The ensuing conversation covered all the expected topics: kids ages, where the kids were in school, extracurricular activities, plans for the summer, all those perhaps mundane but real facts in their lives. And then, slowly and inexorably it swung around to the parents and the explanations started with Alan and the loss of his beloved Maddie. Lynn sensed this man across from her was still in mourning to some degree, accepting of the reality but unhappy with the outcome, dealing with each day at they came along. His girls seemed well behaved and happy enough, giving their father a bit of sassy repartee but staying within what appeared to be their agreed upon limits for such backtalk; they were engaged in so many things she wondered how he managed to keep track of all their activities. She caught herself wondering if there was anyone else in his life, maybe someone he saw now and then for his own mental health, yet he mentioned no one.

When the telling time came around to Lynn, much as there had been personal sadness in his telling, her telling was far worse because the action had been pseudo-voluntary. Where a force of nature had beaten on Alan, it was a nasty bit of human nature that had beaten on her. She recalled in vivid color that day when her husband walked into their kitchen as she prepared dinner, told her he was leaving, and departed, gone, period. There was little recompense; she would only infrequently receive the child support or spousal maintenance ordered by the divorce court, but she soon learned that was not at all uncommon. She was not cheered in the slightest when she learned that the father of the naïve 18 year old her soon to be ex had met at work and had impregnated beat him very nearly to death before others intervened to stop the severe damage being inflicted; the furious father didn't kill her ex but his open hatred of the man would remain intact. Regardless, her ex would spend a week or more in the intensive care unit, then nearly a month in rehab before he could manage to live on his own again. His resulting disability and meager income left Lynn alone to face supporting her boys. It was true the parents of the newly beloved threatened to sue him for support, but it wouldn't result in any significant amount in his reduced circumstances and they soon stepped back from that unrecoverable expense. Lynn did understand and felt badly for the girl but her own struggle ahead of her with the two boys would be steep uphill. She managed, but barely. They had moved because she needed to reduce their expenses and the newer three bedroom house they were living in was more than she could afford on what she could earn, plus day care expenses and all that sort of thing. Her parents helped out when they could within their own limited means, but not the parents of her former husband, half of her sons grandparents, who blamed her for inciting the divorce; any one day in her present life could be touch and go at best, but for the moment she was sitting stuffed to the gills with delicious hot pasta and pizza, kids having a good time with new friends, and this man sitting across from her had to face burying a wife he quite apparently loved very much and spoke of in subdued tones. She had resisted when he first suggested going for pizza, but somehow doing so seemed right and she went, absorbed his conversation with her, and for the first time in what seemed like a very long time, relaxed as the momentary cares of the day eased a bit.

Back in the van, they seemed to be heading home via a circuitous route known only to Alan, but somehow the van found its way into the parking lot of a frozen dairy treat store. Van occupants unloaded and with preferred dairy treats in hand they sat at one of the picnic benches and enjoyed the evening. Lynn did take a moment to protest.

"Alan, you can't keep doing things like this, you just can't."

He seemed confused, conflicted, but was neither, not really. "Is there something wrong with the ice cream or maybe not enough sprinkles on it? I see some kind of bare spots; I can get more sprinkles if that's the problem. Is that it, you need more sprinkles?" It was hard to do but he managed to keep the concerned look on his face instead of the grin that was trying to break out.

An unsuspecting Lynn took the bait. "No, of course not. I have lots of sprinkles, plenty. The ice cream isn't a problem at all..." Looking up at him she realized his lip line was turning up in spite of his best efforts at frowning and knew, she just knew, he was gently teasing her. Accepting the situation, her inner being pushed forth her own warm smile as he continued.

"Good. Then, enjoy. Scared me there for a minute. While you're doing that, is there anything else you need to get done in the house to make it habitable for the evening?"

She did reflect back on the mess at the house, realizing in the process her line of thinking was much clearer now and that he would help her get settled for the night if she asked. The little house wasn't exactly overflowing with their limited amount of belongings but they had adequate furnishings and by the time he got the beds reassembled the occupants were about ready. Taking their leave, the Behr's wished their new neighbors a good night, saying they would see them in the morning. The two parents, finally retired for the night, found they each had good memories of the past evening and a hint each would like more conversation with their neighbor. In their own beds, the last thoughts of the day ran parallel tracks, Alan reflecting that perhaps Lynn could be that adult female voice his daughters needed to hear now and then, while in her mind her boys now had a good man to look to and from whom to learn.

Chapter Two

Unexpected Opportunity

"Eric, I have to tell you that was not my personal shining moment. You know my shop is attached to my house, right? My girls carried my lunch in here yesterday noontime or so, and while we had a bit of father daughter time they were looking at what I was doing. I had already written up my findings on the problem but they pointed out something I missed: if this appliance is to be used by kids, it needs a fail-safe of some sort, maybe a stop switch they can easily reach and that is obvious to even a blind person. I'm not saying it is unsafe under the present configuration, probably not for adult use, but you and I both know kids often don't think in terms of consequences from their actions. I'm just saying I think it would be really easy to add maybe a hold-down safety button under where the hand would rest; that way if the wand gets dropped the machine shuts down; probably not a bad idea for adults to have that feature as well. Adding a pneumatic button is less than three dollars per unit, hose and end switch included; I did the math and researched the hardware. After I thought about it a bit, I realized there are a lot of homes out there much like my own here where the kids do some of the housekeeping chores; we should keep that in mind when designing things they may be using in the future. The thought also occurred to me that we should keep in mind the elderly and their slower reaction times or maybe limited hand strength. So, what do you think?"

Eric Hempstead listened to what Alan was telling him. They were in this discussion because Eric was the product manager for this line of appliances and he wanted no unexpected issues to pop up after they started distribution and major marketing. There was the company's good name to protect, which translated directly into sales figures, and what if the operator dropped the wand and as a result was sprayed by a nozzle discharging something the company could not control beyond making recommendations. He had even heard of a customer using one of their earlier models to spray defoliant on a neighbors prized hedge in a not so friendly dispute; how bad would that be for getting a face full? He knew his response.

"I think you may be on to something there from a liability standpoint, so I'll run it past legal to see what they think. Those guys are always paranoid about something no one else can see, but this time it's very tangible." There was a pause in his speech but Alan remained silent, sensing from the pause there was more to come. Sure enough, his caller continued. "I don't know if I should tell you this or not but I guess I've sort of started anyway. College roommate of mine called a couple days ago. We see each other at class reunions now and then, sort of stay in touch during the year, even do some technical talk now and then just to air our thoughts about some product line, whatever. Anyway, he asked me about product testing and how we get that done, if we use an in-house team or consultants. You know we actually do some of each depending on the specific product, related a bit to product purpose and maybe the environment in which it may be operated, ancillary uses or possible misuses, that sort of thing. He told me they do much of the same processing but that he senses it isn't enough in some respects, maybe not really appropriate to the need. For example, they use a consultant for testing of kids products, and while the consultant does hire kids and observe their interactions with the products in question, the consultants in charge are all adults; they are subject to inadvertent biases just like all the rest of us adults when they form their observation conclusions and recommendations. In addition, the kid testing is done in a controlled environment, not the real world; I know the real world testing could become very problematic in a heartbeat; however, the reality is the products will not be used in a controlled environment but in the real world. I don't think he's out of line with that sort of reasoning, remote though that may seem; you and I both know nature always sides with the hidden flaw; it's Murphy's Law. So, I gave him your name. I will admit I am a bit unsure why I did that because I know you don't have a test lab sort of arrangement, but maybe you could just talk to my friend and see what he has in mind? Sorry for not asking first, but our most recent conversation on the stop switch just proved me right. We good?"

Alan heard it all and digested it quickly. "We are good although I might have to recalculate my bill after this discussion. That's not to mention I may have to share the proceeds with my girls; it was their question that sort of started this whole discussion. Did I hear you correctly that this other person manufactures things for kids?"

"Yes and no; they do some limited amount of manufacturing in one of their own wholly owned places but contract out other things here and abroad. We both know there are only a handful of actual manufacturers out there; those same people make things for multiple sales lines and whoever has the money. In this day and age the key to sales is a product line all somehow related to a movie or successful TV show for kids. So, one glitch in the line and the whole thing can come to a screeching halt if word gets out. I don't know if you'll get a call from him or not, but it's up to you what gets worked out. You have the two girls, right?"

"Some days it seems like more than two." Alan's mind lit up: neighbors. "We did meet our new neighbors yesterday; she has twin boys the same age as my girls, so maybe I can branch out. Thanks for the heads-up; if he calls we'll talk and see what happens. I do agree with your observations on the consumer testing process; no matter what they do, it's still an adult controlled environment; that has to impact the findings at least a small bit. And remember the safety switch, you know, the reason you called to begin with."

Eric would remember. In the meantime Alan went back to work on another item he had received. It was broken, well, not really broken but was starting to crack a tiny bit; could he tell the sender an easy fix to stop the cracking without having to retool the entire assembly. That was something Alan Behr did best, solve problems in a reasonable manner. There were a few times no good simple solution would emerge but even if his recommended fix cost a bit it was still less than a general recall and all the bad publicity and lost sales that could invoke. Lunch time came and went, followed by a mid-afternoon knock at the front door. The girls answered, found Lynn and family before them and walked them back to their father's work area. Alan looked up at they came in and welcomed the group.

"Hey, hi; welcome to the mad scientists lair. How are things going today?"

Greetings were completed as the girls showed their new friends the assorted "playthings" in the shop, Alan heard the reason Lynn was there.

"Alan, thank you again for yesterday, for all you did for us. I'll admit I was pretty close to being frazzled out with everything when you arrived. I don't want to ever take it out on the kids, won't take it out on the kids; what happened isn't their fault in any way, but I guess now and then I just need some adult reassurance I can get through this so I can keep going."

He did understand, and said so. "What I did, we did, it's just being good neighbors; besides, I know the girls helped you put some things away in the kitchen so you might never find them again, not ever. That happens here now and then but we cope somehow. So, how are things with your place today? Getting settled?"

"We are, but some of the outlets in the kitchen aren't working and the garage door thing doesn't do anything; I can live with the garage door problem for now, don't want to spend the money to get it fixed, but the outlets are sort of a problem getting appliances to work where they're needed, like the toaster on the counter, things like that. I was wondering...yesterday you did offer to help, although I think we burned up a lot of that good will with pizza and ice cream; I don't want to use up any good karma we might have here, just in case something else fails, but could you maybe take a look in the kitchen for me, please?" Lynn did realize it was a lot to ask of a neighbor she didn't really know very well at all after a single late afternoon pizza and ice cream run. But, he was looking at her and smiling; maybe she was catching the break she needed to keep on the positive side of life.

"So long as we keep it simple, okay?" Seeing her facial appearance become questioning as she tilted her head slightly, he continued. "I say that because engineers tend to over complicate things and right now I can do the routine and mundane but not the complex. Okay?"

It was okay with Lynn, and with Alan now armed toting some tools of his trade they went back to her house to review the problems. Within the next hour he had directed the girls to go find a couple of new electrical outlets from his stockpile of things, replaced the broken outlets, and restored power. The garage door was even simpler, being turned off against inadvertent opening by the departing owners; a little grease on the screw and even the mild opening chatter subsided. Dinner time was approaching but found Lynn with limited resources; she did feel a need to at least make the offer in light of what Alan had done for them.

"I guess it's my turn to invite you to dinner but all I can find at the moment is hot dogs. Not much to offer after what you've done for us again. I haven't had time to go shopping..."

Alan knew she was trying with little on hand and interjected his own thoughts. "Neither have I recently. How about this: I'm pretty sure we have some hot dogs and buns and some of the mac and cheese we can nuke. How about I stoke up a fire in the pit out back while you nuke the mac and cheese in our kitchen? I think we might have some left over Texas sauce. I usually go for chopped onions on dogs but I'll live without if need be. Okay?"

"You know you're bailing me out again, right? I guess I can stand being bailed out one more time if you're sure about that. Chopped onions I can do but what's Texas sauce? Don't think I've ever hear of it."

"I will admit it is a concoction sort of my own making, variation on a meat sauce I build from a basic recipe that goes over the top of hotdogs to spice things up. So, we on? I have enough roasting forks somewhere; I'll get the girls to go look with your boys helping."

It was all that simple, open pit roasted hot dogs in buns with a savory sauce, and in one case chopped onions over the top, joined by steaming mac and cheese. It was getting to be toward sundown by the time the kids had finished their games and needed to be headed toward baths before bed; the two parents had taken advantage of the time to learn more about each other. She learned he was an engineer by training but in many ways more than the traditional engineer in his abilities; he rather dismissed having any special powers, saying he simply applied what he knew, used some logic, and hoped for the best. She was unsure if he was telling the whole truth but would learn in time that is indeed how he saw things. For his part, he learned she worked in an accountant's office doing some clerical things. Helping to set up accounts for new clients and that sort of thing took her hours; in a financial sense she was getting along but did mention the scarcity of monthly child support payments. Reducing her house payment would be of considerable help. Alan did note for memory she knew about things accounting, something certainly not high on his list of abilities. He had helped her; maybe she could help him one of these days toward a better bookkeeping system for his shop; it was something to consider. By late evening six people were down for the count and would awaken the next day, Saturday morning, rested and feeling good about life in general. Each in their respective beds, Alan and Lynn were starting to have thoughts that ranged over more time than the next few hours and a bit into the future relationship and where it might lead. The path ahead was unclear at the moment but seemed to beckon them toward exploring just a bit.

Technically, Saturday was sort of a day of rest, but not really for people who spent five days a week in paying jobs. Saturday was a fix it, wash it, dry it, clean it, go shopping sort of day and both parents were busy in their respective houses. With their own minor tasks completed for the day the four kids shuttled between two back yards checking things out. The boys had retained precious little from their prior life while Alan's daughters were just a bit spoiled in his over compensation toward the loss of their mother. Still, there were some rules, not real restrictive rules but rules that were to be observed; the trampoline could be occupied only in the presence of an adult and there was to be no climbing on the roof of the utility shed or back garage, not ever. No running the battery play car on the street and remember to plug it in when done so it would be ready for the next outing. If he was mowing the lawn they were to stay away lest they be struck by some discharged object, and in the fall if he raked up a large pile of fallen leaves they could jump in it but would have to help clean up in the aftermath. All in all the rules were only marginally restrictive in any sense. The boys were barely acquainted with such rules but would learn quickly and without resentment. Their father on his best day was barely a father to them; most of what they had learned, how to get along, to share when needed, and how to respect others, came from their mother; she taught them well but knew in her mind her own judgment had been faulty in her marriage choice. Her ex was one of those men who seem to be anything and everything any woman could ever want; had she looked under the veneer the scene would have been different but she didn't look, didn't even have a thought to look, which was exactly that which enables such men to succeed in their quest at the moment. The veneer dazzles, blinds one to the underlying faults, the selfish attitude that peeks out now and then, a misshapen ego that would skew performance from acceptable to mildly unacceptable, at least at first, then to unacceptable in the end. That was behind her now, even the disabled ex husband who may or may not have deserved the beating he had been given. Lynn didn't spend any energy on that thought; she had enough to do at the moment.

There was something else that happened on the weekend, usually on the weekend and not during the week; the girls knew the routine and when the first "customer" arrived went in to find their dad. A glance out the window told Alan all he needed to know as he plugged in the little air compressor and prepared to air up one more bike tire; he would carry the small but heavy unit outside once it had pumped up and the girls would air up the tire for the neighborhood friend. Lynn's boys watched and learned not only how to air up a tire but how to be a good neighbor at the same time. Others would come and go during the day, sometimes needing a bolt tightened or a missing screw replaced in a favorite toy, all things their own parents could have done but which they opted to be done by a "professional". Alan didn't mind, in fact enjoyed the reality other kids found his yard to be a safe haven for play.

Noon time found Lynn coming out her back door looking for her boys; she had agreed to let them go to the Behr yard but no farther until she knew a bit better the general area. Sure enough, the boys were there and deep into the learning process of bike riding; on any one given day the girls were unsure who actually owned the bikes or how many there were in the back garage but it didn't seem to matter much anyway. Seeing her in the yard Alan came out, greeting her as he arrived.

"Hi there, neighbor Lynn. How are things by neighbor Lynn this fine day?"

"Things by me are good, really good; I still have to go shopping as we are out of just about everything. I have to say, I looked out the window now and then as I tried to get the kitchen better organized after some nice man fixed the electrical outlets for me; your back yard looks like a day care: bikes, toys, kids, lot of traffic. How do you manage to keep it straightened out?"

"I just do one thing at a time. While we have a moment here can I talk to you about something starting up next week?" Seeing her nod, he continued. "There is a little church a block or two over we attend with fair regularity; I can't even tell you if it is some specific denomination or not; it's sort of low key yet effective. Anyway, they have a vacation bible school starting up soon and I was wondering if you might be interested in signing up the boys. I know it might sound bad to phrase it this way but the girls have been there the past two years and it doesn't seem to have hurt them in any way. It runs two weeks with an optional third week that has field trips and similar events. Cost isn't all that much considering what is provided. So, anyway, we will be walking over there tomorrow for services and I was wondering if you might like to walk along, scope out the situation, sort of a trial run with no strings attached. Okay?"

It was okay with her. "I'd like that only...Alan...I'm almost broke, again it seems. This move had to be made to drive down our fixed expenses but it has put a crimp on the finances. I do want to take a look but may not be able to afford it. I'm not complaining, just trying to explain how things might have to play out for now. I pay one day at a time for daycare, but without knowing what the church camp costs...well...you see my problem."

"I do indeed, but let's take one day at a time. Ah, one more thing before I forget, again: I meant to bring this up a couple of days ago; short term memory something or other. I know you aren't really familiar with what I actually do to earn a living, so let me explain a bit. Clients send me things with problems that need to be solved, maybe a cracking case due to some unforeseen stresses, or like the other day a spray wand that needed a safety switch installed; it may be a product teetering on the edge of an expensive and negative publicity recall. I study the situation, engineer a solution that is both effective and affordable, transmit my finding, and send an invoice. In short, I make a living by providing fresh eyes to problems, maybe a different perspective. A few days ago a client of mine told me he referred someone else to me, someone who may or may not call; the more important issue was they feel their product testing whether in-house or contracted out is not at a level they find totally acceptable. I have not heard any more since that phone call but I did want to mention it to you; he knows I have two girls, but I told him about your boys moving in next door. You know and I know boys and girls play with things very differently. Point is, if I get a call to do some 'real world' testing, would you be interested in having your boys participate? Never ever would it be anything even the least bit hazardous; I can assure you of that as I would no more hazard your boys than I would ever hazard my girls. No, I have no idea what we might be called on to test or try out or whatever, but are we still having a conversation?"

Lynn heard his words, remained a bit unsure where all this might be leading, but had an urge to trust in him. He said he would protect her sons as much as his own daughters and she believed him. "Yes, we are still having a conversation although I remain unsure what it might be about. It must take a world of training to do your job; mostly I'm sort of a glorified file clerk but your job sounds all complicated. You do seem to be comfortable with your life and your girls are doing great so I guess it all works for you."

Alan grinned at her for the moment. "It all just goes to show I'm not smart enough to know when I'm in way over my head. There is something to be said for blind luck and superstition after all."

Lynn rejected his contention but the two continued the conversation for a while, finally going each to their own way to continue their tasks. On Sunday when Alan tapped on her door they were ready to walk along. When she heard the cost of the bible school and seemed to draw back a bit, Alan stepped up, looked at her with a finger to his lips to quiet her, and wrote a check for all four kids for three weeks. Lynn did stay quiet for the moment, avoiding the appearance of being contentious with her benefactor, but knew she again could not let something like this go without comment, without protest at his actions. As soon as the two of them were outside earshot of the signup table she found her voice.

"Alan, you just did it again. Do you not remember when I said you couldn't keep doing things like this for which I can never repay you? I won't lie and say I didn't want this to happen but I have to live within my means and..."

"Stop already, Lynn." Alan knew he was about to lie to her and knew full well she would know he was lying but he forged ahead anyway. "I do remember you saying something like that but I thought it only applied to sprinkles at the ice cream store." Seeing her grimace and head shake he knew for sure he was about to lose the point but intended to stay the course if for no other reason than the good feeling he had about being in her presence. That alone was worth the loss of a discussion point. "Look at it this way and you'll see how good my reasoning is." Another grimace and head shake from her; she knew he was somehow about to make all of this okay. "I can't be with my girls 24/7, especially if they are away at some church camp activity. Now, I would not allow that to happen if for a second I had any misgivings about church sponsored activities, but it is in my own best interest if I hire some muscle to accompany them during the day. Paying for your boys...that's the muscle; done deal and besides, for three weeks you can avoid day care expenses. See how this all works out to everyone's advantage? Lynn, you need to relax, unwind for the next three weeks, okay? I got this covered."

She was not buying his spiel although it was difficult to not let a laugh escape her lips at his inane reasoning her boys could provide any sort of "muscle" to protect his girls. "Alan, you can't really expect me to believe that, you just can't. My boys, muscle? They do exhibit some strength when shoving pizza wedges into their mouths, but muscle? Really?"

"Yes, really. It may not be exactly the traditional definition of muscle but I'm sure you know about the concept of divide and conquer, right?" Seeing her tilted head and quizzical facial expression, he continued. "I know full well my girls are more than capable of getting into things now and then they should leave alone. I am also sure your boys are equally capable of maybe bending the limits here and there. So, added together, each pair can serve as a distraction to the activities of the other pair, thus deflecting any negative reactions on the part of staff. See the reasoning, how sound it is? Without your boys attending, my girls could end up in trouble, so I bought some diversionary insurance, some muscle. We good now?"

Lynn was right in her thinking: he was going to deliver some cockamamie skewed reasoning she couldn't refute without seeming argumentative and perhaps ungrateful. "Okay, okay. Please do not hit a defenseless woman with arguments like that, arguments that make no sense at all but which somehow seem so reasonable...I give up, I do. I guess I just have to be careful about what you might try to talk me into next." Fleeting, very fleeting, that's how fast her next thought flew through her conscious being, followed instantly by the warm feeling she felt as her face reddened. The thought had been unintentional, groundless, without reason, but there anyway and it was too late to squelch the blush. Maybe he wouldn't notice...but he did.

Alan heard the words and saw her face, sensing all the subtle meanings she accidently conveyed; he was not immune to similar thoughts in her presence, but she needed to know his reality. Stopping in their walk, he turned and looked directly into her eyes, voicing what she needed to hear. "Lynn, I would not ever do that, not to you. You and I have no history past a handful of days, but I will not jeopardize future possibilities by squandering the present; I won't do that. You will be free from hazard in my presence, I promise. That may not mean much..."

"It does; I believe you and I want to see tomorrow and the next day. I'm sorry I responded in a negative way; it was unintentional. Some days I seem to have difficulty accepting positive things in my life. Can we just delete maybe the past minute or so..."

"Done. Now, I have this really nice roast in the refrigerator but no real good idea how to cook one other than in the crock pot. Could you maybe help me out here?"

She could and would help him, realizing in the process it was a set-up on his part but to her benefit; that felt good, posed no hazard to her being, but did add just a bit to her unrecognized and concealed even from herself hopes and thoughts about the future. It was a very good weekend. On Monday morning and for three weeks of mornings thereafter Alan drove four seven-year-olds to church camp each morning, to be retrieved by Lynn as she returned home from work each day.

Chapter Three

The Construction Crew

It took a few days but the call did finally arrive from a Gill Lanham at the company Eric had mentioned. The sound of the man's voice told Alan this was no kid on a quest but a more mature individual with some on the job experience. For all that, Gill was a bit unsure exactly what he needed done. He did know the advertising his company had been putting in place didn't seem to be doing the job any longer. It was true he was the large item line manager for their toy sales but the marketing was done by others in a different department; those others seemed to dismiss his thoughts on changes they needed to consider as sales slowly decreased. His ideas trading on the "so easy a child can do it" for assembly were deemed ineffective, useless by a cadre of marketing "experts" who liked to wave their diplomas about, even a masters degree here and there, but who at the moment were less than effective in earning their own keep. Gill needed an end run, something to get him stirred up and back on the right track to at least slow the decline in sales and maybe get a growth cycle started. Eric, a long time associate, had suggested the call to Alan Behr, a man known for innovative resolution of thorny problems even if they were more physical in nature than the ephemeral term "marketing" could define. On Gill's end of the wire the sound of Alan's voice also rendered some assurance this was not a kid. The conversation started.

"Good morning Mr. Behr. I'm Gill Lanham. I believe my associate, Eric Hempstead, talked to you, gave me your name. He assures me you may be able to give me a hand with something. I know from what he told me marketing is not exactly under your umbrella of expertise, but I have to tell you the marketing people here have been less than helpful in getting this sales slide turned around. I'm sort of at the end of my own ideas and frustrated with our marketing department at the same time; my most hopeful option at the moment is to ask for a few minutes of your time to run my ideas past you. Then, if we find no common ground I will accept that I have done due diligence on the issue and reluctantly let it go. Does that work for you, sir?"

"It does work for me, but I'm Alan or Al, not Mr. Behr. Eric did tell you mostly right; I take things in and try to figure out how to forestall the inevitable failure that may or may not seem evident. I don't know much about marketing, but being a father I do know about putting things together. Did Eric mention I have two daughters, twins really, seven years old, plus a pair of seven year old boys who just moved in next door to us. I don't know what you have in mind but you have my ear for the moment. I will admit to having a curiosity about many things; this may turn out to be something I can really get into, but for the present no promises; I will listen and then we'll decide what road to follow. Work for you?"

"It works for me. In brief, I have been having thoughts about somehow capitalizing on how easy it is to assemble our line of kid's things, especially for harried parents trying to hold down a job and home and all that sort of thing. I just can't seem to deliver the baby; thoughts sort of float past but I can't get a grip on them; even if I do get hold our marketing will tell me I'm losing my grip...probably on my own sanity.. Does this make any sense to you at all?"

"It does. Tell me more, and without wanting to seem argu-mentative, might I ask if your concept of 'easy' is a reality for all or just for you? See what I mean about being argumenta-tive? What might be easy for the two of us could be a real bitch for someone else, it just could. Worst still is that I think once that frustration sets in for a single project, or even just the first step of that first project, it manages to carry over into a lot of other things, you know, that sort of 'oh, he's just not good with his hands' kind of perception of individuals. Are we still having a conversation or have I burned that bridge already?"

"No, no bridge burning; in fact, I'm getting the feeling I may be seeing a whole new bridge. Here's what I've been thinking about." It took nearly a half hour for the two men to flesh out the situation, often times during which Alan heard the frustration in his counterpart's voice. Finally, Gill summed up the situation in so many words: "I think we have something going here. To be truthful, I made this call because I promised Eric I would do so, but my hopes were not exactly soaring high;

I think that may have changed in the last half hour. At the moment I need to let this simmer in my brain a bit until I see all the colors, but I assure you that you have not heard the last of me, however frightening that may be."

"It would be a foolish man to not be frightened at least a little bit by the unknown, but not so much he won't take that first step toward accepting the challenge. I have enough to keep me busy for a while, so whenever you feel prepared to move forward let me know and we can map out the trail. We on?"

"Yes, sir; we are on. It has been a pleasure talking with you. I may not have my answers yet but I do feel better about asking the questions. I should be ready to advance this cause within a few days; talk to you then" and Gill was off the line.

Alan sat back and pondered the situation; what he had voiced about being frightened was actually a valid thought for him, perhaps not fright as such but that little twinge of trepidation as he embarked on a new task in perhaps unknown territory. This situation did hold some interest for him, and he resolved to be patient until his counterpart could gain his own stability against which to push in moving forward. Time was running.

Nearly two weeks later, as Alan was walking into his shop to start the morning, Gill Lanham called, apologizing for the early hour but excited even at that start time. "Alan, Mr. Behr, Gill Lanham here. I didn't think things would happen this fast but I just learned of a situation that I think will play in our favor. Can we talk for a minute? Sorry it's so early in the morning; I just can't take a pass on this deal without at least trying to work things out."

Caffeinated morning person Alan Behr was fully engaged after hearing the first five or six words from Gill Lanham. "Not a problem. You seem excited so please say on. What's up, Gill?"

"I dislike using this term but my company is sort of in a repo situation with a customer. We learned they knew nearly a year ago they were going to file bankruptcy, close their doors, take the money and flee the country. Thing is, that company didn't bother to tell anyone else; they ordered in a lot of stock, marked it down to fire sale prices to drive cash flow, and planned to take a walk on our invoices and the invoices of several other suppliers. I don't know how the scheme was uncovered but they were stopped dead in their tracks. To get to my point, my company has a lot of stock sitting in a warehouse there we need to reclaim, a lot of which is smalls, little items without much wholesale value but substantial retail mark-up. There are also some larger items you and I would have interest in for our own purposes. So, I am trying to make a deal with shipping to relocate some of the larger items to your place instead of back to our regional warehouse; I need to know if that is all right with you. I don't want this stuff to end up sitting on a curb because the shipment was refused. It's worth mentioning that every time we have to move an item the costs go up and the margin goes down; simply put, we can't raise prices to compensate for something like that because the competition is still out there. So, what else can I tell you? We on?"

Alan was a bit bemused by the rapid development of events, but it did sound like an opportunity was presenting itself, an opportunity not to be squandered by indecision. "How much are we looking at and does the value change hands or how does that happen? I'll admit reluctance to accept the debt I guess, much as I want to see this move forward."

"I don't have an inventory in front of me at the moment but I will say we would not burden you with more than one of any specific item. As to debt, we would consider it stored, not sold or awaiting invoicing, so there would be no transfer of value and attendant liability. We good?"

"We're good. Please just make sure the delivery people call ahead to verify we're actually here. Now and then I spend time in the field; I'll give you my cell number."

It was that easy. It was mid-afternoon on the last day of the third week of summer church camp when the call came. 'Would someone be at the house to receive a delivery'? Yes, Alan would be there, but unprepared for what was about to happen. Half an hour later the rental van arrived, driver knocking on the door to verify he was at the right address, and his helper already starting to open the back of the truck. Alan was floored; the truck, while not a giant size van, was full to the back doors and flush with the roof.

"Um...guys...how much of this comes here? Looks like a really big pile."

"All of it, Mr. Behr, unless we hear different. We really need to start unloading now; where do we put things?"

Alan was still in shock; this was not what Gill Lanham had implied, or was that the elusive truth? He didn't actually remember Gill defining the situation any better than saying they needed to make a decision quickly. And then he did remember that statement Gill made about not leaving more than one of any specific item; wireless in hand he hit speed dial for Gill Lanham. "Gill, do you have any idea how much stuff is on that delivery truck? I mean, the truck is full and it's a pretty good sized truck. I don't think we can get all of it in the house even if we really work at it. I remember you saying there would not be more than one of any specific item, but how many thousand items does your company sell? Guess I should have asked. Now what?"

Gill stayed calm, although he acknowledged to himself he also did not know the limit of the material to be reclaimed. "Sorry, Alan; this just happened so fast I had to make some decisions before I really knew the reality. Let me talk to the driver, please." Alan walked the phone out to the patiently waiting driver, then stood nearby trying to not listen as that conversation unfolded, the delivery person frequently shaking his head in the negative. The driver finally signed off and handed the phone back to Alan.

"Mr. Lanham told me to leave as much here as you can stand, then for us to reload at the store to fill up the vacant space and take all that back to the company warehouse. So, can you come out here and show us where to store things and what you want? He seemed anxious for you to receive a lot of it; I just have to keep some track of what goes where. Gotta tell you there are some really nice yard things for kids on the truck that people would love to have; I hate to see them go to waste."

"They won't be going to waste, not if I have anything to do with them. Okay, where do I start, and if you give me the list I'll mark off what is to stay here."

The unloading commenced, to continue just long enough for four excited kids to arrive home with Lynn. Eyes widened as they realized Alan's shop was nearly half full, the spare bedroom also contained a number of boxes and there were a few in assorted other places in the house. Alan did allow more than one of some items, like the play houses; he would talk to Gill about that at some point. Lynn also stood gaping at the procession of boxes, finally finding her voice.

"Is this what you were talking about the other day, you know, the marketing thing?"

"It is, only I never expected anything like this to happen. What Gill is telling me is that one of the retail outlets ordered out a load of stuff, cut prices to get the cash coming in, and never planned to pay for any of it, just grab the cash and run for the border. His company went in to retrieve what they still could. He saw an opportunity to position some of it here for us to experiment on and here we are. At first the driver was going to unload the entire thing here; would have filled up the whole house, but I called Gill and we got that resolved. Now if I just had some idea what to do with it things would be better. I know: I think better when I'm not hungry. Soon as the unloading comes to a halt, what say we load up the kids and head for pizza?"

"Only if you let me pay for at least my kids if not for yours as well. I know you saved me a ton by fixing those electrical outlets, and a lot of other things as well; it's the least I can do. Anyway, sounds good to me; I seem to remain a bit disorganized in the house as regards the food supply; really need to get my act together. In the mean time, pizza it is. Boys: Mr. Behr thinks we should go for pizza; is that okay with you?"

Boys, girls, all together thought it was a good idea to go for pizza, concurrently holding out hopes the dairy treat store would be next on the list. Alan was right about one thing: with distractions removed for the moment, full belly, kids in the playground, and Lynn by his side, his mind turned toward what Gill might have in mind. Telling Lynn all he could remember about the conversations with Gill, he sought her guidance as they planned to move ahead in life. Equally sated and feeling comfortable in his presence, her mind turned to the problem at hand.

"Tell me once again what this Gill person defined or perceived as the problem with their marketing. I know it had something to do with adults having an influence maybe over what their test kids were reporting, sort of modulating it to fit their more adult perception or what they felt the requesting party wanted to hear rather than that of the kids. Am I remembering that rightly?"

"You are indeed. I do know he is frustrated with the company marketing department, that he gets a feeling he is being either ignored or totally dismissed and disrespected. I have been giving it some thought but I'm no marketing person; I don't even know how I managed to let him talk me into this to begin with, and now I have a house full of things to prove the errant ways of my agreement. You know and I know I could use some help with this problem, a lot of help, some of which should include reducing the size of the stored pile. How would you like some yard toys, maybe several of each?"

Lynn heard his words inviting her into the puzzle. The whole thing had been sort of mythical to her when Alan first described to her what Gill had told him, but at the moment she knew reality had visited big time. Kids, that was where the answer had to be; these were things for kids, yet somehow adults interfered with the learning process, or at least Gill thought so. What could she tell this man sitting across from her with a hopeful look on his face? Slowly, very slowly, an ephemeral thought started to condense into a solid being; her thoughts gained voice.

"I'm sure the boys would love some yard toys but I don't see exactly how that solves your problem, not at all. I think...I don't know...somehow this has to do with kids and how what they perceive is altered by the adults in the communication pathway to marketing. That results in the marketing effort being turned in the wrong direction, or at least not really in the right direction. I know that sounds a bit simplistic but isn't that what your friend is telling you?"

"I do think that's what he sees happening, a modification of the reported reality. Given that, the toys are marketed to what that department is told, not necessarily to what the kids are actually finding on their own. So, tell me neighbor Lynn, how do we get past that, or can we? Like I said, I'm no marketing person, not at all; my competency such as it is lies in other directions. How do we bridge that gap, get the adults out of the way?"

She knew, she just knew he had delivered the first step to solving the problem. "Alan, that's it, that's the answer, at least a part of the answer. Get the adults out of the loop. Please do not think I've gone loopy on you but there is something running around in my head I can't quite grasp, not yet, but I know it's there. We need to find a way to get the adults out of the loop, leave the kids alone or maybe not totally alone but protected from harm and left to develop things on their own, discover things. Am I getting way off track here?"

"No, not at all. Only thing is, what we have to work with is already manufactured, ready to go for some frustrated parent to try assembling in the dark of night or with swarming mosquitoes before the kids wake up."

Lynn sat bolt upright, enough of a sudden change it got his attention. "Alan, that's it; that's the answer, part of it anyway I'm just sure of it. What you just said about the parents having to put things together, that's the last step and the only one we have in front of us. All those boxes in your house have things that need to be put together, at least I'm guessing there is some sort of assembly required. What if...I'm just saying...what if we let the kids do the work, see what sort of a reality that engenders?"

Somehow that seemed quite reasonable to Alan Behr, let the kids prove out that "so simple a child can do it" slogan, or perhaps disprove it and force moving to a different reality. "Neighbor Lynn, I do believe you may have hit on a workable solution. Please, tell me more."

"Alan, I truly would like to tell you more but I don't really know any more. It seems to me we don't prove anything unless we can show evidence; we can claim all sorts of things, but no show is no go. How do we get past that problem?"

He didn't really know, not at all, but mouthed a somewhat flippant response anyway. "I don't know, shoot a video we can sell people on how to assemble the stuff, show kids doing it maybe to prove the point?" His own words seemed unreasonable to him at the moment, but were they?

Lynn took the bait. "That's it; we do a video of the kids at work. We'd have to rehearse them a bit, but we can't do much or it defeats the whole purpose. How do we manage that?"

"We do a bait and switch, that's how." Seeing the questioning look on her face, he continued with his explanation. "There are at least two different play houses in that stack of stuff. Suppose we have them do one while we observe for sticking points, then switch and start over with them doing it on their own. Only problem with that is that I think my video camera is a bit marginal for any sort of adventure like that."

"Not a problem, at least I don't think that's a problem. Would you agree with me this has to be done on a professional basis if we are to make good the point?" Seeing him nod in agreement, she continued. "I have a friend who is a videographer, does weddings, all that sort of thing. Would it be all right if I at least talked to her about this, get her perspective? I understand it would just be exploratory up front, that doing a full blown video shoot could be really expensive. Would that be all right to do?"

It would be all right to do, and a few days later Alan, Lynn, and videographer Paige met in his workshop to discuss the possibilities. Lynn was right about one thing: it could be expensive, but Paige helped to ease the problem. "Let me see if I have this right: you do a run through to sort of check the sanity of this whole idea; if that comes up in the positive, we set up and do a shoot of the activity, I will do the editing work, we review the final output, you send it off to the customer, and we hope for acceptance. Let me ask: is this a one shot deal, or just the trial run? That could make a difference in the expense level generated."

Alan didn't know but ventured a response. "To be truthful, I just do not have a good answer to the question. What I think we are talking about here is somehow convincing the customer to include a DVD when the product ships, or maybe just putting it up on a website the customers or customer's kids can access. Maybe we're headed down a wrong path here; I don't know."

Paige was less negative and saw some potential the others had not observed. "Suppose, just suppose, this whole crazy idea works; it could revolutionize marketing kids stuff and probably a lot of other things people have problems with. Do you see that, the idea that one could call up a website and actually see someone doing what you need to do? I think this has some scary potential, maybe in either direction, but I'm willing to take the chance, be the innovator. I will shoot the video, do the finishing work, and we see what happens. You do know if this flies like I think it has the potential to do, I'll be back with invoice in hand. Okay?"

It was okay with Alan and Lynn as the potential for this idea sprouted, took root, and bloomed.

Chapter Four

The Shoot

"Kids, always remember people will see only you, not us big people; just imagine we aren't here at all; can you do that?" and seeing the group nod in the affirmative, Paige continued. "This will be just like we practiced the other day; this is a different play house, same style and all that so the directions may be a tiny bit different but not more than that. I'm telling you so you pay close attention, and read the directions and cue cards carefully; no cussing or swearing, none, not even one word; okay?"

The giggles abounded at her anti-swearing caveat although in her own history that was not quite true. More than once she had heard her husband cut loose when trying to assemble something that frustrated him. During the course of the event she would come to understand that much of the frustration was related to the small size of the fasteners and the large size of his hands; it was a comparison worth noting, but at the moment there were other issues and she had a video to shoot. Bringing in her assistants was a necessity to handle the cue cards; the shoot called for two fixed cameras plus a portable for getting close-in shots. The previous day's run-through had been successful with four quick study children. Today it was for real. The workshop was well lit, so there would be no extra lights to trip over, and all the cameras ran wireless, so no cords on the floor. The big box was in the middle of the room and the little tape X's on the floor remained in place. The kids knew everything worked around those X's; it had taken a few starts and stops during the rehearsal, and a few aside moments when Alan explained how the fasteners worked, but there was an air of comfortable relaxation at the moment as Paige activated the multi-channel recorder and the cameras. The division of labor had worked well, each child being given a function; Ally would read and Anna, treated like the reliable and respectful child she was, had been handed the battery powered screwdriver, a first for the household. Alan and Lynn had taken the four kids shopping the previous day on his unsubstantiated but accurate hunch they would find appropriate costumes in a local toy store. Sure enough, his memory served well and they obtained kits that yielded child sized orange hard hats, OSHA green safety vests, and even tool belts with pouches for carrying "things". Thus armed, the play started.

Stepping into the field of the lens and right onto her "X", Ally led off: "Hi; I'm Ally, one of the Construction Kids. I read the instructions."

Next arriving on his mark was Brad. "Hi, I'm Brad. My brother and I find the parts Ally says we need and in the order she says."

"Hi, I'm Ben. I help my brother find and hold the parts in the right position to be fastened."

"Hi, I'm Anna. Today I get to install the fasteners my sister tells me about that hold everything together, and, I get to use this power screwdriver. You don't need a power screwdriver to do this but it is a lot faster and we don't have all day here you know." Her grinning face at that last remark would become a memorable moment.

Brad: "Sometimes these boxes can be really hard to get open, so ask an adult for help. Let's be safe here. Okay, Ben; time to sort it out" as the two boys carefully upended the large box, slid the contents out onto the floor, then spread out the parts in sequence so the little applied stickers with the assembly numbers were visible. The final product would fade to black for a few moments as that process continued, but soon return to view. As soon as the parts were laid out, Ally continued her reading with Anna taking action.

"The first thing to find is the bag of small parts and pieces. Anna has it so we're going to put all the small pieces into this big plastic container we found in the kitchen. The container will allow us space to sort things out and keep them safe from getting lost while we build. I have the list of parts we need here, so let's make sure we have all the parts before we start to build." The final product would fade to black at that point but return in seconds to show the container contents sorted into piles of each type fastener.

Step by step, piece by piece, never missing a beat the process continued, while the unblinking camera eyes took it all in.

Alan and Lynn stood well back from the process, although there were a few times when young eyes did a darting glance their way. The rehearsal paid off, giving the kids the confidence they needed and the self-assurance they could do this; less than twenty minutes film time from the start the four went into the new playhouse right after they had lifted the roof assembly onto the side walls and Anna had quickly installed the retaining screws. With faces now appearing sequentially in the side window of the playhouse, just like the previous days rehearsal, the four finished up their task for the day, one voice at a time: "I'm Ally." "I'm Brad." "I'm Ben." "I'm Anna." And the four in unison added: "We're the Construction Kids. Welcome to our new Green Garden Play House." A few seconds into waving they heard Paige say "And...cut." The show was over. Paige was ecstatic, contained but clearly ecstatic, in the knowledge she had a product on tape that would be like refining gold already in a pure state. The costumes had been a definite asset but the crowning jewel was four kids who had a good time, interacted well, and who assembled a new play-house in less time than anyone would have thought possible. It was true there were four pairs of hands making things go well, and from time to time the picture would fade to black as activities not needing further explanation or demonstration were taking place, then quickly return; regardless of the time saving video outages, the process was clearly defined as the structure took shape.

The video crew was packed up and headed out the door when Paige paused to deliver one more thought she felt relevant. "It will be a few days before I get this refined into a finished product, but believe me, this is like striking a vein of gold. Those kids...what can I say. There is one thing I need to bring up, nothing critical at the moment but still something to be considered; as soon as we have an agreement on this product, that is, all of us agree to the basic premise of the final version, I am going to file copyright papers. Admittedly none of us knows at this point what the future holds, but the copyright assures we won't get run over in the process. We've all see the copycat ads companies run after the competition has a successful launch. There is no way to keep all of that from happening, but a copyright helps keep the gate closed so to speak. I will admit to high hopes for this project and want to ensure it is protected. Good to go...no, wait; one more thing: I know this may sound bad, but call your lawyer and let him or her know what is going on here, just in case; okay?"

It was okay with Alan and Lynn as Paige headed out the door. With the four kids now in process of dragging the new play house outside, the parents stood back and watched the teamwork. It was a moment Alan thought maybe he could use to his advantage in her somewhat euphoric state.

"Lynn, we're the adults here, right?" Seeing her nod in agreement, he continued. "I think it important that once in a while we reinforce that condition. We do a lot of kid things because we have kids; that seems to make sense to me I guess. But, we also need to do something adult from time to time to retain our status. Otherwise our kids could run over us. Right?"

She knew he was going somewhere with that line of talk but didn't have any clear direction as yet. "Seems reasonable to me. So, is there something you have in mind way past grocery shopping or some similarly exciting activity?"

He did have something in mind. This would be the first time Alan Behr had ever addressed her as a woman and not just someone living next door over. He had made no previous comments that could have been interpreted more than one way, she had never seen his eyes wandering over her contours, nor had she ever entertained thoughts past mildly wondering upon occasion if there was a significant other in his life. There was no significant other in her life; in fact, she still had some bitter thoughts about the divorce she had suffered. So, what was this present situation all about?

"I was just thinking to retain our status, if you went with me to a concert at the Country Club this Sunday it could help maintain status quo. It's not a big deal, not really, just a hot band I like for listening, cash bar if one wants, and..." for just a moment she though he had decided to study his feet in some detail, "Um...maybe dinner in the club dining room after the concert. Does that sound like something we could do to retain our adult status? Just asking."

Lynn sensed the warm feeling start within her. Yes, the visible premise of his proposal was just so they could retain their status as the adults in the two family association, yet it felt like more than that, maybe a bit more personal, more man-woman than just two single parents. The bitterness of her divorce would not win out, not this time. "Yes, I'd like that very much, but you don't have to feed me as well. And, we would need to find a sitter..."

"Not a problem. Yes, I do have to feed you so you don't get faint or anything like that, and I know a sitter we can use who can handle all four kidlets at one time if I provide enough in snacks and other amenities for her. Concert runs 2-5 so how about we head out early enough to get good seats? Dress is informal at very best. We good to go?"

"Yes, we are good to go and I very much look forward to this. Alan, thank you; I don't get to do grown-up things very often these days; this means a lot to me, it really does. Can I at least buy my own ticket?"

"Not a chance. I have been buying two season passes every year since my wife and I...but you don't need to hear all that. Let's just say I think this is the best investment I've made in recent history. Okay?"

It was okay with Lynn, but there was one more thing on her mind. "Yes, okay, but Alan, this whole thing about the video, Paige sort of cautioning us about something unknown...is this going to be alright? I've never been involved with something like that and I guess I'm a bit unnerved by the possibilities. Are we safe, all of us?"

He sensed as much as heard the bit of concern in her voice and knew he needed to step up, to reassure her. "I'm sure we're safe. I heard what she said and I think I understand the issue. If this goes as well as we hope it will go, we're talking a lot of money here; that can make people do strange things. I will call my lawyer and have a chat with him but please be reassured you and your boys will be included in that chat. Come to think of it, that TV commercial for Big Flags that seems to run continuously, that was done by some girls here in town, two of them under age at the time, and I'm sure Ari handled that case. Anyway, I'll call. Okay?"

It was okay by Lynn, eased her concerns knowing he was aware of the potential problems but had said he would take care of them as well as his own family. Hearing the words felt good. On Sunday the two enjoyed reinforcing their status as the adults, heard some great music, and dined in a leisurely manner followed by after dinner drinks on the club terrace. Even at that it wasn't very late when they returned to his house so she could claim her boys. As Alan and Lynn walked into the house they were both aware the four children were acting very much like one family, not separate entities, piled up against each other on each side of the sitter as they watched a video. The snack bowls were devoid of snacks. Within a short time the group had disassembled, with Lynn and company headed toward their own home for the night. There was just that one little incident none of the kids saw as the party broke up, when Lynn one more time turned to Alan and voiced her appreciation.

"Alan, this has been a really nice day for me and I want you to know that. My relationship memories aren't very good, but I think today...I don't know what to say."

"You say 'good night' for now Lynn. I want to see where this is going, but I don't ever want to get ahead of your comfort level. Will this do for today?" as he took her hand, raised it to his lips and kissed it gently.

She never saw that coming, the gentle kiss on the back of her hand, no pressure in any direction, just his simple demonstration of affection. What to say, how to respond. "Yes, it will do for today, but Alan, I think maybe this is only a start." A glance at her face saw the trickle of a single tear as she took her leave. It had indeed been a good day, a good week, and so far a good summer, with the promise of more to come.

Chapter Five

Going Camping

"Daddy, can we go, pleeese, pleeese? We'll do everything to get ready. The boys have never been camping, not really, and we haven't been in a long time; pleeese can we go?" The twins knew how to make their case known chanting in unison, virtually one voice from two people. Their father easily recognized the double teaming his girls were laying on him; it was hardly the first time they had tried that ploy. He also knew the rate of success for such a presentation was reasonably high provided their request was mostly sane and within reach. This time around things had changed a bit; they were including the two boys living next door.

"Girls, I'll think about it; alright? Anyway, you both know I would need to talk to their mother before we make any inclusive offer; she might not be at all interested for her own reasons. The other thing is, do you have any idea if they have any camping equipment? I don't think we can jam six people in our tent, spacious though it may be, so before we get any farther you two need to find out if they have any gear at all. We have enough gear to sleep the three of us, and plenty for cooking and things like that; I guess I could take a look at the big canoe but let's do this one step at a time. Let me know what you find out, but even then, no promises without talking to their mom first, and you two know this will cost you something, right?"

The girls were winning the debate and knew it, but there remained that veiled threat of a consequence from their father, his comment about it 'costing you something'. Ally wanted at least a hint, even though she knew in her own mind she and her sister would continue on their quest. "We're already your slaves doing all the laundry and stuff. What else would we have to do? You know we don't have much free time after all the stuff you make us do."

Alan remained unmoved toward sympathy, knowing in his own mind his two beloved daughters were hardly slaves in any sense of the word. "I'm thinking maybe extra practice time on your instruments, maybe an hour a week for the next four weeks. Okay?"

It was a deal they accepted without question, knowing that they already put in some extra time practicing between lessons. Telling them to practice less would much more resemble punishment. Deal done, off they went to find the neighbor boys and check out their situation. Half an hour or so later the boy's mother would arrive in his shop, entering without knocking as she had been asked to do, and armed with some questions, such as "How did I get into this"?

"Hi, Alan. Why do I get the feeling our kids have ganged up on us again with this camping thing? All four of them were on me. Anyway, is that something for real that your family does? The girls were specific in their questions: do we have any camping equipment and if so what is it and have we ever used it, all sorts of things like that. To answer…it's kind of a long story if you have a few minutes, or is this actually a non-starter?"

"Oh, be warned it is as real as it gets. We haven't been for a while, not since we lost Maddie; that sort of took all the fun out of it, a little fear of the memory I guess would be the truth of the situation. I believe we are past that now. I'm sure that as much as you have distinct memories of past events I also have specific memories, some happier than others. I don't want to sound maudlin about things but she was a really big part of my life and losing her the way it happened …it took a lot out of me. It almost sounds crazy to say it but having to fend for myself in taking care of two young girls probably kept me from sinking any farther. So, anyway, back to the present. I know of a nice place to tent camp and can usually get a reservation there with a little notice. I see you here and you haven't run screaming out the door yet so that tells me we may have a working plan in process. I have time for the long story if you have time and a willingness to tell it to me."

"I'll leave out most of the bad parts, if that's okay with you," Seeing him motion with his hands for her to continue, she did so. "Right after we were first married, pre-kidlet time, my ex came home one night after a drinking bout with his buddies, one of many such nights; this time they had been talking about civil war reenactments and that sort of thing. He had agreed to go with them the next weekend, never asking me; that was sort of his way. So, we acquired what we thought we would need for the three day adventure in the way of food, equipment, necessary things. It was out on this big farm over on the state line, hundreds of people there; we set up camp...let me rephrase that...I set up camp, put up the tent, lugged the cooler from the car...thank god it had wheels on it...while he drank beer with his buddies. I did get a chance to meet some of the other wives and girlfriends, talked to them to sort of learn the routines. Mostly they were a contented sort and supported what their menfolk were doing, staying in camp and reading or doing some sort of craft thing while the men did the reenactment. Not so for my manfolk; if the reenactment required a lot of beer drinking and eyeballing the other women there, he was all game, but actually taking part in marching around in costume and helping move a cannon about was not in his sights, not a bit. We spent the weekend with him mostly drunk, complaining about everything, even his buddies for getting him into the situation; I packed us out at the end of the third day and we never went to another reenactment; in fact, the one we attended was never ever discussed in the house. I guess to answer your question, yes, we do have some camping gear; I would have to dig it out and see what's there. Might I ask what we really need for this adventure?"

Alan had listened to the long narrative, hearing in her voice the disgust she was feeling even after all this time. If they had a decent sized tent, maybe a few other things, they would have enough equipment for a trial run, maybe two days. "I feel badly your experience came out that way; reenactments can be a lot of fun if one is prepared to participate; for sure we can change that memory. If your tent can sleep the three of you, we have enough cooking equipment, things like that. The site I have in mind does have restrooms and other amenities like showers, but they are a fair walk from the camp site I prefer; I have a sort of a chemical porta-potty we can take along; takes about one minute of instruction to learn the process; I just don't like it when the girls get too far out of my sight. I'm thinking about weekend after this, partly because I need some time to root out the gear plus check the big canoe; the site is by a lake, fairly wide spot in the river actually, so taking the canoe along is a plus for an activity."

"I thought canoes were sort of small things, maybe two persons. Have I been watching too many TV ads or reality shows?"

"No, not at all. We have two actually, a small one I use now and then for fishing or exploring, and a longer and wider one all of us can get in. I'll probably need a hand getting it on the car top carrier but it isn't really all that bad to handle. With enough paddles maybe we can even get the kids to paddle the two of us around. I have a basic list of food to bring along and will amend it to account for doubling the head count; maybe we could go this weekend and get some of it. The perishable I leave to the very last minute. You still with us?"

"I hope so. I'll need to find our tent; I'm sure it's in that house somewhere. Once I find things should I bring them over here so we can do a joint inventory, sort of make sure what we have?"

Alan grinned at her. "I'd say you're with us, thinking ahead like that. Yes, that sounds like a good plan. I need to make sure we can cram all that into the van, or decide we need to take two cars. Basic shopping this Sunday?"

Sunday shopping would work for her. Four kids were lit up big time.

Two Friday's later, mid-afternoon, the six of them managed to jam everything into the Behr family van, canoe and a cooler strapped down on the top rack, every corner filled with something, and off they went for a few miles to a well run camp site location. Alan was able to reserve his preferred campsite by calling as soon as the two families had an agreement on the event. The van was left in a small turn out at the side of the road, not far away from the fairly flat camp site by lake side; it did take multiple trips, not to mention toting the big canoe to the water, but the work was soon done and two tents stood erect, within a few feet of each other. Shoeless kids already had their feet wet, then with shoes back in place were sent into the surrounding woods to find firewood. Alan already had a stash of firewood and the site itself had a small pile provided by the facility management, but giving the kids something creative to do kept them involved in the process.

By evening time the site was in full operation. They did scout dinners for their evening dining experience; it was a whole new concept for Lynn and her boys, cooking dinner by putting foil wrapped packages of selected food directly on the edge of the fire; dessert was the anticipated s'mores. The entertainment for the evening was finding assorted constellations in the clear night sky and hearing the story behind each arrangement. Bed time came with no protests, at least not protests with any conviction, and soon six people were sound asleep.

Saturday went well. Although the four kids didn't paddle the big canoe very long, they did some exploring of creeks that fed the stream, explored a rock outcropping they found, and walked around on the tiny mid-lake island. Evening time found much the same routine as the previous evening plus a mildly off-key sing-along, and before long the day's activities took their toll; one at a time they folded and climbed into their respective sleeping bags. Shortly after 3 AM things changed, really changed.

Alan heard the summer rain storm blow in but didn't concern himself with the issue. Their tent had gone through storms before, it was on fairly flat ground that sloped gently to the lake, and the tent itself had sort of a floor, turned up edge that would take several inches of water to breech. There was some thunder but the wind was the issue; even then he felt reassured his skills at putting it up would stand the test. And then he heard the voice calling his name.

"Alan, please, can you hear me, please say you can hear me; I need help." Lynn's voice, sounding strained and a bit frightened, brought him to full awareness in seconds as he reached for the tent flap zipper.

"I'm here, Lynn; what's wrong? Talk to me." Hearing him respond was like finding a life preserver in a turbulent sea.

"Our tent, I know I put it up right but the wind...I don't know what happened...it's got a big rip in it now and getting worse. I don't think we can stay in it much longer, not in this rain. What should I do? Can you help me...please?"

"Sure; take a breath and push it out slowly. Hang on a sec while I get the lantern turned up a bit." Alan reached for the little battery lantern hanging from one of the tent poles, turned it up so there was enough light to see the interior, then scooted the sleeping girls around to make a bit of room. Within seconds he had slipped on a plastic poncho, unzipped the front flap and felt the rain in his face as he stepped out. Lynn was there in front of him, drenched in the downpour. "We can do this, okay? I need you to keep this flap closed to keep the water out; a little getting in won't hurt but it's really coming down. I'm going to get the boys and bring them over here, so let me in. Ready?" Seeing her nod in the affirmative, he stepped through the rent seam in her tent, and flipping the sleeping bag top flap over the first boys head, scooped him up gently and carried him to the Behr tent, placing him where there was a bit of room. His brother followed, leaving precious little room inside. Alan had a plan for the clearly soaked Lynn.

"Okay, that went well; now for you, mom. You can't stay in the wet clothes; get in here so I can zip up." Lynn was grateful just to be out of the deluge but had no idea where she could lay down her dripping body. "Lynn, get into this sleeping bag." Seeing her hesitate, eyes wide, he verbally pushed her. "Listen to me, Lynn; get in the bag, then take off the wet stuff and hand it out to me, okay? Nobody is going to see anything anyway and I can't let you freeze in the wet clothes. Get in." Directed by his reassuring but commanding voice, in she went and by wiggling around in the roomy bag managed to get her wet outer clothing stripped off and handed out to the waiting Alan, leaving her shivering in her wet but tolerable underwear. Gathering the wet pile into a bundle and stuffing it into a plastic bag, he remained in the poncho as he reached for the zipper one more time. "I'll be right back, okay, I will. Stay in the bag." and out the flap he went.

He was right, it was only a minute or two before he returned carrying something in yet another plastic bag. "Here, put these sweats on; I know they'll be a bit big but they're clean and dry. We need to get you warm." Dry sweats in hand she once again wiggled around in the big bag and managed to get both the top and bottom on; the change in body heat was instantly noticeable. She watched as he folded the poncho, turned down the output from the little lantern putting the tent again in near total darkness, and wondered where there was any room left for him. The answer came sooner than she expected as he parted the top of the big sleeping bag and slid in beside her; Lynn couldn't decide if she should panic right then or what to do as his arms went around her and he pulled her body close to his own. He felt her body stiffen and heard the sharp gasp of air from her. Time to clarify.

"Lynn, you need to be warm. I do not want you to catch something and strand me with four little kids when I can barely cope with two. As of this moment I am contributing body heat; I have no plans or intentions of contributing anything else at this time; perhaps another place and time that might change but for now, be warm and go to sleep. We'll deal with the tent in the morning. Good night." She heard his voice and knew he was right; the shivering had stopped and she could feel the heat from his body pressed against hers radiate into her being. But there was that other problem she was sensing, the reality she was feeling really good at the moment and wondered where this might lead. Her next thought was that other curious thing, the smell of coffee and that bright light. Morning had arrived,

She was right: she did smell coffee, she was alone in the sleeping bag, and there was sunlight streaming in through the unzipped flap. She sensed a reluctance within herself to slide out of the warm bag but just had to talk to Alan, to somehow thank him for his response to her early AM call for help. Remembering what he had done, a quick glance around the interior of the tent disclosed the still sleeping boy girl girl boy stack of kids; for just a brief moment she debated awakening her boys and moving them to their own tent before the girls awakened, but decided there was no harm being done and let them sleep. Once she ventured outside and surveyed the damage to their own tent, she realized it would be futile to try to use it for any sort of shelter with the whole side seam ripped out. Besides, there stood Alan Behr looking at her as he reached for another cup and the coffee pot hanging over the fire. He opened the conversation.

"Good morning, neighbor Lynn; sleep well?" It was voiced as a question but the grin on his face said he knew the answer.

"I did, thank you, although somehow during the night I seem to have changed clothes. Alan, what can I say...besides saying I'm sorry for my reaction when I felt you beside me in the sleeping bag. That was uncalled for; I had no reason to..."

He interrupted before she could get her whole statement of contrition out: "I beg to differ; we really don't know each other all that well; I could be a serial hugger for all you know and sure enough, the first thing I did was get my arms around you and reel you in next to me. Right? So maybe I should apologize for scaring you, or could we just exercise short term memory loss and put that all behind us? Your call."

Lynn thought about if for just a moment, decided to go with the short term memory loss suggestion, but had a caveat. "Okay, okay; I'll agree to the short term memory loss exercise and we go on with the rest of our lives, but Alan, I think there's a part or two I want to keep in long term memory if you don't mind. I can't tell you which parts; that's my secret, but is that okay?"

It was okay with Alan Behr as he also had some warm remembered moments of that night he wanted to keep in his mind. For the moment he poured her a cup of coffee and the two talked about the remains of the day, what needed to be done, when they had to pack out and so on. Neither was prepared for the wail they heard coming from the Behr tent.

"Daddieeeeeee, there's boys in here; how did boys get in our tent?" He couldn't tell for sure which twin was doing the complaining as it was apparently coming from a sleeping bag covered head. The wail continued: "I need to go to the bathroom but they'll see me in my pj's. Can you make them go away so I can get up?" Alan knew by then but also knew all four kids would be awake after hearing her loudly voiced complaint.

"Anna, you wore your regular clothes to bed last night, okay? You can get up any time now." and within a minute or so a tousled head poked out of the tent flap, followed by a scamper to the porta-potty. Alan and Lynn refrained from laughing at the sight, but it was indeed food for further thought. Alan voiced his idea: "I think we're good to go here today, but we need to remember this won't work in just a few short years, not stacked in a row like that. At least they didn't witness the trauma of seeing their parent sacked out with another parent from a different family. For the moment I need to get the griddle over the heat if anyone wants pancakes this morning."

Another voice came out of the tent flap, male this time: "I want pancakes; are we really having pancakes?"

Alan looked at Lynn and spoke very quietly: "I wonder how much they heard about anyone sacking out? I think we just got away with one, not that there was anything wrong with what we did, but...you know...kids can draw errant conclusions at times...even if...never mind. I'm just rambling on and on." She did know what he meant; their shared sleeping bag event would be kept between the two of them.

Mid-afternoon saw them packed out and on their way home, ripped tent and all. Alan thought he knew where they could get the repair done for a reasonable price. He did admit to himself the thought of being in a sleeping bag with the woman next door, wet or dry, didn't hurt his feelings any, not at all, even if the likelihood of that happening again was very remote.

Chapter Six

A Bit Closer

True to form, Alan had awakened with a potential answer swirling around in his thoughts. It was not at all unusual for him to retire for the night to "sleep on it", a process that as often as not had worked to resolve the problem of the moment. The key element was getting the idea down on paper before it sort of evaporated from his thoughts. It didn't always work out to the positive but the track record was rather enviable for the most part. At this moment he was busily drawing a sketch of the modification he believed would solve the "glitch" in the item that had been sent to him. It was one of those crazy things, something that didn't gum up the works every time but often enough so the history of consumer complaints was extensive. It was well known in manufacturing circles that once the consumer got a negative feeling about an item with a specific brand name, say Brand A, the negative feeling would carry over to all other Brand A products deserved or not. He had dismantled the assembly the previous day and watched the internal parts move freely, except for that one time they seemed to stick together; nothing was readily apparent to cause the problem, and he gave it up for the moment to "go sleep on it". It worked, and now he could see the issue as he drew out what he would modify to solve the riddle. It was also not unusual he would arise when the idea came to him regardless of the actual time, sort of a "strike while the iron is hot" process that continued to bear fruit. By the third cup of coffee resolution was well in hand; the light tap on the outside door surprised him just as he glanced at the clock hands reading 6 AM. Stepping over to the door, he unbolted and swung it wide as the form of neighbor Lynn came into view. He spoke first.

"Well, good morning. This is a surprise, a bit of an early surprise; to what do I owe this visit?" He had spoken just as he realized she was carrying something with a towel draped over it.

"I really hope I'm not disturbing you; I saw the light on in here and thought...maybe I didn't think at all. What can I say to excuse this early morning intrusion except that I did bring you something. Can I set this on the work bench? My hands are getting a bit warm."

"Sure, right here, and no, you aren't disturbing anything. To be truthful, I've been up for an hour or so; woke up with this in my head and I needed to get it down on paper before it escaped. So, welcome; what have we here?" Alan watched her set the pan on the workbench and carefully withdraw the covering towel. "Wow, just wow! Are those really iced cinnamon buns, and hot ones at that?"

"They are one and the same, right out of the oven. I know this is a bit screwy but I sort of had the same thing happen with me, woke up with cinnamon buns on my mind for some reason and next thing I knew I was in the kitchen. Obviously the boys aren't up yet, so I thought I'd share with you, if that's okay. We good?"

"No, we're way past good." Opening a cabinet, he extracted some napkins, then reached into the pan for the first of what would be several times. He did take just a second to ask if she would like a cup of coffee and poured one at her agreement. The two stood stuffing themselves, unable to do anything else for a few moments, but finally, sated appetites, started a new conversation, Lynn lead off after hearing his profuse thanks.

"Alan, you know I live alone, well, not exactly with having my boys there but as an adult I live alone. I don't want to get all deep here and psychological and stuff, but now and then I get questions in my head that don't seem to have answers, at least not sane rational answers given the circumstances. I know my situation isn't rare at all, divorced and so on; I know what happened and how I coped with those events, but sometimes I wonder how people cope with much more tragic events. I don't want to be rude or insensitive here but can I ask you something?"

"Sure, go for it. I don't think you could be rude or insensitive if you tried. What do you want to know? I have few secrets, except maybe that one about how to get into a sleeping bag with the next door lady."

Lynn was taken aback at his statement for just a few seconds; the sleeping bag incident was far from her mind but came back quickly, even the feel of his arms around her as the warm memory swirled through her mind. "I think the two of us need to keep that one secret for a while yet. What I want to ask is a little touchy, I guess it would be to me, and if you chose to not answer I can understand that. I know you must have some very real memories of your late wife, and I hear your voice change when you talk about her. I'm sure you really loved her a lot, so how did you manage when you lost her? You seem so stable and sane, all that, but it had to have come at a cost; how did you manage so well when I seem barely able to manage my own lesser circumstances? If you don't want to talk about it I can understand that but..."

"I have no reservations talking about what happened, not really. Coffee refill?" Alan poured for both cups, taking just a moment to consider what he was about to relate. "In a lot of ways it seems like yesterday, even though I know time has passed. We didn't have any sort of long drawn out courtship; when we met at a casual house party I knew she was the one for me and I guess she felt the same way, so the reality was we didn't waste much time dancing around the issue, just got married as quickly as was reasonable to do so. Nine months after we agreed it was time to start a family, the girls arrived right on schedule. We knew there would be twins, so no surprise there, but it was an exciting time for us. It wasn't very long before Maddie started saying things like it was easier on a mom if the kids were closer together in age; I got the hint alright, but then nothing happened. That seemed strange to us since we had barely made the decision to start a family when she was pregnant with the girls. Did some testing and we discovered she was no longer fertile but with no apparent reason for that to have happened. We talked about it now and then, maybe adopting, something along those lines, but it wasn't long after that the early symptoms of the tumor started to manifest themselves; while that explained some things we were then on a quest to get it treated, stopped, killed off before it could do any more damage. The docs did manage to extend her life by probably a few months but the side effects were damned near as bad as the tumor itself. She quietly slipped away one night while I sat with her...I need a minute...I'll be okay."

Lynn had been listening in rapt attention to every word he said, even as he put his head down and went silent. Somehow inside her being she sensed the power of his emotional turmoil at the moment. She had never ever been witness to an outpouring such as this man was telling her, not before her marriage and certainly not during or after her failed marriage. She would wait quietly as he gathered his thoughts and after a minute or so continued.

"Maddie knew what was going to happen even if I could never quite come to accept the inevitable. She was my strength and when she was gone I had to find my own strength, had to carry on for the girls, certainly not as well as Maddie would have cared for them but each little crises would find me trying to do as I believed she would have done. I know I lack her wisdom and I miss her every day, but I have no choice other than to go on. This may seem harsh or crazy and I don't mean it to be either, but it is the reality that when she died my life actually became easier in some respects. You see, when she was still alive each and every day I could believe there would be some miracle before us, something that would make her whole again, some new discovery. When she died all that hope died with her and my energies had to go into parenting as best I could. I knew that day as surely as I know today that I can't have her back no matter how much I want that to happen. Sorry about that little pause I had to take; things just sort of sneaked up on me. Anyway, that's about it, how I manage on a daily basis, why I manage on a daily basis. End of story I guess; what more can I say?"

Lynn had to pause herself as the emotion of his narrative seeped into her being and her own tears were close to falling. "Alan, thank you; I don't know what else to say. I do know the trials in your life make mine look rather trivial in comparison; I don't know how you can..."

"Lynn, don't say that. Our trials aren't so far apart, not in reality. I know you lost a spouse, maybe through different means but it is a loss anyway; he's gone and I would guess forevermore. You have to make all the decisions that should be joint decisions, try to do what you believe is best. It is true my remembrance of Maddie and how she was seems a far cry from what I perceive your memories could be but at the end of the day each of us is alone in many respects, our life fabric torn through no fault of our own. Do you agree?"

Lynn considered his words and agreed with the reality of what he said, with one exception: "I agree, but there is one thing: please don't take this out of context or read more into it than I intend: today I don't feel quite as alone as I did yesterday; okay?"

Alan understood her meaning, had a brief flashback to the sleeping bag incident, and realized he felt the same way. "Yes, okay. I read about the dissolution of marriage in the paper and know some of the assault data over a pregnant teen, but if you want to tell me more I'm right here. In fact, I think my fingers may be sugar glued to the workbench, but I'm not complaining."

Perhaps it was the opening she sought to unburden her own thoughts, or maybe she just felt this man who had suffered a painful loss would understand where others might not. "I think you may know almost as much about what happened as I know, but to set the stage a bit better I guess in truth it was also my fault to some level. He was big-man-on-campus, well known, physically attractive, outgoing personality, all that, even with sort of a reputation with the ladies that may or may not have been true. It was all a projected persona, some of it not real, but I didn't see the man pulling the levers behind the screen that was the real person. I was thrilled that he could even see little old me, not realizing other women on campus saw him for what he was. He proposed and I accepted; in a way I'm almost ashamed to say this but I had decided to sleep with him one way or another; getting a ring confirmed my decision but truth is it was probably just the luck of the draw the boys weren't born much sooner than they were. I wasn't very smart but of course believed I knew it all. I didn't see the warning signs, the reenactment fiasco, the missed dinners when he didn't show up home; somehow I made it all good in my own mind and when he announced he was leaving it was a total surprise to me. Somehow I think my mind already knew the reality, that I was entertainment to him, nothing more. But, your point about loss of a spouse felt very real to me. I had been totally dedicated to making it all work and when it didn't somehow a good part of that I believed was my own fault. I had excused but had no more excuses, not to myself. I had some thought it would all be good, but it wasn't. I suffered the loss from my own lack of maturity and relational blindness. Does it ever go away, the pain from realizing the loss? I know your loss was not at your own hands while my loss rested at least partially on my hands. Alan, will I feel this way forever?"

"No, you won't but it isn't up to me to say when it will start to feel better; it will be up to you to make that decision...Is that a light I see in your house?"

Lynn followed his gaze and knew in an instant their early morning therapy session had just come to an end. "Yep, it's on in the boys' room and I have to get going home, but thank you so very much for this morning. I'm going, I'm going, but I want you to know I think I feel better already, maybe just a little bit but better. See you later?"

"I think you can count on that...and Lynn..." he paused as she looked back from the doorway "I think maybe that 'feel better' works both ways, okay?"

She knew in that brief moment there was a connection forming between the two of them, a very real connection, tenuous at best but existent nonetheless, shining a ray of hope into her being and lightening her burden just a bit. "Okay."

Alan heard the music start in the girls room just as the door latch clicked in Lynn's wake, realizing they were going at ask about the half pan of still warm iced and sticky cinnamon rolls on his workbench. He would tell them it was about being neighborly, caring and sharing.

Chapter Seven

The Reprise

"Alan, hey, Gill Lanham here; sorry to be calling so early but this just broke loose and I want to get out ahead of it." Gill was right about being early, at least for normal business hours, but Al grabbed the phone on the second ring, glancing at the 8 AM on the clock as he did so.

"Gill, good to hear from you. To be real truthful here I've been up since about five trying to get an idea down on paper before it faded away into the mist. So, where are we with things? I take it the big boys liked the DVD or should I tamp down my expectations a bit?"

"Like it? That's an understatement for sure, but they want to sort of put their mark on it, you know, their own version; that's why I'm calling before anyone can maybe rethink their proposal. So here's the deal: my company's legal guys will send you a contract with all the terms, comprehensive, to hire the kids to shoot a new video here in our playroom. I don't have all the details yet but we wanted to get in line just in case word of this whole new tack on advertising gets out in the industry. The kids do a really great job and our marketing guys see the potential here. Anyway, just a suggestion: you might want to take this to a lawyer for review. I don't know that any of our legal eagles would try to slip anything past you but people sometimes do things they shouldn't, inadvertent or not. Okay?"

Al had been down that road before when as an inventor he was not well protected from the wolves of industry. "Sure, got it; thanks for the reminder. I have to tell you, I need to get the agreement of the boys' mother before this can go anywhere; I don't think that would normally be a problem but she is still recovering from a bitter divorce and some financial ruin; she's a bit gun shy if you know what I mean."

Gill, a multiple divorcee, did understand. "Sure, thanks for telling me, but I have faith in Al Behr, I do. The papers will probably come by currier direct to you, with several days in the response limit. You're a smart guy; I'm sure you will see through any smoke screen, but again, I recommend referral to your lawyer, someone you trust. Okay?"

It was okay with Alan; he would await the arrival of the contract but did think to call his lawyer, Ari Schoenroth, and let him know the situation. It always impressed Al that he knew Ari had handled some very large and complicated cases with a multitude of people and details all tangled together, yet Ari had won out, made a lot of people well, developed some major contacts, and above it all seemed more excited about being a father, again, than anything else. Like most people in his town, Al was unaware just how deep Ari's contacts went, and Ari had no motivation to brag on the fact. The reality was that it seldom had any impact on cases he handled, but now and then he would wield the connection like Thor's hammer, with similar results. Talking to Lynn would have to be much gentler.

With the kids from both houses now into full play mode out in the connected yards, Al walked the few steps over to tap on her door and found Lynn opening it before he could even raise a hand to knock. He opened the new conversation.

"Hey, Lynn, gotta talk to you about something that just popped up. Got a few minutes to spare?"

"Sure, come on in. I sort of need an engineer this morning anyway and sure enough, one arrived here just in time. My clothes dryer...I don't know...something went wrong with it; it sounds like it's running but doesn't go around, I mean, if I open the door it would stop anyway but if I'm quick I can see inside before it stops. It isn't moving, not at all that I could see, and it doesn't sort of rumble like normal. Am I making any sense at all?"

Alan Behr had to laugh at her mildly futile attempt to explain the situation before them. "You are doing just fine, you are; I'll look at it in a few minutes; probably a broken belt, not a big deal. Anyway, remember we sent in that demo DVD of the kids building the playhouse?" and seeing her nod in agreement continued. "The company guy called me this AM about it. He's telling me their marketing people went nuts they liked it so much. But...and it's a big one...they want to shoot another video of I guess the same thing but in their company playroom. Their legal department will send us the proposed contract and allow some days for us to review and sign; at the moment I need to know where you stand on the whole idea. I think their company playroom is in LA so we're looking at an airplane ride plus at least one night in a hotel, maybe two depending on what we can work out. Also, I need to tell you I will sign nothing until my own lawyer has a chance to read it over. I guess I can wait for your decision to opt in or out until after the contract arrives but you know it takes all four kids, so if you opt out the Behr bunch is out as well. Just as a guess, how are you feeling about the idea?"

Lynn let his words soak in a bit before responding, refilling their coffee cups as she pondered his question, and finally arriving at a cross roads. "Would you be there with them? I can't just send my boys out any more than I'm sure you wouldn't send your girls out. How is this going to work, the plane trip and so on...never mind all that; I'm just rambling, but I do have a question for you that I really need answered: where does Alan Behr stand on the idea? Tell me that and I'll have an answer."

"Depending on what the contract says and how my lawyer feels about it, up front I think I want in for at least this first go around. And, we go together, thee and me and four kidlets, or we don't go. My contact warned me to take precautions, legal and otherwise just so there is no chicanery by design or accident, and I can assure you I will be as protective of your boys as I will of my girls. If you want out, it all stops and right now; if you want in, we will go see my lawyer when the contract arrives. I should tell you they are anxious enough about this to be sending the contract by courier no less; there is apparently some level of paranoia this new concept will get out to their competitors. So, how's Ms Lynn feel about this?"

He was looking straight at her when he asked the question; Lynn needed to answer and would do so but with a caveat. "Speaking for my boys and myself, we're in, but I say so only because I trust Mr. Behr to take care of us. Am I asking too much Alan? I do trust you but I know I may be out of bounds here with something this big, and I don't want to..."

Alan broke in before she could talk herself into a corner "Lynn, stop already. We do this together, read the contract together, see my lawyer together; if you want to talk about trust, do you want to talk about being in a sleeping bag with me, or have you forgotten that little incident? This is only a contract to shoot a video; being in the sleeping bag with you...whole different subject. So, we good to go, take at least this first step? Look, I know this is important to you and I want you to know...um..." Alan Behr didn't want to say more than he intended but it was important to him this woman knew where he stood as concerned her. "I will protect and defend you the same as I would do for my own family; at the same time, I think we need to stay out of that sleeping bag, at least for now. Okay?"

It was okay for Lynn as she smiled back at him, feeling inside her being he had given her reassurance beyond what she had asked, and had done so with an apparent willingness.

The contract arrived two days later, by courier, hand delivered into the hands of Al Behr, signature required. Although he did read it over with Lynn in his presence, it was a performance contract and very unlike other contract forms with which he was familiar. A few hours later and the two were sitting in the presence of Ari Schoenroth, lawyer, as he read page after page of the document. Finally satisfied he had gained enough understanding of the document, Ari opened the conversation.

"First of all, please let me clarify that this sort of document is not my forte; in a few minutes I will return to that issue for clarification and my recommendation. Lynn, if I may call you that" and seeing her nod in the affirmative, continued "I don't want you to think I'm just plain nosy but it would be helpful to me if I know a bit more about you, some background perhaps. Alan has already assured me you are his partner in this adventure and that I am to represent both of you at this time. I don't want a lot of details, just some general information so I can feel comfortable in the process; nothing you say will ever leave this office unless I have your permission, not your name, nothing. To best represent you I need to know you better, okay?"

It was okay with Lynn and over the next few minutes she filled him in on her status, what she did for a living, her boys, the divorce, all those things that made her world go around. The ever observant Ari Schoenroth knew by the end of her life story summary that she had an interest in Alan Behr that went beyond the present situation, perhaps not very far past the present and perhaps it was in gratitude as much as loneliness, but he could hear the nearly imperceptible change in her voice when the traffic between Lynn and Alan was mentioned. There was no mention of the sleeping bag incident. There was, however, a moment when Ari picked up on a specific point in her monolog and wrote a quick note to himself for later pursuit.

"Thank you, Lynn. It helps me to know how you might react to different situations, good or bad, that may arise. I do not anticipate any bad situations but neither am I blind to the reality things do go wrong from time to time. Now, we move on to the more legal aspect of this visit. For the actual performance part of the contract I am going to refer you to a gentleman known as Sol Kaplan; it is your choice, of course, to work with him or not, but you did ask my opinion and I feel it would be in your best interests to at least talk to Sol. If you are familiar with the Big Flags commercials running on TV these days, those girls in the ad are his clients; his representing them netted a nice income over the next few years. Sol...this is kind of hard to explain given how some people are these days...Sol looks down the road, way down the road. He could have taken a cut up front, netted the girls some quick cash, then taken a walk, but he didn't. Every time for the next few years one of those commercials is aired, they are paid a royalty. I don't know if that would apply here or not but I wanted you to know how good he is and how he looks after the best interests of his clients in the long term. For my part in this, can I assume both of you will be making the road trip?"

Alan picked up the conversation, glancing at Lynn as he did so, "Yes, both of us. Is that somehow a problem?"

"No, not a problem; in fact, I would strongly recommend it. I'm not saying these people are good or bad, only that we need some checks in place. I know this may seem odd but I am recommending each of you serve as legal guardian for children of the other person in that adult person's absence." Seeing their questioning looks, Ari continued. "Both you two and your kids will be in with a lot of other people; suppose, just suppose, one of you needs something as simple as a bathroom break or has to step out for a phone call, or even gets lured out of the room somehow by one of the other people, who then speaks for your kids? With a guardianship in place you two can trade off as needed with someone always watching over the kids. I am not a paranoid about this, just being a realist. It sounds like these people will be spending a lot of money and they will want every bit of control they can get and then some.

Okay, that's the first thing we need to put in place. Questions at this point?"

There were no immediate questions; over the next hour Ari explained other steps they needed to take, then with a phone call handed them off to the offices of Sol Kaplan. Ari had been right about one thing for sure: meeting Sol Kaplan for the first time could be a test of one's courage. Shown into the man's office, Lynn and Alan were motioned to seats while Sol read the documentation they had hand carried to him, sometimes going back a page or two before forging ahead. Not a word had been spoken up to that point but Sol was now ready and opened the conversation.

"Same old crap from the legal guys, everything for them and damned little for you; we're gonna fix that. You two did good going to Ari for the guardianship; believe it or not, that has to go before a judge to write the order. And another thing, did he talk to you, lady, about severing all ties to the ex-hubby? You need to make a clean break here, make sure there is no coming back on you. I have no way to know if this will have any significant financial reward or not but you need to be prepared, just in case. Is he current on his child support, things like I am assuming you were awarded by the court?"

"Please, call me Lynn if you would, okay? And the answer is he is way behind on everything and in no position to ever catch up. Why is that so important anyway?"

Sol explained as well as accepting her name as her name and to be used when referring or speaking to her; she had made that known. Sol in fact was impressed she had stood up to him on that issue. "It could be important. I'm handling a case at the moment that will reap thousands and thousands in income for a pair of underage boys; their birth father is a weasel, never supported them in any way, but he would have come back on their mother if he had any sort of leverage to get at their bank accounts. We slammed that door and sealed the lock. If you agree, I'll talk to Ari about the situation." Lynn nodded as he continued. "With your permissions, I will become agent for your kids and negotiate the situation. There is no guarantee this company will come through but if we don't ask, we don't get; it is in their best interests to save money; it is in our best interests to get some of that money. You may note I use the term 'we' and I do mean it; as their agent I will be paid a percentage, so you can see it is in my own best interests to do well. In contrast to that process I will not in any way ever cause any harm to come to my clients, not ever. That may seem a bit altruistic on my part but the reality is that even if I didn't care about them as individuals, it could cause me a subsequent loss of income; I would not like to think of myself in solely those terms. Now, on to our agreement."

Half an hour later the two parents walked back to his ride and headed back to the Behr home. Quiet while riding along, once they arrived at the house, Lynn made her wishes known.. "Alan, could I come in and sit with you for a while, maybe...I don't know...gain some level of comfort with all this, please?"

"Sure; come on in. I sort of have the same thoughts. We need to talk this through until we are sure we are both on the same page, the kids are safe, all that. Up front, I know you are about to ask me about the money thing with the lawyer; let me handle that, okay?" And so it went until they were agreed it was the thing to do and that Ari and Sol were two good people to have on their side. Al did finally remember a conversation with a friend of his, Jeff Banning, a fellow engineer; Jeff was married to the eldest sister from the Big Flags commercial trio of sisters and had commented one time on the mildly abrasive personality of Sol Kaplan; that abrasive trait gave Sol traction to negotiate, a lot of traction. Jeff even remembered Sols' counterpart saying if he could survive Sol, he could survive anyone.

Within a few days the paperwork headed the other direction but with major modifications. The rewritten contract spelled out specifics on treatment primarily of the children, work limitations for them, expected accommodations, rate of pay, details a less motivated person may have skipped over; Sol Kaplan was motivated in the positive. Concurrently, Ari went to family court and obtained a total disconnect between the ex-husband, Lynn and the two boys. In exchange the ex-husband was let off the hook for thousands in support he had never paid. Two days later Gill Lanham called again in the early morning.

"Hey, hi Al; Gill Lanham here. Jesus, what did you people do to that contract we sent you? I gotta tell you our legal guys totally blew it off at first; I mean there was no way they were going to accept those terms. One of the guys I know a little bit even called to tell me the whole thing was a bust, that they would never accept terms they didn't set down. It was looking bad for a while there..."

"So, they got a little tense? Gill, those contract terms...we talked to the kids' agent about all that; your legal guys may not know it but Sol is the agent for the Big Flags TV ad running these days. I get the feeling he is not to be screwed with. Even better, the girls in that ad live here in town; I had a chance to talk to the oldest sister who is now married to a good friend of mine; between that and the recommendation of my own lawyer, that's how we ended up with Sol Kaplan as the kids agent. Anyway, we out of business now?"

"No, not at all. I was gonna tell you after they calmed down a bit and did their own homework they realized the contract was written by professionals with some real clout in the business. The guy even admitted to me they disregarded the guardian-ship part your lawyer sent, until they looked him up. Hey, he's a small town lawyer, you know, someone they thought they could just run over at will, until they read that little reference on the bottom of his business card; the guy has contacts with more power than the Pope for god's sake. So, you will be getting a signed copy back with no changes to your proposal; our travel people will be in contact with you over the specific arrangements to be made, and I gotta tell you the marketing people are nervous about this getting out. Are you sure there are no other copies of that DVD floating around anywhere just by accident?"

"No, no copies to the best of my knowledge. Our videographer who did the taping did tell me she had filed for copyright, just in case, and was required to send a copy of the DVD by wire with the application, but she is confident it is all kept safe. Okay?"

"Sure, okay. Man, I'm getting to be as nervous as the marketing people, but we're one step closer to getting this in place. I really do believe our sales will fly once this hits the market place. Take care of those kids, okay?"

Alan laughed at the comment. "I think you can count on that, but remember, they're kids and things go wrong from time to time. Will you be kept advised as travel plans are put in place?"

"I will. I probably shouldn't tell you this but just so you know, the marketing people are not happy a sales person like me discovered what may be the magic key to jacking up sales;

they do not like being upstaged, not one bit, hence my earlier comment about not trusting them too much. But then, you saw the contract they proposed, all for them and little for you, so I'm sure you have an idea of their mind set. And Alan, I do look forward to meeting you in person in the not too distant future. Talk to you later." And Gill was off the line.

Three weeks later, early one morning the Behr van approached a side gate at the Conyerville airport, a place with a slightly longer runway than their small hometown airport featured. Motioned to stop by a guard at the closed gate, Alan was informed that was not a public gate and asked what he was doing.

"We're looking for the restaurant this morning."

"There's no restaurant at this gate, sir. What were you going to order?"

"Mile high meringue pie."

As the gate swung open the guard motioned them in, pointing to a parking place they could use. Greeted by another airport staffer they were informed the corporate plane was already on final approach and they should be boarding within minutes, the van would be fine where it was parked, and in case it mattered there were restrooms just inside the building. Fifteen minutes later, passengers seated and belted, the corporate jet again reached for the sky. Once at altitude and on cruise, the second seat officer came back into the passenger area and opened a conversation.

"Good morning; I'm first officer Tony Burcham; welcome aboard. I had to be up front for the takeoff but now that things are a bit less hectic, is there anything I can tell you? There is a bathroom right back there, just in case, but I have to tell you it isn't very big and using it if we hit any air turbulence...well...you can see the problem. Anyway, I understand someone will be meeting you in LA and you won't be going through the main terminal. We'll call ahead to make sure all that is in place as we go along. Now, any of you want to see what goes on up front?" Tony Burcham was nearly caught in the stampede as four little kids all jumped up at once. He would be patient as they examined the flight deck, answering questions only little kids could think to ask and resolved in his own mind to talk more with his own sub-teens when he got home that night.

Stopped in front of a private hangar in LA, the ladder extended itself and the travelers prepared to debark. There was a limo, sort of mini-bus, apparently awaiting them. Two steps off the plane and Gilll Lanham make his presence known.

"Mr. Behr, right? Gill Lanham at your service. Welcome to LA; good flight I hope?"

Alan assured Gill it had been a good flight, introduced the rest of the group, help unload some minimal amount of luggage and boarded the mini-bus for the ride to their hotel, all the while Gill went on about the schedule they would be following. By plan, Gill would make sure they were settled in comfortably at the hotel, treat them to lunch at a place sponsored by a major toy manufacturer, then back on the bus for a brief tour of LA highlights. They would not go to the play room until the next day, would spend the entire day there if needed, return to the hotel and on the next day fly home, just like the schedule said would happen. The hotel was a bit of a surprise in itself, expressed by Lynn as she stood in the adjoining doorway.

"Alan, this is almost too much. Are you sure these are the rooms we are supposed to be in? The key card worked, all that, but look at this place, two whole rooms in each suite, large rooms, two queen beds in that area, basket full of beautiful fruit that I guess is for us, this door that joins the two suites, all that..."

Gill knew the answer and responded for Alan. "Lynn, my company keeps these rooms on reservation for visiting buyers, people like that we really want to treat right and show our concern they have a comfortable stay. And I might add, the goodies in the refrigerator or snack bar or wherever are all yours to enjoy. Once I realized how paranoid our marketing people were about this I knew I had the leverage to get the room usage; please, enjoy. So, take your time to unpack a bit, freshen up, then back on the bus and we'll go touring LA. Okay?

It was okay with all. The evening meal was at a fine dining establishment, one where the wait staff was accustomed to dealing with the children of high rollers, some well behaved and some not, but these children of Alan and Lynn were smart and knew how to get along, how to smile at the right time, how to say please and thank you, and how to change the seating arrangement from time to time just to confuse everyone.

Returning to their rooms for the night the parents decided to leave the adjoining door open a bit between suites, finally settling in for the night. Lynn did one more time express her thanks to Alan for his part in getting everything in place and taking care of them. In turn, he looked her right in the eyes and said his only disappointment all day was that there was no double sleeping bag to share that evening; she would retire for the night wondering if he was serious about his closing comment, and as sleep overtook her realized she would most likely have been a willing partner to that arrangement, ready or not.

While the first day of their adventure had gone well, the same could not be said of the second day, not at all. The play room was full of lights and cameras; each child would be wearing a microphone; the videographer was pushy to say the least, an expert in everything except working with children, and worst of all, the playhouse they were to assemble bore no close resemblance to the ones they had previously experienced. The director of the production didn't like the yellow hardhats or safety green vests they had brought along and insisted they not be worn, no one could find a large plastic container in which the small parts could be sorted, inventoried, and separated, and there was no battery screwdriver to speed the process. For all that was wrong, there was one point where rights needed to be established before progress could be made. The director of the production made her demands known.

"Okay, we don't have the plastic container so you will just have to use the floor, and I don't know what sort of battery thing you think you need but we don't seem to have whatever it is; make allowances for that if you have to. We need to get on with this, so mom and dad are going to leave the room now and we'll get started shooting." Alan saw Lynn's immediate glance over to him, eyes wide; he made their point.

"I need to inform you on behalf of our children and their contract that mom and dad are going nowhere and especially not out of this room." The director opened her mouth to protest but he continued before she could speak. "If you had bothered to read the contract, and I don't believe you have" he was guessing in that fact but was right "then you would know that at least one of us is to be here at all times in observation. We even have reciprocal guardianships in place for our respective children so either one of us has full authority. Now, having cleared the air, please feel free to continue with your work, and by the way had you bothered to talk to Mr. Lanham you would have known a battery screwdriver can make life much easier and faster doing one of these assemblies." Alan glanced briefly toward Gill Lanham and realized his new associate was trying to stifle a guffaw over Alan's defiant speech.

Everyone in the room at the time held their breath, just sure this pain in the butt director would chew up Alan Behr and spit him out like so much confetti. It would not happen. For all her bluster and demanding take charge personality, she looked directly at Alan Behr and thought better for her own safety from the look on his face. Clearly he was not afraid of her in any way shape or form and seemed to know she had not read the contract. What else he may have known about her shooting technique was unknown to her but there was that consideration in her own mind he might just know she was a borderline child abuser in getting them to do what she wanted, especially in the absence of parental supervision. She caved in.

"Okay, fine with me, just please stay outside the lens field of vision." Shooting began, they broke for a catered pizza lunch, then resumed. Alan was keeping track of the time, was well aware of the contract limitations for child labor, and with only thirty minutes to go so notified the director.

Shooting ended as time expired and all retired from the area for the day, Gill taking his group back to the hotel for the evening, making apologies as they went along. Alan did not push the issue as he was aware four kids were nearly ready to fold from a long day when nothing seemed to go right. In a sense that was true although they had done enough run-throughs of each step that a whole video could be pieced together in the lab. That also would come back to haunt some people.

Between Alan and Lynn they decided the last night in town would be spent in their respective rooms, but as compensation and by agreement with Gill Lanham, the kids could order anything they wanted from the room service menu. The event did not turn out to be a junk food orgy, although it did come close in some choices; the kids did know what they wanted, mostly sampler platters of appetizers, and at the end of the meal very little was left. Wise parenting suggested the kids could stay up but first should change into their pj's; in their willing compliance, Anna forgot all about her complaint voiced during the camping adventure that boys would see her in her pj's. Four small persons were totally gone before nine PM. The plane ride home the next day was uneventful although the crew let them sit up front one at a time. Gill Lanham continued to apologize for the director but was assured no offense had been taken by any of the group. It would be some days before they would hear from him again although the checks arriving in Sol Kaplan's electronic mail box for distribution were significant.

Chapter Eight

Best Use

With the video somewhere in production, life returned to near normal for the neighbors, almost. Alan was in his shop working on a solution for a new problem that has been shipped to him overnight from a good client. It would take some time to find the snag causing a problem in the consistency of operation, but he would find it in good time; of that the client was assured. Mid morning Ari Schoenroth called, but not about the video process.

"Good morning, Mr. Behr. How are things going for you today?"

Alan knew something was going on when Ari used the more formal introduction. "Okay, Ari; it's Alan, remember? When you get formal I get nervous, so give; what's up?"

"It's about your associate, Lynn, but nothing bad. I know this is sort of off the beaten path but I have a couple of questions in mind, then I can tell you the motivation behind the call. Okay? Again, this is nothing bad, just sort of a very informal off the record fishing expedition."

Alan agreed to the informal off the record chat and would soon learn the reality of the situation as Ari continued. "Okay, I think I know all I need to know for the moment. You're telling me she is apparently a lot more capable at accounting, things like that, than her present position would require, that she may do some upper level tasks but for the most part is paid at a rate more appropriate to the lower level work she completes. That about the situation from what you can see? And let me say your answer isn't a go or no go response for what I will propose but does carry a lot of weight."

"Ari, I'm no accountant; some days I can barely keep my checkbook straight, so I'm no expert in the field. I do know she has had some formal training, though not as much as she would like; that divorce issue really messed things up for her both work wise and financially. Her ex, as you well know, never contributed, which left her scrambling for the essentials. She seems to be doing better now; in fact she moved in next door as a cost saving measure, got out of that bi-level or whatever that was costing a bundle in house payments. Is that info of any use at all? I'm just sort of rambling here I guess."

"It is useful, and now the reason for the twenty questions. When the two of you were in here about the guardianship and all that, I remembered her talking about what she did for a living. It sort of made a connection in my head with another issue of which I am aware; it's taken me a while to put some data together, plus I wanted to give you time for the road trip and recovery thereafter. I have a sometimes client who is looking for someone in this area with some accounting expertise, not anything real formal at this point, just sort of in the inquiry state for the moment. Do you think Lynn would be amenable to a job change if the money and perks were there? Like I said, nothing formal; just asking at this stage."

Alan thought it over for a moment or two before responding. "Ari, I wouldn't rule anything out; I do know she has a strong work ethic but I also know she has had some hard times and there would unquestionably have to be some assurance of job longevity for her to make a move. I do not believe her situation is as desperate as it once may have been, but I will also admit to doing what I can in the shadows to help her out a bit. It just seems to be the neighborly thing to do, so I do it, no ulterior motive, nothing like that. Okay?"

"Yes, okay; I understand and I agree that at this point you are in the good friend category with her, perhaps the very good friend category, but not a friend with benefits. So, I plan to call her this evening when I know she will be home and talk to her a bit about a company position that may be opening up in this area if they can find the right person for that position. I know this is a bit out of the ordinary, looking for the person first then defining the position, but they have a record of doing things like that in the past with significant success. If you want, I can call you tomorrow and give you an idea of her response. This isn't some secret mission, nothing like that, just an informal way that may lead up to a formal process while keeping a low profile. My client is very particular in selecting persons to interview and in general does not accept walk-in's. That said I will tell you it would be a long line if they openly advertised for this position. Okay with Alan Behr?"

It was okay with Alan, although the entirety of the plan remained a bit of a mystery. If Ari knew some way to make life better for Lynn, Alan was all in, even though he remained unaware of why he was so motivated, or even why he did those things in the background to help her out. Maybe it was, like he believed, being neighborly, like repairing the drum belt on her clothes dryer when it broke; he knew how to do those things, actually enjoyed doing things like that, and would have done the same for anyone else had they asked; somewhere along the way he failed to realize that, yes, he would do the same for anyone else, but in all likelihood would not have early morning chats with them in his shop. Maybe it was the iced cinnamon rolls...

It was early evening and once again getting ready to make s'mores, Alan was stoking the fire pit in the back yard to get the heat built up. The four kids had come to him asking to make the treats; he had sent the boys home to check with their mother. Having received her assurance via the returning boys, he set to the task after making sure all ingredients were on hand as the heat started to build. It didn't take long for the group to assemble and start in the process, enjoy the products of their own efforts, and feel the warmth of family, maybe not all the same family but close enough anyway. With the process completed and the fire one again stoked up a bit for sitting around and enjoying the warm quiet, Lynn took a turn in the conversation as the kids started an undefined game of tag of some sorts and left the parents to their own company.

"Your lawyer friend called me this afternoon, right after I got home from work. Can I talk to you about what he told me, maybe ask a question or two? I have no idea what to think or which way to go. I know you seem to have a good opinion of him, and he sure took good care of that DVD adventure, all that, but this is something really different and I'm nervous. Okay?"

"Lynn, just so you know, Ari called me this afternoon about whatever it is he wanted to discuss with you. I don't know to this minute what that subject is other than it somehow involves a job position; even then it was sort of hazy at very best. He did say he was working on behalf of a sometimes client, but little beyond that. I don't know if I can be of any help or not."

"Okay, I understand; Ari suggested I talk to you about what he was proposing. What he told me is that his client is looking for someone with accounting experience to do some work in this area, sometimes involved in helping to define a new system or upgrade an existing system, then to go back in and help with the installation and training. I would work out of my home, be paid mileage, maybe do a minor bit of travel, other things like that but with no broad scope specifics defined until they have the proposed candidates capabilities better defined; I have never heard of any company doing things that way, not ever, finding an employee first and then defining a job to fit the employee. It works the other way around and I don't know what to think, I don't."

"Ari sort of told me the same thing he told you, that the company intends to find the person, then define the job, and that they have a successful track record of doing things that way. Ari is no fool; he knows this mystical company and he knows you, so he must be connecting things somehow and coming up in the positive. Has he defined any other activity, anything?"

"Nothing other than talk to you. He said he would call back in a day or so and see how I was feeling about things. What should I tell him, Alan? I guess I need to make some sort of a decision to agree or not agree with whatever he has in mind."

"Lynn, what do you want to tell him, that you're interested if it would better your life and that of your family? My suggestion is that you at least talk to him if you have any interest at all in what he might be proposing. Ari can be very secretive if he wants; your present employer will never know about the conversation unless you tell them. If you need me to sit with you for an interview, whatever it takes, you know I will do what I can to help you out, to see you do well. I don't know what else to say, to tell you. That is about as much as I know, except to say one more time, Ari Schoenroth is no fool and if he has something in mind it will not be a fool's errand to pursue that idea. Does that help you at all, Lynn?"

"It does help; I agree that he does not seem the sort of person to go off in random directions. I'll wait for his call, then let you know what happens." She paused for a second as he remained silent, sure there was more she wanted to say. "Alan, I know this is crazy, but the man has me thinking about things and getting excited in spite of probably knowing better. Thank you; I'll talk to him when he calls. What would I do without you?" Even in the fading light he could see the blush reddening her face when she vocalized much more than she intended. Alan Behr eased her embarrassment.

"For the moment let's not find that out, okay?" It was okay with her.

On Thursday Ari called back, letting Lynn know his client was interested in learning more about her and her talents. They were aware she worked full time during the week and were prepared to make allowances for that restriction, not to mention some additional allowances she had not considered as yet. Ari illuminated the situation.

"Lynn, this idea is starting to get legs, but let me suggest something here if I might. I know you are nervous about what I might be proposing so to ally that concern suppose we do this: my client is prepared to bend their own rules and take a meeting with you this Saturday morning if at all possible; it is not a life or death crises if that can't be done, but one of their operating standards that has always placed them in good stead is that if a situation is favorable to their operation they want to adopt it as soon as possible. I think, I'm rather sure, they see this opportunity being placed before you as also being good for their operation. Please be aware they will not trade your well being for their own well being, never; that is not how they operate, standing on the bodies so they can see over the next hill. They don't do that sort of thing. To be very blunt, if they do not see this opportunity as being a positive for all con-cerned, an offer will not be made; the reason for that decision will be clarified so you will not be left wondering if you made some sort of error. So, back to the original premise; would you entertain taking a meeting with them at their place of business this Saturday, say eleven AM or so?"

Lynn's nervous concern remained firmly entrenched. "Mr. Schoenroth, Ari, I don't even know what these people are proposing for me to consider, I don't know where their place of business might be, and I'll admit going in there alone wherever it might be gives me the willies. I want things to get better for us but while my mind wants that my spirit is pretty weak after the divorce and all that. I will admit that taping episode in LA gave me cause for hope some good things can happen for us, but there is one factor that remains steadfast in all this: Alan Behr. Without him we would not have been in LA no matter what was being promised. Please do not read more into this than is real, but I think if he can be with me to give me courage, then I can do as asked. Where is this place anyway that you keep talking about?"

Ari Schoenroth had a bite, a solid bite on the bait; she was game if he could make the conditions right. That took all of a few minutes when he asked her to check with Alan to see if he was available for the Saturday adventure, and upon learning that information told Lynn he would formalize the arrangements and get back to her within minutes. Ten minutes later he called back.

"Okay, here's how this happens, and by the way my client knows you have the twin boys and Alan has his twin daughters. Please do not misunderstand me; these people don't spy on others but they do their homework. They were not surprised when Alan's name popped up, not at all, and they readily agreed he should be with you. And by the way, you are to bring the four kids along; there are people who will see to them during your meeting time; I have been to this place with my own kids and will tell you the only downside is they won't want to leave. So, we good to go? Wait, one more thing: if you are asked to stay for lunch, no matter the outcome of the meeting, stay, whatever you do; you will not be disappointed, I guarantee."

They were good to go. Saturday morning, leaving in time for the eleven AM meeting, the Behr bus as it was known, headed for Conyerville and a place they had never before seen in spite of having been in Conyerville to board the plane for the LA trip. Sure enough, if one knew the landmarks by the road the big gate emblazoned with one word "WINDMERE" was right there as they turned in. Keying the call box Alan made their presence known, was directed where to go once they entered, and he watched the huge gate close swiftly behind them; he would learn over the course of time the gate could stop any vehicle from entering, even crushing a small car into useless junk. Stay to the left at the fork, go past the beautiful and ornate house and dive into one of the marked visitor parking spaces; someone would meet them, and sure enough, someone did. As the six piled out of the van wondering what was next, a huge man appeared from a side door in the house, identified himself, and asked them to follow him.

"Good morning, folks. I'm Dennis, your tour guide for the moment. You're maybe ten minutes early for your eleven AM meeting; that's a good thing. Let's go to the kitchen, get comfortable, and I guarantee the meeting will start at eleven as promised. Now, you kids ready for some fun and games?" and seeing four anxious faces looking up at him, continued: "You'll meet Amanda and Jack in the kitchen and will be with them this morning while your parents are in the meeting. They live here and know all the rules so no problem there. Here we go, you kids grab seats over at the short table and we big people will be here, okay?"

It was okay with the four as they met their playmates for the morning while their parents perched on the tall stools and watched a young woman approach them.

"Hi, I'm Leslie, Les for short. I got called in to work today because we have some sort of big shindig later this afternoon, bunch of people, so I got called to help out a bit. Now, what can I get you to drink while you wait? Never mind; I'll be right back with it."

Two adults sat there wondering what had just happened, finally asking Dennis the situation and learning they were not the first to be amazed by the ever cheerful Leslie. "She's actually a housekeeper for the place but she likes to come in here and play waitress now and then; we'll lose her pretty soon as she finishes up her EMT classes and joins the fire department; certainly no one here begrudges her that success; she's had a rough go of things but that's behind her now and marrying a really great guy ahead of her in the next few weeks. Here she comes."

Returning with a small tray Leslie set a large mug of aromatic coffee before Alan, and a cup of hot green tea with a small crock of honey before Lynn. "Please, try the tea and honey combo; it's sort of a trademark beverage here. I need to get back and see what Doris needs me to do in the kitchen but if you need anything Dennis knows where to find me. See you." And Leslie was gone just that fast. It was then the parents realized there were no kids to be seen in the area, none, not a one, but Dennis let them know all was well.

"Amanda and Jack know the limits here, where they can go and where not to go. Technically I'm not at work but will keep an eye out for them anyway; to tell the truth, work here is often times more fun than work should be to be called work. One thing I can guarantee for sure: they will be back in here for lunch, do it yourself taco's today and the kids never ever miss that adventure. Looks like its that time; I'll walk you back to the meeting room." The three headed off into the house following along as Dennis led the way. It was amazing how much the house seemed to contain, even a really large meeting room containing a huge inlaid Oak table that could seat multitudes. A few steps more and he pointed to an open door to a smaller room. "They're in there. See you at lunch for sure."

The two stepped into the doorway to find three people awaiting them; introductions were done all around as they learned Ryan and Laura Williams were the owners, while the third person present was Jillian Andrews; her presence would be etched in the mind of Alan Behr for a long time with her blouse open an extra button down and the blouse contents threatening to rip off a couple more buttons, not to mention the long blond hair and other prominent Norse features. All took places at the table as the meeting convened, Laura leading off.

"Thank you so much for coming in today. I know this is rather out of the ordinary, at least for us here at Windmere. We do not believe in working longer or harder to get ahead, just smarter in every way. That is sort of why we are here today. We do know you two are neighbors and that your kids spend a lot of time together. Never do we actually spy on people, but we would be fools to not use easily obtainable data. So, I will admit this is none of our business and has no relation to our business here today, but would either of you tell us what that trip to LA was all about? If you don't want to for some reason..."

Lynn broke in. "We would be happy to do so but I have to say my curiosity about this meeting is gnawing on me pretty seriously at the moment."

Laura continued. "Agreed; we'll back burner the LA trip for the moment. Now, on to the reason for today's meeting. First of all, Jill is here because this is directly related to her own work load. Windmere is full into providing accounting systems for our clients; some want support, some want us to do everything for them, some want results with no further involvement; it varies all over the place. At the same time, we also survey and design new accounting systems for clients, sometimes to make their lives easier, sometimes because the IRS can make one's life miserable given the right circumstances, and I will even admit a time or two when it was purely one-upmanship, no doubt. Let me broad brush this first with an overview of WINDMERE." An organization form appeared on a wall screen. Within minutes the guests has a good overview of what Windmere did and didn't do, the nature of their far flung empire, and the reason they were there. Jill took over the narrative.

"By degree, I am a forensic accountant; I hold Masters Degrees in both accounting and criminology and am a CPA. I know those two degrees may appear to be disparate subjects but they seem to come together more often that we would like. Upon invitation, I will go into a business, survey the operation, design a business plan for upgrading, call out the supervision needed on our part and if the contract is signed off, return as needed to make sure the project is completed to design specs. Business has been good, almost too good; we don't want to turn anyone down but as an individual I cannot be all the places I need to be on a timely basis; I need a helper, in a sense a partner. So, we put out a feeler, let some people like Ari Schoenroth know we were looking around; he was on the phone to us within minutes of you leaving his office that first time. He believes, as do we, you can be that partner if you are so inclined. So, tell me if you would what you like about your present position, what work you enjoy doing. Once we know that we'll see if we can to build a position to match your abilities. Okay?"

Lynn was stunned. "I don't understand. I thought positions were defined then people hired who fit that description. What am I missing here?"

Jill continued: "You are missing nothing. We do things this way, construct a position backwards in a sense, because we know the more you like about a position the better you will perform in that position. Will all be perfect? Never happen, but we can get close, and the closer we get the happier everyone is, so, again, what do you like to do, and please do not think we do not want to hear the downside either; not everyone likes the same things, so please be honest and we will do the same. We truly believe in finding the best use of your abilities and remain assured at this point those abilities are not being used to the extent possible under your present circumstances. We may be able to change that situation."

The one hour was barely enough to contain the discussion about what Windmere staff could and would do to make Lynn happy in the position being considered. With a little encouragement Jill got Lynn talking about things in her life; along the way Jill also learned somewhat through osmosis that Alan Behr loomed large in Lynn's life. No mention was ever made of the sleeping bag incident but there were plenty of other indicators Lynn trusted this man, especially considering she would not be in that room had they not agreed he could join them. On top of that, they learned about the LA trip and the need for guardianships; only a trusting parent could execute such a paper; Lynn had trusted him. And finally, there was one more thing Laura needed to cover in the process as she reentered the conversation.

"Lynn, we will document all this discussion so we know for sure we are all on the same page. There is one more thing I need to mention, and let me preface that by saying we are not above sweetening a deal to move it along. We do want you to be comfortable and accepting of this situation; it appears we are achieving that goal but I want to offer just a bit more incentive. If you decide to come aboard the WINDMERE ship of state, we will make provisions at your local junior college to pay all the tuition, book rental, fees if any, all that, up front so you can continue your education. We are aware you would like at least a bachelor's in accounting; your junior college already has connections with the state university to provide professors for bachelor level courses in aviation; we have talked to them about the accounting situation and find them amenable. There are a number of persons who would like that bachelor level process to be available. It would not be paid company time but the expenses would be covered. Does that hold some interest for you, Lynn?"

In her being Lynn felt the emotions rise unexpectedly at this new information; this whole thing was becoming dream like. "I don't know what to say, I don't. Sure, I've had hopes but this seems way too good to be true. I'm already very intrigued by the opportunity I see before me; you don't have to do anything like that..."

Laura interrupted: "Lynn, remember when I said that if we see an opportunity favorable to WINDMERE we take it as soon as possible? Yes, I'll admit it is a bit selfish on our part but the reality is the more you know the better off we are; it is really that simple, a solid return for our investment. Now, we are aware our financial contribution is not 100 per cent, that there are still some vesting costs on you for things such as child care for night classes, things like that..."

It was Alan's turn to break in as he looked directly at Lynn sitting beside him: "I will trade a pan of hot iced cinnamon rolls from you every so often in exchange for the boys staying in my house on those class nights. Deal?" Lynn managed a positive head nod as her eyes met his.

Laura continued: "So, Lynn, it looks like everything is coming your way. I know you need to take the time to read the position description, proposed pay statement and list of perks like vacation days, things like that, but for our planning purposes what is the possibility we could get a tentative agreement from you, nothing more formal at this point but an idea of where you are with things at the moment, what you see as your path ahead? I ask because if the response is positive then we will stop expending hours on the recruiting process."

Alan very quietly leaned closer to Lynn's nearest ear as he spoke in a whisper: "If I have a vote, it is a yes, but you do what you need to do for Lynn, just you."

It was nearly too much for her to absorb at one time, so many positive things happening, then one unexpected thing gave her the strength to rise to the occasion. This man beside her had told her very quietly how he felt, but it was when she felt his hand slide over hers and clasp it in his that she knew her answer. It did not go unnoticed by Laura Williams but she already had thoughts about how things were between the two seated before her. Lynn had to voice her response and did so with a slight tremor in her delivery: "Yes, please; I want this position even if I don't know for sure what I'm doing; what can I say?"

Laura closed out the meeting. "Then we are in agreement: we want you aboard, and you want to come aboard. The finer details will all be reduced to writing on Monday and will be sent to you by whatever means you find acceptable. Should this process continue to fruition as we expect it will, we would want you to give your present employer the standard two week's notice. Now, I do believe lunch is calling; please join us in the kitchen. As much as I enjoy do-it-yourself tacos, half the fun is in watching the kids do the assembly for themselves." Five persons headed for the kitchen.

Ari Schoenroth has been right when he encouraged them to stay for lunch. Just as Lynn and Alan arrived with Jill, Laura and Ryan, some grubby and well worn children arrived through another door, were stopped by Leslie and sent to wash their hands before sitting down. It was the same scenario that had played out a hundred times before in the big kitchen, with the same results. As the kids returned, hands hopefully much cleaner, food started to arrive on a long low table along one wall; there was a riser board in front of the table so small people could reach everything reasonably unassisted. Hard shells and soft shells in yellow corn, white corn, and wheat, tortillas in a warmer, three kinds of diced peppers (red, green, yellow), two kinds of diced onions (white and red), shredded purple and green lettuce, spiced corn compote, cilantro, two colors of diced tomatoes (red and yellow), bowls of shredded chicken, shredded beef and pulled pork, and three dishes of shredded cheese of various sharpness, all followed by three bowls of topping sauce (marked regular, Ryan and Fernando). With the head count now numbering in the teens as more arrived, the kids went first and the adults had to agree it was fun to see what happened as the table top became littered with stray pieces of food. Lynn had to restrain herself from intervening when her boys hit the line, being cautioned by Laura sitting at her side to let them learn the process on their own; they would be helped a bit by the ever present Leslie when they seemed to falter. Shells jammed to the hilt the kids retired to their area and the adults started through the line. Although tempted by the unknown, Alan listened to the suggestion from Dennis Anderson he try the "Regular" topping sauce with some of the "Ryan" on the side as a sampler. His taste buds told him he was grateful the suggestion had been voiced as the fire was nearly unquenchable. A double stack scoop of ice cream from the dessert table helped ease the heat.

As the clock approached one PM the party of six, escorted by the party of four, walked back to the Behr bus to depart. While the others loaded in for the trip, Laura worked her way around to Alan's side, standing quietly as he settled in for the drive, then breaking her silence very softly so Alan could hear but others could not. "Alan, thank you for bringing her to us; we are aware her life experiences have been difficult and only with your support is she able to do those things she most needs to do. I sometimes see or sense things others do not; while it is in our best interest and, we believe her best interest to sign on with us, it is more important you take care of her for your own interests and I believe hers. I'm no fortune teller, but I did see you take her hand when she faltered; it told me you care about her and that a simple touch of her hand on your part gave her the strength to do what she needed to do. Please, take care of her; she just might be a keeper." With that Laura walked away before he could answer, although at that exact moment he was rendered virtually unable to speak at all.

The four kids were asleep almost before they rolled out the gate as they headed home. The two parents remained quiet for the first few miles, with Lynn finally opening the conversation. "Alan, please tell me that what just happened at that place actually happened, that I am not having some sort of illusory taco hot sauce induced fantasy, that I may be looking at my own highest ideal of a job I would love to do every day. I don't even know the pay rate or if there are any benefits but I think I already agreed to take the position. Is this real or just some figment of my imagination from which I will awaken and probably cry?"

Alan glanced over at her as they drove along, knowing what Laura had told him he would keep to himself for the moment. "When all this came up I called a couple of people I know and asked some questions about this WINDMERE place. I know where Ari stands and do not doubt his position, but I also knew I would feel better with a second or third opinion. It was sort of guessing on my part but I found several people who are well familiar with WINDMERE for assorted reasons, one as a part-time contractor and two as customers for the accounting service. Everyone agrees the whole operation keeps a very low profile for their own reasons, but they are also known to be up front and honest in their dealings with others. I was encouraged to make the trip and to encourage you to make the trip. To a person my associates told me that even if this doesn't work out in the long term, that it would not have any negative consequences, that WINDMERE does not do things that way. On Monday I guess you will find out the more mundane details, like pay and bennies. If you want, I can read over the contract with you, but I suspect it will be comprehensive in every respect, no hidden 'gotchas' anywhere in there. I don't know what else to say except maybe to offer congratulations."

"Thank you; you know I would never have made that trip without you beside me, and then just as I was feeling rather overwhelmed by it all I felt this hand on mine giving me strength to forge ahead. I do know I saw Laura glance at our hands when you did that; she didn't say anything about it, just seemed to smile and continue on without pause. I don't know if you saw it or not, but as we were walking toward lunch I saw her hand slip into Ryan's hand; she didn't even look to see where his hand was, just connected; I'd guess it wasn't the first time that has happened. Oh, one more thing: you passed the Jill test."

Alan was lost. "What are you talking about, the Jill test? I was impressed she listened to every word you said, even seemed to absorb it directly; she didn't even talk to me very much, there were no questions, nothing like that but I'm not the candidate anyway, so what test?"

Lynn laughed as she continued. "The Jill test is what she called it, told me about it at lunch while you were refilling your plate for the umpteenth time. You know and I know that blouse she was wearing had plenty of buttons, but she made sure it was open far enough down that you could get a good look at her Norse assets, even a bit of black lace peeking out of the plunge. We know you looked, but you didn't stare for long minutes wondering if that next button down was going to give it up and go flying off into space, you just did a quick survey and returned to business. She told me she does things like that because in about five seconds she can get a very accurate read on the depth of people's interests in the issue at hand. She even laughed about it, telling me more than once she has caught men staring then asked them some pointed and complicated question and watched them go down in embarrassment as they fumbled and crashed. She doesn't do it to be mean, just as she described it: one more tool in her armament. Now, just so you know and won't feel neglected, she told me to tell you everything you saw is real, no enhancements, no augmentation, no genetic modifications, none, just Jill."

Alan shifted a bit in his seat but didn't actually squirm at her observation. "I won't lie about it; yes, I did look but Lynn, the woman rather made sure I would. I'm not saying she flaunted anything but it sure was there in front of me; she is one really healthy person but enough of that. How are you feeling at the moment, and by the way I did mean it when I volunteered to keep the boys on class nights." It was slow and subtle, his hand sliding slowly over the top of the console as it neared her hand, then touching her hand as she realized what he was doing and placed her hand in his. It was a simple act, hand holding, but the powerful connection it evoked was very real. There was more conversation as they drove along but none so powerful as a simple touch of a handhold.

By early evening they were once again seated around the fire pit just because they could. The four kids were involved in some sort of hide-and-seek with other kids from the neighborhood, leaving the two parents on their own for the moment. After returning home from the road trip to WINDMERE, Lynn had busied herself around the house doing minor chores; she realized it was busy work to give her hands something to do while she thought about the situation before her and the one question that kept surfacing in her thoughts again and again. Maybe now was a good time in the quiet of the evening to slake her thirst to learn an answer or two from this man sitting beside her, almost but not quite touching her, while lingering thoughts of the touch of his hand on hers were still with her. She asked her question.

"Alan, I know I always seem to have more questions than answers but sometimes the same question seems to circle around and come up time and again. Can I ask you something?"

Warm and comfortable in the evening air, sensing her close presence even without physical contact, he turned enough to look directly at her for the moment. "Sure, go for it. I have few secrets to hide. Ask away."

Lynn felt sure what she was about to ask had a not so subtle danger to it; what if he didn't want her to know how he felt about anything, that it was none of her business and she was getting too close for his own comfort level; what if her quest for answers caused him to push her away to arms length; what then? She needed to know, get at least a hint so she would feel better about a lot of things. Courage tightened up, she continued.

"Ever since we moved in next door, every day it seems, you have been there helping us in some way or other; I get all that; you're being the good neighbor even if it doesn't pay so well. You even feed us at times, more often than I would like to admit, and all the things you do make our lives so much better. I know in a financial sense having you next door has helped me dodge a lot of expensive repair bills; I do understand and accept that as your good will nature. But today, when we were sitting there and I was virtually in a frozen panic, I felt your hand touch mine; everything seemed to change at that moment. My fear somehow transformed itself into a force for good, pushing me to go forward, your hand on mine. Alan, you get nothing from doing things like that, being my foundation to stand on when I'm weak and unsure. I know sure as this world that no matter what I might ask you will somehow make my concerns unfounded; I remember all too well trying to understand why you had just fed us and we were then at the ice cream treat store; somehow you made my legitimate and concerned question to be about sprinkles and nothing more." She turned to face him and reaching out took his hands into her own as she plied her question, "Alan, please, I want to know what is going on here. I do not for a second think you would ever endanger any of us or harm us or cause bad things to happen to us, but I also don't know why you do some things when I see no motivation, no reason, no sense of anything to be gained. Please, tell me, help me understand."

She fell silent, his hands still in hers held firmly, as she hoped with all her might she had not just breeched the thread she had felt growing between them. Maybe there was no thread and it was all in her imagination; maybe she was driven by some hidden need to "get even" for the deeds done her by her former husband as her mind replaced him with this man before her. It was not so; Alan Behr had motivation, unspoken to this point but motivation.

"Lynn, this isn't easy for me, trying to clarify my own feelings about things before us, and I do mean 'us'. After Maddie died I lost all interest in social contacts; she was my all, my everything, and without her life seemed to have no meaning. Sure, the girls were with me and caring for them became my focus. I will not lie about what happened; other persons did everything they could to hook me up with some, I'm sure, wonderful sisters, cousins, whatever, but I was having no parts of it. I did miss the companionship Maddie gave me, all those things that can grow between a husband and wife, but I had no intention of replacing her. Then one day there you were next door and everything I thought I knew evaporated in front of me. I had not looked at a woman as a woman and not just as another person taking up space since the day she passed from our life. But that night as I was in that twilight zone before sleep overtakes us, somehow, I can't explain this, I felt a release; it was almost like she was telling me to get on with my life, that others needed me and I should get back to living. So, that's it; that is what is going on, that is why I do those things for you and the boys; I know this sounds a bit selfish but it seems to be almost as good emotionally for me as the end results are for you. You are not replacing her in my memory, and with the girls in front of me I know that will never happen, but you're like a second chance for me. I have no clue why I am being given a second chance, but please let me see where this is going, please."

Lynn had listened to every word he said, known he was not doing some dancing around the subject but heading directly into the core. What he said sounded so much like what she was going through in the wake of the divorce her understanding was very real; they could lean on each other. "Alan, thank you. I do understand and believe me I have had that 'second chance' thought more than once. I do have some hopes but do not pretend to know the future, only that I hope you are in it with me as we discover this new reality before us. What else can I say?"

"I think it best at this point to say good night, to retire each to their own digs, to let all this soak in a bit, and as to your question about what to say, do you agree you are in this with me until we figure out the road ahead, where the rainbow might touch down for us?"

"I agree, but there is one more thing; okay?"

"Sure; after venting my soul to you what more would you like to know?"

"Only this:" as she leaned in and kissed him gently but surely, learning the answer she wanted to sense and feel and revel in. He kissed her back, no question, as he raised a hand and touched her face with his fingertips. The thought, however fleeting it might have been, was that the sleeping bag would no longer be a safe haven for them.

Chapter Nine

Reality Replay

The ring tone for an incoming call was insistent as Alan picked up the handset in an almost involuntary reaction. It was early morning and once again he was in his shop taking an idea from sleepy thought to active reality. It was a reprise of one of those times when a dream of sorts in the twilight of sleep had come to him, a dream that virtually awakened him and prompted the move into the shop where he could investigate the realities. He had enough established that the phone would not derail the process, but the voice coming forth did as he voiced a simple "hello?"

"Mr. Behr, Alan; Gill Lanham here. I am really sorry to do this to you at this early hour but I need to tell you some things while I'm still employed here. Can I have a couple of minutes, please?"

Hearing that voice set Alan Behr back on his heels it was so unexpected. True enough, he did expect to hear the outcome of the commercial shoot the kids had done, but even just the time difference made this illogical. "Gill, what's going on here? It's barely past five AM in your time zone. I expected to hear from you but not at this hour of the morning. I'm guessing there is some sort of crises, and what do you mean by saying 'while I'm still employed here'?"

"Okay, okay. Look, the shoot out here was a bust, a total bust in my opinion. We had a meeting late last week to view the end product; I was actually invited to sit in, which surprised me a bit; they had a room full of expectant people including the senior VP who oversees marketing activities among other things. If you remember, the director wouldn't let the kids wear the hard hats or safety vests, and ran a product in on them they didn't have a practice run on, no battery screwdriver, not even a container to sort parts in. There was little to no explanation with maybe a caveat on the screen, you know, something for instance saying 'pause the video here until you get the parts identified and sorted', anything like that; nothing. It was disjointed and I think maybe even out of sequence at one point. Alan, I would be ashamed to show that DVD to anyone, but they did it anyway. The only possible reason I can come up with is that they wanted so very badly to discredit an idea that came from outside their coven walls, from a sales rep of all people."

Alan listened, stunned at the information. "But Gill, even if the brass didn't like it, how could that affect your job security? And besides, aren't any of those persons smart enough to know a sandbag job when they see one, that the marketing guys were trying to discredit your idea so later on they could claim it for themselves? Makes no sense to me."

"There's more, a bit more anyway. It became clear to me the idea for the video was being piled on my plate, giving others present the impression marketing staff had done the best they could with a lame idea. I was sick, knowing the original DVD was a virtual masterpiece that they somehow tarnished and trashed into oblivion. The reason my job here may be over is that I thought about it over the weekend and decided I would not take the beating for something I didn't do. I came in here about an hour ago, went into the corporate office area while no one was around, and popped the DVD of the original shoot into the tower for the senior VP who had been there at the presentation. The system will see the DVD as something new when he does the morning start-up of his system and will hopefully start to play it before he realizes what is taking place. I know I'm going to fry for doing that, especially if the marketing guys find out, but Alan there was no other way to give it a chance to succeed. So, there you have it. I have done what I believe is the best I can do for the idea, and in good faith I will tell you I still firmly believe the video is a clear winner. I don't expect to be here much longer for what I did once my boss finds out, but those kids are wonderful and deserve a chance, a far better chance than they have been given. I can tell you that I have already done a bit of research on who else might be hiring in my line of work. I haven't fully given it up yet but the odds of my remaining here are slim and none from what I can see. It's gonna be a head hunting hate fest once the marketing people find out what I did. What else can I tell you?"

"Gill, this is hard for me to get my mind around You have risked your own well being for us when these others should be punished for what they did to you. I know things are not always fair but to not even give it a decent hearing is just out of the park in being mean, especially when they took a valid idea and made a mess of it to protect their own overinflated egos. I can only say all of us here are thankful we at least had a chance, that you gave us that much. Maybe it's time to go shopping around with the other major suppliers of kids things; I do know there are only three or four major players in the field, if that many. I am truly sorry this has come down this way, but maybe no one will ever find out about the relocated DVD; your secret is safe with me. What happens now; any idea?"

"Not much, I guess, just that I loved working with the bunch of you and hope for the best for all of you, especially those kids. They are just so...I don't know what they are except to say they are fast studies and about as photogenic as can be; I will always remember that closing shot where they appear in the playhouse window one at a time, saying their name, and then did a chorus of 'We're the Construction Kids'. So, maybe one day in the future...who knows; I guess I should probably start packing up my things. I don't really think anything will change, but if it does, I'll let you know."

In a minute or so Gill was off the line to Alan Behr, then sat back to ponder the remainder of the day ahead of him. There remained the possibility he would be escorted out of the building as had happened to a few other people, almost like a 'perp walk' sort of thing. He remembered one former employee being shown out when he was caught selling inside infor- mation to another company. Gill admitted to himself he had often wondered how that person could afford such an extrava- gant life style; in Gill's own mind the cost of that lifestyle was not worth it in the end. For the moment he had other things to do; after all, his tenure might be cut short but he was still being paid to do his job and intended to continue in as normal a manner as possible. That changed a few hours later when a "suit" appeared in his doorway. Gill recognized the head of corporate security; the knowledge gave him no comfort beyond knowing at least it would be a familiar face walking him out to the street. The "suit" spoke.

"Mr. Gill Lanham, right?" and seeing Gill nod in the affirma- tive, continued. "Come with me please. Someone wants very much to talk with you. I have no idea what is taking place, only that I was tasked to determine who might have performed a certain act, then find that person and deliver them. You won't need anything, just yourself. Can I verify one thing first?" and seeing Gill again nod, posed his question: "Are you the person who placed a DVD in the computer tower of the senior VP early this morning? I should tell you we have the video surveillance and a log of doors opening and closing, not to mention seeing your car in the parking lot at 4 AM or so. We can pretty much track your path though the building at that hour just by seeing which doors open and close. So, how do you answer?"

Gill knew he was caught. "Sure, I did that, kind of as a last resort to salvage something that went south on me. No sense denying anything when you seem to have the goods on me. So what happens now; where are we going?"

"Back to the top floor. I do know the DVD has something to do with this but that is all I know. The senior VP called me after finding the DVD and wanted to know who might have placed it in his drive. He had accessed his system from home yesterday evening, which narrowed the time window substantially. It took all of maybe ten minutes to winnow the possibilities down to Gill Lanham, and now you've confirmed our findings. I know this might seem strange to say but you don't seem like a bad guy, even owned up to what you did; the VP didn't seem to be angry, just anxious that we find you, almost like he was afraid some corporate enemy would find you first. Into the elevator and up we go."

Two minutes later Gill Lanham found himself back on the top floor; he got the feeling there were a lot of eyes on him as he stepped out of the elevator onto the deep pile plush carpet. A few more steps and he stood before the office door of the senior VP. His escort made their presence known.

"Mr. Touhy, this is Gill Lanham. You wanted to see him?"

Terrence Touhy looked up from his desk. "Okay, good. I have him now, Chief; you can go find the other person I mentioned earlier but no big hurry on it. Please come in, Mr. Lanham, and have a seat. Anything I can get for you, coffee, Danish maybe, hot tea, anything?"

Gill Lanham, delivered feeling more like a culpable criminal of some sort, stuttered over his own words as he stood in the doorway. "Mr. Touhy, I don't know what's going on here. I've admitted I placed the DVD in your drive, so what's the point in my being here? I should probably be gathering my things and getting ready to go find another job; truthfully, that's what I thought was happening when security arrived at my office, that I was about to be walked out the front door."

"Nonsense. Please, come in, close the door, have a seat, and I'll try to explain. If you want coffee, bottled water, pastry from the kitchen maybe, anything to make you more comfortable, please let me know and I'll have staff see to it. By the way, I think formalities are overrated at best; please, call me Terry and I'll call you Gill if that works for you. First of all, you scared the hell out of me this morning, not because the system fired up playing the DVD but because of what I was seeing after watching that worthless piece of crap last Friday. There was no way in the world I could sanction something that bad with our company name and logo on it. Then, I come in here this morning and there before me is everything I could hope for to launch a new ad campaign, catch the competition with their pants down so to speak. Just one thing before we go any farther, call it my need for assurance in counterpoint to my own paranoia: can you name the kids in the video, however many there are?"

Gill Lanham managed to move from the now closed door and took a seat in a plush leather upholstered chair as he answered the question. "Four kids, of course: Ally and Anna, Brad and Ben. Two sets of twins. The girls are Alan Behr's daughters; the boys belong to the lady who is next door neighbor to the Behr's. And one more thing: the reason they have so much product is that I had it left there when we had the repo event at the Deer Run shopping center; there was no sense having it all trucked back to the warehouse just to gather dust. This whole thing has been a pure accident that sort of grew legs."

"Tell me more, Gill. Why do you say it was an accident?"

Gill Lanham spent the better part of a half hour explaining the initial contact with Alan Behr through a mutual associate, the crazy idea to show the simplicity of assembly via the video with the kids, and his own involvement with the situation. He mentioned that the kids now had an agent and that the parents had reciprocal guardianships on the kids, even mentioning the futile effort by the director to separate the kids and their parents at that filming. Gill ended up by making yet another apology for what he had done and hoped Mr. Touhy would understand the situation and Gills motivation.

"So, my apologies for doing that which I should not have done; it was a last ditch effort on my part to see something good come out of all of this. After the treatment they received at the hands of our marketing people. I'm not sure if the parents would consent to a new video shoot or not. And one more thing: they come as a package, four kids and two parents; I don't know the relationship between the parents but get a feeling it is more than just neighborly friendly, further undefined than that but best left alone and unquestioned. So, now what? I need to make some calls; like most everyone else, I can't afford to be without an income for very long." Gill stopped talking just as there was another announcement from the doorway. The Chief of Security had returned with someone in tow.

"Mr. Touhy, here's Mr. Grubb just like you asked. Do you want to see him now or should I keep him on standby for later?"

Mr. Touhy responded quickly. "He's mine, Chief. Mr. Grubb, come in please and have a seat; we need to talk about something."

Phil Grubb paused before entering the office. He could see Gill Lanham already in there and just knew this was serious business. On the other hand, maybe Mr. Touhy was looking for added ammunition to fire Mr. Lanham with no repercussions; Phil Grubb would be an eager participant if that turned out to be the case. Regardless, he had been summoned and in he went, taking the second chair before the big desk. Mr. Touhy continued as he fiddled with his keyboard and displayed the contents of the DVD on the wall screen; the DVD opening scene played out before them.

Mr. Touhy continued: "Mr. Grubb, Phil, have you previously seen this video on the screen?"

Phil Grubb was caught. It was quite evident the senior VP knew the entire story now; that damned Gill Lanham had to have blown the whistle in some misbegotten effort to save his own job. Phil intended to extract his revenge on Gill Lanham within the hour, just as soon as he could find Gill's boss. "Well, sure; I've seen it but it's not very well done and probably not by professionals. We thought a reshoot was best to try to salvage some of the investment in time and energy. Really, when one looks at it there are all the trappings of it being a Saturday morning cartoon of some sort. Who would believe anything like that, four young kids? When you look at the credits, is that anyone we know to be professionals in the ad business? We did the best we could with what we saw, so can we move on now?"

Terrence Touhy was unmoved. "We are going to move on alright, but I'm not so sure you will be with us, Mr. Grubb. Both of you need to plan on attending a session in the kids play room later this morning; it was supposed to be about some new products but I'm going to have staff find one of those playhouses and ask the kids to put it together. We'll see the realities and move forward from there. In fact, we have enough kids coming in that we will run both videos and see the outcome, keeping them separate of course. Be in the viewing room at 10 AM. Any questions gentlemen? Hearing none, we are adjourned for the moment. Ten AM."

Two minutes later, as soon as Phil and Gill left the office and were out of hearing range, Phil vented: "Lanham, I don't know what in hell you're up to but I do know you know nothing about marketing; I'm going to bury you for doing this to us; just as soon as I can find your boss you're gonna be history to this company. You are not going to make fools of us, not a chance."

Gill heard the words but pushed back. "You better hope those kids are plenty smart enough to follow a simple video; see you at ten."

By noon it was all over. First to be run was the original DVD, including the built-in pauses to sort parts, pauses that made sense in the process, and the play house grew from a pile of parts to a useable structure, maybe not perfect but close enough. Gill had asked that a container for sorting parts be made available to match the DVD scenario; that would not happen for the reshoot. Neither shoot had the advantage of a battery screwdriver. The worst thing to happen was some tears being shed by frustrated children trying to follow a video that made no sense to them. Terrence Touhy had his answer; no one knew about the earlier call he had made to Gill Lanham's boss, a call in which he had made it clear Gill Lanham was of significant value to the company and should be protected from any predatory activity in the area. Gill's boss understood the intent if not the reasoning, and knew something significant was taking place just outside his sensory range. Back in his office with Gill and Phil seated before him, Terrance Touhy cleared the air of any question that might remain.

"Mr. Grubb, you and your people very nearly cost this company a significant advantage in the marketplace. Had I never seen the original DVD I might have been tempted to go with the reshot product and not known the difference. Suffice it to say we currently have nothing like that in our product line, yet I can savor the advantage it could give us. Mr. Lanham, I am thinking more along the lines of an advertisement than something in a product box just to make the life of the purchaser easier doing the assembly. I realize that was the original intent of the effort and believe we should follow through with that aspect. At the same time we all know as soon as the competition sees what we have done, they will follow suit within days if not hours. I am proposing this, information to be kept confidential at the moment: we have a totally redesigned kid sized battery ATV coming out for the Christmas market. Longer life battery, larger wheels and higher torque motors, more bells and whistles on the dash to include sound effects, a CD player and radio combined, cup holders even, room enough for two small riders or one larger rider, everything the response cards we received have told us the consumer wants. It will not be inexpensive, not at all, but we believe it can be one of those 'mine is bigger than yours' type situations that drive sales through the roof. I believe a new video, maybe not the entire assembly process but enough to put that foundational 'so simple a child can do it' thought into the head of the adult purchaser, should be produced. So, here is what I want to see completed within the next five working days. Gill, Mr. Lanham, I want you to contact the parents or the videographer or the kids agent, whomever you need to contact, to verify the potential for this process to occur. At the moment I have no way to know if they would even be amenable to such a process given the poor treatment at the hands of Mr. Grubb's staff at the earlier event. Mr. Grubb, if we can confirm a real possibility this can happen using the original cast, you and your staff will support Mr. Lanham in any and every way he needs support, including but not limited to providing HD equipment, staff assistance, whatever, and it might be of benefit to see what including a battery screwdriver in each box would cost us; I suspect that would be a pittance when compared to the final cost of this new product. At the same time it could give the purchasing parent a tiny bit of incentive to purchase with the lure of a new gadget just for them. We will meet here in one week's time; I hope to see some significant progress at that point; time is already getting short to prepare for the Christmas shopping season. I do have one last question, at least at the moment: I do not believe the original DVD was shot on these premises, while the reshoot was done in the play room area. Either of you two know where the original was shot?"

Gill responded: "I know for sure it was shot in the shop of Alan Behr, the shop attached to his house. It's kind of hard to explain what he does for a living; he has this workshop he needs to do investigative work he is hired to complete for various clients. They apparently cleared out an area for the shoot. The whole thing was done with probably one stationary and two mobile cameras, one of which was the close-up unit. It's just a suggestion on my part but I do recommend any replay be done in Alan's shop, for several reasons: the kids are in and out of the place all the time so it's like home to them, it is easily accessible being in a residential area, and although the last trip was successful in most respects, the kids will be in school full time pretty soon; convincing their parents to take the kids out of school could be a difficult sell. If we opt for maybe a Saturday or one of the weekend holidays I believe we would have a better chance of reaching agreement. All that goes without mentioning the kids had a bad experience taping here they won't soon forget; we need to avoid that trap if possible."

Mr. Touhy agreed. "Gill, make such apologies as are needed, sweeten the deal, do what you have to do. And Mr. Grubb, I should mention we have a vacancy in the first floor mail room should I find any lack of enthusiasm on the part of yourself or your associates; do we have an agreement on that issue?"

Phil Grubb was mortified this VP had just threatened to demote him in front of an hourly peon, well, maybe not such a peon at the moment. "Yes, sir; we will make every effort in support." The thought he had been having about seeking out Gill's boss for revenge faded to black.

Gill did have one more thought to voice although where it may have come from surprised even him. "Can I say one more thing here, Mr. Touhy?" and seeing the nod, continued. "I remember something being said about the original shoot being like a Saturday morning kids show cartoon. What if, I'm just speculating here, what if the new video can be shot so it can be separated into pieces, you know, like a TV serial, with a little more progress over each of a few days until the final product is revealed, build the suspense a bit? I know parents have to put forth the purchase funds but building a strong demand on the part of the potential recipients I think would be a good thing. I agree with Mr. Grubb I don't know much about marketing but isn't a product ad campaign all about convincing people to make the purchase, and even more so if their kids are clamoring for the new item? I may be way off track here..."

Terrence Touhy could hardly believe his ears. This sales rep in front of him had a better understanding of marketing than any number of the professional he knew, and in the process of just asking for a fair hearing had created an entirely new line of thinking. Indeed the new DVD could be shot in segments for airing as a part of a commercial, yet combined into a final product assembly instruction video to be shipped with the ATV. This Gill Lanham was clearly an asset to the company, an asset to be protected; Terrance Touhy would call Gill's boss again and make sure Mr. Lanham loved his job with some new perks and income. "Mr. Lanham, you are indeed correct; please keep that in mind as we go along. I only hope we do not see a burning bridge before us we set on fire ourselves by our poor judgment; please keep me advised as things change." The meeting ended

As the two men walked out of Touhy's office, even knowing he was already on very thin ice, Phil Grubb had to do one last dig into his perceived adversary. "You screwed us over big time, Lanham; I won't forget that any time soon so be careful."

Gill Lanham felt way too good to be bothered by such a petty threat but he also could not let it pass without recognition, even in his somewhat euphoric state: "I suggest you learn where my office is so you don't lose any of my mail in your next job." It turned out to be a valid recommendation on Gill's part when he returned to his office only to discover his boss sitting there awaiting him. His boss clarified.

"Gill, I don't know what in hell is going on with you, what you might be into; in the last half hour or so I have had two calls from Mr. Touhy in corporate. He ordered me to find you an office in the outer ring, with at least one and preferably two windows and a workable door, a system printer so you don't have to walk to the copy room, a useable A/V system with on-line capability to view things, and I am to give you a gate card for the mid-level manager parking area. On top of that he called back and said he was processing paperwork to give you a 25% pay raise starting today. You and I both know you left here hours ago with the Chief of Security, and now this happened. I guess maybe I don't really want to know the details, but can I ask if my own job is now somehow in peril for some unknown reason?"

"No, sir; I do not believe there are any issues with your job. This whole thing had to do with that video shoot I was involved with a few days back, a marketing video. To tell the truth, I didn't know about any of the things you just mentioned until you said the words; I didn't complain or ask for a different office or the printer or anything. Hell, I was just glad to keep my own job, but I can tell you one thing of which I am fairly sure: Mr. Grubb in Marketing will be much nicer to us peons in sales in the days ahead. Beyond that, I guess we go as Mr. Touhy directs." Gill moved the contents of his office two days later to an office in the outer ring, with two windows and a workable door, new printer, mid-sized but very capable internet ready A/V system, and a small but important plastic card for the parking lot gate reader.

Chapter Ten

Hired!

Every so often Alan would check for traffic on the desktop system that sat in his shop area. He did learn while traveling from their site visit at Windmere that Lynn had no such system in her own home. The system she had acquired when first married had grown old, then quit entirely as software storage space needs overcame its limited hard drive abilities. Alan had agreed during the meeting to accept e-mail traffic for her on his own system, and sure enough by mid-afternoon, as promised, a message entitled "Lynn" popped up. He didn't open it or the attachment, deciding it was hers to see first. He would log onto the system but then essentially turn his back as she read.

By late afternoon Lynn cleared her work area and headed home. The day had gone well enough but again she was paid as a file clerk while being asked to do tasks that required a much higher level of expertise. She did think about that every so often but in her reality it was important just to have a job and a steady income. This whole thing with the people at Windmere might be blown smoke and nothing more; she did have a quite favorable memory of the interview and had a feeling the issue would be resolved in the best interest of Windmere operations but perhaps not to her own favor; over time she would learn the error in that thought process. A few minutes after arriving home and doing a brief catch-up with her boys, she crossed the driveway and entered Alan's shop.

"Hey, hi Alan. Anything new or are we still in the waiting room? I'll admit that has been on my mind most of the day but I have refused to speculate on the outcome or daydream about what life could be like."

"Hi,neighbor Lynn; there is an e-mail for you on my system from Windmere, Inc; looks like it has an attachment or two. Just so you know, I have not opened it; this is your mail so once I get logged back on I will leave you alone to call it up for a read. Okay?"

It was not okay with Lynn; this man had been at her side and given her strength when she needed it. Sharing with him was important. "No, not okay. We need to read this together, then you can hand me the tissue to dry my eyes."

"Lynn, I don't think that will be the case, that these people would make some phony offer you couldn't accept just to say they followed the rules. Remember Laura saying they take action based on the information they have on hand, and if they make a mistake they take fast action to correct the situation. They do things quickly because if the decision is good for all involved they want to reap the benefits sooner rather than later, the same for making corrections that might be needed. I think this will be a valid offer; should I print it or do you want to screen read it first?"

"Screen, please." The two started the read with the message sized up, moving to the attachments as they finished the cover letter. Lynn was becoming speechless, finally managing to get some words out. "Print, please. I may not be reading this correctly off the screen." The printer belched out five pages and the two started the reread with the pages spread out on his workbench. It was every bit as comprehensive as it could be: hourly rate, three month increase, six month increase, one year increase, overtime provisions, vacation hours accrual, sick days accrual, family health insurance plan, flex time hours, available family life insurance plans, mileage rate, company stock purchase options. 401.k plan, mention of the rare occasion when she might be called in for extra work and recognition of the child care that might entail, general working hours, and two pages setting forth the next three months activities in which she would be expected to participate. The financial arrangement with the local junior college was set forth. She would be provided with a cell phone on the Windmere system, plus a new home based system for entering date and a portable gadget of choice for field data entry. There was a request for any questions on her part to be sent back to Windmere by e-mail and they would answer as quickly as possible. There was the suggestion that if she was nervous or perhaps didn't fully understand the contract provisions that she have someone more familiar with the hiring process read the provisions and advise her. It was in plain English, not convoluted or laced with double meanings but straight up in intent. The work schedule was clear that there would be some limited amount of travel toward the end of the first month of employment, and at least one period of not more than four days she would be out to town entirely for training; she would report to Jillian Andrews as her immediate supervisor but given a whole list of people to call should Jill for some reason not be available. Lynn sat down, almost afraid she would somehow awaken herself to discover this was all a daydream of some sort.

"Alan, I have never seen anything like this offer. They answered any and every question I could think of and a lot I never asked. And look at that pay rate, nearly double starting out over what I make now with specified increases. Do you think maybe they sent the wrong attachments to the cover letter? I know the storage reference in the bottom corner of each page tells me these pages are all held in my e-file at Windmere, but is this real? And what about that travel schedule where I have to be out of town a few days; how do I manage that? What should I do, Alan? I'm kind of lost here; I want to believe but there is nothing in my life for comparison. Now what? Help me, please; you always know what to do, what's best for me. Talk to me, please?"

Alan did understand her dilemma but within his own reasoning could not help her. "Lynn, I can't tell you what to do, or even if this is truly valid. I think it is valid; these people don't mess around. I have to admit something here that is a bit difficult for me: I can't advise you in this because...I care about you very much and I think it could blind me. Let's do this: let's send this to Ari Schoenroth and see what he says. Okay?"

It was okay with her and after Alan called Ari to let him know what was taking place they sent the message on for him to read. Half an hour later Ari called back and was put on speaker in Alan's workshop.

"I did as you asked, read the proposal, did some homework, and I believe in good faith I can tell you, Lynn, the offer is quite valid as written. You will have to make the decision neither Alan nor I can make for you. It is very clear Windmere wants you in their fold and they have done a lot of sweetening to make that happen. I'm not saying they are giving the store away but it sure looks like the candy counter is open. They are very astute people and I feel quite comfortable telling you they see something in or about you they want aboard. So, it remains your decision to go or no go. And by the way this is actually after office hours so technically I can't charge for my time. Besides I owe Alan for figuring out that heating problem at my house. Okay, I can't just leave this subject, Lynn; on a strictly personal basis, not a professional basis, I really believe you should go for it; there are people who would sell their next of kin to get on at Windmere and can't get a toe in the door; Windmere has opened the door and asked you in. Trust me, things just do not get any better than that in a job search, not with Windmere anyway. And one more thing: they have you reporting to Jillian Andrews, Jill. I have had occasion to work with her several times on different cases; Jill is as consummate a professional as you will ever see; she will never place you in harm's way and will see to it you are given every tool in the book, honed to her sense of perfection and precision. This decision has to be your call and I do wish you well in spite of the company you keep."

Lynn laughed at the reference to Alan. "Mr. Schoenroth, this man in my fortress. Thank you for your input. I believe my decision is made." Within the next minute Ari left for home while Alan and Lynn did one more read of the proposal.

"Lynn, you need to know Ari is no fool; I understand he does do work for Windmere now and then but he is his own man in that regard. His reputation is spotless or his Chicago associates would have nothing to do with him. This is your life you are deciding; I will abide by whatever decision you make. About that four day road trip: I do have some parenting skills, nowhere near yours in quality, of that much I am sure, but we can house the boys in the spare bedroom if we excavate some of the things stored in there. Good to go?" While he had been talking his hands had reached out to hers and now held them firmly in his grasp, his eyes looking directly into hers.

In her own mind she already knew the decision she would make, had to make for herself and her boys, couldn't pass up with all that it offered, but needed one more little push to set it in stone. "Alan, I want this so much I can hardly stand it; I would be a complete fool if I let this slip away while I stayed in a dead end job; this is like every dream I ever had and I haven't even started it yet. I know you won't make that decision for me, can't make that decision for me, but I have one question to ask of you that can make everything all right. I'm scared to death, I am, but when that happened to me at Windmere I felt your hand take mine and the power of that touch gave me strength beyond my imagination. Will you do that for me in this, hold my hand when I need it, pull me along when I falter, pick me up when I fall..."

His grasp of her hands tightened just a bit as he interrupted her to make his own thoughts known. "Lynn, you will not falter or fall, I'm sure of that, but if now and then you need a reminder of your own strength, I will be there." He stopped speaking for just a moment but she knew there was more on his mind; it was almost strange in the few months they had know each other each could now sense so much in the other person. "I would like to be there with a hot iced Cinnamon bun in hand, fingers glued together, lips burned from the molten icing. Can we make that happen?"

The craziness of his diversion did what it needed to do, broke her concern, and Lynn knew all was well as she laughed with him in the moment. Thirty minutes later she drafted her response and wired it to Laura at Windmere: Lynn had signed on. In the morning she would give notice to her current employer; by lunch time they counter offered but it was a fruitless gesture; she realized if she were that valuable to them why had they not paid her better to begin with? She did opt to take her few accrued vacation hours at the end of the two weeks, allowing her to start at Windmere a day or two earlier than anticipated. Two days after her acceptance of the position, the boxes arrived at Lynn's home, to be assembled for her by Alan, a new computer system and all the accessories including a color printer/scanner/fax that would order it's own ink refills via a Windmere account. It amazed her that the very first time she activated the assembly the screen lit up with a message welcoming her to the system; she would discover in later days that it didn't matter where she might be, the rocket fast server at the Windmere home place could find her in about half a heartbeat. The system also recognized when the more portable device was in the area and would ask if Lynn wanted to download more data. The two families celebrated at Mama Leoni's that evening; while the kids didn't particularly know what the celebration was about, it hardly curtailed their appetite there or at the ice cream store. The boys did sense there was some slight change in their mother but made no specific note of it. They would learn later the size of the step she had just taken.

One working day later Jillian Andrews called Lynn's new cell phone for the onset of a long conversation. What day would Lynn feel comfortable starting her new position with Windmere, and could they meet at Lynn's home so it was more comfortable for them? The two planned to make a day of it, agreed to call a well known sandwich shop for lunch if they felt like it as Jill would lead the parade with Lynn following her. There were some routine forms that could be filled out on line and they did have a discussion about those very rare occasions when Windmere would call staff in regardless of hours to meet some need. Jill explained as she referenced an incident in the not too distant past.

"First of all. the odds of you getting one of those calls is slim and none because you don't live in Conyerville; time is usually of the essence at that point in discussions and the need for you to travel to attend would counter that. The one I got three months ago, the first call in over a year, when I got to the house and entered the main conference room, it looked like a NAFTA trade conference for both Americas. Turned out I was called because I speak Spanish with some fluency in Portuguese, Tex-Mex and other assorted language derivations. There were translators from each language to English but none with three way capability. I know this sounds crazy but they wanted me there to give each translation from English into each of the other languages being spoken and vice verse so each country could be assured they were being told the same information as the others present, that some translator wasn't muffing the job. Anyway, we got things settled down some time in the early AM and the pact was signed near as I know. They were meeting at Windmere so the national press couldn't find them until after the fact. The only reason I remember it so well is because I got two offers for road trips and probably a lot more from a couple of the attendees; I strongly suspect my Norse heritage had a lot to do with the offers, that and I sort of hurried to get there after I was called and was wearing more of a summer dress than I would normally have selected for a meeting at that level. I caught a couple of them outright staring at me, parts of me anyway, and you know I used that as leverage. So, I do not believe you need be concerned about that issue; besides, it looks to me like you rather have a built-in child care sitter in your neighbor, Alan. True?"

Lynn knew this woman talking to her was a fast and thorough study of other people; there was quite probably little she didn't already know about Lynn and the potential for a relationship with her neighbor. "It is true, at least I would like to think it's true. When I first read that part about the four day road trip I had concerns, but he reminded me he has child care experience with his two daughters, and a spare bedroom to house the boys. Some time back he told me the girls were given the option of each having their own room but that they declined. My place only has two bedrooms so my boys are used to each other. Somehow every time something comes up that could cause me concern or derail some process, Alan pops up, slays the dragon, then convinces me he didn't really do that much." It was a good point to relate the story about the ice cream sprinkles and Lynn did so. Jill added more to the thought.

"You do know that at the interview when you sort of froze, I saw his hand cover yours and give it a squeeze; it was apparently what you needed to move ahead. This is just a suggestion, only a suggestion; Windmere has no part in this observation, only me, myself and I: don't let him get away; he gives you strength. Maybe it won't work out long term but I think the odds are it will. I see how he looks at you; I suspect he is coming out of a shell after suffering a significant loss in his life. Those of us at Windmere don't really snoop into other people's lives beyond maybe seeing if there is anything negative that could somehow derail a process. Did he suffer a loss of some sort, something major?"

"He did lose his wife a few years back; he even admitted the girls kept him going when he wanted to withdraw in the face of the loss. We've talked about all that, my divorce, all the messy details. I do believe we are drawing a bit closer but there is a lot of distance to go, no hurry just a bit of distance. Now, just between the two of us, you have to promise to keep this secret probably forever; okay?" Jill voiced her agreement and Lynn related the sleeping bag incident, omitting nothing except a feeling or two she had to keep sequestered even from herself. To Jill the story confirmed her thoughts about this man.

"Lynn, he may not be the only man around who would do something like that, or to be more accurate would NOT try to take advantage of the situation, but he is the one closest to you; I'm guessing he thinks about that incident now and then without regret. I believe that someday when that situation again presents itself, you'll know what to do about it. In the meantime we have work to do; in a few days we make our first site visit; your job will really start to unfold before you then and you will be able to better see what you have gotten yourself into. Okay?"

It was okay with Lynn, even more so when she retired for the night in the realization she was now part of a power house team, well protected by a number of persons, and warmed by the thought Jill believed Lynn had a future with Alan Behr.

Chapter Eleven

Made for TV

Gill Lanham's boss received yet a third call from corporate: Gill's tasks were to be reduced to a level where he could concentrate on some sort of project with which he was associated. Gill had to take time to explain to his own supervisor what Gill was being tasked to accomplish, even if he didn't know for sure how it all could be worked out. Trying to make progress as the calendar days to the Christmas shopping season were flying by, Gill called Alan Behr for help; Alan was the idea guy in the beginning, maybe he could help again. He made the call in the early morning, knowing because of the time difference Alan would be in his shop but hopefully not yet fully immersed in the problem solving of the day. Gill was in his office with two windows and a door when he made the call, looking out one of the windows at his car parked in the front row of the midlevel manager's parking lot.

"Hey, Mr. Behr! How goes it this AM?

"Okay, Gill; I hear that voice inflection and term of address so I already know something is up. You are calling me probably from your home at this hour, maybe even still in your pajama's. If this is about attempting to shoot another video at your place of business, I gotta tell you it's not gonna happen, I don't care how much sweetening is applied. The money is an incentive but those kids are mine, at least the girls are mine and I will protect the boys just as much. I do believe I can speak for Lynn here and the answer in NO. Now, last call you made to me you suggested you were about to be fired. What happened?"

Gill needed over ten minutes of non-stop talking to convey what had occurred at his place of business; he ended with what had taken place when the two videos were screened as action videos, including a comment on the tears being shed. "Alan, I am neither in my pj's nor sitting home; I am fully dressed, in my new office with not one but two windows to the outside, even a door I can shut if I want, and get this: I can see my car in a part of the reserved parking lot that takes a key card to access. I get the feeling I am in way over my head here; the idea of what we are trying to do is sound; I believe that much, but I'm a sales rep, not a tech guru; I need help and where do I turn but to the person who started this whole process. So, can I come see you, meet with your team at your place? The senior VP handed this to me, even threatened to fire one of the section chiefs in Marketing unless he goes all in to help me, but I don't even know the questions to ask. Help me?"

Alan did believe the sincerity in what he was hearing, realizing this man on the phone had a desperate sound to his voice. Alan also realized he had something this corporation wanted or he would not be having this conversation. Maybe there was opportunity here, maybe not, and either way he would have to inform Lynn; he needed her acceptance before moving ahead, even taking the time to listen to the proposal. No Lynn, no project. Gill had to be so advised.

"Okay, I do think this opportunity needs to be considered, but before I take the time to listen to the spiel, I need to talk to Lynn about the boys participating again. Without her acceptance, no deal; we both know we need all four kids to make this work, whatever this new project might be." The sound of a latch being opened caused Alan to look about as he saw a pan of iced Cinnamon buns entering his shop in the recently held hands of neighbor Lynn. "Hang on just a minute if you would, Gill; you're going on speaker. Lynn just came in with a bribe, a whole pan of right out of the oven super hot iced Cinnamon buns. Lynn, say 'hi' to Gill Lanham, the trouble maker who got us into that whole fiasco in LA."

Lynn placed the pan before Alan on the workbench top and pulled back the cover. "Hi, Mr. Lanham; to what do we owe this honor?"

"Good morning, Ms Lynn. Alan has already accused me of being in my pajama's and sitting at home, but it is not so. He also reminded me the last conversation we had by phone was me telling him I was most likely about to be fired from my job for jumping the chain of command big time. Don't know if he told you what I did; in brief after the big guys had seen that misbegotten piece of a video shot here on site, I slipped the DVD of the original into the computer tower of the senior VP who has say over marketing and that sort of thing. I was about to tell Alan what happened after that, about the Chief of Security coming to get me and taking me to a meeting with the senior VP; I had every reason to believe it was the start of a perp walk out of the building but was dead wrong, totally dead wrong. To say Mr. Touhy loved the original would be a serious understatement. I do try to not gloat, but I am sitting in my new office in the outer ring of the building, two windows to the outside and a workable door, new gadgets to make my life more than livable, and it all comes down to my ability to deliver a new video to Mr. Touhy. You both know I have no idea how to do that and worse still is that he wants it to air in time to hit the coming Christmas ad market. I stipulated the video work would NOT be done on site here, not after what happened last time; as I explained to Mr. Touhy using your shop only makes sense, Alan. The kids are apparently quite accustomed to being in and out of it, feel at home in a more low key environment, and I believe that makes the video a bit more believable, more of a warm fuzzy experience sort of thing. I have given this much thought, and my own peril aside for the moment have one thing to ask of you, probably the two of you representing the four kids: can I come visit and bring a couple of people with me, people who can get this done before Mr. Touhy finds out how inept I really am at this sort of thing. What say you parents?"

Gill heard Lynn laughing out loud just as he finished speaking, a laugh carried over into her speech pattern as she tried to answer. "Mr. Lanham, Al can't talk to you right now. He's..." more laughter came out of Gills speaker phone "he's got a mouth full of Cinnamon roll and the icing is burning his lips." More laughter, with a muffled grunt or two in the background, followed by the sound of a door opening and more voices. "The kids just came in; I think the smell of Cinnamon buns attracts them like flies. I usually get over here a lot earlier in the morning but I just changed jobs and the hours make my life a lot better. Kids, one at a time please and you probably need to wash your hands first. I'm sorry Mr. Lanham; this thing has gotten out of control, really out of control..." Gill heard her lilting laughter again as she tried to continue "but I wouldn't trade it for anything, not for anything. I'm sorry, really I am."

Gill managed to keep from laughing himself as the picture of the scene in the Behr workshop played though his mind. "Please, never apologize for having fun with your kids. As for

Alan, he's old enough to know better than to ingest hot sugar icing. He did tell me earlier that any agreement to do a new video would depend on your participation. I also know the kids now have an agent, a real bulldog from what I hear; any way I can meet with all those persons at one time? I have already talked to Mr. Touhy about the need to make this site visit if for no other reason than to smooth some ruffled feathers; he is on board with the idea but reminded me Christmas is coming sooner than we realize. Please, if we can work this out just give me a time and place and I'll be there." It was a good point to stop talking and Gill did so.

Alan Behr was still trying to cool scorched lips but with hot coffee as he tried to speak. "Gill, I think you have our agreement to at least meet." He saw Lynn nod as he looked at her while talking. "My hours are flexible; Lynn's hours in her new job also seem to have some flexibility, so lay it on us. Even if we do finally agree, I realize the timing is really short to do all the taping, that sort of thing. And by the way, I do know better that to ingest molten icing, but that is easier accomplished than avoided with the Cinnamon aroma in the air and a whole pan in front of me. I get the feeling this proposed video may be a bit different from the original; can you fill me in?"

Gill Lanham could do that and spent the next few minutes outlining the intent of the shoot, to do a segmented video that could also be used in advertising. He would make every effort to obtain one of the new ATV's to show the kids, even mentioning the idea of including a battery screwdriver in the shipping box. About ten days later, on a Saturday morning when the kids were out of school, a group of people descended on the Behr workshop, sitting on hastily borrowed chairs, some roosting on work benches as they tried to grasp the task before them in the available time frame. One of the new ATV's, still in its shipping box, was in the center of the room. Gill Lanham, nervous about what was soon to be the collective finding started his pitch.

"Thank you all for coming today. I know the timing is a bit unusual but the truth is we just have no time to spare. Some of you are aware of the schism between the original video shot here and the one done in LA at my employer's place of business. This proposed video will be shot here; it will be designed to serve as both an in-box assembly tutorial, a fact we will brag on a bit, and will also be used in active TV, internet and print advertising. With me today are persons who know how to make that connection; their purpose is to coach the videographer in the process, not to control the process but to coach toward meeting our interconnection needs with the proposed media presentations. Above all else, you all need to recognize that two people here today are all powerful, really nice people but holding final say on what happens, Lynn, the boy's mother, and Alan, the girl's father. You will meet the kids in a little bit so all can get a better feel for how this is to happen. I know Sol Kaplan, the kids agent is here, and look forward to crossing that bridge yet today; their family lawyer is here, Mr. Schoenroth, and Miss Paige, the videographer of the first shoot. I want all of you to see the original video, how this played out and why my company is so excited to expand the process. The kids ATV you see before you is being manufactured in this country; it is bigger, stronger, faster. has a longer lasting battery, and has more gadgets than any preceding model; the existence of this specific item is at this point a company secret; we ask that you maintain that secret. The task before us is to watch the video and see how that can be translated to this new toy. Let's watch."

The assemblage watched the original video and caught the excitement bug it delivered. It did amaze some that four kids in early elementary school delivered performances one would expect from older and more trained actors, but that was the whole point: they engendered warm feelings in just watching them, and the closing act was memorable. Half an hour later, after a lot of questions were answered, Gill asked Lynn and Alan to invite in the kids. All around general introductions were made but while they remained polite and all that, four kids eyed the box on the shop floor. They did recognize Gill Lanham as being their benefactor in LA, the person who had shown them the sights and let them order what they wanted to order off the room service menu that second night in town. He started the explanation of what was taking place.

"Good to see all of you again, kids. I see you looking at the box here, so let me tell you the deal. I know you have a battery car or two for use in the yard. In the box is a brand new ATV battery quad-runner. It is bigger, faster, better battery, all the good stuff, but unassembled. What I want to learn today is if the four of you can put it together like you did the play houses; this is a lot more complicated than a play house, plus it has all sorts of decals to put on, trim pieces, all that, but it does come with an instruction booklet to follow. You can take all the time you want if that would help, so tell me: are you interested?" Gill knew there were four sets of eyes glued to him at the moment but they swung back to the box the second he stopped talking. With their heads turned away a bit he could hear a voice but knew only it was one of the girls.

"Do we get to keep it when we're done?"

"Yes; it is yours to play with, but you know the rules: head protection, shoes, the usual stuff. So, you want to do this?"

Again he couldn't say for sure who spoke but knew it was one of the boys. "Can we start now?"

Gill looked at Alan and Lynn: "What say you mom and dad? Do we get out of the way and let them have at it, no cameras for this first go around?"

Alan looked at Lynn, saw her nod, and gave their answer. "Go for it, kids, if that's what you want to do. Your call; okay? Battery screwdriver is in the charger if you want to use it."

The instruction reader, Ally, virtually took over at that point as the perceived leader of the quartet. "Brad, Ben, I need the instruction book out of the box; get it, okay? Anna, I think I saw the big container under the sink in the kitchen; we'll need it. No! Wait! Wait! We need our Construction Kids stuff." Pleading look on her face she spun around to face her father. "Daddy, where's our stuff, our Construction Kids stuff?"

Alan knew: "Spare bedroom, in a box right inside the door" and watched as four young bodies tore off back into the house only to return in less than a minute with vests and hard hats in place. The boys found the instruction booklet after upending the big box, handed it to Ally, then went back to work matching numbers on parts into some semblance of order. Anna found the battery screwdriver and slipped it into a holder on her tool belt. The race was on as the adults present moved back out of the way lest they interfere with the process. It was quite clear the four kids were now in a whole separate mind set; Alan even wondered if the Construction Kids outfits were somehow responsible for the change. In the meantime, others present were busy formulating their plans to forge ahead with the project.

Over in a corner of the shop, out of the way, Gill met with the kid's agent, Sol Kaplan, and made his plea. "Mr. Kaplan, I know you represent the kids. I don't want to give away the store here but I need to throw myself on your mercy; I'm a sales rep, not some marketing guru; I sell toys for kids, some pretty big toys but toys nonetheless. I don't know squat about any of the financial aspects I should have under control; I don't even know what all this is worth to my company, even if it has any worth or not, only that I have been told to get it done and in time for the Christmas rush. I guess what I'm asking is that you be fair with us in the face of my own ignorance, do what you need to do for the kids of course but please do not leave me abandoned at the side of the road. I don't even know where to start, what to ask."

In spite of his perceived persona, Sol Kaplan was not an unreasonable or unfeeling man. He heard what Gill was telling him and believed the story, that Gill had been thrust into this position but had zero traction in his ability to bring things to a successful conclusion. Sol would help, driven by his own sound perception of the situation.

"Mr. Lanham, Gill, take a breath, calm down; I'm going to get us through this. Clearly I do have my own motivation here and that is to do the best I can for those kids, but I like to think a bit more long term. Let me give you an example: you familiar with those Big Flags theme park commercials that run on TV now and then?" Gill nodded. "I know you think what you see was made somewhere around the LA Great Flags park; it wasn't. All that video of the girls flying around in the rides and wearing all that Big Flags logo clothing, even that yellow Jeepster convertible they are seen riding in, it was done within about forty miles of here. In fact, the Jeepster is about six blocks from here at the moment unless the younger girls have borrowed it from their older sister, again. They do love that car, they are indeed sisters and I'm their agent. I could have negotiated a larger payment up front but held out for residuals. Every time one of those commercials airs, and I do mean for all seven parks across the country, the girls get a few cents, each and every time. So, seven parks times the dozen or so times each ad is run during a day times a year's worth of days times the probably three year life expectance of the ads themselves and we're looking at full college tuition in the bank and then some. The oldest sister, now married and pregnant, has started a college fund for her children although the first one to arrive is still a couple of months away, My point is that I will not gouge you for your lack of experience, not because I am some sort of nice guy but because I see the potential down the road. I said three years for the Great Flags ads and I am already seeing a quartet of replacements for the three girls, four kids presently in this very room. Do you see where I'm coming from, Gill?"

Gill Lanham had a really good feeling in his gut, probably due to the releasing of the knotty tension he had felt up to that point. He could team with Sol and both of them could come out of this real good. "I do see, and thank you for the explanation. Like I said, I'm in sales; I recognize your expertise in a field about which I know nothing. Alan and I guess Lynn came up with the original idea for a video; the videographer is a friend of Lynn's. A business associate of mine recommended I call Alan to sort of pick his mind about our declining sales figures. Alan isn't into marketing either; maybe Lynn is, but either way this thing has legs. Thank you, and I truly mean that. Shall we observe the magic going on?" The two men turned their attention to the assembly process for the moment.

Over in another corner but where they could closely observe the kids in action stood Paige and her corporate counterpart. The woman was explaining to Paige what had gone wrong with the LA shoot, that she had done as told by the director and given the option would not have done it at all as she had been directed. The director remained behind in LA. What Paige had delivered as product was impressive, more so perhaps because she was seen as a small town operative not to be confused with big town experts. As the discussion continued, Paige commented on the specific equipment she used to do the original shoot, was asked if she could use the services of a gyro stable camera unit and an additional technician if the project continued and agreed the two women had much in common in their end goals: to deliver product of a most excellent quality.

By this time the kids had the wheels on the ATV and were in process of applying the decals. There had been one little hitch when the instructions called for the use of a specific wrench in addition to a screwdriver. It took some doing but Ally read back through the instructions and located the part that told them where to look for the wrench; it was not to be found in the parts bag but taped to the underside of the piece for which it was needed for installation. The process continued. Alan did notice that in applying the decals his much larger fingers would not have been able to reach into some of the small crevices where the decals resided, crevices like the bars on the grill, places like that. He wondered at the time how a parent was supposed to get that part of the job done without any specialty tools; it did occur to him perhaps doing an assembly should be a joint venture between child and parent. Maybe it was worth mentioning to Gill, adding something about the parent-child teaming on assembly. The marketing people would bad mouth the idea when it was mentioned, but it surfaced in a print ad anyway and was given recognition as the positive suggestion it was.

It was drawing close to noon when the battery went into the container under the cowling, the signal all was complete. Alan recognized the moment and started to applaud. Those who had remained for the entire operation also clapped as he made known the forthcoming reward.

"Kids, you did great; I didn't hear even one cuss word, not one" giggles broke out "so, here's what we're gonna do. I know you ate a lot of the Cinnamon rolls but how about we do lunch at Mama Leoni's? You agree Mama Lynn?" It was not as though she had any other choice, and within minutes the six were loaded into the Behr bus and heading down the street. Alan did take a minute or so to explain to the others present what was taking place, that they were going to lunch before all else, that the others were more than welcome to join them but that for their own safety they should stay out of the way of the kids first surge toward the serving table. One other thing he did as they were leaving was to plug in the charger for the ATV battery.

Gill insisted on paying the bill at Mama Leoni's, something he was actually more than happy to do; the morning had been a watershed event for him and quite probably for his tenure with the company. He realized that while he didn't really know how to do any of this he did know people who could handle the tasks and respond in kind; Gill Lanham had become an able manager, unconscious though he might have been of the fact. The group returned to the workshop to finalize the day and work out the future events. Gill led off.

"Once again, thank you, all of you, for making this day happen. We have seen proof the kids can do what is needed with little coaching; they were even chanting that 'righty tighty, lefty loosey' thing at one point and having a ball doing it. I know this might sound a bit nuts but did anyone else here sense the change in the kids when they put on contractor outfits, maybe like they were dropping into familiar roles? I know there was no question about who was to do what; it was beautiful to watch. I know this was only a practice run; when can we do a taped run, anyone know?"

Alan had an idea. "I know time is running on this; next Friday the kids have a day off school for some teacher's event. That would give us a three day weekend although I have to say if this takes three days I think we need to bail right now. I'm mostly thinking Friday with a bit of time on Saturday for reshooting a scene or two if something does go wrong. Work for everyone? Lynn, I know your own schedule might interfere but I will be here for the kids."

Alan's time frame was accepted by all and those assembled started to head for home. Gill needed Alan's ear for just a moment.

"Alan, that went really well. Sol did tell me if the kids have to work on Friday that I need to pay them time and a half. His explanation was that their normal task, their job, was to attend school; they were being given a day off, a vacation day by any other name, but a vacation day that was related to the school district. So, in effect the kids were still working for the school, just having a vacation day; that implies they were doing school hours on Friday and anything more than that would constitute overtime. I don't know if he was serious or not but I am filing the expense sheet for time and a half, okay? And one more thing: I'm going to have three more units shipped here just as soon as I can. Would you have the kid's assemble another one during this next week when they have time, plus make sure all the batteries have a full charge for Saturday?"

"Can do. I am a bit amazed today went so well; I hoped it would but these are all different people from all different perspectives and sometimes that doesn't work so well. And by the way, thanks for lunch. Can the kids use the quad-runner now or is it off limits until after the taping?"

Gill hadn't thought that far ahead but there was the machine in front of him. "Let them ride it; if it's gonna break I want to find out now rather than later."

Four kids rolled the new machine outside and rode it until the battery did finally weaken hours and hours later. At some point during that time Lynn and Alan stood side by side watching the kids fly though the yard. She thanked him on behalf of herself and her boys, stole a gentle kiss when no one was looking, and wondered how her life had come so far so fast in such a short time, all the while knowing the answer was Alan Behr, the same Alan Behr who had warmed her when she was cold and wet, leaving a memory she replayed from time to time while wondering what lie ahead.

Friday morning with the extra technician and the gyro stable camera at the ready, once again the kids were called upon to do their thing. The three additional quad-runners had arrived Wednesday, with one being assembled per Gills request. Construction Kids costumes in place and recording started, the four were even smoother than on the original run through, shaving a few more minutes off the run time. The adults stayed out of the way but watched closely as the process unfolded. Some briefly noticed the additional person who came into the shop very quietly and stood back out of the way; their attention remained focused on the kids at the moment. Again it was a successful adventure as the machine took shape, the battery that had been sitting to the side with the charger plugged in was inserted under the cowling, charger packed into a niche by the battery, and the cover buttoned up. As the cameras coasted to a stop after "cut", Alan started the applause and praised their effort..

"Kids, you did great, really great, but you know we don't expect less now. Gill, that make you happy, even a bit faster today? Practice must have worked!"

Gill was happy and started to say so, then for just a second looked back to see who had come in so quietly during the shoot. Whoever it was coming in didn't cause even a tiny ripple in the kid's performance, but it caused a tsunami in Gill Lanham. "Mr. Touhy, I didn't know...I mean...you know...what can I say?"

Terrance Touhy had a wide smile. "Gill, all this process going on during the past week or so I guess got to me a bit here and there. If you think about it, this is the most unorthodox approach to an ad campaign I have ever seen; I think I needed to assure myself it was all sure enough real and not some folly I would come to regret. I am happy to tell you I have no regrets about this, none. We spend literally millions with ad agencies and I think they all just got upstaged more than a little. Now, can I meet some of these people?"

Introductions were made all around, including the people from their own company who Mr. Touhy would have had no cause to meet otherwise. The four kids, now immersed in consuming the few remaining cinnamon buns, remained pretty much unimpressed but had no call to be otherwise. Mr. Touhy had a request and talked in general to the crew but more directly to the kids. He was well aware their one parent present was watching closely, recalling for a moment that the hand-shake of Alan Behr was somewhat akin to that of a gorilla.

"I was just wondering...I'm sure someone kept time on each step of this process. It is really important we stay within the limits of short TV commercials. I know when you're waiting for a show to return the commercials may seem a lot longer than they really are, but it is very important. So, do you have enough strength to do this one more time, kids, if I promise to buy lunch wherever you might want to go?"

Ally spoke up as apparent foreperson for the quartet. "Mama Leoni's?"

Mr. Touhy looked up at Alan, received a positive nod, and answered. "Mama Leoni's."

Anna continued the conversation after looking at her twin: "We can do one more but do we get to keep this one too?"

"You do. Crew: ready?"

It took a few minutes to sort of reload and get ready, but the action was even faster when they got started, shaving a couple more minutes off the end product. Mr. Touhy was well pleased; he was even more pleased at discovering low small town prices for that much pizza and drinks and bought for all present. What he was unprepared for was the finale Gill had in mind when they returned to the workshop. Gill explained.

"Okay, kids; I know you have done your part and done it quite well. I have one more thing I would like to see this afternoon. Let's take this fourth machine outside while I talk to the video people and make some preparations. Okay?"

It was okay with the kids as they wheeled the machine outside before Ben climbed on and slammed the pedal down for full power, tearing off across the drive like a shot. Alan looked up just in time to see Lynn and Jill return from their site visit tour. More introductions were made as Gill busied himself doing some measuring in the driveway, suggesting to Paige where the cameras could be set up for whatever he had in mind, then walking off and returning in a minute with a grocery bag. Much as he had done inside the shop, he had placed white x's on the driveway apron in front of the garage, each apparently carefully measured from the next. By the time he was ready he had to request assistance to get the kids back in one place and separated from the other battery riders in the neighborhood that had arrived from time to time; the four Gill needed were on their new quad runners.

"Kids, we're ready to go so here's what I want you to do for me. First, follow me to the front yard so we can get you in the right order." Once in the front yard and out of sight of the others Gill made known his plans. "Ally, you get the pink car, Brad the blue, Ben the black, and Anna the orange. Now, here's what I want you to do; you need to have your headgear on, of course, and your Construction Kids vests and tool belts, so get those on and come back, okay?"

It was okay with the kids and within minutes they were back, properly clothed, and in the order he had requested. He gave them the timing order, then went around the corner of the house to the driveway and walked back toward the videographer. Gill finger twirled in the air and Paige knew to start the taping without even knowing what was taking place. Sure enough: within seconds the pink quad runner sped out from the front of the house into the driveway and flew toward the camera. Just as instructed, when the right front wheel hit the X Gill had placed, she turned hard right, popped her foot off the pedal, and the machine went into a four wheel broad slide, coming to a halt a couple of feet from the camera. Hot on her heels was Brad on his quad runner; he also saw his mark, turned hard and let off the pedal, going into a broad slide and stopping just as his wheels touched hers. Ben and Anna followed suit as the adults with mouths hanging open stood and watched the four kids pose wheel to wheel. Lined up as they had done earlier in the shop, the kids did their closing.

"I'm Ally, I'm Brad, I'm Ben, I'm Anna; we're the Construction Kids. Bye!" Within a few seconds, Paige had once more yelled "cut" and the four sped off on some sort of wild chase.

Gill saw the stunned looks and started his explanation. "I know what you're thinking, hazardous, all that sort of thing, but it isn't that way. Remember the grocery bag I had and seeing me sort of scatter some stuff on the ground? It was cracked corn, tiny pieces of hard corn; that lubricated the concrete in a sense so the quads would slide. I did test it out first in my own neighborhood with a couple of kids there. Face it, people: this quartet has high asset value to all of us in one sense or another; there is no way in this world I would ever cause harm to come to them. So, what do you think about the finale?"

An awed Mr. Touhy was able to speak, at least enough to make a brief observation. "Mr. Lanham, Gill, had I not seen that I would not have believed it. How in the world did you come up with that ending, and not only that but you featured all four colors the quad is manufactured in. And another thing: you have girls riding quads; do you have any idea what that can do to sales? I know all about the mis-conception girls are dainty fragile little things to be protected; these girls eradicate that idea. I'm not saying they aren't feminine, all girly at times; I'm saying this shows them in a positive light as much as the video itself shows that positive light with Ally leading the charge. Now, I want to see the final product as soon as I can and we need the commercial segments identified and started in that process. And Gill, there isn't much more I can do for you without causing some personnel issues, but I won't forget this, I promise."

Gill Lanham was on a high. "Mr. Touhy, I just feel vindicated after all this. You met Al and Lynn, the real problem solvers; I just jumped on the bus once I saw which way it was going. I love being in sales and I agree this is gonna be big, but can I ask one thing?"

"Ask away, Gill; you've certainly earned that right."

"When we get more new things, new toys or whatever, can I run them through here first to see if they are really worth the effort? It just seems to me this has really been worth the time."

Terrance Touhy could recognize a gold mine. "No question, Gill; none. Anything you believe can benefit from this process, let me know as soon as you can. My door is always open to you. Let me propose one thing here, just because I can. Parents, would you let me know when you might have the time to bring these kids to our factory, whichever one they want to see. My company will stand all the expenses, provide travel and spending cash."

Alan and Lynn agreed. Later that day, fire pit sticky with s'mores residue and four brand new quad runners parked for the night, chargers plugged in, neighborhood kids disbursed to their own homes, the two parents had a moment or two to savor each other's presence in their life as the kids were sent in to get ready for bed. The day had been exciting, sometimes a bit goofy as when Gill explained he used cracked corn because birds would clean it up for him, their moment of panic as that first quad runner at full speed approached the camera, and the assurance of Mr. Touhy there would be more to come. Alan had rescued an old glider from a junk heap and the two slowly rocked in it, warm in each other's presence. Lynn opened the conversation.

"Alan, again I don't know what to say, how to express what I feel about all this craziness with the kids. That Mr. Touhy, nice man but you and I both know his suit alone cost more that I make in maybe two weeks or so. I did have a chance to talk to Sol a bit about all this; he says getting the kids paid for their performance is one thing but being in line for residuals, that's where the money really comes into play. He's talking thousands here, not hundreds; I had no idea but then I have no experience in things like this. You seem pretty calm with everything that happened; am I just over reacting?"

"No, not a bit of it. I may seem calm but it is just my way of dealing with the unknown, sort of a game face I guess. When I saw Ally come tearing around the corner of the house at full speed it was all I could do to not yell for her to stop. I did feel Gill had this all planned out, so I guess I trusted him to keep the kids safe; when you think about it, he knows full well without all four kids he's out of business. I did hear the discussion he had with Mr. Touhy about testing new items here, so I don't think we have seen the last of him. What I am really waiting for is the end product, hoping it will end up on TV and not somewhere in a trash can. I did sort of talk to Sol myself; he reminded me he was agent for the Big Flags commercial and that those girls were reaping the fruits of their labors every time the ads run. For the moment I think we need to get some kids in bed but I do want to hear all about your day with Jill; tell me tomorrow?"

"Yes, I will tell you tomorrow, probably as we watch the quads fly past. I did see some of the neighborhood kids using the girl's older battery cars plus some of their own. Some days I wonder how my boys and I came to be here wallowing in all this good fortune, and then I remember: Alan Behr and family are next door. You're right; time to get them to bed, but first things first."

"First things?"

"Yes, first things," as she leaned into him and kissed him, perhaps with just a little more feeling and just a little longer than ever before. It was the end of one really great day.

Chapter Twelve

Lynnette

The original hiring documentation gave Lynn some options as to the specific day she would start work for Windmere, Inc. At the outset it wasn't known exactly what days she might have coming from her previous employer; once her resignation was posted, and she had heard and rejected their counter offer, she knew the specifics. She opted to take the accrued vacation days rather than cash them out, closing out the need for her to be physically present on-site for the full two week notification period. She was surprised to learn from Jill Andrews that the long phone conversation they had enjoyed was paid time by Windmere, that Lynn was considered to be an active employee at that point. Jill was currently immersed in some other activities but assured Lynn the orientation to Windmere ways would start on or before the end of the two weeks. That call came well within the two week notice period but during the vacation time. Jill clarified.

"Lynn, I just had a change in my schedule, a window of opportunity as it were, and I really want to start bringing you up to speed with the ways of Windmere, Inc. I know you are technically still employed at the accounting firm, but could we maybe use one of those vacation days to our benefit in getting you aboard? If you have something going already, no problem, but if you don't, what is this coming Friday looking like? I believe that is your last day with them anyway. Not a crises either way. The time window opened a bit for me to make a site visit with you, probably several sites if we can; there is much you can do without me being there, but I thought if we can manage this it would be one day closer to you being more of an independent operator for us."

"I can do that, I can. Much as I don't want to miss the video shoot being done here that day I also don't want to miss this opportunity. Besides, Alan will be here to watch over the kids. I know this may sound a bit paranoid of us but we have reciprocal guardianships for our kids. We did that before the LA trip just to make sure there was always a parent present, realizing that presence without a guardianship in effect is pretty useless. I digress. Yes, I can do Friday. May I ask what we will be doing?"

Jill explained. "First up I think we need to sit and just talk a bit person to person, employee to employee, some Windmere history perhaps, anecdotal evidence of the craziness that can take place from time to time, nothing immoral or hazardous; it can be at times fattening if one is not cautious about the volume ingested, especially in Doris' kitchen when she's in a baking mood. There is much about this place that you won't find documented in some manual, but it is just as important. Sometimes it is as much a feeling as anything else. We can talk about that Friday before we go wandering around. I still have to make some calls to get a visit or two set up; we're not talking some in depth study of anything, more like a meet and greet as I try to shed some of my hours onto your shoulders. See you then?"

Assured she would indeed see Lynn Friday morning, Jillian Andrews disconnected and started making the necessary arrangements.

Lynn had awakened early on Friday morning, popped an extra pan of Cinnamon rolls into the oven, drew a fresh cup of coffee, and sat for a few minutes at the kitchen table to reread the information on the Windmere job offer documentation. It was all still there, written plain as could be, all those perks that went so far beyond her previous experiences, accrual rates for vacation days and sick days, even an investment paragraph about buying stock in Windmere and the governing rules for that option. Her mind wandered back to that one particular time she felt so tired, needed a shower after a long day, depressed a bit, unable to find food she knew had to be in the house somewhere so she could feed her sons, then answering the doorbell when she didn't really want to but was driven by a need to be civil; there stood this man, daughter on each hand; she protested but he would not be denied their joining his family at a pizza restaurant, then at an ice cream treat store before she could protest further. He had lost a beloved wife; she had shed an abusive husband. He held her hand when she needed it held; she kissed him first but he did not withdraw. She remembered being cold and shivering in the pouring rain, but remembered even more so the feeling when his strong arms went about her and pulled her close to him as his heat poured into her and warmed her being. He had been her stalwart rock when she interviewed for the career upon which she was about to embark, when she faltered but felt his hand take hers and pour his strength into her being. He had asked for nothing in return but her presence at his side now and then, maybe at a concert or just sitting somewhere watching the kids at play. Her mind had other possibilities these days, things she would not have considered before they met, but which were becoming possible now should he ask. But, he didn't ask, at least not today or yesterday or the day before that, and she didn't know how she would respond, whether it would be an act of repayment or self-gratification or what exactly it would be. The insistent tone of the oven timer broke the spell for the moment but the memories would remain fresh, especially of his lips on hers. Hot Cinnamon buns ready for sticky icing, most to go across the driveway to the shop of Alan Behr as he hosted the scheduled replacement video shoot. She had wanted to be present but he had assured her all would be well, he would be there for her sons should they need him, and that she needed to do what was needed to better cement her new relationship with Windmere, Inc. And then she heard a car door close, and went to the door for a look. Jill Andrews was nearly an hour early.

"Hi, Lynn; am I too early? I just sort of got up this morning and headed out, habit of mine I suppose. Am I interrupting anything?"

"No, not a bit. I didn't expect to see anyone at this hour but please come in. I have fresh coffee; I do need to finish icing these Cinnamon rolls and carry them next door, but would enjoy some conversation during that process."

Jill entered the kitchen and took a seat on a stool, filled coffee cup in hand. She got to observe the boys as they turned out to start their day, consuming everything their mother put before them then bolting out the door as she admonished them to use the safety equipment during the shoot. That statement prompted a question from Jill as to the nature of the activity. Lynn explained.

"Today is a reprise of the trip to LA, only without certain parties. I'm still a bit hazy on what went on out there, but I understand the company is bringing staff that will augment local staff, not replace them. Alan will observe, which is why I can do other things. I remember in LA when the director said something like 'mom and dad are going to leave now' and Alan slamming the door shut on that idea. I have never seen him angry, not even really upset about anything, but I don't think I ever want to see that anyway. He just stays so calm and collected, gets the job done without any excess fuss, and I think maybe he can read me pretty well in the process."

Jill knew the answer to what she was about to say but talked anyway. "I get the feeling you really like this man; that is a bit of a surprise after what your ex put you through. Mind if I ask how you made that transition, or was it that easy after all?"

"The truth of the matter is I don't know what or when anything happened; just all of a sudden I realized I want to be around him...a lot. Jill, the man has never ever tried to, you know, put a move of some sort on me, not once." Jill looked at her new associate closely as Lynn's face clearly showed the beginning of a blush. "Now and then I even think back to that sleeping bag incident I told you about and wonder what I would do if that happened today. I think I know, but I also know he is very stable, protective of me and the boys as much as he is of his girls. I may never find out what could happen, but I think I want to, I think that, I do."

Jill could see in Lynn's face the reality of that statement and the intensity of meaning; to her it meant Lynn also was already in love with Alan; she just didn't know it yet. In the meantime, Jill had a new employee to start training in her own image. "It may take a bit of patience with him to discover what goes on in his head; I think he might be having a difficult time trying to move you in where his late wife resided, not realizing the mind is adaptive and can handle you both if that is what he wants. I know you might not be aware of the situation at Windmere with Ryan and Laura, but it is quite similar to that in which you find yourself these days; he lost his beloved Mary but found his equally beloved Laura; she managed with some difficulty to shed an abusive husband but accepted Ryan as her second chance at a good life. I do know you probably noticed the hand holding when they walked anywhere together; that goes on all the time, nothing more and nothing less when they are in public, but the kidlets seem to keep arriving in their household. For the moment we need to do some Windmere work instead of burning time gabbing; I do believe the more you know about the company the better you will adapt, the faster that will happen, and the more you will understand about what principles govern their way of life and their decision making. So, ready for a bit of field work?"

The rolls had been delivered, boys admonished to behave, and the two women departed in Jill's car just as the additional personnel for the shoot started to arrive, even Gill Lanham who waved to Lynn as he walked up the drive. The first stop was at a place Lynn didn't know existed, or at the least had no awareness of its existence, Wilson Cartage Company. Jill drove straight to the big chain link fence, pushed the CALL button, when the voice asked their business she said "Jill Andrews and associate to see Lindsey Borders please" and watched the big gate roll open only to close right behind them. Seeing Lynn's questioning look, Jill explained.

"Now and then they get cargo in here that is of really high value, so the gate stays shut. All the trucks have openers and staffers have gate reader cards if needed. A couple of months ago we added a register and sensor to the system to keep track of open and close events. There isn't any good way to know if maybe a portable opener is moved from one vehicle to another, at least to the extent of knowing where specifically it ended up, but a little known reality of the portable openers is that if the back of the device loses touch with a visor, something like that, it sends a signal to the gate system head end that essentially says 'I'm lost' until such time as it again senses the supporting structure. We have some work to do on expanding that feature but today we'll just talk about the system they use a lot. We'll be seeing Lindsey Borders, the new Ms Borders of only a few months. Come on in."

The two entered the office area just as a colorful semi-tractor rolled through the gate behind them; Lynn just had to say something.

"Pink, a pink truck? Wow; never thought I would see anything like that." The woman sitting behind the counter responded just as another woman came out of an office.

"You are so right you haven't seen one like that before; the whole point is you're not likely to forget seeing it. That's the Pink Petunia by name, and we have a second unit just like it on order. The really important thing about all that is that our two female drivers operate the two pink trucks and have matching hard hats, head bands, nail polish and lip gloss; none of the guys seemed interested."

It was a fun moment as the four women laughed about the comment, finally being ended as the fourth woman spoke to the group. "I'm just guessing here but since I already know everyone else, you're Lynn, right? Welcome to the madhouse we so lovingly call Wilson Cartage; I'm Lindsey Borders, co-owner with my hubby Rich who is back in his inner sanctum somewhere. Come on in please and have a seat. What can I tell you today?"

Jill continued the conversation: "Our accounting system workload has continue to expand; demand is now approaching a point where it will exceed available hours, probably in six months or less. We decline to short change problem resolution for anyone, which leaves us with the options of reducing demand or increasing available hours. Reducing the reality of that demand seems selfish of us, while increasing available hours has a whole separate set of parameters to be observed. A month or so ago we fielded our interest in hiring to some of our familiars, persons such as one I believe you already know: Ari Schoenroth. We asked them to keep an open mind and to let us know if someone came into their sights who displayed at least some of the attributes we were interested in. Sure enough, this very nice lady was in Ari's office for an entirely different reason but he quickly checked off our list, and referred her to us. We did due diligence, and here she is. I should add that she already holds an AA in accounting but will be returning to the classroom for her BS in accounting. In addition, we are sending her to Hartford for orientation on our preferred systems, a sort of boot camp although she is hardly a beginner. In a couple of months, probably sooner, she will become your 'go to' person for accounting systems. I will keep myself available on-call as needed and you always have the right to call Laura Williams if all else fails. I should add that Laura is pregnant, again, but believed this pregnancy also will go as planned and she will be able to stay active most of the time. Please let me assure you Windmere has your best interests in mind as being in our own best interests. What else can I tell you that might make this go more easily?"

Lindsey picked up the conversation. "Jill, that first day you walked in here I knew things were going to happen, good things for this company. We made the call because of the new

IRS demands for filing taxes; we are so far ahead of that little issue I find it hard to believe. Back then I was running the office; today I'm running the whole company, most of it anyway, while Rich does other things more suited to him. Connecting the load monitoring software with the trailer GPS and with the accounting system...genius." An insistent tinkling sound rang in their ears as she tapped her headset. "Sorry, gotta answer the phone...Wilson Cartage; how can I help...?" She was apparently cut off by the caller and stopped talking for a moment but then continued. "Got it. Our driver said he heard on his radio there was an accident on State Route 29, the route he was on. He did a quick reroute, dived into a side road, and is presently on County Highway 3A. All in all he may be a quarter hour late getting to your place but he is in full flight on his way at the moment...no, I'd rather not say his present speed; let's just say he's making good time...fine...if that changes I'll let you know. I would have called earlier but was waiting just a bit to make sure all was going well on the reroute...sure thing...thanks. Bye."

Disconnected for the moment, Lindsey used the event to explain how the system had performed, giving details to those present on how she knew exactly the location and speed of the truck, noted the arrival time at the destination was continuously calculated by the system so it was always a real time display, explained why the arrival time at the delivery point was so important to the customer, and a few other items of interest. When Jill raised a question about why Lindsey would not repeat the trucks speed, Lindsey did tell those present it was running a bit over the posted limit at the moment; there was no sense airing that information and tempting fate. For just a moment or so the narrative was distracted when an older very well kept woman popped her head in the office door, told Lindsey she was headed out to retrieve someone, and disappeared just as quickly; that also warranted a bit on explanation.

"Sorry for the interruption; that was my mom telling me she was here to pick up her all time favorite truck and go rescue another driver; I do know the details since both of us here listened to the call for help when it came in from the field. Her husband is probably already on scene in his own ride. They would normally be together but he must have been delayed for some reason and left late. Mom is retired mostly but now and then the two of them…it's hard to say…I think they do this recreationally. Anyway, back to the moment."

Winding down the meeting for the time being, Jill did a brief summary. "That was great, getting a real life event to unfurl in front of us. Lynn will have all the system narrative and such in front of her within a few days; she will have a lot of reading to do but please let me assure you as an owner we will never, and I repeat, never send someone in to do a job we feel is not prepared to do that job and do it well. Now, having said that, I will also tell you that in spite of what you may think at times, I do not have all the answers either; no one I know of has all the answers all the time, but we will support, support, support. Okay; we're on to the next site but thanks again for allowing us in and for that accidental show and tell event."

A bellowing exhaust stack going by nearly drown out all conversation for the moment. Lindsey explained. "That's mom. I think she truly does love that behemoth of a truck, probably something about all that power; no simple semi tractor for her, although Jesse her husband did buy an antique semi tractor for her to show and tell I guess. The Osh Kosh is one of the few around anywhere, at least in that configuration. It is sort of our last resort in pulling power. Anyway, thanks for the visit time; those of us trapped here in the office don't get much of that; there is one more thing I might mention just in passing: Laura isn't alone in being pregnant."

With congratulations offered about the pregnancy, five minutes later Jill and Lynn were back on the road and headed for Bowman Auto Plaza, a dealership in town that would seem to the casual observer oversized for the population served. In reality it was right sized for the volume of traffic passed through those doors including large unit count fleet purchases. Jill was recognized by the office staff as the two walked in and headed for the office of Veronica Weston, owner. Motioned to enter, the two took seats as Veronica finished a phone call, disconnected and opened the conversation.

"Hey, you two. Jill, is this person the promised guru to come? I think everything is all right at the moment but you know how paranoid us owners can be with this magical machinery. It's Lynn, right?" Seeing Lynn acknowledge the observation, Veronica continued. "I don't know if Jill told you or not; my real name is Veronica but I go by Roni unless I've been bad, which is just never, at least not these days. What can I tell you about the goings on here?" Roni glanced up for a moment at someone outside her office window, gave a thumbs up, said 'thanks Billy' and kept the earlier conversation going, all essentially in one breath.

Jill laid out their mission at the moment: familiarize Lynn with what the system did for Bowman in some detail. That took a significant amount of time due to the diversity of the operation. Lynn was told the story of how the system had virtually saved Bowman from some parts theft going on right under their noses, but even that revelation didn't quell a notion stirring around in the back of her mind a notion that finally surfaced and wanted answers. Lynn made her question known to those present.

"I get all that, or at least I think I get enough of it to be nervous about my own abilities in comparison. Guess that will take some significant study time on my part but it does seem to be quite comprehensive. I do have a question or two but totally off the track; I think once I get these asked I will return to clarity on the system before us. Funny how some things can get in one's mind and stir up dust. Can I ask something off the wall?"

Roni responded as Jill looked on, wondering what her new constituent was thinking. "Sure, ask away; nothing asked nothing learned."

"There are two things really. Where did the beautiful car in your main showroom come from? It is a work of art, it is, and I'd bet draws some customers in, right?"

Roni knew. "My grandfather handed this business directly to me when he died; the house we live in was built as a part of the business and never legally separated. It's a long story but there is an old barn on the property; when my husband got the yard in general under control, one day we got the barn door open just out of curiosity; inside were about 40 cars stored there, some packed so tightly we couldn't even get the doors open to look inside. What you see is one of the cars we managed to get out of there, rehabbed, restored, and ready for sale; it is a 1934 Pierce-Arrow Coupe, in running condition. Billy Hansen, a mechanic retired from here works in a bay we set aside here for him doing the restoration work. That's who was outside the window a moment ago, telling me he had finished a minor repair on my own ride, my Cord; I just love that car. So, what else can I tell you Lynn?"

Lynn did have another question as Jill sat beside her and soaked up what she also was learning about Bowman. "Roni, you and I just met, but I keep thinking I know you from somewhere, I don't know, maybe something in the paper, something that has me going."

Roni thought maybe she had the answer. "I get that now and then from people who come in here. I think it comes from the TV news story or the one in the paper about when those two idiots stormed in here and assaulted a couple of us some time ago. My Ron saved me even if he didn't know the whole problem, getting shot in the foot for his trouble. The controversy continues on whether Rhonda, who runs the parts department for us, actually called out 'Billy, help me' or not; he did go to her rescue but will not to this day tell anyone what it was he did to her assailant, the ex-boyfriend. Billy laid the guy out cold, trussed him up with zip ties, then simply went back to his bay and continued to work. Neither of those guys will be around for a few years, my assailant, my ex-husband, much longer as the feds want him next. End of story."

Jill continued. "So no lingering after effects? That was quite serious business; I know about the foot shooting; your ex was armed and I guess ready to do you bodily harm when Ron took him down, the gun went off and Ron got hit. Everything back to normal?"

Roni seemed to hesitate in responding but with a smile starting to form on her lips finally started talking. "Yes and no. I don't think this has anything to do with the present discussion, maybe down the road a bit as things develop; I'm pregnant and so is Rhonda. It was almost funny that Billy told her they needed to get married right away 'in case anything happens.' She was living at his place anyway, not with him in that sense, just in another part of the house. The story is after he saved her from a serious beating, she told him she wanted to give him something for saving her: a baby. I guess he was stunned, but then something happened, no one seems to know; Ron and I stood with them when they got married, we changed places and they stood with us when we got married. And now...all's well, so far."

Jill just had to confirm what she was hearing. "I know both of those persons, and I've seen them interact when they think no one is looking. They do seem very happy, but Billy has, what, maybe thirty years on her, Roni?"

"Somewhere in that ball park; I even talked to Rhonda about that just a tiny bit but she did the math and had a really strong case; guess it worked on Billy.. Her take is that his family genes mean he will probably make age 100 and then some. She is just past 30. Children take a nominal 22 years to put college behind them, so she won't even be in her 60's yet when they leave home. The only thing I don't know is if they plan to reprise this event; I get the feeling this man would go along with that if she is thinking more kids, I don't know about that any more than I can quite explain my own condition. It's just that...I want this man, this Ron, to know how much I love him and this is one way I can let him know." Roni suddenly turned red faced, stammered but continued with a few words. "Besides, Ron is good,,,I mean...he...you know what I mean."

Realizing Roni had somehow slipped into her own private world for just a few second, Lynn tried to help her out. "You're ahead of me for sure. I thought I had all that going but I wasn't even close. I think maybe somehow I am being given a second chance with Alan; guess I'll find out."

Jill heard Lynn, declined to relate the sleeping bag story, but did note that Lynn had entrusted her beloved boys to the keeping of Alan Behr this day. She did take their leave of Bowman Auto Plaza but not before taking a walk to the Parts Department to say 'hi' to Rhonda and then past the bay where Billy Hansen labored on another antique car, a Reo if the name plate was accurate. Neither Jill nor Lynn had ever heard of a Reo, but Billy Hansen knew.

Mr. Vance Simmons at Citizens Bank welcomed the two visitors into his office. "Ladies, can I get you something perhaps, coffee, soda, water. Please make yourselves comfortable. Now, if you would be so kind as to let me know the nature of our business I'll see if I can provided answers you may be seeking. I know you, Jill, and I believe this is Lynn, new associate of Windmere, Inc. Correct?"

Lynn already liked Mr. Simmons just from the way he did business, evenly paced, never hurried, direct but not demanding, pleasant in his approach but not obsequious in his demeanor. She had no clue how much money he presided over but would have been very impressed. Jill did know a bit more because of Windmere activities in the area and the frequent connections she provided via other operations. She opened the conversation.

"You're so right, as usual, Vance. She recently joined the company; the plan is for her to pick up parts of my operation as she grows into the job, resulting in me having more hours available to do that which I do best: interfere with peoples and companies lives; right?"

Simmons laughed at the suggestion. "But you do it so well, Jill, you really do it so well. Since we first met the coffers of Citizens have grown quite appreciably. We recently passed Metro in assets held, not that it mattered all that much in house. Assets held is a pecking order status symbol in bankers meetings. We at Citizens care less about that than we care about repeat business and the well being of our customers. Tell you what: let me bring in the two ladies who do the on-site training for us; they can tell Lynn about what they do and start to build that relationship. We don't know all the answers either but find if we work with the right people, answers seem to appear to resolve whatever quandary might appear. They just spent some time at Emerson Tree Service getting that on line, an acquaintance of yours I believe, right Jill?"

Jill responded. "True enough. Emerson had some real issues in more ways than one but I am happy to say it is all resolved. Lynn, now and then you may run across something you perceive or maybe just sense is wrong in an organization. It can't always be well defined. We didn't talk about it much during our Bowman visit, and it wasn't that difficult to curtail with some astute software gymnastics, not to mention law enforcement; Emerson Tree Service is a whole different story. It is, of course, their business and we will remain mum on the details; suffice it to say the new system had a hand in the resolution of the issues. Having Kevin Emerson take over the reins was the best thing that could ever happen to that company and then when he and Margaret Shafer,,,well...that's another whole story for another day. They are doing quite well."

Lynn remembered something from out of the past. "Did you say Margaret Shafer, big woman, fairly reclusive? I sort of remember her from my high school days, even a story about her no one knew was true or not. That Margaret?"

Simmons knew. "I think you just described someone who existed at one time but who no longer exists with that persona, same body perhaps but different person. The Margaret Shafer I once knew is now Ms Margaret (Kevin) Emerson and holds a titled office at Emerson Tree Service. I also heard there will soon be more Emersons. Enough said."

The conversation continued for some time as Lynn learned how Citizens software could mesh with Windmere software into a seamless comprehensive system. They didn't talk about any additional individuals but did use Emerson Tree Service as an example of how things could be handled. Simmons continued.

"So, you see, once Citizens software is linked to the Windmere system at Emerson, all they have to do for payroll is to enter employee hours worked for the pay period. Even that is automatic to some degree since time clock activities are on electronic files anyway, all the IRS data and such is in the Citizens computer system, all that detail, and our system processes it through to payday, sends e-mail statements to those with e-mail at home and hard copies to the few others at Emerson. They did make an exception recently when they had us send them checks to print for a bonus they were paying employees from some big project. Easily done for a customer of Citizens. I think that about covers it, ladies. Anything more I can tell you?"

There was nothing else the two needed to know for the moment. Jill suggested they enjoy a quiet lunch at a place she knew so they could talk about the day's findings. A full hour later, dessert consumed, the two made their way back to the home of Alan Behr and arrived as activity with the commercial shoot continued. Seeing the four kids perform their broad slide trick for an alternative finale was enough to cause heart stoppage in anyone, but true to form, Lynn glanced at Alan standing nearby, didn't see him flinch, and kept her mouth shut. What she didn't know at the time was that Alan didn't have enough time to react before it was all over; he had experienced instant misgivings but also knew Gill Lanham was not about to jeopardize this potential golden goose.

Introductions were made all around, then the two women retired to Lynn's kitchen for a sort of wrap up to the day, with Jill opening the conversation.

"Today was a cross section of what you can expect to be doing for Windmere and our clients. We do not have a canned program so to speak, which is what makes our system so desirable. We don't say 'our system can't do that so you'll have to adapt', never ever. We make our system do what the customer wants. I will say sometimes we need to help the customer along a bit in deciding what is best for them, but in the end, if they insist, we perform. Now, I need to get a stack of books out of the car; sort of forgot to bring them in with me." Jill departed but returned within minutes carrying a large box. "Here are some of the manuals for systems in this area. I suggest you should perhaps start by reading over the narratives for Wilson Cartage and Emerson Tree Service. I do so because those are really new systems and we may not have located all the bugs as yet. You know and I know any large system can have a glitch here and there, maybe nothing really bad but we need to make sure to keep any channel through which unauthorized access could be gained closed and sealed off. You have a couple or three weeks before the Hartford trip; the more you can soak up here the better that will go, but please do not fret about it, not for a moment. It is just one means we have to push progress along. Okay. How are you with all this now that you have seen some of the actual operations?"

Lynn needed to summarize but the morning had been a wide scope of activities and she was unsure. "I'm not going to lie and tell you I'm all good to go with this situation. Jill, I did understand much of what I heard, but then I also realized some of it was way out of my ball park. I want to do this job, I really do, but I don't know if I know enough to not get into serious trouble. I sure don't want that to happen, not ever, never. I don't want to let Windmere down, not after all of you have given me a chance of a life time, a chance I thought I would never see. What can I say that could better explain my feelings?"

"You don't need to explain. I understand, Windmere staff understands; we will not allow you to let us down. I don't mean that as a threat, only to say if things go south on something and you feel you are in over your head or are maybe just nervous about some aspect, tell us, tell us right then, and we will be there for you. We can't replace that feeling you get when Alan takes your hand, but we'll try, we will." Jill paused for a moment when Lynn looked at her with a puzzled look on her countenance. "Lynn, there is nothing wrong with hand holding; I'm rather sure you saw Ryan and Laura doing that any time they could. Those hands just seem to find each other like Alan's seem to find yours at just the right time. Trust us as we trust in you. It works that way at Windmere. Time for me to head home but you have my connection data; call me if you need, but in the meantime have a good weekend."

It would be Saturday morning, invited into the Behr house and kitchen for pancakes and sausage, that Lynn and Alan finally had a few coherent moments to talk about the day spent with Jillian Andrews. Alan could hear in her voice two distinct tones, one saying she was already immersed in this new job and would give it her all, and the other saying she was a bit frightened by it all. The moment was pure magic when he took her hands in his and heard the fright dissipate, the unsure sense become more stable, and he knew she would be fine, perhaps not perfect but at the least a major asset added to the Windmere portfolio. Her hands clasped warmly in his, both remembered the darkness of the previous evening when their gentle kiss as they separated for the night grew into something with a bit more strength; both realized they were on a road to somewhere, hand in hand; both wanted very much to see where that road would carry them. The dreams were becoming a bit more graphic.

Chapter Thirteen

Wonder Week

At some point during the Friday activities, Alan did ask Gill about all the yard type items he still had stored in #3 bedroom of the Behr home, a nearly full #3 bedroom. Gill had managed to forget all about the items, but realized he had a golden opportunity to achieve resolution of the situation. Taking Mr. Touhy for a walk, Gill refreshed Touhy's memory of the bankruptcy store closure and the need to recover items from the store; his explanation of why the items were here instead of back at the company warehouse serving that area did make sense. Mr. Touhy needed a bit more information.

"Gill, get me an accurate inventory of all this stored material. To tell the truth, I think most of it is from last year and no longer marketable at list price. I do know we have changed some color combinations, things like that, so mixing this stored material in with the new would not be a good idea. Anyway, get me that inventory and I'll make a decision on disposition. Just as a quick guess, do you think Mr. Behr would take it off our hands, or are we already asking too much by taking up an entire room in his house for months?"

Gill didn't know. "I don't have time to do the inventory right now with the shoot going on but I do recall Alan maintained a running inventory of what is here, which items they have assembled and moved out or somehow given away. I should be able to get an inventory from him Monday when things around here have returned to more normal conditions. And by the way, there is some more out in the back garage, not a lot but it all needs something to happen to it."

Alan said he would fax Gill an accurate inventory on Monday morning. Gill was right that things needed to return closer to normal at the Behr household; Alan made sure that happened. The four kids did protest a bit Friday evening when their two parents agreed on a time and sent the four to get ready for bed; it was a rather weak protest, hardly worth the effort. With Alan and Lynn following suit shortly thereafter, when each parent looked in on their kids all were sound asleep already. It was no surprise when the parents had over two hours of quiet time with each other Saturday morning in the Behr kitchen before the first youngster arrived following the scent of cooking sausage. Pancakes and sausage consumed, with her earlier agreement to his proposed plan in mind, Alan suggested the six of them take in a rehabilitated and reopened city park with rides and assorted attractions like a petting zoo. They would spend hours there, find lunch there, continue the play time and roll past the ice cream treat store on their way home. Late afternoon and evening would find the new quad runners and a gaggle of other assorted battery riders in some sort of follow the leader circus like event. Some other parents out for a walk stopped by to ask why their child suddenly had a used but serviceable rider in their driveway; Alan could explain, and did so, pointing to the four new units currently racing about the yard and around the house. Dinner was sort of a "what do we have to eat" seek and find exercise but no one left hungry before resuming play

Sunday found the six walking the short distance to the little church they attended, Lynn's hand safely in Alan's while the kids wandered along up ahead a bit. It was a fairly low key sermon and lesson, as usual; Alan stayed awake in spite of the warm temperature inside. He was also listening when the minister mentioned the church was hosting a fund raising sort of flea market the next Saturday. It would include the usual home baked items plus whatever else the parishioners wanted to sell off; Alan's mind was filled with pictures of kids play houses, swing sets for toddlers, and other assorted things he had stored at the house. He made sure the inventory was accurate and early Monday morning sent it to Gill by fax in spite of the time zone change. One of his reasons was that he enjoyed the quiet time each morning with Lynn as they imbibed a cup of coffee, chatted a bit about perhaps nothing in particular, then set out upon their day; on this day she would retire to her own kitchen table and dive back into reading the narratives for systems in the area that would eventually be hers to tend.

With Lynn gone and the kids off to school with much to tell their friends, Alan settled in to continue research on an item that had arrived by courier on Sunday. Courier delivery, and on a Sunday, meant one thing: the customer was in a desperate situation for help; this situation was apparently no exception and his phone had already sounded off once with someone calling to make sure the package was in his capable hands. He assured them he was on the study already and would do what he could as soon as he could to help them stave off a serious marketing issue with a malfunctioning toy. Around lunch time the phone sounded off. Gill Lanham was calling, inventory list in hand.

"Good morning or whenever, Mr. Behr. I have news for you about that mountainous inventory you are storing for us. Are you ready for this? Gonna tell you anyway. Mr. Touhy says to get rid of it any way we can without causing other problems. You can sell it, haul it off, whatever, and he says if you run into costs doing that to send us a comprehensive bill, all costs included. I'm gonna send you a letter documenting all this, just in case, but unless you have some other plan, the inventory is yours to do with as you please and as of this moment. Questions, sir?"

"Easy Gill, down boy, down. I do have a plan but I need your blessing or someone's blessing on it to make sure I'm not violating some rules from a body of government of which I have never heard. Here's the deal: there is a church sort of fund raiser next Saturday, neighborhood church we attend; if no one protests, I plan to take some of the material there and see if we can sell it off for a donation to the church. If it goes well, with my SUV I may have to make a half dozen or so trips but in the end I get back a bedroom, maybe even a garage. Now, do you see anything wrong with that plan, Gill?"

Gill did not see anything wrong and in fact thought it was a great idea. "Once again I stand impressed by the great Alan Behr. That is a very reasonable approach to this problem and not only that but it stands to make some people very happy. I know you have to figure out some sort of cost basis of those items, so I'll see if I can find the original price list and you can mark down from there. I'll get a letter of agreement done this morning and sent to you. And Alan, thanks for Friday; this is gonna work, it is. I don't want to say how much Mr. Touhy was impressed but I'm getting a new wood desk this afternoon to replace this high mileage metal monstrosity sitting here, glass overlay to protect it just like the big guys, credenza for the back wall, decent new curtains on the windows, and two leather upholstered guest chairs. And one more thing before I let you go: rent a truck if you need one; I'm going to send you a rental agency account number to apply so it won't cost you anything. Good to go, Alan?"

"Good to go, Gill, and thanks. Any idea when we might get to see a finished video product? Not a crises, just asking as the kids ask me now and then. I guess if it makes it to the small screen we'd know."

"I'll see if I can get a timetable. That Sol Kaplan person put a clause in the contract that requires the parents approval, your approval, before anything is aired. Guy is like a Doberman around those kids, maybe even more than their parents, but we know it's all about protecting them."

"True, but we both know I'm the calm cool one; tangling with Lynn over her boys could have fatal consequences. Let me know when you need to do the screening. I'm guessing Sol will have some say on that since he is the kid's agent. Thanks for being so steadfast in pursuing the video goal; I know you put a lot on the line, put yourself in jeopardy and your job on the line. I'm sure you're right about this being a go situation; I was watching Mr. Touhy now and then as things progressed, saw him interacting with the kids not to mention the size of the tip he left at Mama Leoni's place, and that alternate finale that nearly gave me a heart attack. I need to get back to work for the moment as I have a nervous customer who has already called me once this morning for an update on progress. Time to earn my keep; let me know as things change."

"Will do, and Alan, thanks for your apparent trust in what I was trying to accomplish. I agree with what you said about Lynn, but I also know every time there is some sort of issue, large or small, I see her look at Alan Behr before she responds. I don't know her history but I get the feeling she has found a rock to stand on, at least for the moment. Am I right?"

Alan was reluctant to admit anything going on between Alan Behr and neighbor Lynn but didn't go out of his way to deny the connection. "Gill, she's had a tough time of things in the past, ex husband issues, all that; I just try to be there for her, that's all, act like a good neighbor and be there for her to maybe lean on a little now and then if she starts to waver. This job she just started with Windmere is something I believe she has wanted for a long time but the opportunity just never came her way; truthfully I can't even explain what Windmere is or isn't as a company and there is little to no public information on the operation. I believe they will be a positive force in her life. Gotta go before my client calls back again."

Connection terminated, Alan turned back to the offending piece on his bench and reached for a hex driver to start the dismantle process; somewhere along that process line he thought to find the spare battery for the powered screwdriver Anna used and put it on to charge. It didn't take very long with the piece disassembled until Alan discovered the tiny scuff mark on the otherwise shiny interior of the plastic housing, just enough to cause the reported problem, the failure of the mechanism to recoil and reset every time the air burst was fired. All it really did was blow a puff of air out the muzzle to launch a foam missile. The scuff was tiny, barely visible even under his exam light, but enough to cause the slide to rub and lose momentum in recoil; on the converse, with the mechanism disassembled the problem went away and the source of irritation was not readily visible. It took very little effort to remove just a fine layer of plastic from the interior of the housing, leaving enough in place to avoid failure in that respect; reassembled, Alan cycled the toy a number of times, wrote his finding and a recommended fix to the manufacturing facility management and sent a fax, along with an invoice.

That was something else he had intended to address one day, his own archaic method of bookkeeping; that thought train prompted the next thought : neighbor Lynn. In turn that thought quickly gave way to a momentary consideration of the feeling her lips bestowed on his lips and coherent thought paused for a moment of pleasurable feelings in the memory. Alan did think from time to time that he wanted this woman to stay in his life for a very long time, but he had a reluctance to initiate any activity that might enhance that possibility. She had kissed him first, and he didn't back away. Much of his problem with the situation was that he knew she had suffered trauma at the hands of her ex husband; Alan Behr was reluctant to chance rejection because of that trauma, remaining unsure of his limits with respect to and for this woman. He did recall upon occasion that she had an opportunity to run screaming from a damp sleeping bag when he climbed in, but she didn't and he was left unsure if that meant tolerating his presence was preferred only when compared to going back out into the cold rain. It was hardly a warm thought, yet now and then when for some reason the event would find its way into their verbal discourse, she did not seem to be displeased in any way for the experience. If nothing else, maybe he just needed to accept the fact he was falling for her, slowly but very surely, with no idea of what her consideration might be as regarded Alan Behr. Hearing the outside shop door latch click, the present reality flooded back in, along with neighbor Lynn. Alan opened the conversation.

"Good morning again neighbor Lynn; how is your morning going?

"Quite well, thank you. I just thought I should mention I somehow managed to cook too much bacon just now and was wondering if maybe I could lure you into my kitchen for a BLT or two and maybe some sweet tea to wash them down. Interested?" She was already reasonably sure she knew the forthcoming response; he met her expectations, at least on the issue of BLT's.

"I could maybe help you by consuming at least one BLT if that is agreeable. Should I bring along the chips, maybe the onion flavored ones?" Chips, BLT's, or not, he wanted to see more of that beautiful smile of hers.

"We have a deal. Five minutes, my place? I need five minutes to get the place in some semblance of good order; you know how kids can leave things...oh...never mind. I forgot: you have those neat and clean girls."

"Yeah, right; neat and clean girls. Wanna take a look at what they can do to a bathroom, not to mention the laundry pile, just getting ready for school? The frightening thing is when I realize some day they will be teenagers with the diverse trauma that can bring."

The chatter did go on some, and was resumed five minutes later when he walked into her kitchen with a bag of onion flavored chips under an arm. At her suggestion he finished off two BLT's and a half quart of sweet tea. The conversation finally swung around from food and kids to their activities that day, his success with the mechanism he had received, and the fact he had submitted his report...and an invoice. The mention of the invoice prompted her memory a bit as the stray thought floated through she believed she had promised this man a long time ago she would look at his system; maybe today was the day. Then it came to her how beneficial it might be for her to learn the basic Windmere system foundation by setting up this fairly simple system and building on that knowledge.

"Alan, I do sort of remember a long time ago promising to help you get your accounting system up into this century. But, that was back in my days as a file clerk with an AA degree in accounting and no pay grade to show for it. Sorry; that sounded a bit bitter and I know those days are well behind me now. I was thinking maybe if you allow me to do so I would talk to Jill about up grading your system, using it as a learning tool for implementing the Windmere process. I know it would be a basic system when compared to some others in the area but it would be start to finish, all the little details that can raise havoc with the unprepared. Can we at least talk about it some?"

Alan Behr jumped on the wagon. "I'm pretty sure they are well paid for their services. I have talked to a few other persons sort of in my situation about upgrading. They tell me it is the thing to do in that costs can be captured, defended if need be, and the IRS kept happy at least most of the time. The advantages acquired offset the initial cost; that may not be true for a one person operation but there is something to be said for looking more professional in the processes. Besides, who else would I trust with my deepest darkest secrets if I didn't trust neighbor Lynnette? Make the call; do what you have to do to initiate the activity, but please let me know a bit ahead of time on the finances so I don't get embarrassed, okay?"

It was okay with Lynn as she reached for her phone, thought better of it and asked Alan if they could make the call from his shop with the speaker phone. Her reasoning, carefully explained to him with a smile on her face, was that she wanted the process to be as transparent as possible, partly because if she steered into the deep end he could head her off. It was true he would watch the process unfold but with explicit trust she would protect him. Lynn placed the call and within seconds heard Jill respond.

"Hey, hi, Ms Lynn. I believe you are in Mr. Behr's shop, right? You did list this number as an alternative to your cell. So, what brings this call? Finish those manuals already?"

"You are so right; Alan is here with me. I wanted to use the speaker phone because I want him to hear every word of what I am about to propose. No, I have not finished the reading but I did finish Emerson, Wilson, and Bowman Auto Plaza. Those are some really complex systems in what they do, especially with Bowman and the parts supplier's interconnect. Anyway, that's not why I called. I have a proposition for you if you have a moment."

They heard Jill laughing out loud as she responded and quickly realized how things sounded. "It would not be the first time I've been propositioned and probably won't be the last; I do suspect what you are about to tell me will be more business than pleasure no matter how much those two activities can be intertwined at times. So, let's hear it."

Lynn continued. "I know, I know. I no more than said that than Alan nearly convulsed in laughter even if he was quiet about it. So, here is what I have in mind, start to finish." Lynn did take some time in relating her plan, covering every aspect that came to mind as she went along, even to some limited degree the financial aspect with Alan Behr, ending up saying she really believed there was much to learn and that it would be a good experience for her. Jill agreed.

"I think you have something there, Lynn, a golden opportunity to learn vertically from the ground up. I'm actually going into the office today for a while so will have an opportunity to talk to Laura directly about this aspect. I am but a wage slave; she can make the heavy lift decisions. I say that because this is not something to the best of my knowledge Windmere has ever tried, yet it warrants a serious look as perhaps an aspect we have overlooked but should consider for future applications. I have no idea of a time frame here; it depends on when Laura can take time to talk with me about this idea. Should I give you a call back at this number or to your cell?"

"This number, please, for all the reasons I mentioned earlier. Alan has already told me he will reveal all his innermost secrets but only to me; I very much want to keep him in the loop so if there is any confusion about what I am doing we can stop, correct, explain, whatever is needed. He does need to get up into this century with his accounting; I believe this would be a way to do that while improving my own future with Windmere. Sound like a plan?"

Jill agreed. "Yep, sounds like a plan. I'll get back to you." Jill disconnected, leaving Lynn and Alan looking at each other for the moment. Lynn continued.

"Alan, I really think this is going to work to both our benefits. I remember someone saying Windmere likes to try new things, and while I do know some accounting, this is a whole new experience for me. I hope we get the nod from Laura but either way something has to happen; I do know the IRS wants to go all electronic; I even hear they plan to sort of force the issue by threatening audits of payers if they don't go paperless; it isn't written down anywhere that will happen but I believe the IRS is the least regulated of all government entities and does what it wants for the most part. So, I guess for now I need to get back home and continue reading through that big stack for documentation. Yell if she calls back, okay?"

"Okay, I can do that, but before you run off there is one more thing. I talked to Gill Lanham earlier today about the material they have stored here; I am to dispose of all of it by whatever means I choose; end of story from his point of view. I was thinking if we take a lot of it to the church flea market we might be able to reduce the pile a bit. Gill is going to get me a price list so I have a starting point for pricing it out. What got me going at the moment is you mentioning Wilson, the trucking outfit. I'm pretty sure they don't rent trucks, or maybe I just don't know about that at all. Could you possibly tag up with someone there and get their recommendation on who would be a good company to call for a rental? I'm thinking you already know them a bit; work for you? I'd appreciate it. See, this Windmere connection has benefits already."

Lynn did agree it was the thing to do although she would deny any strength of connection to Wilson at the moment; she had been there and they did know she would eventually be their go to person for accounting issues, but much was left to be proven in practice. Still, what could it hurt if she just asked her question? She had already taken the time to load phone numbers into her cell as she had made the rounds with Jill; it was a first step in her ascendency. Phone in hand she scrolled down, hit SEND, and listened as the call was placed.

"Wilson Cartage. How may I help you?" The voice was pleasant sounding but in Lynn's memory didn't quite match the voice of the women she had met on site.

"Hi; I'm Lynn from Windmere Inc looking for Lindsey Borders this afternoon. Is she available?"

The voice continued: "She is here but she's on an important conference phone call at the moment, video meeting sort of thing about a new extended trucking contract. Perhaps I could help you with something?"

Lynn was a bit unsure but gave it a shot anyway. "I asked for her because I was there Friday with your usual rep from Windmere; I am in training to take some of that burden from her, Wilson Cartage being among my eventual charges. Anyway, this isn't really about that. I was going to ask for advice on a good truck rental place we could use to move some things for a church fund raiser this coming weekend. If she's busy I can move on."

The voice continued: "Please tell me more. We may be interested in supporting a charitable event if it would be within our operating parameters. I do have to tell you the person who usually does this job is off on her honeymoon at the moment; I'm Lindsey's mom, Helen Schatz."

Lynn remembered: "I saw you, well, sort of saw you while I was there visiting. You went by in this huge truck of some sort; I remember Lindsey saying you were her mother. It was a really big truck with a lot of wheels." She could hear Helen laughing, then listened to the reply.

"Yep, I was escaping at the moment. That was the Osh Kosh, brute of a truck and I'll admit my all time favorite ride. I'm actually retired for the most part; that is a whole story in the telling; I was not in the trucking industry, at least not for very long, but I digress. Tell me what you need to move and we'll see if we can help, okay?"

"My neighbor has this stack of kids play houses, things like that, all still in their original cartons. How they came to be there in his house is in itself is a long story. The things are from last year and have no commercial value but are brand new. The company has told Alan, my neighbor, he can dispose of the things however he wants. Then, Sunday the announcement was made about the church flea market and we thought it would be an ideal place to move product. The boxes aren't heavy but they do take a lot of room; I remember Alan saying he could get maybe five of them in his SUV at best but I believe he is storing thirty or so play houses. His company contact told him to rent a truck if he needed to make things easier, so here I am out learning that process. I'm not complaining; Alan has been the best neighbor in the world so I want to help him out. He suggested I call Wilson because he knew I had been here. And that's the story; we need to move some boxes."

Helen thought about the situation for just a moment before responding, only a few seconds really. "I'm just here on phone duty to help out a bit; as soon as Lindsey is off the conference call I can ask her. We do have a couple of small box trucks that I believe would do what you need, and I can tell you Lindsey is pretty charitable. My son in law is much the same; technically he does still own this outfit but Lindsey runs it day to day. Let me get back to you as soon as I can talk to her. We're looking at this Saturday for probably some hours to get there and maybe return some items, right? And what sort of time frame are we covering?"

Lynn described the Saturday event hours, locations involved, and gave Helen several phone numbers for her response, signing off after Helen acknowledged and verified the information. Alan had been listening so no repeat was necessary. It had been a busy day and was only half over; more importantly, they were making progress, perhaps not always in the chosen direction but progress anyway. Mid-afternoon Lynn came back into his shop, explaining her presence.

"I just need to stop for a few minutes; my eyes are starting to hurt. At least I don't feel so left out of things as I read through the narratives. I'm not sure but I think Laura Williams writes most of the material, or at least has final say. It is straight forward and down to earth narrative that makes sense as it unrolls down the road. Have you heard from...that the phone?"

It was indeed the phone as Alan hit the speaker button to answer; the sound of Jill Andrews voice came forth in greeting.

"I heard the click, so I'm on speaker, right?" Hearing Lynn confirm the speaker usage, Jill continued. "I ran this idea past Laura; she is all for the whole concept. I am to supervise the effort at least somewhat; here's what has to happen. Lynn, you are to keep an annotated time coherent log of the whole process so we can learn process speeds from it; Windmere does not currently have any programs specifically for sole proprietorship operations, so we need to learn the difference between that and a larger operation with perhaps multiple entities. How much more does the large corporation require and where can that excess be removed for a single person operation, even a partnership? We want to learn and the best way to do that is for you to document, document, document. Because this falls under the category of training, there is no cost to the customer; that will not be true for an operational program, but this is a learning process from which we stand to profit in the future. This is considered to be in place at this time, Lynn, so any time you are engaged in this process you need to keep time. Alan, if you're listening, I want to tell you this is a good deal for everyone involved. Your associate is already proving her worth to the company and I don't think she's even been paid yet."

Alan aired his comment. "Jill, I'm here listening. I agree with the whole thing, and let me just say she had already done much to improve my own life. I look forward to moving into this century with her."

Jill had one more comment, uttered with her finger poised to end the conversation: "And I'm guessing hand in hand; right? Bye!" She was gone just that quick as Alan and Lynn looked at each other, then burst out laughing. It was obvious Jill knew something was going on between the two but had no problem with it. Other consideration aside for the moment, Jill was aware the connection between Alan and Lynn would make the program even more workable. Lynn headed for the door to go resume her reading but paused for a moment as the phone rang again. Alan answered.

"Behr residence, Alan speaking."

"Hi; this is Helen at Wilson Cartage. I'm looking for Lynn; she gave me this number to call. Is she there?"

"She is here, and you're on speaker. Is this about renting a truck?"

Lynn joined in. "Hi, this is Lynn. What do we know, Helen? Where do I go from here?"

Helen knew. "Lynn, you need go nowhere. I talked to my daughter as soon as I could; we will support your activities this Saturday by sending a truck and driver for the day. Our yard foremen is familiar with the materials you described and believes the small box truck would work out great. It has a fairly low floor for ease in loading, even has a ramp tucked up underneath if needed. It will be at your place 9AM sharp. Does that work for you?"

Lynn's answer was enthusiastic. "Yes, that would be great, even just to haul the stuff there in the morning. Hopefully we won't have that much to bring back here at the close of day. We'll get it ready first thing in the morning so we don't hold things up in case the driver has to go elsewhere. Thank you so very much for this; it helps out a lot, really a lot."

"Consider Wilson Cartage to be on board for Saturday, 9 AM your place. Talk to you later." Helen Schatz was gone that fast but for a conversation of less than two minutes, she had delivered a great message. They had transportation.

Once again Lynn thought to head for her home but paused for a moment to reflect on something. "Alan, am I just being silly about all this or is there something going on I can't see, maybe something I'm blind to but should recognize anyway."

Hearing her voice her concern offered no explanation of the issue. He had to ask. "What are you talking about Lynn? What's wrong; what has you going?"

She had to think about her answer for a moment, unsure what she actually wanted to know or if in fact he might have any answers for her. His hands reached out and took hers. "Alan, now and then I get a bit scared in thinking about what has happened to me, to us, my boys and me. You and I have talked about this before, how down and out I was just a few months ago, hardly getting by, barely able to feed my boys, and look at me now. This big corporation talks directly to me about the boys sometimes, even took us to LA and they have come here on their own to do business with the two of us, kids included of course. Jillian Andrews is a force all unto herself, yet I asked and she went to bat for me, ran the bases, and delivered on the promise. I know the call to Wilson was nowhere near that level, but again something positive happened. I agree they may well be charitable people but they don't know me, they don't. What made them agree to a truck and driver? Was it my association with Jill? I'm just trying to understand the last few months, from down and dirty to where I am today, with Windmere and with you, with things coming my way I never expected. Help me understand, please?"

It was Alan's turn to pause and collect his thoughts as he held her hands in his. "I don't know if I can explain or not, or even really understand some of this. Windmere people are no fools and neither is Ari Schoenroth; he flagged you to them but once acquainted Windmere staff maintained the connection. They believe you can deliver for them and in the process become one of them in a professional and maybe even social sense to some degree, confident in you and your abilities; I do not believe for a second that would be a bad thing, for you to be seen in your own right as smart, honest, capable, forthright, all traits I believe are associated with Windmere staff. As to Wilson, you stated your need, explained the situation and things happened because they also believe in you; I don't know what Lindsey might have told her mother or vice versa, but you're getting a truck. And I want to say one more thing that may muddy the waters on everything I just said." Lynn looked directly at him, concern showing on her face; was he about to take a walk away from her to ease his own life? "Lynn, I'm falling for you, I am. It may be slow, will be slow, but I remember thinking I want you in my life for a very long time; each day that call is stronger. I just ask that you give me some time to not abandon the past memories but to put them in a safe place to remember but not control. That's all I ask."

Lynn sensed his need for her to stay in his life; she needed to let him know she very much wanted that to happen. "Mr. Behr, I can't let you go, not after you pick me up, protect me, take care of me." She laughed softly at the next thought: "even feed me at times. I need to resolve my own past, not let it affect today or tomorrow; you are not alone in your fall, not alone." It was a good place to stop talking, and she did so as the distance between the two narrowed, lips touching, arms encircling, and emotions soaring. It was probably fortunate the insistent telephone ringing slowed the moment.

"Behr residence, Alan." The responding voice was familiar, friendly and excited.

"Hey, Alan; it's Gill. Look, I got a deal for you, I hope I have a deal for you. Mr. Touhy got poking around in the system and found some more material that needs to go out of the distribution center serving your area. I know, I know, but Alan, this is better than what you already have. He found a cache of riders no one has ever been on, never left the warehouse. Now, they are two years old and that model is no longer produced, so we can't sell them. The batteries have been discharged for too long, so we will replace all of them. I have three quad runners, a bit smaller than the ones we did the video on but in the five and up age range; I have four smaller ones for the three to four age range, and two two-seat Escalade SUV type riders. You and I both know these things have major appeal and can serve to draw people to where you are showing the play houses. If I can get them into your hands in time can you move them for us? Truthfully, I don't want to see them fed to the dumper when we both know there are some kids who would love to have one. What say you, Alan Behr? And by the way, I understand arrangements are being made to screen the video this next week for sure. I don't have any of the details yet but didn't I hear that Lynn is going to be gone for a week coming up pretty soon? I don't think we can afford to let time slip away that far; Christmas ad season is bearing down on us. Sol will let you know. Now, about my riders: can I ship to your place, live demo maybe?"

Alan looked at Lynn, face questioning the whole thing, only to see her give him a thumbs up gesture instead of a vocal response. She must have heard something he didn't, or perhaps missed, but her indication was "yes" and he would agree.

"Gill, this is crazy. I already have a pile that hasn't moved in recent times, and now you want to add more to it. I do agree those riders have a habit of drawing a crowd, and Lynn seems to think this is a good idea. The flea market is this Saturday so you have precious little time to spare. After that point storage would have to be elsewhere. I think we're in but only if you can manage with that time limit. I'm gonna need to use that spare bedroom one of these days."

Gill was a good salesman and knew his pitch to perfection. It worked...again. "I can have them on your doorstep tomorrow afternoon; will that work? Soon enough?"

Alan knew something was up. "Gill, how are you going to manage that, shipping here in one day? I guess so if you really believe that but I think there are issues." Gill came clean.

"I put them on the truck today before they started on their route. Truck will be there tomorrow, and thanks, Lynn, for the support. Raise those funds. Sol will be in touch on the video screening; I think he has some place he uses that is private but spacious. Anyway, I'm gone if there are no more questions, and thanks people; I know some kids are going to thank you as well." No questions came forth.

The bevy of battery riders arrived the next afternoon by truck along with a box full of replacement batteries; all were stored in Alan's shop very close to the exit door. He did take the precaution of finding a large painting drop cloth sizeable enough to use for the assembly process, the plastic container that had found its way back to the kitchen, the box containing Construction Kids outfits, and early on Saturday morning placed the battery screwdriver and both power packs into the plastic container. He had taken the precaution on Friday of digging out a set of instructions for the quad runners and handing it to Ally to review, just in case, then had the kids carry some of the stored boxes into the shop area to cut down the loading time. The girls were up early Saturday morning and convinced him they would need the extra energy pancakes and sausage would give them; their next ploy was to tell their father they shouldn't eat that much sausage because it might not be good for them, but it shouldn't go to waste and if the boys next door came over they could help the pile disappear. Alan agreed, having purposefully cooked enough for all six people anyway; Lynn and boys appeared, along with a pan of iced cinnamon buns right out of the oven. At 8:45 came a knock at the door; Alan answered.

"Good morning. Can I help you?" The man standing in the drive was no kid and exuded a confident maturity in his approach.

"I'm Jesse Schatz from Wilson Cartage; the truck is here but we need to know how best to pull in for loading." Alan motioned him in and pointed to the pile by the door for starters.

"That pile has been added since the original conversation. Over here are the boxes for the yard playhouses, about half of them we moved in here to save time. Out in the garage there are about ten more in storage. If we can get it all in the truck, fine; if not, we'll take what we can and deal with the rest later. I'm just glad to see this stuff grow feet; it has been here a long time already although that also has had some benefit for us. Your truck, your call."

"Well get on with it then." Jesse stepped back out the door. Alan followed, saw Jesse turn to face the street end of the driveway and wave to the driver, turn sideways and pat his rear end, then back to face the truck as he motioned it into the drive. Per instructions, the truck moved into the street then slowly backed into the drive. Inside the kids were directed to pile the dishes in the sink before they came outside, and did so. Lynn walked outside to stand by Alan and was there when the truck was motioned to a stop and the driver climbed out. Lynn was lit up.

"Helen! I didn't expect to see you. What a pleasure. Lindsey isn't forcing you into involuntary servitude is she?"

Helen Schatz laughed, big smile in place. "No, not a bit of that stuff. My daughters truck so I get to drive. Jesse and I are both retired and thought this might be a fun day. He wants two of the play houses already for our house and hasn't even seen them. Jesse, suppose the two of us work the truck while they carry, probably four in the cab over, then a flat stack on each side and vertical up the middle to stop the sliding around. And look, the kids just keep coming out of that door. Lynn, how many kids are there?"

Lynn was already laughing at Helen's exuberance. "Only four, but before you ask: two sets of twins, okay? Boys are mine, girls are Alan's. Now, ready for boxes?"

They were ready for boxes and kids started on the shop piles while Lynn and Alan carried more from bedroom #3. With a steady stream, all boxes were safely in the truck, including those formerly in the garage. True enough, the truck was jammed full to the top. Alan made sure the other things he needed were placed in the Behr bus, told the kids to climb in, and along with Lynn headed off to lead the truck to the church parking lot. There was already a lot of activity to get ready for the 10 AM opening of the event, but with eight people involved the play house display was ready to go within minutes. Alan had prepared a large temporary sign that announced the assembly demonstrations of the quad riders would take place at 11AM, 1 PM and 3 PM. With a couple different play houses assembled by the kids, they were prepared for the opening time. Alan had also prepared a sign showing the original list prices for what they had on display, then what they were asking this date; he had opted for a nearly 60% markdown, and if things didn't move fast enough would opt for an even deeper discount; that option would prove to be unnecessary.

With the drop cloth spread out to define the work space and the other items needed in place, safety vests, hard hats and tool belts on young bodies, the first quad runner box landed in the middle of the space; Ally started reading the instructions. They had with purpose not shown the quads prior to that point, keeping them in the truck until the time was right. The crowd watched with interest, and within a few minutes had swelled to include nearly everyone at the event, interest high in watching the performance; they were impressed that these four kids had things all together and were working like a well oiled machine as the toy fleshed out from a stack of parts to Anna jumping on to test the foot pedal. The machine was sold two minutes later, with a second buyer telling them he also wanted one and would pay an extra $20 to have it assembled for him while he waited. The third large quad was left in the truck for the moment as a part of the overall plan; they would get it out when they felt the time was right to rebuild interest in what they were vending. Two more play houses were assembled for show and three were sold off in the original boxes. Jesse and Helen had stayed with the group so the truck could be used for storage on site, but in reality enjoyed being around kids much like their grandkids. Lindsey with husband and children arrived at some point, as did other persons the group knew.

At the 1 PM showing the third quad was assembled and sold within minutes, along with one of the smaller riders and one of the two-seaters. The play houses had continued to disappear steadily, some assembled and some in boxes. By the time Alan needed to start considering the 3 PM showing the truck was empty, bone empty; there was nothing left to sell. The reverend Jack Hodge could be considered wired to the max with what had been taking place. Flea market events were not known as big fund raisers, being more social than monetary, but other flea markets did not have a truck load of valuable merchandise to vend. The cashier ladies had taken a moment to advise him of the size of their haul for the day; he was impressed and wanted to let these people know his feelings. Walking over to the group he realized Jesse Schatz was there, his financial mentor who had put the church on an investment track not generally available to others. The reality of Jesse Schatz was not that he was a heavy haul truck driver; he did that for recreation. Jesse Schatz was a financial wizard in every respect and while the reverend Jack Hodge might not have known the extent of what Jesse could do, he did know the church funding was safe and growing like a weed. In counterpoint Helen Schatz did love to drive a truck, but only certain trucks, those that appealed to her for some reason, like the brute Osh Kosh or the box truck they were using this day; in fact, that specific box truck was the first truck she ever drove for hire with a revenue producing load to be delivered. Jack Hodge made his appearance known.

"Mr. Schatz, what a pleasure to see you. All these your grandkids?"

Jesse jumped in. "No, not even relatives, but I will say I would adopt them in a second. I didn't see you at either of the battery quad runner assembly sessions but I'll tell you I was impressed with their organization and work division. I did hear they are in process of doing a commercial for a major toy company. So, how is the Reverend Jack Hodge these days? Get any more offers?" Jesse was aware Hodge had been solicited by the church hierarchy to move up in the organization, bigger church, more congregants and so on.

Hodge replied. "I did get another nudge by the big boys in church corporate. They see the books and are after me to tell them how our interest on investments piles up so fast. They'll not get a word from me, not ever, never. And, I don't plan on moving any time soon. I was given this facility as my first church because it was aging out, sinking into oblivion. Thanks to persons such as yourself, and of course that Marty Roberts woman who books weddings in here as a 'go to' destination, we are up and running just fine. You can probably see the construction taking place over there; that's our new community center and meeting place. I was a bit unprepared for that to happen; one of our elderly parishioners wrote a big donation to see it through. His knees were giving out and he didn't want to miss any of the group hug type meetings in the church basement so he decided we needed a ground level hall he could access. He came to see me, told me what he wanted to do but didn't bother to tell me it was already in process. That realtor Randy Shaker saw me two days after that to tell me the land purchase was complete and the construction contract let. I'll tell you for sure, corporate need not take up any more of my time. But tell me, how did you get involved in this? Looks like the space is empty, nothing left to sell."

"True enough, nothing left to sell. Partly that is because of the kids and their performance but as much because what we had was brand new in the box and the price was right. Helen got me into this, really; that lady over there talking to Helen is the boy's mother; she had met Helen's daughter Lindsey on a professional basis. When the truck need came up, she remembered Lindsey, made the call, and here we are. We have had a ton of fun. To be clear, everything we sold today was a donation; do you know these people?"

"I do see them regularly but had no idea about all this. I understand they are close neighbors and the kids play together, but I haven't looked into things beyond that. Maybe I need to get out more. Think so?"

"Couldn't hurt. I only met them today but my opinion is pretty high. The other thing is, if you look close, you'll see the woman's hand is in his hand; any time they are that close together the hands are joined. I'd say that is a good sign. Anyway, time to gather things up and take the truck home. Let me know if anything changes in a financial sense, anything I can do."

The conversation ended and Jesse walked over to help close out the site. Some time along that process it was suggested everyone go to the ice cream store for a treat, then on home after a long day; it was a suggestion easily voted in. Within an hour all were returned home, well satisfied with the day, pleased with themselves, and ready to quiet down for the evening. Alan was particularly thrilled bedroom #3 was empty of storage; there was again some vacant space in the back garage. The next big event was four or five days away; Sol would let them know.

Chapter Fourteen

The Ad DVD

True to form, Gill Lanham called early Monday morning to hear how the disposition had progressed. Alan let him know everything was gone but brought in money in the process. More importantly, when was the screening to take place? Gill Lanham didn't know but again made it clear Sol Kaplan was the man in charge of that evolution.

Two hours or so later Sol did call for Alan or Lynn or both; he would accept any combination of parents so long as those present could sign off on the video work. The showing would take maybe an hour start to finish; Sol had made arrangements to use a theater like setting, gave Alan the address and a phone number for just in case issues, said they would start the process at 1 PM on Thursday and would that be a problem. Alan assured Sol that would not be a problem, but thought to himself he needed to take action and rather quickly to liberate the four kids for the event. After all, they were critical to the process and stood to benefit from it. Lynn arrived for her mid-morning break a bit later than usual; Alan filled her in on the time and place and the need to start the process to get the kids out of class in time Thursday; that would turn out to be the most difficult thing to complete.

"Lynn, I think we need to start that process yet today if possible. I'm sure it will take both of us even with the guardianship document still in place. I truly do not want the wheels to come off the bus at this point; should we go to the school this afternoon?"

It was good for her, taking some time in the afternoon to handle the process. She had been spending her hours wisely doing the reading of processes Windmere used to make their system function in a variety of ways. She discovered it was much like the way they had described their problem solving process: break it all down into small pieces, see what fit best, reassemble the whole from the parts and pieces, and continue onward. They would go to the school in time to catch the kids as they got out of class. Alan had been right about the difficulty of springing a child out of the school other than at a designated scheduled time; they were there nearly an hour proving their case, starting with id's and working up from there. Finally, and with apparent reluctance, the principle signed off although the two parents suspected she didn't believe their entire story, even after they provided phone numbers for substantiating corroboration; no one, just no one, had ever signed a child out to go review a commercial DVD they had starred in. It would take some time, weeks later, when the ad ran on television, the principle made sure everyone knew those kids were in her school.

With two parents and four kids, the Behr bus made its way to the given address, passing through the drive to the parking promised at the back of the house. Kids cautioned to be on their best behavior, the six made their way toward an entry door, finding Gill Lanham motioning them into the house, with a warning.

"There's a really large dog inside meeting people but don't worry about him. He's friendly enough, okay?"

Lanham was right, to a tee. English Mastiff Clyde did greet everyone who came in with a sniff or two; all passed through without incident although the kids did want to stay and pet him for a while; they would get their chance a little later in the afternoon. Entering the room referred to as the A/V room, they found it filled with large comfortable recliners toward the front and a meet and greet clear space toward the back; trays of finger food were being consumed and the bartender kept busy but with soft drinks only. Alan knew, he just knew, the barkeep looked familiar.

"Hi; I'm Alan Behr. You look really familiar for some reason. Have we met?"

The barkeep responded. "We have met; I'm Rob Roberts. I was in plant engineering; I think you were more in the research area of the plant, right? We both took a hit when the plant shut down. I'm doing quite well at the moment working mostly for an outfit called Windmere doing energy studies at their multitude of facilities. This is actually my wife's place of business where she runs a sort of seek and find operation for people with too little time and too much money, now and then hosting meetings such as this one, and feeding Clyde, of course.. Our daughter will be home from school about the time this wraps up; technically, she's my niece but I adopted her when Marty and I got married. How about you? Doing well I hope?"

"I am doing well. Now that you mention it, I do remember you from the plant. I had a sort of sideline going when the plant closed and managed to parlay that into a full time occupation, mostly doing trouble shooting on consumer products that don't work right and are teetering on the edge of a product recall. You mentioned Windmere; Lynn, my next door neighbor, is just starting out working for them in accounting; it's kind of a convoluted story how that happened but...isn't that Ari Schoenroth over there, just came in? He's our lawyer for several things but mostly at the moment this commercial we are here to review. By the way, the girls are mine, the boys are Lynn's, just so you know."

Rob did note the explanation given. Alan was right; it was indeed Ari Schoenroth, invited by Sol Kaplan, along with videographer Paige and her crew. Mr. Touhy was standing back toward a corner engaged in a conversation with Marti Roberts about her operation in the home, including a brief discussion on Clyde's origin. Marti took a moment to explain to Mr. Touhy what she did for a living, in the process telling him her daughter Emily had another pet, one that was a bit more nocturnal in nature: a North American skunk named Keeper. It was a good point to stop as the meeting was called to order by Gill Lanham standing by the big screen at the front of the room.

"First of all, thank you all for coming today. As you might imagine, we are pushing toward releasing this material in time for the Christmas ad rush; that process starts earlier every year, whether we like it or not. Our plan this year is a bit different, and I have to tell you it makes us nervous to a man...or woman...as the case may be; we will use what you are about to see but will not start the full blown push until after the competition completes their initial blast, touted what they believe will be their big seller, that sort of thing. You and I all know the market for toys is driven by media, what's hot, what's not, fame that can fade with the sunset, really fast turnover, red hot to what's not measured in little more than seconds. Our intent is to wait in the bushes, then leap out with something so different the competition won't be able to field a comparative item until sometime after the market closes. Even if they do manage to compete, by the time they get to market we will be there in the cat bird seat. Now, a bit of explanation: the first part you will see are the short 15 second bursts we will air to drive interest, pique the curiosity a bit on what this might be leading into. There are four of those we will sequence over about three weeks. Next will be the more explanatory ads, showing what the kids are assembling, and then the entire sequence of ads shown one commercial break after another and repeated until time runs out. We will also provide the full blown video to be used during kids Saturday morning shows. It will cost us dearly to run something that long but we were able to leverage some interest among the hosts, even promising to some degree to include them in as the response grows. We are that sure the response will grow. Okay. Everyone ready to watch?" With the attendees seated in the recliners, Gill motioned for the video to be started.

Gill was right in how he described the segments and how they would work. Only the few present who had done the actual taping knew what to expect as the process unfolded. The others learned quickly and saw how the process worked, how the little segments left the imagination running; after all, those kids in the video were having a lot of fun and those watching wanted in on the fun; the fact they were adults and not kids said much about how the product was being marketed: parents were made to feel they wanted their children to experience the joy this product could deliver. As expected, the final segment of the long version, that of four quad runners sliding to a stop wheel to wheel, prompted a lot of open gasps, followed by applause as the video faded to black. Gill Lanham was lit up as was Mr. Touhy and any number of other persons in the room; the four kids were less impressed as they had been there done that for real; maybe there were some snacks left on the finger food trays.

The group would spend the next hour talking about the process. Daughter Emily arrived home some time during that time period and joined up with the four kids, introducing them to her pet skunk, playing catch with Clyde, and other amusements she enjoyed. The adults, including in particular Ari Schoenroth, reviewed the contract to be signed; Ari had received a copy the previous day for his review, a copy that spelled out all the details, pay rates for actual work to be completed, minimum standard perks to be provided, royalty rate, nominal schedule of airings, all those details, including but not limited to reimbursement of the parents for any and all support they might be called upon to provide, all those things. It was a good contract offering and in an aside meeting with Alan and Lynn, he recommended they sign on the line; Sol had been thorough in his specifications; the kids would be well cared for in every respect. There was also a section on public appearances that called out parental presence at all times, no exceptions. Why there was a section like that was lost on the parents, but not on Sol; he knew if this whole thing went as hoped, his small clients could well be called upon to make televised public appearances on behalf of their product; it could be a gold mine and Sol knew how to dig.

A mandatory call at the ice cream shop was completed before the group returned home. Alan and Lynn remained engaged in conversation about the event and in particular about how Ari and Sol were so supportive of the children; true, it was their job, that for which they were being paid, but it seemed to be a step above that due diligence in every regard. The two also talked about her upcoming road trip and how that event would be handled.

Sitting by the fire ring as they watched their scout dinners cooking, Lynn again assured Alan her mother could come stay with the boys during the five days she would be gone. In counterpoint Alan assured her he could manage the four and that he had the advantage of knowing the school location, the dairy treat shop, Mama Leoni's place, and had the guardianship papers close at hand, just in case. Assured and comfortable in Alan's parenting abilities, she cautioned her boys to behave as they left their house for school Monday morning but would return to the Behr house for the four nights to come. True to form, Alan planned out ahead, knew the five day menu and bought the needed supplies, told the girls to use the bathroom off his bedroom so the boys could use the guest bathroom, and was well prepared for what turned out to be a fun time after all. With the kids headed to school, he took Lynn to the Yorkville airport, a slightly larger and better served facility. It turned out to be a fruitful four days in the class room with only ten other attendees. One of the things she learned early on was that Windmere carried a lot of weight at the training facility and that Windmere IT operations were frequently on the cutting edge of available technology. Alan took the kids along to meet her return at the airport. They would talk about her experience at some length, with Lynn again wondering aloud about the events that seemed to propel her forward and upward; she was not complaining in the least but at times wondered if her perceptions of reality were somehow altered. One perception that remained was her lips on his as they retired for the night; she had come to the conclusion, as had he, that the separation clearly defined for them their need to remain close.

Chapter Fifteen

Side Effects

Two weeks later, just as retail stores and on-line shops started their seasonal ad push, the first assembly ad went live on cable and on-line at the same time, most frequently being seen with children's show programming. Questions were raised about what the ads were trying to show in the 15 second blurbs, who were those kids, how old were they, were they really the twins they appeared to be, were they all related maybe, was that pile of parts really that large and what was the stuff in the plastic container, lawyers salivated over thoughts of child labor law violations and maybe some OSHA violation concerning that power tool thingy the one girl wielded, why did this brief ad look so organized and professional, and many more questions. No other vendor had a similar ad and a mad scramble was on to replicate the process before this one ad series had the entire audience in tow. The second assembly ad went live a week later, right on schedule. Juvenile viewers weren't doing it but bets were being placed on what it was the kids were assembling; their professional demeanor was impressive even if they did look like they were having fun. They had a locked in audience for clips three and four as the ATV took form, and then the featuring of the entire assembly DVD contents by running in sequential ad slots over a couple of hours, day after day; the ending clip with the four in full broad slide drew juvenile rapt attention. The bar was raised to a new high in kids advertising; this was not simplistic fodder for this product with all hype and no real substance, but a very real presentation by real persons on a real product. The competition went nuts just trying to discover the source of the ads; they would be successful in the discovery process but it would take a lot of time and net no cooperation in resolving their own dilemma.

About the fourth week in after the initial airing of the first assembly ad, Gill Lanham called Alan mid-morning with an update. Gill had learned the schedule between Alan and Lynn, and knew she would most likely be in Alan's shop at that specific hour of the morning, probably with some of those Cinnamon buns right out of the oven; his mouth watered at the very thought. Gill Lanham was excited, really excited.

"I gotta tell you two...I don't even know how to say this and remain calm; sales of the quad are out of sight. Us peons in Sales have become some of the most popular people on the planet, right up to the point we have to tell some Purchasing Agent we can put them in line for a shipment of quads but that the line is getting long, Hell, the factory is running 24/7; they've even shut down a couple other lines and shifted to making quads. To tell the truth, I'm wondering if we need to shut down the ad campaign a little early before we cause a riot. I do know sales of other riders are way up and we're packaging an assembly DVD with play houses, the original DVD; I know, I know: it's copyrighted so we are prepared to pay those royalties but with sales this good the royalties are a just reward for delivering us out of the wilderness. One more thing: we have been getting calls for kid interviews, public appearances, all kinds of stuff, plus a lot of product endorsements in the mix. Sol will be giving you a call real soon; I have to tell you he predicted this happening after seeing the assembly DVD. The other thing is, he will protect those kids like they were his own, and in a sense they are his own, at least for that part of their lives. So, there you have it. Oh, I should mention the guys in Marketing here are asking to sit with some of us Sales people in the lunch room; guess they're looking for a new home since their boss is on pretty thin ice these days. Gotta run for now. Things go to hell, you know where to find me." Gill was gone, leaving Alan and Lynn fairly speechless in his wake, neither having said a single work in the process. Neither had time to recover before the phone sounded off again; Sol Kaplan was calling and led off the conversation.

"Good morning and it is a very good morning. I can see those royalty checks from here, even if I know after the holiday season they will become a bit scarce. The kids are going to do quite well in this fairly short but intense burst of ads, and there are always the coming summer months ahead of us. I get the feeling once this company sees the bottom line, we will get more calls. Anyway, that is not why I called; I just like to bask in the sunshine now and then. My real reason is that I have been getting calls, lots of calls, once people discovered who did the work on the ads and who is directing that traffic. I know you have probably talked to Gill Lanham about calls he has been getting since the ads broke, right?"

Alan jumped in when he could. "We talked to Gill just before you called. He is super excited, told us the factory is running flat out and losing ground. I agree this will taper off when the holiday season is behind us, but in the meantime what a gift. He also said there would be calls made and that we could expect to hear from you. So, what's up this AM?"

Sol continued. "First of all, as I review the proposals I will not accept anything that has even the remotest potential to cause harm to my clients, your kids; even a hint of hazard is a no go. I have one before me I think we should consider as soon as we can. It's from a soup company and before you think I'm nuts, here's the tie-in: snack time for hungry quad riders. Quick summary: kids park the quads, store their brain buckets, and head in for something to eat; this company markets soup in pouches suitable for nuking, enough in a single pouch for two kids; the kids read the directions, nuke the soup, dishes in the sink, back outside. I suspect this started out to serve single adult persons, but it does have potential for this application. I know you travel a bit, Lynn, so here's my pitch: can we a meet at Alan's place yet today, say after 5 PM so all can attend including the videographer? If we're going to do this, we need to move quickly."

Alan looked at Lynn and saw her nod. "We can do that and we'll call the video person. I know this also might sound nuts, but can you bring some of the product so we can see how complex the prep is, and by the way, if it doesn't taste good, I believe I also speak for Lynn here" Alan saw her head nod in agreement with whatever limit he was about to place "if it doesn't taste good it will be a no go. I do not want our semi-celebrity kids to endorse something they don't like. Okay?"

It was okay with Sol, and after they completed an agreement on the kids being interviewed by a teen magazine via video, the call ended. The local media was also given an opportunity to interview after they called and asked; one of the TV reporters finally figured out who those kids were when his own kids watching the quad ad mentioned the four being in their class at school. The two parents talked about the situation a bit before Lynn had to leave and make a site visit on behalf of

Windmere accounting. Each day her confidence level notched up just a bit, not soaring yet but certainly no longer unsure of her own abilities. Jill came through every few days and would add to the store of knowledge Lynn was piling up, in a subtle way enabling Lynn to take on more complex issues. Lynn also reveled in the reality her customers welcomed her as the being she was and the company she represented; that in itself was a good feeling, that she was welcomed as a person, not just a lifesaver at the moment. One thing she had not considered in any depth was that her ex husband would also see the ads; even though Ari Schoenroth had handled the guardianship documentation, she remained leery of what her ex might consider doing in this new situation. It was true he had virtually renounced any trace of parental connection in exchange for waiver of his monetary responsibilities, but in his own mind those facts were not necessarily connected. Her thoughts also reminded her she was doing really well these days in every sense, even had an undeclared boyfriend, while her ex remained limited by the results of his own stupidity.

With all gathered in Alan's shop, including the kids, the informal meeting started with Sol painting a picture of the situation; he ended up by opening the lid of a cooler and asking the kids to pick out what they wanted, then see if they could handle the prep work required. It was no challenge, none at all, even if they did pair off and pick out two different varieties; if anything was unusual it was that the kids had paired off boy-girl, boy-girl, in what was the very first time anyone had seen that happen, even their parents; Alan and Lynn looked at each other when the pairing occurred, eyes meeting and a silent agreement made to keep any eye on the situation; their concern at that point was unfounded and solely due to something they failed to keep in mind: not everyone likes the same flavor of soup. Directions read, the very literate kids knew two bags could be done together if the time setting was followed. Five minutes later, at a table set up for that purpose, the pouches were cut open, the contents divided half and half into bowls, and spoons went into action. No one needed to ask if the kids liked the soup; it was gone in an instant even if the crackers and condiments had yet to arrive.

Paige needed time to write the cue cards and review the process, but a Saturday AM shoot was scheduled, completed in well under an hour, edited, polished, copyright documents filed, and contact made with the requesting company on the following Monday. Four days later, with negotiations completed and a contract in place, the soup video was released and hit the airwaves, placed as often as possible right after the quad runner spots aired. It was costly, that placing by the quad ads, but the company knew sales projections would handily cover the increased cost; they erred a bit on their estimates and were soundly yelled at when grocers couldn't keep the frozen pouches in stock; there were other equivalents available, but lacking the link to the quads they stayed on the shelf. Those royalty checks would start to arrive in thirty days, again tied to the seasonal sales of the quads but appreciable as the seasonal good times rolled. The local interview went well, mostly simple questions like "Do you like to ride your quad" and "Where did you learn to assemble things so fast?" and "Are you really twins?" with a number of color pictures taken to be published with the by-line article. The broader based interview was conducted by sending in a person to conduct the interview on site while the cameras rolled; that interview nearly collapsed when Anna asked the interviewer if she wanted to share some soup they were about to make; after all, it was mid-afternoon and time for a break by Anna's standards. Sol had calls stacked up with potential customers, but remained adamant in his stance of safety for the kids, their financial improvement, and their future in the process. No lost school time was allowed; this was extracurricular activity, and while it was indeed profitable, school time remained all important; the four enjoyed an increased popularity but remained on a par with their peers and did not tread on their own fame to gain position. Sol even worked out a Saturday live appearance on a nationally aired kids show; that did require the four plus parents to fly to the west coast Friday evening, do the show live Saturday, tour the town in the remaining time, and fly home Sunday in time to make school Monday morning; Gill Lanham did the hosting at their request. Monday morning was also important: Alan rearranged things in their freezer to accommodate the several cases of frozen soup pouches that arrived by messenger.

Residing in his less than desirable accommodations, the ex saw the soup ad when it first aired, noting it was in addition to the quad ad already running and made the connection "his" kids were making a killing in revenue. He had no idea of the reality Sol had created. Sol was reluctant to get into product endorsement unless he knew for a fact a specific product met his expectations in every respect before being presented to the kids for their vetting. It was a good practice and would remain in place. Meanwhile, life in other areas continued to unfold.

Chapter Sixteen

The New Customer

Syd Long lay back into her husband's arms, comfortable in the warm feeling as they rocked slowly in the old glider on the back patio. They often sat this way, with his arms draped around her, his hands softly touching the growing rise in her midsection; it was just a good time for relaxed talk, air things out if need be in a calm and thoughtful process. His work running Precision Machine Specialties was a handful for anyone but Ed could handle it with skills deftly applied. On the other hand Syd headed the US based marketing shop for Tallright Corporation, a division of Tri-Norse industries. One item of particular interest for her and her staff was to make sure the consumer appliances Tallright wanted to sell in the US were suitable in every respect for the US audience. As the new shop was being created they received a shipment containing multiple assorted consumer units for use by the marketing staff. There were a few obvious items right up front that had to be changed; with that taken care of, the campaign was kicked off, sales increased, the marketing effort was clearly a success, upper management was happy as was Syd Long, but now and then some gremlin would appear. Syd could always refer such issues back to Oslo, but that took time, exacerbated by the time zone difference. There had to be a way to shorten the response curve, get back to the consumer faster, at the same time remediating the issue for both the satisfaction of the consumer and to avoid further issues like a limited recall of some sort with the negativity that could cause. Syd voiced her concerns to her husband, partly just to vent the idea and maybe even find a response in the telling.

"See what I mean? Sometimes it isn't much of anything at all, maybe just a misunderstanding of the specific application. I know you're up to your ears already with two work cells churning product, plus there is always the remote possibility someone would think I have accepted a fix just because I love you so much and am carrying your child; so, I'm not asking you to bail me out, just airing my story in the hopes you might know someone who could possibly help out. Um…do you maybe know someone like that?"

Ed took her bait: "Not right off the top of my head, but let me ask around a bit, okay? There are a number of really good engineers living here, some I see regularly at chamber open house events. I haven't been in town all that long, you know, just long enough to find the job of my dreams, the woman of my dreams, and pretty soon the family of my dreams. I'll ask around once I get to work, okay?" It was okay with wife Syd.

As promised, Ed did start making some calls, the first one to Ron Weston at Applied Dynamic Technology. Ron was rather innovative himself but knew he was starting a rebuild in one area of the plant he managed; his time would be limited, very limited to expend on anything but the renovation. Ron's problem was less the technical nature of the renovation, he could handle that easily, but because the project was to accommodate the needs of a new federally funded guidance system for the military; the Pentagon would demand a lot of his attention, warranted or not. Ron voiced his sympathy, declined the task, but did suggest Ed call another engineering associate of theirs, Rob Roberts. All of the men knew or knew of each other partly because of the Chamber "After Hours" events they attended each month at various facilities.

Rob turned out to be a good source of information, although he was about to start on a road trip for a week out of town doing energy management work for Windmere Inc, one of his employers. He was well known as a problem solver but this problem would have to go the end of the line; Ed declined the loss in time. It did turn out Rob, as a home town guy, knew a lot of people and posed a reference.

"Ed, do you know Al Behr maybe? What you're asking about is what he does for a living, at least these days. I worked with him before the plant closed, not necessarily directly with me in plant and Alan more in the product development department, but I did know him And one more thing: those crazy commercials with the kids on battery quads we are seeing these days: the girls are his daughters. Anyway, maybe you should give him a shot, see what happens. Wish I could help out; you know how engineers love challenges; I just have to pass this time. Okay?"

It was okay with Ed. With that information in mind he called Syd and told her what he had learned, suggesting she should do the calling to Al Behr since she was the customer and Al Behr appeared to be the solution at the moment, or at least a source of a solution. Syd placed the call.

"Behr residence. May I help you?"

"Mr. Behr, this is Syd Long. I think maybe you know my husband Ed Long. I work for Tallright Corporation in marketing their consumer appliance products in this country. You may know we just really got going in that respect, good sales, all that, but as usual this little gremlin popped up on one of the products. I'll admit my staff here is technologically incompetent; one alternative I have is to refer the problem back to Oslo but that takes time I don't want to lose in this campaign. I will admit I am making this call because I asked Ed to find someone who could help me; I do know he could problem solve this but there is always a concern about how that might be seen if the solution had any unseen issues. So, here I am. Mr. Behr, now that you know the issue and a bit on my time constraints are we still having a conversation?"

Alan bit, quickly. Here was a new customer with the potential for international connections. "We are still having a conversation even without me knowing the nature of the beast. I do have a fixed rate schedule for shop time, plus parts if that need arises, but will document each parcel of time I expend; I say that because problem solving upon occasion includes walking away from the problem for a few minutes or letting it ferment over night. There are times that is the only way things get resolved, or at a minimum the decision can be made the issues cannot be resolved by any normal means and we need to step back. Given all that, are we still having a conversation, and by the way, I go by Al most of the time, not Mr. Behr; okay?"

"Yes, certainly. One question: if I have this item delivered to your shop, can you give me an idea on when you can take a look at it? As noted, I have a time crunch."

"About ten seconds after I hand your delivery person the document saying I have possession of whatever it is. I'm not saying my problem solving abilities are anywhere near that fast, but I do have a window at the moment I can dedicate to this issue. May I assume this item will arrive here sometime in the near future?"

"Possibly sooner than you think. Travis just went out the door. And thank you so much; I am aware this may not be an answer but at this point I barely know the questions to ask. Will you let me know what you think? I should mention I sent along the few written comments and copies of the e-mails we have received about this item; it isn't in some sort of flaming crises at the moment but we want to avoid that by all means possible."

"I'll let you know as soon as I find anything; okay?"

"Yes, okay, and by the way Ed told me the two girls in that ride on thing commercial are your daughters. That had to take some courage on your part to let them do that one trick, the sliding sideways thing as they bumped into each other."

"I have to admit Lynn, the boy's mother, and I were as stunned as everyone else when that took place. In his defense, the person who set that up had run that specific scenario with some other kids and knew exactly what would take place; what you see is the first time our kids actually did the trick; I'm not sure Lynn and I could have withstood a replay. Anyway, I'll take a look as soon as Travis gets here. Talk to you later." The conversation ended.

The appliance looked innocent enough when Travis carried it in along with a handful of paper. Alan filled out the form of receipt, handed it to Travis, and as Travis departed took his first look at the device. It was pretty simple, a bit ingenious in concept, and took only a few moments to decipher. Meant to hang on a wall, Alan found a way to suspend it, then read the forms and started his examination of the issue. There wasn't much on the forms, a few comments about a little sticking sense on a slide switch, especially when moving to the "off" position; that could be problematic and Alan quickly saw why the complaints had been filed. Pulling the hand held device off the base, he took note of all the fasteners first, then started the disassembly. The odds were no one else would have seen what he saw, one screw tip with just a tiny bit of plastic shred clinging to it. Slide the switch, look for a tiny mark or scratch, and there it was, just that fast. Calipers in hand he measured the thread length of the screw, then very carefully ground the tip off back into the first complete wrap of thread by using an abrasive wheel. Reassembled he exercised the slide switch a number of times, sometimes pressing down hard to deflect the plastic case a bit toward the screw point; smooth, every time. It had taken less than half an hour, for which he would charge one full hour as the minimum shop fee, reassembled everything, and called Syd.

"Good morning again Ms Long. So soon again we are talking I almost feel guilty about taking your money. Would you like to have Travis come back to pick this up for you? I'm all done here with the problem solving."

Syd Long was floored. "You're done, already, after this has gone on for weeks? What happened, what did you find?"

"Almost the usual, a little slip of the spec somewhere, failure to measure correctly, I suspect no ill will toward the product, but a mismatch between what is needed and what was used. I don't have the correct fastener to use but I did modify the original to serve the need. I'll write up my findings but thought you should know resolution has been achieved The culprit is a case screw that is just a tad too long, probably a standard length from what I can see and most likely the choice of fastener because it is off the shelf in boxes of a hundred. I ground the tip off the original screw but it remains fully functional in holding power, just doesn't drag any more. The original is a socket head, not commonly used in this country, so your Oslo people need to know that is the issue, just the one screw. I almost regret to say my one hour minimum shop fee will kick in but maybe that isn't bad compared to a recall notice."

Syd laughed. "You know how true that is. It isn't even necessarily the administrative cost of doing a recall but the cost of the lost confidence in the company, things like that. It can run into the millions. So, charge away Mr. Behr, charge away, and please understand you are now a permanent resident on my phone listing; no escaping. Thank you so much for giving me one less thing on my mind. Talk to you later?"

"Talk to you later." Again the conversation was ended but the thought process for Alan Behr continued for some minutes. He had just been assured of a permanent contact with Tallright via Ms Long; there was no good way to know for sure what the future would bring in the way of work for his shop, but statistics alone told him there would be work coming by the very nature of the process. That in turn made him think once again about the future. He had always been cautious about the family finances, using Maddie's life insurance settlement to set up college accounts for the girls. His own retirement account held over from the factory employment days was not large by any means but was growing at an acceptable rate. Alan Behr was doing well in most respects, but something seemed to be nagging at him just a bit. It took a bit of reflecting about the present moment before he realized the hitch in his plans was Lynn and her two boys. When he had first met them, even without knowing for sure, he believed them to be on shaky financial ground; he was painfully close to being exactly right. It was not his responsibility to provide them monetary backing, but he also realized the number of times he had included his neighbors in a purchase; the summer bible study camp was a fine example of how he had paved their way, not necessarily from some sense of obligation but from a sense he wanted to ease the burden on this woman, lighten her load a bit, and maybe in the process get to know her better if her worries were tamped down just a bit so she could interact on a more social level. Today he realized that had all changed and for the better, at least for them. It was true he didn't want to build a relationship with her where her dependence on him would somehow alter their relationship, yet he did want her to know he was there to support her. He remained unsure if he actually loved her or was just acting out some remnant of being lonely at times after Maddie was gone. Certainly Lynn had everything coming her way at the moment, good job she enjoyed and was good at, potential to grow with the Windmere group, a job with benefits unlike any she had previously seen, and two boys who would be reaping the benefits of an hour or so of work for at least the next year. There were other ads being proposed, interviews, all that, but Alan Behr still wanted her to know he was there for her. Maybe he needed to just tell her how he felt, but then again, what if that made her run for the door from a complete lack of reciprocity; then what would happen. His answer was out there somewhere, closer than he thought.

The beauty of the growing relationship between neighbors was that they could operate on the familiarity usually found in families. The four kids seemed at times to be running the show, although in reality they would check with their parent before making their proposal. This afternoon's proposal, fielded late afternoon, was to do a cookout for the evening meal rather than dirty dishes. Alan was at his bench while Lynn was coming home after an early afternoon meeting; a quick survey told the kids this could be done and they set about making things happen, running inventory on supplies needed, and getting the burgers out of the freezer to warm a bit. They were resourceful, recalling what they had seen their parent do and making sure all was ready by the appropriate time. Finally, with the meal brought to a successful end, the kids and some other neighborhood kids were engaged in some sort of non-tackle tag about the area. Alan and Lynn sat by the fire ring soaking in the warmth and the peace of the evening as they engaged in mostly idle conversation. Maybe it was a good time for Alan to bring up his thoughts on a bit of their relationship.

"Lynn, I was just thinking about how much things have changed for you since we first met not all that long ago. Here you are with a job the likes of which people salivate over, benefits all over the place, employer people might not have ever heard of but just can't be beat, all the good stuff. So, how does Lynn feel about all that success; excited I hope."

"I am excited, every bit of that, but what excites me most is having an employer that is welcoming, expecting the best for me and from me, and reasonable belief this will last for a long time. I would be a fool to not recognize that the intangibles are a least as important as the tangibles and probably more so. And then there is Jill, the Jill who comes by now and then not to say 'you made a mistake' or point out errors but to show me how things could have been done differently to the same end, the Jill who seems to revel in my own success. For the first time in a long while I feel I'm standing on solid ground. But Alan, I haven't forgotten who had a hand out to keep me from sinking until all this happened, kept me afloat and my spirit buoyed and even fed me and my boys countless times. I remember that vacation bible school sleight of hand where you paid for all four kids and when I tried to back out told me it would mess up your checkbook something awful; you were lying and I knew you were lying but somehow you made it all right and good. So, yes, I'm excited, I am."

"Good. I guess my point for the moment is I want you to know that even though you are on solid ground, if any potholes show up, I'm still here for you. I agree things have changed since that first meeting and I don't mean to downplay any of that success in any way; I just want you to know what I felt that first day about putting a hand out...that hand is still there, just in case. I still want to be your neighbor for sure." He stopped talking for just a moment but Lynn remained silent, sensing there was more on his mind; there was and after a brief pause he continued. "Lynn, I think I want to be more than your neighbor, but I don't know what you want and I don't want to make any mistake here. I'm not afraid of making a fool of myself but I don't want to scare you off in the process. I don't know..."

"I do know, I'm not scared, and you are no fool. Alan I want to be more than a good neighbor but my foundation in that area still has some scar tissue to get past; I will get past it, I will; I want that part of a good life and with you in it, Now, what are the odds if we make s'mores for the kids our lips will get stuck together again? I sort of look forward to that you know."

It was a good place to end the conversation and move on to other things.

Chapter Seventeen

Having a Blast

Mid-week, mid-afternoon, all present in both families, and it was time to go do a local radio show interview. As a part of a national campaign, the local interview would most likely not bump the sales figures one way or another, but they did feel some onus to support the local talk show host. Less than an hour later the show was behind them after much giggling and so on, as promised they went on to the dairy treat store for some burgers for dinner, then on home for the evening. Turning into their street, Alan was amazed at the collection of fire trucks, police cars, an ambulance, and assorted other official looking cars, all flashing lights like mad, with people everywhere. Kids looking over his shoulder the questions started, to be stopped when a policeman waved them to a stop.

"Sir, this road is closed until the emergency is over. Please turn around."

Alan needed to know; he could see his own house seemed to be intact but hers remained mostly out of sight: "I see all this but what is the emergency officer?"

"The house over there blew up; whole backside is gone. We're still trying to figure out what happened. Anyway, you need to clear the area, okay?"

"Actually, I believe the house you are talking about belongs to this lady sitting here with me, the house right beside mine. I think maybe we need to pull into my drive and see what's going on. Okay?"

The officer remained unmoved but curious: "You are...?"

"Alan Behr. Lady with me is Lynnette Albert; her house seems to be having the problem. I think we need to go see; okay?"

The officer did understand as owners they had a right to see what was taking place with their properties, and motioned Alan into his driveway. Cautioned to stay close to their parents, the four kids also climbed out, impressed with all the equipment and people on scene. Walking to where they could better see the scene they discovered the back wall of Lynn's house was missing and there was debris all over the back yard. Seeing the people who appeared to be the homeowners, fire inspector Burns made his way over to them.

"You folks the owners?" and seeing Lynn nod in the affirmative, continued. "I can explain what happened after I took a look at what was once the inside of the house. That specific area wasn't originally enclosed; doing so isn't the problem, but doing so improperly is the problem and caused this accident. An hour or so ago the gas company, along with us as fire protection specialists, got calls that there was a heavy natural gas odor in this area, calls from several homeowners. The gas company checked and found their metering station a couple of blocks over was running over pressure downstream; apparently the pressure reducing station failed somehow. Normally that wouldn't cause too big a problem as each home is fitted with a pressure reducing station as well as a safety valve. Those items are outside the home where some venting doesn't matter. In the case of this particular home, the original equipment was outside, but when the utility room was extended and closed in, the equipment ended up inside. That also is not a problem provided the safety valve is piped to the outside of the house; here that was not done and when the gas supply went over pressure the safety valve opened and vented into the closed space. When the water heater relit, the gas ignited and the outside wall took the brunt of the force. I have a structural engineer on the way to check out the remainder of the structure just to be safe; it looks fine but there's no way to know for sure until she takes a look. Sorry to be the bearer of bad tidings but I understand no one was home and no one was injured, so that's good news. Anything else I can tell you folks?"

Alan and Lynn looked at each other, a bit shaken by the news but equally grateful no one was injured. Alan had a question: "What are the odds we can at least get inside to retrieve some belongings for the night?"

"I can give you that answer as soon as the structural person is done, probably a half hour or so. I can make a call to find you a place to stay for the night if that's the problem."

Alan answered for both parents: "No, but we appreciate the offer. I live next door here and we can manage; may be a bit close; her boys stay with me from time to time anyway and my girls don't seem to mind too much. But, we will need night clothes, things like that, and eventually other items. So, if you would let us know the outcome it would be helpful."

"I can do that; I see her here now and need to go talk to her but I'll let you know what she says about getting in."

That was pretty much the end of that conversation. Alan suggested to Lynn she call Jill to let her know there might be a break in what Lynn had been doing for Windmere, and that Lynn should also call her insurance agent right away; that call would turn out to be rather negative. Lynn did call Jill, to be informed Jill was in town and would be there in two minutes or less. The agent was less positive, telling Lynn he was busy and that anyway he never paid claims in less than 30 days at best, regardless of what anyone else said. Both Jill and Alan heard Lynn comment on that statement, with her phone now on speaker; the agent sounded as though he didn't care what Lynn wanted, never asked her if she was okay or the condition of the property or anything else. He seemed, at best, to not care, period. Disconnected, Lynn sighed in acceptance of her apparent fate, prepared to face what needed to be done regardless, and then felt a warm hand take hers as strength poured into her.

The structural person finished her survey, telling others the building was safe to enter for purposes of evacuation but that it would not be considered to be repairable from a cost standpoint. The blast had pushed the roof upward, freeing it from the walls below, which were a bit bowed because they lost their top restraint for a few seconds. With that news, Alan turned to face Lynn directly.

"We need to get enough stuff moved into my house to make it through the night, maybe a day or so, until we can get it all relocated. I can get us some help tomorrow to move the excess furniture into my garage or the back garage for temporary storage. It may be a bit crowded but the dressers and such can go in their respective bedrooms for now until we get things better figured out. I plan to relocate myself to my shop or the living room for sleeping, one or the other, whatever appeals to me. So, there's my plan; we need to get started right away. Okay, neighbor Lynn?"

She had been unprepared to hear his plan, thinking to herself she needed to do something, maybe seek shelter in her parent's home, but the rejection by the insurance agent still had her seething. "Alan, this is my problem, it is; you don't have to do that."

"Neighbor Lynn, remember what I said about a helping hand? It's out; please do not bite the fingers off. Let's get a move on, okay?"

It was a clear plan and Lynn decided she needed to go along, at least for the moment. Evicting him from his own bedroom would not be her choice, but it was apparently his and the move from one house to another started to get ready for the first night together. It would turn out to be a long day, ended up with that promised kiss a few moments after 'smores ingestion and stuck lips. In the meantime, two people remained a bit displeased with how Lynn was being treated by the agent.

Jillian Andrews, once she was assured Lynn was safe for the night, speed dialed her own boss, Laura Williams at Windmere, Inc. She relayed the situation with the insurance agent to Laura, telling her that Lynn was an asset of growing value for the company and that if Laura knew of any way to maybe help resolve the insurance crises and get it out of Lynn's mind, that would be a good thing to do. In the process of the two women talking, Jill had managed to send an electronic copy of the policy front page to Laura. Laura didn't have an immediate response but did know if she hurried making her next call maybe she could still do some good this afternoon. Hit the speed dial, listen as the system threaded its way to Chicago and the offices of Dewey, Cheatham & Howe. LLC, Attorneys at Law, ID-ed herself as the caller when the administrative assistant answered, and asked for J. Lawrence Dewey, Principle. Mr. Dewey was on the line in seconds.

"Good afternoon, Ms Williams. To what privation do I ascribe this honor today?" J. Lawrence Dewey enjoyed a good conversation,, and particularly enjoyed a conversation with this important client. Laura relayed what she had learned, in the process forwarding the policy cover sheet for his review. J. Lawrence Dewey scanned the sheet, told Laura he would indeed look into things in the morning, and would do what he could as a personal favor to Windmere, Inc.

In the meantime, Alan was equally concerned with the lack of insurance agent attention to the woman beside him. Thinking about what he might be able to do for her, there appeared to be few options to force the agent to take action. Then Alan remembered an access he had seldom used in the past to meet his own personal needs, hitting speed dial for Ari Schoenroth. He caught the lawyer wrapping up his office for the afternoon, but Ari told Alan to give him all the facts and he would at least mull it over to see what could possibly be done. It was first thing the next morning when Ari placed a call to his contact point at DC&H: Mr. Watkins. Mr. Watkins listened with interest to the story, agreed it was not a pleasant situation, said he was unsure if DC&H could help or not but would relay Ari's concern up the chain. Half an hour or so later a call was made to J. Lawrence Dewey about the situation; the second call reaffirmed the situation and J. Lawrence Dewey took action.

"Becky, get me Sal Victorio at United Frailty on the line please; thanks Becky." Less than a minute later the voice of Sal Victorio came forth.

"Larry Dewey, since when do you make calls from the golf course and don't bother to tell me you're in your office this hour of the morning. I know better. So, this business or pleasure; what did we do wrong this time?"

Lawrence Dewey was not amused but restrained himself. "Sal, this is business, serious business. One call and I think maybe one person is upset, out of sorts for some reason, a confirming call on the same subject and I start to worry. Becky is sending you a copy of the cover letter for the policy in question. This agent of yours totally blew off a policy holder, a private dwelling homeowner holder to be sure but a policy holder none the less. Given that, you might want to ask what else this clown has done to your reputation. Anyway, he told this single parent woman he wouldn't pay any claim in less than thirty days; worse still is that there were others standing nearby who heard his blow off comments and surly tone like she was interrupting his day at the beach. Her goddamned house actually blew up making it unfit for human habitation and he blows the whole thing off like it's nothing. Sal, I can't tell you how to run your business but I will tell you if anyone at DC&H treated a client that way they would be gone so fast they'd get whiplash. I will refrain from mentioned how many of your major policy holders might be clients of DC&H but it is something for you to think about, okay Sal?"

Sal was stunned at hearing the words coming from a business and personal friend. It was quite clear J. Lawrence Dewey was steamed and it was over a single home owner. Sal also realized perception is everything and if DC&H perceived United Frailty as less than honest and supportive of their clients, in particular a defenseless single parent client, that could be costly, very costly. What could he say?

"Larry, I had no idea. You and I both know we have thousands and thousands of policyholders, large and small, private and commercial, all that, but I agree a single bad agent is like that single bad apple in the barrel. It sounds like this one person got everyone's attention; not that it would ever excuse his behavior, but what happened anyway?"

"Like I said her house blew up. I understand there was an issue with the natural gas system in her area and because her home had been improperly modified the gas built up inside and blew. You might have some recourse via the city inspectors for letting that happen but you know no one gives a damn if insurance companies suffer or not. Sal, people deal with what they see, not necessarily with the reality of a situation. If they see United Frailty being the bad guy, that is all they will remember. You and I both know one 'aw crap' wipes out a hundred 'atta boy's' every time. I do understand the action of one agent would be difficult for you to monitor but if the right tone is set at the top, then that agent has clear guidance and there is no excuse. I'm not sore at you Sal but I do believe this is a teachable moment for some people. Okay?"

"Yeah, okay Larry. I understood the deal up front, but you sure do get excited. I'll find this guy and take care of things, make us look like good guys again in the process and thanks for letting me know. Deals like this have closed some companies for not paying attention to consumers needs; I won't let that happen. So, we playing a round this weekend on the links?"

That was the end of the important part of the conversation, but the ripple started downhill within United Frailty.

The local agent was sitting in his office talking to the city inspector and a city code enforcer, having a laugh over what he had done to a single parent policy holder the previous afternoon. The poor woman's house exploded and clearly she would be due the maximum policy value, but he had every intention to making her wait until the very last minute even if there was no such policy. The intercom on his desk spoke forth:

"You have a call on line 2."

"Tell whoever it is I'm busy and will get back to them later."

"I don't think so. The caller said he wanted to talk to you right now and if that didn't happen then I was to tell you that you have been terminated, period. Your option."

The three in the room gasped at the announcement as the agent realized her voice was dead serious in the message delivery. He reached for the phone, identified himself, and was told to listen, then follow directions. The speaker identified himself as the agent's district supervisor and commenced speaking.

"I have been totally and thoroughly reamed by higher ups in corporate; they are very irate to say the least over what you have done. Here is what is to happen and in this sequence. You will find Ms Lynnette Albert and apologize directly to her in person for what you have done. You will ensure she under-stands you are at her beck and call for any and all insurance coverage she may need now or in the future. You will present her with a check for the full value of the home-owners policy plus a ten percent premium for what you have done. You will apologize again, ask if there are any questions she might have, respond accordingly if necessary, assure her all will be taken care of, and will inform her that her auto policy premium is waived for the next twelve months as of the next due date. Do you understand what you are to do? I need to add this will all be done today or you are terminated with loss of everything."

In spite of having two other persons in the room with him, the wayward agent was truly scared to death at the flat somber tone of the speaker; this was not a joke. "Yes, sir; I understand and will call you back as soon as I have everything done. I'm sorry this happened, really sorry."

"You need to be sorry. Even the CEO is hot over this. Keep me informed or clean out your office; your option." The connection was terminated.

It took a minute or two for the agent to fully realize what had just taken place. The noose was around his neck and he was standing on the trap door. There was no way to know the whistle blower or blowers in the situation but that didn't really matter. What mattered was that corporate was hot and he was in the kiln. Turning to his two associates he summed up the situation.

"Guys, I don't know who this woman knows but clearly she is in the care of someone with ungodly power. I know what I have to do, but suggest each of you take stock of your own position in this matter and make sure you haven't done anything and won't do anything to irritate her in the slightest way. Maybe we can meet here again tomorrow AM to sort of review things and make sure our liability has been reduced."

The others agreed and all left to pursue their own duties with a dark storm cloud hanging over their heads. The insurance agent prayed he could find Lynn before time expired; he got lucky, locating her in the house next door to her own house. Asked to enter the room, he saw that neighbor man standing there with her, asked her if the man was to stay and was informed the man was her rock and would stay, period. The prescribed scenario was carried out as he had been told, including handing her the check. Lynn looked at the amount and knew there was a significant difference from the face value of the policy she was holding in her hand.

"I don't understand. This check is for more than the maximum face value of the policy by a substantial amount. What's going on here? Is this a joke of some sort and the whole check is bogus from the get go? Truly I have had enough from your company and you." Lynn was not a happy camper although she had no idea what had been put in place in her behalf; for present company any negative change in her acceptance was seen as a death sentence. He needed to explain as panic set in over her upset condition. He had no way to know the id of the whistle-blower and damned sure didn't want it to be her.

"No, please, no. I can explain the difference. United Frailty is providing a ten percent premium because we recognize you have not been treated in the best manner possible. You are the policy holder, and without policy holders United Frailty is just another empty building. We have done wrong and want to make amends. I was directed to add the ten percent to atone for our poor handling of this situation. Please accept it as a token of our apology, please."

It seemed sincere enough in all respects and within minutes the agent was gone while Alan and Lynnette faced each other wondering who had pulled what strings. The agent was clearly scared out of his wits, apologized more times than they could count, and the money felt good in her hand. The two would spend a few minutes talking about the situation, to be interrupted by the city building inspector.

"I know this visit may be a little premature but we all know that house needs to be demolished in view of the high cost to remediate major damages. I'll do the abatement testing today although I don't expect to find any issues. This is the form you need to hire a contractor, along with a list of city approved contractors; I've filled most of it out already and approved it just to save you time. Please give me a call before the demo starts so I can get here and make sure all is well. The code enforcement people have waived all issues as they know you are not the owner who made the inappropriate changes. When you decide what to put back in place, please call us at your convenience for the plan review process; we can get that wrapped up rather quickly with a little notice; okay?"

It was all okay with the two as the inspector departed; Alan had an observation. "I have been around those guys a number of times in my life. I'm not saying they don't do their jobs, but they don't hurry with anything, nothing at all. Lynn, the guy was scared to death. Who did you tell about the agent blowing things off?"

"You and Jill were standing there listening, no one else, but I know you're right about the situation. Who do you think pulled the trigger and ratted him out?"

Alan gave thought to the subject for a moment or two. "My guess is this: I called Ari Schoenroth and asked him if he knew any way to help, and I'm betting Jill called Laura Williams; somehow those two calls merged along the way and someone really up there took a look. Like everyone else, these people have someone they report to, who reports to someone else higher up. I'm betting someone higher up is unhappy. Don't know for sure but it looks that way to me; maybe someday we'll find out. In the meantime, feel free to bask in the attention."

Really for the first time in her life, Lynnette basked.

Chapter Eighteen

Creative Kids

The tap on the door was barely audible, but enough to get his attention. Bruce Albert was in his unkempt one bedroom subsidized low income apartment thinking about the upcoming weekend and if he needed to run and buy more beer to be prepared. There was nothing of which he was aware that caused him concern...except the beer supply if his buddies came over. He was aware his married friend's wives specifically did not like him; his unmarried friend's girlfriends specifically did not like him; in fact, other than his drinking buddies the only person who really liked him was the beer salesman at the package store. His very low rent enabled him keep himself in drink; it was true there was work he could do, and if the money got really tight, he would hire on for very light physical labor, maybe sweeping a warehouse or dock, something like that. It was barely a living but he didn't really care much one way or another; he was well aware this situation was of his own making the day he walked out on his wife and family; the beating he took from the pregnant girl friend's father had healed for the most part and he had acquired no additional financial burden as her parents kept him at arm's length in every regard. Still, there was that tap on the door; he managed to roust himself out of his chair and go pull it open, only to be unprepared for what he saw, or more correctly who he saw: the sister of Lynnette Albert.

Jennette spoke first, realizing the stunned look on his face. "Bruce, you gonna ask me in or what? We need to talk about something really important, unless you prefer living like this day to day."

Recovering from his momentary speechless condition, he responded. "Sure, come on in. I haven't had time to clean the place yet this morning; you know how busy some people get at times these days. Didn't think I'd ever see you again after the divorce."

She knew full well he was lying, that the place hadn't been cleaned in months, if ever, but that was not her reason for the visit. "Yeah, right, the divorce. You are aware those are your sons in that commercial running all over hell and gone these days, right? Some people are even forming clubs around those four kids and their personas. Do you have any idea how much money they make on residuals alone; tons and tons of money. So, are you still paying child support, all that, got an iron in the fire?"

Bruce flashed back to that moment when being released from child support payments seemed so important and such a good idea to him. "Um...no, not really. She went before the judge with some lawyer and said they would trade my complete release for waiver of child support and maintenance. The boys have my name but that's all, no visitation, none of that stuff. Why?"

Jenn knew: "You know what a dummy you are? When did she go to the judge? Was it before or after the commercials started to air? I ask because I suspect she found out how much money the boys are making once it hit the big time and wanted to make sure you couldn't cash in on it. I don't know for sure but I'll bet the money is rolling in and she's seeing a lot of it. We need to find a way to get you reconnected so you can cash in. That's why I came here today, to find out. I want some of it as well but don't know right now what I can do to leverage my way in; something will come up, I'm sure of that

"I don't know; haven't thought about that. I do see those ads a lot on the TV, even saw the local interview show. Those kids are riding high, that's for sure. Then the local news said there was an explosion of some sort couple of days ago that damaged one of their houses; I think they live next door to each other and all are in one house now. That's about all I know about it."

"I don't even know where they live now since she moved from your old place. Can we do a drive-by and take a look?:

They did a drive-by, using her car because his was out of gas...as usual. The proximity of the two houses gave a clue and with the knowledge all were living in the Behr house now, Jenn began to have some ideas. The two returned to his place to continue the discussion, as Jenn led off.

"We need to think this through, figure out a way to get the pubic on our side or at least not on the other side. I think having kids involved gives us an advantage. The ads are selling wholesomeness and all that sort of thing; if we can find a way to leverage that, we're in. I was thinking that avoiding a good scandal would be high on their list; that for sure would drop sales through the basement. Suppose, just suppose, we take the four kids into protective custody claiming we are somehow protecting them from parental abuse. On top of that, if my sister and this guy are sleeping together in a house full of kids, I know that would not go over well in the public eye; most of the time people wouldn't even think about it but with kids involved...you can see the difference, how that might be seen, especially by kid program sponsors. So what do you think?"

Bruce was unsure; it sounded good and he liked the idea of having a lot of money, but what would they have to do to make this all work in their favor? "Okay, I like the idea but Jenn I don't see any way in hell anyone would cooperate with us. Besides, what do you get out of all this?"

"Easy. Once we get that wedge driven in you are restored with fatherly rights and I get myself appointed as guardian, let the good times roll. All we really have to do is grab the kids and hold on to them for a day, probably not even that long, so we can leverage the parents. I don't know anything about the girls dad, but I do know my sister; she'll cave in a heartbeat; if that happens he'll be right behind her, I'm sure of it."

"Jesus, Jenn; that's kidnapping; we could go up river for twenty years or more for that."

"No, not at all. We grab the kids and sequester them somewhere safe, then call the cops and tell them we have done an intervention for the kids personal safety, protective custody sort of thing for their own good. I think citing that one scene where they are sliding into each other on those rider things should be proof enough. In the following inquisition, I will bring up the parents setting a bad example in their own behavior at bedtime; I just know the public will go nuts over that sort of thing in front of little kids, even if the public itself isn't exactly as pure as the driven snow. This will work. We need to rent two cars to confuse things and avoid being tailed, then find a somewhat furnished rental house in a quiet neighborhood to hold the kids for a day or so. Now what do you think?"

He could see some light in the plan, some distinct possibility of success on his own behalf ; whether Jenn made any gain or not was not his concern as far as he cared.

During the next few days they scouted out rental houses, finding a furnished one in an older quiet neighborhood, with a connected garage they could drive straight into without exposing themselves in the driveway to unload. The cars were next, a passenger mini-van and a non-descript sedan. With some snacks and such loaded into the house, their plan was put into action; it was almost too easy, telling the four kids as they walked home from school that their parents had been badly hurt in an accident, every cliché in the book kids are warned about, but with a valid parent in the form of Bruce Albert present plus Aunt Jenn it made the scene plausible and believable; if the boys believed there was no reason the girls should disbelieve in spite of their years of training about such things. Once inside the van, the kid locks snapped down before the little ones could ask about the paper over the van windows; it took all of about ten seconds for the kids to realize something wasn't right. Anna asked first.

"How come the windows are covered over? We never cover the windows in our van, and besides, we're supposed to be in car seats, not just sitting here like this."

Jenn realized these were smart kids and they were most likely onto the scheme of things already. "It's an emergency and you don't need car seats. We covered the windows so it doesn't get too hot in the sunlight; okay?"

Brad was next in line. "How come we're going this way? The hospital is the other way; where are we going? What happened in the accident? Mr. Behr is a really great driver; he would never be in an accident."

Jenn continued but felt the hole getting deeper under her feet. "The accident is this direction and the EMT's are administering first aid on scene. It wasn't Mr. Behr's fault; he just got hit; sometimes things happen."

Ben was next up. "Which car did they have and how come mom didn't go on the site visit she was scheduled for today? She always tells us if she might be late for dinner so we can plan."

Jenn continued to bail. "Not sure what they were driving; besides, maybe she got busy and just forgot to tell you her plans. Okay?"

It was not okay with Ally. "If you were at the scene how come you don't know what they were driving, and besides if you weren't there how do you know where to go. I don't like this without car seats, not at all."

Jenn threw it in. "Okay. Listen up you four. We are not going to any accident scene; there is no accident. We are going to a house where the four of you will stay for a while; us big people need to talk to your parents and get some things straight. We are protecting you from harm by keeping you away from your parents and some other bad people until we get this worked out. You could have been hurt doing that sliding thing trick; we don't want that to happen so we have staged this intervention and are taking you all into protective custody. So, sit back and shut up; once we get to the house you will not be permitted to leave unless we say so. There is food at the house, television, and enough furnishings to get by. I want all your cell phones and right now. This should last only a day but might go longer if your parents don't play ball with us. Give me the phones."

Phones were reluctantly handed over as the van rolled into the dark garage. The kids realized they were prisoners. The girls had picked up on the fact the male was the boy's father and the woman was their aunt; she even looked a bit like Lynn but hardly seemed as nice a personality. Settled for the moment Jenn started on the next step by calling her sister; enough time had gone by the kids would normally have entered the Behr house by this time of day. The call was quickly answered.

"Hi, this is Lynn." The caller ID provided no clue. It had not dawned on Lynn yet the kids were running a little late getting home from school. On the other hand, once in a while they stopped off at the play park for some fun with their friends before finishing the trek home; they did know not to stay too long or to call home and let their parents know. Today neither thing had happened and Lynn was unprepared for the voice she heard next.

"Hi, sis. This is Jenn. Are you missing some kids by any chance?" Lynn knew something was terribly wrong at that point, motioned to Alan, and hit speaker on her phone. This could not be a good situation.

"Not really; they just aren't home from school yet, that's all. Nothing unusual. What do you want. Jenn? You always seem to want something but you know that divorce cost me, really cost me a lot."

"This will cost you even more. Bruce and I have your kids in protective custody until we can get all the details worked out. Now, don't go calling the cops or anything like that or I'll have to break your little public bubble. The kids are safe for now, well protected. We need to meet. By the way, we have those two girls as well so I guess we want to talk to that guy. You have tonight to think about this; we want to meet in that little city park nine in the morning to talk about this. Okay?"

Lynn felt the furor rising in her body but kept her cool. "What are you talking about? There isn't anything for us to talk about other than what crime you are about to be charged with, including kidnapping for starters."

"Oh but there is a lot to talk about. I've seen those commercials and all the hype being built around the kids. All I have to do is call the news media and tell them I have some dirt on all that perception of a wonderful bunch of kids. First of all. I'd go for child abuse; you have to know that trick of sliding the quad runners was hazardous at the least; the kids could have been hurt or killed so we have to ask if their parents approved hazarding their own children just to make money. Then, I know you all live in one house now; I don't think the public gives a damn about what goes on in private most of the time, but one word that you and your boyfriend are sleeping together in the house and setting a bad example for the kids and it's all over. The public loves to see the mighty fall. You starting to get the picture here? You play ball, let Bruce back in as a parent and me as a guardian and all will be well, the kids come home unharmed and we all live happily ever after. I'm sure you're getting enough money to keep everyone happy. You getting the big picture here, Lynn? And remember, no cops or I can't guarantee the kids safety."

Lynn was still furious, but quite sane. "Jenn, Alan and I don't get any of that money, none of it. It all goes into a college fund. You can ask their agent; he knows the situation, so no matter what we might want to do, that deal is made ad infinitum. Now, we want our kids back, right now, understand me, and if anything happens to any one of them, even the slightest scratch and I will be on you like a mama grizzly. Got it, sister?"

Jenn had not expected anywhere near that much pushback from her formerly mild and passive sister. This guy must be having some effect on Lynn. But, it was too late now; the kids were under lock and key and Jenn realized maybe, just maybe she had overplayed her hand. For the moment she needed to retreat to shelter. "Okay, okay. Here's what's gonna happen: we have the kids and we'll keep them overnight in a safe enough place. The four of us meet tomorrow at the park, nine AM, to talk about this. No cops or you'll never find out where the kids are being held. Tomorrow, park, nine. "The line went dead.

For the next few hours Bruce and Jenn were forced to listen to a continuous stream of complaint from four very verbal kids, even the usually quiet Anna. The pizza they brought in wasn't from Mama Leoni's and barely fit for human consumption, the soft drinks were all wrong, there were ice cream treats but not in their favorite flavor, they had no pajamas for sleeping, no tooth brushes and they had been raised to brush after every meal, no electronic games to play, so on and so on. The two adults finally ordered the kids to bed just to get some quiet for a few minutes to do some planning. They would go to the park by 9 AM, leaving the kids in the locked down house; Jenn was starting to rethink her ideas but they were into it already and the difference between protective custody and kidnapping was starting to fade just a bit. Still they had the kids as a major bargaining chip and they were the only persons who knew that location. Their investment thus far was safe. The thing that wasn't safe was Jenn Houser; as the two adults contemplated with unbridled elation the forthcoming riches and consumed a significant portion of the ample supply of beer in the house, their physical interaction at the time seemed an appropriate extension of the festivities. As partners in crime it couldn't get much more personal than what they did without really thinking things through. She would discover the results of her neglected oversight in a few weeks; what should have taken place on a routine basis...didn't, to be confirmed in the next month. Worst still was that by the time the diagnosis of weight gain by pregnancy was confirmed, she would be all alone in the process; Bruce Albert would be of no help in any respect beyond the initial glandular contribution, not ever, never.

Sent to their room for the night, the four kids stalled with bathroom visits, anything they could think of but finally capitulated to the late hour. Although it harkened back to that day camping when they found themselves all in a row, somehow it seemed like a better idea for this night and the four piled together in the double bed, off to sleep in a few minutes, warm and comfortable through the night. None of them snored, a trait to be developed later in life.

In the Behr household the decision was made to call for reinforcements. With Lynn in agreement and based on a long term familiarity, Alan called Officer Jack Bailey, a friend since high school days. Jack was a patrol officer most of the time but it was because he liked being a patrol officer out in the public seeing different things every day. Finding Jack in the station house Alan opened the conversation.

"Jack, this is not a friendly call; it's a call for help but I really want to make sure this doesn't get out of control and endanger anyone, no SWAT team, none of that stuff. Just hear me out please, then we can talk about the situation, okay?"

It was okay with Officer Jack and over the next few minutes Alan related the events taking place, assuring Jack he did believe the kids were safe for the moment, probably unhappy but safe regardless; that was most important. What to do next needed clarification; Office Jack continued the discussion.

"Alan, I agree heroics are way not called for here, none of the TV glamour shot stuff. We need to remain mostly invisible until we can find the kids; that has to come first. I can start that search by hitting the car rentals for vans in town; I'm guessing they would at least be smart enough to not use their own wheels in this caper. So, that's a starting point. I'm going to talk to the detectives now, probably put a nondescript person in the park for observation and at least one by the parking lot to see where the van comes from and what it is for tracking purpose. We may even be able to get a tracking bug on it but those things don't really work as well as the movies show; they can be of some help sometimes and we need to use all means at our disposal. While we've been talking I ran the names through the photo library, so now we know what both of them look like. Neither has any long or felony type record; the woman has shoplifted a time or two and tried unsuccessfully to kite a check; the guy has some misdemeanors, mostly involving hijacking beer from the liquor store, nothing worse. I think maybe their records are about to get lengthened a bit in the near future. I should mention that wearing a wire is a possibility; they don't work as well as you see on the telly but we can give it a shot if you want; thing is, if they discover the wire then they have to assume someone is listening after they warned you about calling us in. I don't think a wire is a good idea, at least not at this level. We will make every effort to follow them once the meeting is over. And one more thing: stay calm. I know you want to beat these persons to death, but a long term conviction is a much worst thing, especially in some prisons. Anything else I can tell you? And by the way, thanks for calling; we will do everything we can to get this set straight."

"Thanks, Jack. You know you have my confidence; I just don't want anyone to get hurt in this situation, I guess even the bad guys. It's about the money, but most things are when the root cause of the discontent is discovered. Keep me posted, okay?"

Jack would keep him posted regularly. They already had discovered the car rental agreements including license numbers and had pictures of the two culprits. The person who would be sent to the park to pose as a quiet old pensioner sitting there reading was in his early 30's, loved entering martial arts competitions, and had a shelf full of trophies.

Meanwhile, back at the rental house, morning had arrived. Four heads poked up enough to realize they were all still in the same bed and maybe that wasn't so bad after all. Still dressed from the day before they made their way as a group to the kitchen and started up where they had left off the previous night. They had no toothbrushes and their teeth would rot out, they used whole milk at home because it had more nutrients, they didn't eat sweetened cereal as they preferred to add to it their own chosen amount of honey from a local source, there was bacon but was it Kosher bacon (the kids did understand the joke in that question; the adults didn't catch on), the toast was the wrong color and why didn't they have sour dough bread, on and on. Bruce and Jenn's nerves were starting to fray just a bit, not a good thing for people who needed to gut it out for their plan to work and the money to come rolling in.

Left alone when the adults went to the park meeting, the kids retraced every inch of the house looking for some way to escape. The adults had done a good job securing the place by adding independent dead bolts on the doors that could be opened only by key from either side, no thumb turns. The window sashes were screwed down tight, leaving only the possibility of smashing a window pane out and then trying to crawl through a glass shard surrounded tiny hole. Nothing, no way, and they retreated to the kitchen to consider the future.

Brad was idly looking through a stack of old newspapers apparently left there by previous renters when he was suddenly sporting a huge grin. Ally had to know as the others looked on.

"Brad, what's there to smile about? We're locked in here while our parents have to deal with these crooks. I heard them talking about how much money they'll have once they get in charge of us. I know we don't see any of it, not much anyway; Mr. Kaplan takes care of things like that for us. So, anyway, why the smile?"

The grin widened even more as Brad contemplated what he was about to propose. "I was just looking at this old newspaper someone left here; it has a picture of our house in the before and after. That's when I got the idea. We have everything we need; I even looked in the utility room where the water heater and furnace are located. All we have to do is break off one of the gas lines, close the door, and find protection. No idea how long it might take for the blast to take place but at this point what else do we have to go for? Nothing, that's all, nothing. You in?" It was a general question that drew three positive responses. Ben added to the scene.

"Suppose we go to the other bedroom and steal the mattress, then pile it up on top of our mattress in the far corner; nothing could get through that barrier." It was a good suggestion quickly carried out, with all the pillows piled up to sit on during the wait. Brad the instigator was drafted to break the gas feeder lines. It was a bit more difficult than he had imagined, getting the lines to part with the fittings, but he managed and with two lines broken off headed for the door, latching it tightly behind him. Into the back bedroom and behind the mattress stack he waited with the others. It took a few minutes but as they were planning their escape from the house they felt as much as heard the heavy WHUMP elsewhere as the house shook. Venturing out of the bedroom they found the place with clouds of dust in the air, a disturbed collection of years set free by the blast. Opening the fractured but mostly intact utility room door they discovered a lot of sunlight beaming in through where the outer wall had previously existed; through the bit of rubble and out through the hole in the wall, the four didn't know which way to go but they did know away from the house was preferably to any other direction.

The concussion from the blast was felt by the neighbors who were at home that hour of the day, rattling window sashes and so on. Fingers sped through 911 from a half dozen or more phones and a police cruiser in the area had the word in virtually seconds. A fire truck was dispatched to the address, just in case; in reality the blast had consumed all the Oxygen in the room in a half second or so and no subsequent fire occurred. All patrol officers had been briefed before heading out that morning although there was little that could really be added other than that it was an ongoing investigation; to an officer they knew who the four kids were although to some it came as a surprise the kids lived here in their town, not some mega city somewhere. Sent to patrol her usual area, Officer LaVonne Adams rolled slowly through the older but well kept section of the city. Before her eyes appeared four kids, all about the same size, on the run and coming out from behind the house address given as the location of the blast. Calling it in first, she dismounted and approached the kids.

"Hi, kids. What's going on with the house back there? Something bad?"

Brad spoke up, proud of his part in the adventure. "We blew it up so we could escape. These bad people locked us in yesterday so they could do something with our parents. I don't know about that but I know our parents never lock us in, any of us, no matter what we do. Do you want to take a look at what we did?"

Yes, Office Adams did want to see, and as the fire truck rolled to a stop they went around the back of the house to find a gaping hole in the wall. There was still the sound of gas escaping but it was out in the open air now and simply blew away. The attending fireman turned off the main valve and the hissing sound quieted out to nothing. Office Adams was in awe, but remembered what Brad had said and turned toward the group for a moment.

"I don't even know your names. Can you tell me please?"

The response was as rehearsed as it had ever been on the DVD's: "I'm Ally." "I'm Brad" "I'm Ben" "I'm Anna." "We're the Construction Kids."

Unable to resist the grin on her face the kids response had elicited, Officer Adams keyed her mike and raised the central station. "I have them, the four kids, Ally, Brad, Ben and Anna, although after what they did I'm not sure who has who. Near as I can tell, their captors had everything locked down, no way out, so the kids made their own way out: they blew up part of the house...no, really...they blew up part of the house, tore a whole section of wall off; it's laying out on the ground. Brad told me he knew how to do that because their own home blew up a couple of weeks ago due to a gas main problem; he listened to what the fire inspector had to say and apparently remembered it well. I'll bring them on in with me. Where are the parents, the real ones?" That question was being answered elsewhere in town.

The little city park seldom saw much activity and some citizens thought maybe it had outlived being a useful tool as a hitching post; the space, while not large, could be used to develop maybe small specialty shops, something like that for bringing in revenue. Had they read the century old charter for the park they would have learned if they took it out of serving as a park, ownership reverted back to the original owners, persons whose family tree still existed in the area. This morning it did see a bit of traffic, with one old man sitting alone on a bench apparently reading a book when four more persons arrived from the parking lot and clustered around one of the tables. Two more persons were at the park but unseen: one watching the parking lot arrivals and recording them on a video camera, while the other was at the edge of the park concealed inside a huge Lilac clump, long lens held back enough so no sunlight glinted off it. The four looked over at the old man but decided he was no threat, possibly not even awake...or alive. The discussion started with Alan breaking the silence.

"I told you people yesterday we don't see the money stream, none of it. Here's a copy of the cover page; it very clearly spells out the process, how it is sequestered and so on. Even Sol can't get the money out, but the kids can, some anyway. Like most trusts, they have to go to the administrator for disbursements. So, if you're having thoughts of getting rich, guess again people. Now that you understand the finances there is nothing we could, would, or should do to aid or abet you in any way. Where are the kids; I want to know right now and you better hope to god not one of them has so much as the sniffles from being without a coat through all this."

Jennette believed she knew the kids location (they were no longer in the house at that exact moment). "You and I, we know things can change hour to hour, so why don't you just tell me you two will agree to our terms of parenthood and guardianship and all will be well. You and this woman, my sister, can get that financial thing changed, I know you can. Not a document written that can't be changed, not one; we need some of that revenue to support our preferred lifestyle; let's get on with it."

Alan looked at Lynn for just a moment as he contemplated his reply; he was stalling for time, hoping in the interim Officer Jack Bailey and friends could find the kids and liberate them. "So, if we did agree to any of this ridiculous scenario, what do we get in return? Anything? I suspect your offerings are going to be pretty slim."

Jenn was puzzled just a bit. He didn't seem to be taking this whole thing as seriously as he should, even being a bit flippant in the negotiations; what did he know that she didn't know and would it bite her for not knowing? At that specific minute none of those present knew the kids were out in the sunshine and looking forward to their ride in a patrol car with Officer Adams. They also didn't know something else lurked that had the giant teeth with which to bite Jenn Houser, something ferocious that would make Bruce Albert look behind himself every once in a while for months to come. The internet was relentless against anyone who might hurt the Construction Kids, as they would discover soon enough when the threats against them came pouring in. She had Alan's question before her to answer.

"When we get what we want, we will say nothing about the child abuse or your shack job with Lynn and the bad example that sets. If you don't play ball, we go to the media and unload the whole thing to some tattler host; they love dirt and taking people down. True or not doesn't matter; that is sure to kill sales and your deal; everyone loses. I agree most people wouldn't care one damn way or another, but these kids have a ton of public clout these days for some reason and anything not in their good favor is bound to have negative consequences. Okay? Ready to play ball, get this over with, and get the kids back?" Jenn did know one thing for sure: she had to be first out of the gate to make all this threat work; her side had to be media established firmly before anything to the contrary could push back against it, and at the moment she was feeling pushback, undefined pushback she couldn't discover enough to squelch.

The scanners at the TV station always listened to the police channel for something to do, maybe a fire or assault, anything they could use to their own advantage. If they ever had something the network actually liked and aired, well, it would never be better than that for the home town station. This morning things seemed quiet, almost too quiet, and when traffic suddenly picked up they were listening. They had the feeling some sort of sting was going on but couldn't better define it, and then there was a whole string of chatter about a house blowing up just like a few weeks ago. The explosion was newsworthy enough and a van and crew sped to the scene to capture some video. What they saw as they arrived on scene within a very few minutes was a police officer surrounded by four kids, kids that looked alike. The producer felt a knot in his gut as he realized these were the Construction Kids, he had an exclusive, and was out of the van before it stopped rolling, microphone in hand and videographer shooting over his shoulder. Take a breath, let it out slowly, approach as a friend, not as someone who was seeing the scoop of a lifetime.

"Hi kids. Are you the Construction Kids we see all the time? What's going on here and what's with the fire truck?"

Officer Adams intervened just as he got started. "I'm sorry sir but this is an ongoing criminal investigation; the less these witnesses say at this point the better. I can confirm in their behalf that they are often seen as the Construction Kids. I can confirm there has been an explosion at this domicile but I really cannot address that further with an investigation open at this time. Thank you; we have to leave now."

It was the end of the brief interview but it was live footage of a nationally known entity, or maybe entities, depending on how one looked at it, one group or four kids. The crew did take time to walk around back and get shots of the missing wall. A lot of the neighbors were now out of their houses wondering what had happened, so the news team ran some tape on them; during one of those brief segments the producer heard something he had not heard elsewhere and would not hear again for some time; one of the boys had reportedly said they blew up the house so they could escape being kidnapped. There was more to the story, a lot more, and they headed for the police station. It would take the hours to dig up the whole truth but they kept digging, finally arriving back with the kids parents and asking for an interview; the interview was granted but only with the parents present in the group. Once again in Alan's workshop, they sat in sort of a row: parent girl girl boy boy parent. The producers questioning was direct.

"I heard one of you told someone you blew up the house yourselves to escape. Is that true, and what were you trying to escape?"

Brad the bomber responded. "We were being locked up because our parents had something these other people wanted. I remembered how the fire marshal described what happened with the gas when our own home blew up a couple of weeks ago. It was pretty easy actually; the hard part was getting the pipes loose but I hit them with the ball bat I found in the utility room and they came right off after that."

"What did the people want from your parents? Do you know, Anna?"

"I don't know. I do know the man is the dad of Brad and Ben and the lady is their aunt I think, but I don't know what they wanted. We never saw them before; they lied to us yesterday to get us in their van. Grownups are hard to understand sometimes."

At the same time interviews in several locations were being conducted, a second camera unit had been dispatched when chatter apparently at a local park was overheard. One comment overheard was something like "She just admitted it's a shakedown of the Construction Kids parents. You get that on tape Kenny?" Apparently Kenny did 'get it' and the next voice they hear said only "Take them down...now!" Where the four stood in the middle of the park it was still not obvious they were the subject of close observation, not until the old man sitting on the bench reading suddenly arose and walked toward them, speaking as he approached.

"All of you, hands up, stand still. No sudden moves, okay?" Two uniformed officers appeared from nowhere. Placing a hand on Jenn's shoulder so she knew he was talking to her, he added: "Hands down and behind your back, now." The third officer did the same routine with Bruce, leaving Alan and Lynn standing with hands up but unshackled. The first officer turned to them: "Sorry folks; you can put your hands down now; we just need to be sure for our own purposes. Okay?" It was okay with Alan and Lynn as the other two were walked off and placed in a suddenly appearing squad car. Turning to the first officer, Alan asked what was going on?

"I don't think I get what's taking place here. I guess you heard the deal they were trying to make, threatening to somehow harm the kids if we didn't play ball. We still don't know where the kids are and Jenn swore she would never tell us if she didn't get what she wanted."

The officer responded. "I do know but you're probably gonna find this hard to accept. They're on their way to the station with an officer at the moment."

"So someone finally figured out where they were stashed?"

"Not exactly. They...um...they sent a signal for help by blowing the back wall out of the house. I know, I know, I didn't believe it either but that's what they did. The one boy said he knew how to do it because his own house blew up and he listened to what the fire inspector told them. They set it up to explode, then hid behind several walls and stacked mattresses for protection until the blast was over. Anyway, they're safe. Only thing to me is that they blew up a house, demolished part of it, but because they're minors can't be held financially responsible for the damage; someone is gonna be unhappy. You'll see them in a few minutes." He was right; in a few minutes the two parents were being crushed with hugs in the reunion.

As the various tapes arrived at the TV station the several producers involved realized what they had: a scoop of a shakedown plus some nationally recognized kids who blew up a house, bad guys now in cells, all the good stuff. Working at a furious rate they edited, built a time coherent sequence, did what they needed to do, and produced a finished product they put on the wire to network headquarters. The response was immediate, asking for confirmation this was not some put up fake job but the real thing, kids actually blowing up a house (real time security footage from a neighbors back yard camera was shown, both the blast and the kids exiting via the missing wall). The network would run it without change as a "feel good" piece at the 6 PM news hour, again at 10 PM, and several more times on their alternate channels. Their phone system was overwhelmed one minute into the first showing. Worse was that social network posts, seeming to appear as if magic, in a few instances were taken down quickly but not before their threatening contents made their point. Both Jennette and Bruce were threatened with dire consequences by a lot of people if they touched the Construction Kids, even a single hair on the kids head; her version of anything about the Construction Kids, child abuse, or shacking up parents, all false anyway and none of which made the airways, would be seen as her desperate ploy to justify her error. Worse to come was her discovery she also could not trust Bruce Albert in any respect, especially forthcoming child care responsibilities.

Sitting in his recliner after a long but very successful day at work, Gill Lanham had the remote in one hand, adult beverage of relaxant in the other hand, feet up, shoes off, and was considering enjoying the fine meal yet to come. Their life was good, really good, with raise after raise he had earned by his own perception of a winning ad scenario with four kids; Gill was comfortably at peace with himself, and then the bomb dropped: there were the four kids on the screen, kids he knew personally but who others in the whole country knew as the Construction Kids; they even rattled off that so familiar refrain: "I'm Ally." "I'm Brad" "I'm Ben" "I'm Anna." "We're the Construction Kids." Rapt attention now being paid, Gill realized what he was seeing was a network piece that no amount of money could buy in advertising power. He did miss the opening explanation but would catch that at the later airing; for sure he knew that something had happened to merit a national airing of the event. Phone, find the phone.

The early news was barely over, time for dinner, this night whatever the kids wanted as a reward for their staying calm at all times, some laughs from parents when the kids admitted they had whined about anything and everything just to be an annoyance to their captors, and then the phone rang to be answered by Anna as being closest.

"Hi; this is Anna; can I help you?"

Gill recognized the voice at the same time he was feeling tremendous relief it told him the kids were safe. "Hi, Anna. This is Gill Lanham. Can I talk to one of your parents please?" What he heard next set him back a bit in the realization Anna was correct in her response.

"I only have one parent, my dad, but Ms Lynn is like a mom. You're on speaker so both can hear you, okay?" Comfortably nestled in her own chair to watch the news program, Lynn heard what Anna said and realized what was happening: they were slowly but surely becoming one family, maybe not in a legal sense but in a relational sense. Anna's words were like gold to Lynn. Gill continued.

"People, I just watched you on the national news; what in the world happened to you?" It took some minutes to explain, much of which was done by the Construction Kids when it came to staging the blast and subsequent escape. All had ended well although there would be legal process as the prosecution of the miscreants began. Gill hardly knew how to accept the reality before him but did realize the impact it would have.

"I have to tell you, I don't even know how to really say this, the consequence from this news story is gonna be monumental, it just is. Any and every parent with kids who has ever heard of the Construction Kids is gonna get hammered; people who didn't know about you just gained the information in a story that has a happy ending, apparently a juvenile bomber, photogenic kids, bad people locked up, every cliché in the book. There is no amount of dollars that can buy that sort of good will advertising, none. But most important is that all of you are okay; I know this may sound a little crazy but you four have become national icons of that old slogan 'truth, justice, and the American way'. My only concern is not your concern; I don't know how we will meet the demand for product that is about to go through the roof. I know none of you planned for this to happen but I thank you for being who you are, the Construction Kids and parents; what more can I say?" Gill closed out the call in the next minute and started preparing himself to field the calls he would get the next day, calls from distribution centers telling him their shelves were bare and stores were screaming for product; even items that maybe weren't previously selling very well were gone from the shelves. Gil Lanham enjoyed his dinner, agreed with his wife she could order the new carpeting for the whole house if she wanted, and realized he personally knew some people who had made the national news in a good sense.

The Construction Kids were allowed to stay up to see the late version of the news but then it was off to bed on a school night, even if they did know how to blow up buildings. Each parent retired to their respective lair with their own thoughts; strange to say, each had a brief stray thought about what things might be like if that shack-up story was true.

Chapter Nineteen

The Plan

The next morning, kids off to school for the day, Alan and Lynn were in his kitchen for one more cup as a start to their own days. She had prepared his breakfast without being asked; in fact, he considered her to be a guest and would never ask her to do that sort of thing. She did the breakfast cooking because it pleased her to see him enjoy her effort; it was that simple, no hidden motive, just a warm feeling inside as she joined him sitting at the table. She knew there were things to be done but for the moment this feeling was to be enjoyed. Alan re-opened the conversation they had started earlier before the kids came roaring in for their own breakfast.

"Lynn, I think we should take some time this morning, maybe right now, to see where we are with a whole bunch of things." He knew what he really wanted to talk about but was unsure of the path to take. "I know you have a lot on your plate as much as I have a lot on mine. How about we start with your house, the one you own or at least share with a bank, the one the insurance carrier got in trouble for mishandling. The city wants it gone, at your expense of course. Anything I can do to help that along?"

"I guess I don't really know what to do. The city inspector gave me all the signed permits, even a list of contractors they recognize, so that's a start. I do owe a lot of mortgage money to the bank, so that also has to be addressed. That screw up by the insurance company left me with more money than the house is worth; I guess I need to call for a payoff on the mortgage, then see what's left. The remaining question seems to be what should I do with a vacant lot on my hands?"

Alan had an answer for her. "I've been thinking for some time I really need to upgrade my shop facilities here. The room was added as a hobby room by the former owners; it has worked well for some years now but as the products I'm seeing become more and more complicated I think I need to get updated, modernized, better test facilities, all those things. I am not trying to circumvent whatever you may be thinking about the house, but I would like to at least have you take a listen to my idea. Can we do that?"

Lynn was ready to listen. "We can do that, but is it really that simple Alan, adding like a one room building sort of thing? And what about the zoning laws, all that stuff. How does all that work for us or it or whatever?"

"It does actually work to allow a single dwelling to be built on the site. Knowing you are more than thorough in your work, I took the liberty of doing some homework. The zoning laws allow a single family dwelling to be constructed on a lot that size, even giving the maximum square footage the building can contain on the first floor, probably so it doesn't encroach on the lot lines. While it does say single family dwelling it is not exclusive phraseology; so long as the maximum limits are not exceeded the rules become a bit murky on specifics. I even called the city inspector about the question and was told I should submit plans for review but that he didn't see any issue provided the general appearance of the neighborhood remained unchanged and provided whatever operates in the building does not call for public parking spaces. My idea is to build a shop that looks more like a house on the outside but with few walls inside, bearing walls where needed but probably no partitioning walls other than for closets, bathrooms, things like that. If I guess correctly, you will demo the house but retain ownership of the lot, maybe even the foundation and slab, that sort of thing. There are things the shop here doesn't have, things like filtered compressed air, nitrogen bottle for dehydrating, more electronic detectors and test equipment, things like that. If we can agree on the price, I would rent the lot from you long term, build my shop and we all live happily ever after. What say you, neighbor Lynn?"

"Okay, I get all that, and I can see where this is heading, but what about the shop in this house; what happens to it? Bigger playroom maybe? And I don't think you should be paying any sort of rent, not after what you've done for us since day one."

Alan knew what he was about to say would choose a future path for them; he continued. "I know this sounds simple. When the new shop is ready to go I move all my stuff over there. Once the old shop here is vacated, I would build a bedroom I can live in, big enough for my needs but not taking up all the shop space by any means. The plumbing is underground but accessible in that area so the probably of a usable bathroom is high. I move out of the living room and into my new digs, everyone else stays where they are until something happens that prompts any further change. Any room I don't need for the remodel remains playroom. Sound like a plan, Ms Lynn? And by the way, paying rent has to happen; otherwise by definition we do not have a contract and you would be free to throw me out at any time you felt; is that your intent neighbor Lynn?"

She was caught off guard, party by thinking someday her family would have to move on, out of the Behr house, and partly by his seemingly convoluted rent statement; her thought had been they would probably move into the replacement house she would build in the empty lot. He had just totally altered that concept but instead of feeling displaced her mindset seemed to be accepting what he was telling her could happen. Moreover, she realized his plan called for them to stay until...whenever...no question about it. He wanted her and her family to stay in the Behr home and would make provision to see that happen. Her mind replayed that Anna comment from the previous night: "Ms Lynn is like a mom." Is that what Alan was thinking; where was he in all this, really? "Alan. I don't know what to say. You have this all planned out, decisions made for me and..."

He couldn't let her say things like that. "No, Lynn, not decisions made for you. I would never do so, make such an assumption; that wouldn't be right. There are decisions to be made no matter what you decide; what I am saying is that this is one option. I don't know where you are in all this, what Ms Lynn wants and hopes for, her dreams for herself and her boys. I know what I want for my girls but is that what you want for your boys as well? At the moment we are sort of locked together by happenstance, a ruined building, some kids that far outshine my own aspirations, all that, but I want to know where Lynn is in the process. I did hear what Anna said last night talking to Gill; I want that to continue for my girls and maybe along the way some good would rub off on me as well. Talk to me, please; what do you want, mom Lynn?"

"I can't lie about last night. When the girls say things like that it does something inside of me, something that is warm and pleasant to sense, something I want to sense over and over again in the future. Much of what I hear you say makes sense to me even if I do think you are short changing yourself in the process. I want us to stay together, all of us, until...until I don't know when but for a really long time. I found myself hurting as much for the safety of your girls as I did for my own boys yesterday; I'm maybe not explaining this very well."

"You are doing fine mom Lynn. Yesterday I couldn't have distinguished which meant more to me, the safety of my girls or the safety of your boys, and then realized there was no difference. Lynn, I have a rather large pile of things to do at the moment and it's gonna take me a while to work through everything, but I promise there will be a day when there is one sole thing before me I need to resolve; I promise. That day will come, a day when all thoughts are clear, emotions observed but not driving the illogical, a single decision remaining to be made aside from all the little decisions yet to come. I want to get there and I want to get there soon; I need that resolution. Will you wait for me, mom Lynn?"

She knew then how serious this discussion had become. "I will wait for you, Alan, but you have to promise to help me along the way so we can go faster. Promise?"

He understood her meaning: she was getting tired of waiting for the next step in their relationship, anxious to make that step, sooner rather than later, and was not letting go of Alan Behr, not now, not ever.

The first major decision they made was over the damaged house. After Alan called a couple of personal and professional contacts and received their suggestions, he and Lynn settled on one contractor and made the call. The contractor arrived an hour later for a site survey, took a look at what had to happen, told them it would take him less than a day to finish the job down to broom clean slab but that they would have at least five days to await the permitting to be completed. His surprise was complete when Lynn produced a signed set of demo documents from the city, then asked the contractor what day he planned to arrive as they wanted to get on with their lives. If they really really wanted him to do so, he could schedule them in for the coming Saturday; the security fencing would go up Friday afternoon, house remains removed down to the slab on Saturday and security fencing removed Monday morning. She accepted, then called the city inspector to let him know it had been scheduled; the inspector did not normally work on

Saturday but these people appeared to be some people other than normal and he was unwilling to push back.

The neighborhood kids were attracted to the security fencing, not to mention the adults who came by and asked about the schedule. Saturday morning saw the Behr yard full of people, adults and kids alike, some hauling lawn chairs, some on quad runners lined up twelve in a row, even little kids in strollers, all anticipating the arrival of heavy equipment. Two boys from the neighborhood asked Alan for permission to sell iced water bottles they had chilling in their wagon; he blessed their entrepreneurial spirit. The contractor arrived mid-morning, as he had said he would, having loaded out his equipment that day, bringing a large track hoe excavator on a trailer plus two big dump trucks and another smaller service truck. It surprised people a bit that the first thing they did was to unroll a hose from the nearest fire hydrant to the demolition site, then charge it with water; it would all make sense quite soon. With the hoe off the truck it started in on the house, first biting a large chunk out of the roof and stirring up a whirlwind of dust from the old attic insulation; the fire hose opened up a heavy spray to settle the dust. First bite dumped into a truck, then tamped down with much snapping and crunching of the wood framing, the process continued step by step, bite by bite until in less than an hour the house was gone, leaving the bare slab broom clean as promised. By lunch time the contractor and equipment were gone, leaving a thoroughly entertained neighborhood audience.

There was one special thing that happened as the process closed out. The contractor, a dad with young kids himself, called his wife and asked her to bring their three kids to the site. When they arrived he walked them over to meet the Construction Kids sitting on their quad runners all in a row with a lot of other quad runners; into the role playing, the kids had their costumes on just because they could. Pixels were consumed, memory sticks filled, phone batteries sapped to zero. And once the process started virtually every parent there had to get in on the act. The contractor, realizing what he had started, atoned for the deed by having the four kids line up on the construction site on their quads, posed his demolition crew behind the kids, and behind all of that the excavator. It was a good day, a very good day, and the first step on Alan's long list of things to get done.

Not one to wait around Alan had already called in an architect with whom he was familiar, telling the man what it was he wanted and that it had to go on the remaining house slab or at least very close to that limitation. The resulting plan presented to the city was a single story two bedroom house with two full sized bathrooms framed out and finished but with no intervening walls otherwise in place. By design, if at some time there was a need to actually create the two bedrooms, the utilities and framing were ready to be extended. The kitchen would be constructed, including appliances and such, but with only the two outside walls in place to define the area; the two interior walls would be missing. Care would be taken to ensure the gas supply safety valve remained outside the building. With a building permit already in hand, the new shop went up in surprising little time, including the dark green metallic roof for which Alan had opted with its forty year warrantee; Alan would move in as soon as he could.

Within the time frame of the house demolition and shop construction, many other things came to pass. The kids didn't miss a day of school but did get interviewed a number of times on the weekend or on the evening of a school day. Alan and Lynn were cautious in their approach to such things and made their cautions known to Sol Kaplan; Sol might be the agent but the parents came first and he knew it. Also during that time, Gill Lanham had at times feigned deafness just to retain his own sanity. His estimation has been oh so right; and products associated with the Construction Kids, even some products that only seemed to be related to the Construction Kids, disappeared from store shelves. Gil didn't want to do so but ended up having to job out some of the work to every manufacturer he knew just to put something, anything on the store shelves. Mr. Touhy also was stunned when he saw the news story about the abduction, blast, and so on; mildly panicked, he called Gill at home, discovering Gill had already talked to the kids parents or someone in charge, everything and everyone was well, and he agreed they needed to go to crises mode on product manufacturing; even with that effort receiving a new Construction Kids logo bearing battery quad runner would take probably six weeks from order placement at very best, way past the coming holiday date but with no order cancellations. Ordering was limited to one per family, although it was pretty well recognized people would lie cheat and steal to get one of the machines; scalpers charged twice the list price and could still sell all they could find. Officer Jack Bailey was interviewed more than once when the press found out he knew the whole story start to finish; he would be nominated as Officer of the Year for the department partly because he had brought positive national vibes to this small department in a fairly small town..

Some of what happened during the construction phase of the new shop was right in line with what the Construction Kids knew best. It also moved the Behr/Albert game pieces closer to the finish line, taking a rather large leap as it were. Lynn had been called to attend a meeting at Windmere, not an unusual act in itself although their management style tended to be more one on one than mass meeting style. Laura Williams had called Lynn herself, apologizing for the need to have the meeting on a Saturday morning, telling Lynn at the same time it was a most excellent opportunity they had not seem coming at them. That in its self seemed strange to Lynn when she truly believed these people somehow were always and forever on top of their own game. In the more casual chatter of the conversation between the two women, Laura also mentioned the new play park at the Windmere home office, a park centered more on the 4-10 year old consumer than either toddler or older children's parks were normally seen. It was actually not a solicitation on Laura's part to have the Construction Kids per se visit the park; just a friendly invitation for a visit while the adults did business. Would Lynn like that and would she be bringing Mr. Behr along with his girls? It was all settled, including Lynn saying she would like Mr. Behr to sit in on the meeting if that would not somehow imperil the situation; Laura agreed to the sit in, basing her decision on the knowledge the presence on Alan Behr in the life of Lynn Albert was an important aspect not to be overlooked; Laura also knew what they were about to propose to Lynn would take some courage on Lynn's part to face the challenge head on, courage Laura Williams also knew could come in part from Alan Behr through a simple hand hold. This would not be a decision point to end all decision points in the life of Lynn Albert, but it was foundational in importance and Laura knew if Lynn faltered, Alan would hold her up until she regained her footing. There was never a thought in the mind of Laura Williams that the challenge they were about to offer Lynn would not be met. What she didn't know was that as much as Windmere believed this process would be successful not only from both business and personal growth standpoints, but that it was exactly in line with what Alan Behr had been thinking for the last couple of months even if it took him a bit of time to realize what was before him: the answer to his remaining question.

On the next Saturday, Behr bus loaded up they headed for Conyerville, Windmere, the new play park and whatever else the day might bring. Alan had readily agreed to sit in on the meeting even if Lynn couldn't tell him the specific nature of the meeting. Rolling along the wide drive inside the gate, the Behr bus parked behind a roadster Lynn recognized as belonging to Jill Andrews, her mentor, advisor, confidant, all those things; there must be some ongoing crises for Jill to be here on the weekend, having stated any number of times Windmere staff worked on the weekends only if the problem was in the range of immanent impact of a nuclear tipped missile targeted to land in the big Windmere conference room.

Kids out of the bus and turned over to the Williams children for the morning, Lynn and Alan were met by someone they recognized, the larger than life Dennis Anderson, former semi-pro football lineman. Others were already gathered in the big Windmere commercial kitchen and informal dining room, even a couple of people who looked familiar alongside Jillian Andrews. Hugs bestowed and other introductions made, Alan and Lynn learned the others present were there representing Precision Machine Specialties, PMS by the familiar acronym, Ed Long and wife Syd Long. In a strictly legal sense, Syd would one day be owner of PMS when it passed from her father to her, but in a practical sense she had no idea how to run that operation and depended on husband Ed to handle it for her; at the same time, Ed was also a percentage owner of PMS, a decision made by her father to keep Ed aboard and closely connected to the well being of PMS. Ed Long had no plans to go anywhere, particularly after Syd had told him the evening before she was with his child. Syd also had her own enterprise to manage as head of the Marketing Department, North America, for the TallRight Division of Tri-Norse Industries. No more had she heard the names of Alan and Lynn and learned their occupations than her mind recalled the in-house problem she had needed to solve; today she was seeing the actual Alan Behr and thanked him one more time in person for his response to her dilemma. There was more on her mind but for themoment Syd would wait her turn. The remaining couple present, also looking familiar, was introduced as Ron and Roni Weston, Ron from Applied Dynamic Technology plant operations and Roni from Bowman Auto Plaza; their two children had joined the others in the play ground. Like Ed and Syd, they also had a child in process; while that was not obvious, they had arrived in Roni's preferred antique ride, a long hooded Cord; that was obvious. The combined kids had already taken their first play break by going to the kitchen for hot chocolate and snacks.

Invited into a conference room, the group settled around the table: Syd and Ed, Alan and Lynn, Ron and Roni Weston, Ari Schoenroth who had finally arrived, Laura and Ryan Williams, and Jillian Andrews. Laura opened the meeting.

"Thank you, all of you, for agreeing to a Saturday meeting. You are all aware there has to be some sort of almost crises level event to get us out of bed this early on a Saturday." Chuckles were heard about the table although to a person there they had been up for hours, mostly due to children. "First of all, Alan and Lynn, I think we all saw that news video of your kids that went viral; is everyone safe now?" Hearing a positive response she continued. "By the way, I guess just for my own satisfaction, did those kids really blow up the house or was that a bit of editorial license?" Assured by Ed the kids did in fact blow a wall out of the hostage house, the reality of which he certified with some parental pride, Laura continued the opening narrative.

"Obviously all of us here this morning are related to the situation at hand, a situation in need of better definition. Some of you may know that ADT does some very secretive work for several government agencies; we are not at liberty to describe which agencies and for our purposes here it doesn't really matter. In fact we don't know which agencies are involved, but again, it doesn't matter. What does matter is that PMS is running a secure manufacturing operation making some parts for ADT, several thousand parts I believe, but again, that is not relevant past a certain point. What the Pentagon wants is total capture of all data related to that process, how much is in process, time to complete the whole thing which I believe is a couple of years at this point, material in the supply line, shipping processes, all that sort of thing. Not directly represented around the table today but also very interested in upgrading the data capture process at PMS is a household products manufacturing company for which PMS is producing parts, again by the thousands. Everyone associated with the ADT process has been cleared via a governmental security check up to the level of SECRET with need to know, the usual caveat; that includes spouses of those directly connected to the process. We learned of that process by default, when an employee of Ed Long's was vetted in an adoption process; her criminal history, minor thought it was, was expunged all the way back through high school library fines near as we can tell. We remain unclear as to whether the feds would have ever told us the whole story or not; we only know we submit names to them for PMS system operators and they bless or don't bless that nomination; so far so good. Now, on to the specific issue before us today: PMS has no recognizable accounting system in a digital sense and the Pentagon wants one; they want to be able to look into the process at any one moment and see exactly where things stand. In contrast, the buyer for the second major operation at PMS teeters on the edge of a crises quite frequently; they are aware if they do not have their very hot consumer items on the shelf right now, they will lose market share; Jill can tell you in the last week she worked with the owners at Wilson Cartage to expand their load tracking system so when the buyer calls, Wilson staff can tell them not only that a load is on the way, but the specific direction the truck is moving, at what speed, and when it will arrive at their dock. The limiting gateway in both these operations is that PMS staff would have to virtually sit beside each process minute by minute and count the pieces ready to ship. Obviously that is not a satisfactory solution to the problem. We have been called and asked to research this situation, connect the dots in sufficient manner to design and install a system that can meet the needs of both clients while simultaneously easing the accounting problems at PMS. The company itself has doubled in size over the last few months with the addition of a building expansion to house equipment provided by Tri-Norse machine tool division. Tri-Norse already has accounting software in place to keep track of machine hours, particularly when the work cell is being operated for the good of PMS. We are met here today to define the basics for the system we are to install at PMS; this is not to define a bid package or do anything like that; we have been told to get on with it by all involved. We will keep notes on this meeting and will wire copies to each of you as soon as they are written. There will be a brief window of opportunity to correct said minutes, discuss among yourselves what we may have read wrong, make any corrections then move forward. We believe with what we know now, the many data streams to capture and process, hardware and software needs, that this process will take up to two months of implementation time at a minimum. We will make every effort to shorten that time frame but believe it to be reasonable based on our prior experience. Now, I should tell you before we get into the actual nuts and bolts of this process, that Windmere plans to staff this project with Lynnette Albert backed up by Jillian Andrews. For those of you who may be wondering why Mr. Behr is here, if you remember from that news item or perhaps from purchasing a battery quad runner for your own children, please meet the parents of the four Construction Kids;. Lynn has the two boys, Ben and Brad; as her son Brad mentioned, he knew how to blow up a house because their own house blew up and he learned from the fire marshal. That said they are currently sharing a house with Mr. Behr and his daughters, Ally and Anna, the rest of the Construction Kids; all the kids are here somewhere at the moment. I suggest to you parents who want to do so that you get pictures of yourselves with the kids; it will enhance your own status at home; trust me on that one. As this unfolds, we want to make sure Alan as her child care provider in a sense understands the need for Lynn to maybe work some long hours. The good news is that at least this project is in their home town, no commuting, and her boys are apparently quite comfortable living in one bedroom while the Behr girls are in the other bedroom. We should all get so lucky our kids would get along that well. Okay, I think that covers it. Who's first up, and I should mention all your laptops are connected via wireless to the interactive board here, so no secrets, okay?"

Lynn had been sitting comfortably relaxed, assuming she would be an assistant to Jill in what was appearing to be a multi-tentacled project at PMS. Just hearing words like "The Pentagon" could be frightening, but Jill seemed calm, so Lynn would remain calm, right up until she heard Laura Williams say the Windmere staffer would be Lynnette Albert; Lynn's mind substituted Jillian Andrews but it didn't fit. She tried again, no fit. Lynn looked at Laura with widening and probably frightened eyes, but in return saw only Laura's eyes looking back at her, a slight upturn of a smile on Laura's face, a subtle wink, and a slight nod in Lynn's direction; that was it, the whole connection saying she was the staffer. Her mouth started to come open just as she felt that hand take hers and squeeze it just a bit; in that moment she understood she was running with the big dogs now. She had to make good on this assignment, do everything she possibly could to make it come out right side up; the hand holding hers was telling her he believed in her abilities, in the process, and what she could deliver in the future. It also gave Alan Behr something he had been seeking without knowing what it was he sought; he had if not the answer, at least the process to that answer.

The meeting went on from the early 9 AM start right up to the noon hour, non-stop, as Lynn gathered her wits about her and started her list of questions: what did they operate now, was any of it automated and what platform did it operate on, how would the Pentagon inquiries be formulated and what data base form did they use, what software did the PMS work cells run on, could that load tracking software be modified into automated reporting, how soon could she meet with staff one on one to learn the specific operations of each client, on and on it went as the project started to take form in her mind; Lynnette Albert was aboard, totally aboard. The good news was that as he had reached out and taken her hand to reassure her, it was her left hand, leaving the right hand to gesture, write notes, move her mouse to point to something on the display board, things like that; her left hand grasped his the whole time, never letting the pressure off, until his hand was totally inert and devoid of feeling. They did take a break about mid-morning, enough time for her to realize what she had been doing to him, making her apologies as she went. Taking a moment to seek out Jill, Lynn found more positive support; it also gave her a moment to ask a major question of her mentor: who in their right mind would give a project like this to a novice? Jill knew the answer: Jill had made the recommendation of Lynn to Ryan and Laura Williams, telling them she had every confidence Lynn could handle the task, could shine at the task, and that Jill would be right there not to do the work or even to closely monitor the work Lynn was to do, but to serve as the backstop against which Lynn could push when she needed to push.

Noon time saw the all time favorite meal again being laid out on the long table in the "kitchen", do it yourself tacos with all the trimmings. It was a reprise of an earlier adventure in eating and served well to refresh that memory.

A major lunch event behind them, the group headed out to the playground to learn what the kid's had discovered. The playground was at Windmere on a trial basis for them to learn the best approach; when approved the prototype would serve as the basis for what was essentially a "kit" for a playground. Several of their owned or operated resorts had seen a significant uptick in vacationers bringing their younger children along. For the older kids it was no problem with game rooms and tennis courts, jet skis, all that, available to them. The playground at Windmere would serve the younger group, trying to keep them entertained and together in one place.

Greetings exchanged and picture taking burning up scads of memory space, the group of parents stood and watched for a while as the kids indulged themselves. As the group finally decided maybe it was time to go home, Laura asked if anyone has specific input to offer on the playground and equipment. Alan ventured a comment.

"Couple of things I'd like to mention, nothing earth shattering. I suggest taking the bottom two rungs off the hand walker, both ends. That way really young kids who could climb up but not be able to access the horizontal run would be safe, unable to start the climb if the bottom two rungs are gone. The one other thing is that the center structure of the merry-go-round be somehow closed off so no one can get in there and push. I know that may sound simple but sometimes older kids will get in there and do the pushing; the resulting centrifugal force on the outer part is really significant, sometimes throwing riders off onto the ground. I decline to tell you how I know that data; let's just say I do know it and let it go at that. Other than that it all looks good to me, pipe ends suitably terminated against snagging clothing, all the good stuff."

Laura thanked him for his input, then walked with them back to load the Behr bus as they prepared to depart. Kids in place, Lynn taking her place in the shotgun seat, Laura worked her way around the van until she was at the driver's seat window. Alan powered the window down sensing Laura wanted to say something to him; he was right."

Laura couched her words carefully, believing in her own mind there was much more to the Alan-Lynn connection than the two principles openly recognized. Voice very quiet as she spoke words for his ears only, Laura said her piece: "Alan, please take care of her. We know how hard her background has been and we know how big a challenge this project is to her, how nervous she may be at the moment; above all we believe her abilities surpass the task itself. When we made the decision we made it knowing you would be her backstop, her rock." Laura laughed softly: "I couldn't see it but I knew when your hand touched hers under the table; her face changed from Nervous Nellie to Lean-in Lynn and I knew for sure we had a contender for the project. So, I believe it is in both our best interests for you to take care of her. Okay?"

It was okay with Alan Behr, every bit of okay with him. He did continue to think about the process as they drove along, listening at times to the chatter from some excited kids, mom Lynn joining in now and then. It did surprise him a bit when things seemed to get too quiet, but a quick look in the mirror told him four kids were asleep with mom Lynn not far behind. Maybe it was a good time to bring up what he had been considering.

"Lynn, this project of yours looks to be really huge, enclosing three different companies, maybe four counting the trucking outfit, each at a different level of accounting. I've been thinking the logistics to support your work have to be improved; I do not believe laying files out on the kitchen table is going to work, not this time. So, here's what I have in mind; please hear me out before shooting me down? Okay?"

"Alan, I would never shoot you down. Why would I shoot down the very element that keeps me safe and sane and on the right road, without whom I would most likely still be clerking in a small and unappreciative accounting firm instead of facing an oncoming train? Why would I do that?"

"Okay, but I have to ask the questions; you know how that works; my plan affects the building residing on a lot you own and currently lease to me for a very nominal fee. I propose to change that building just a bit here and there. What I believe should happen is that we need to finish out some of the interior wall construction for the living room and dining room areas; neither room is very large to begin with, so I suggest we erect only those walls necessary to form one large room with a single door to the rest of the house, not the two shown on the drawing. Overhead lighting would be installed along with plenty of power outlets. I have three banquet size tables in the back garage, plastic tops, ready to go; those would go along the walls, separated as to company or however you would like to handle things. If I can find it, I also have an old drafting table in the garage I can uncover and bring along. I know that may not sound like much of a deal but I do believe you would find sitting at the tilted board easier than a regular desk for processing paperwork. Give it a try anyway?"

She was impressed. His mind was already on premises improvements to accommodate her new enterprise; clearly he was all in with his support for her. She had seen Laura talking to Alan just before they left and rightly assumed it was somehow about her. Maybe that was his motivation for support, but Lynn hoped for more. Answer him, had to answer him.

"Yes, that sounds really good to me." As positive as she tried to sound, her confidence was growing faint as the project reality again grew in size before her and her voice sounded less sure as she went along. "Alan, this thing is like a speeding bus bearing down on me. What if I can't do it; what if I misfire and somehow mess it up? Then what happens? The reward for bringing this project in as a success would be something most accountants never ever would be allowed to enjoy, not on their own at least, yet I seem to be out there running with the big dogs when I'm uneasy about even being allowed in the kennel. I'm sure the Windmere organization is one of the finest management teams around at positive decision making, yet here I am, virtual novice, major project in hand, nerves a bit frayed and the work hasn't even started yet. How do I get through this Alan without losing the battle and maybe even more than that, losing you when I come unglued and take my frustrations out when I should be angry with myself for failing?"

She was wavering from her earlier stance; he couldn't let that happen. Had they been back at the house he would have put both arms around her and held her until the fear passed, but here he was driving, listening to her as her conviction faded. What could he do?

"Lynn, can I say something?"

"Yes, please, anything; I need to hear something to know I'm not nuts, in way over my head. I'm sorry; I shouldn't be going on like…"

"Lynn, shut up; be quiet and listen to me, please." A bit stunned at his stern voiced directive she fell silent. "I understand what you're going through but your thought basis is all wrong. Believe me when I say Windmere does not make these decisions without a lot of thought. They have a lot riding on this as well, and they chose Lynn to carry their flag. Their track record of success is exemplary, ask anyone associated with them, and they chose Lynn. They surround themselves with consummate professionals in every respect, and they chose Lynn. I know this whole project may seem overwhelming at the moment, but I got some advice today I need to pass on to you; it's the key to how Windmere gets things done in a positive sense and why their track record is so stellar. Ari told me he learned directly from Ryan and Laura how they problem solve any and all situations that come before them: they break the situation down into the smallest pieces possible, see what each piece does to fit into the whole matrix, decide which pieces to use, which pieces are relevant to the decision making process, then they reassemble until the original again exists but is understood by all. You already know this universe has three separate entities plus maybe the trucking company, so that's a start on the disassembly. Now, I know what I am about to say may earn me a poke in the eye, but think about the Construction Kids and how they do things; I'd guess none of them every thought they couldn't do what was being asked; they just read the instructions to define the situation, did what was required, then moved on to the next task. And Lynn, I'm sorry I told you to shut up; not very polite of me at all but I really needed to stop you in the direction you were headed. Besides, if you ever believed in omens, I have three tables and you have three companies. We better now?"

She had listened, still reeling just a bit from when he told her point blank to shut up but came to understand why he had to take that tactic. "Yes, we are better, and I apologize for going off on a rant like that and making you shush me. I guess I've never thought about the decision making process like that, taking it apart and rebuilding." She turned in her seat just a bit so she could better look at him. "I needed to know that, and while I don't particularly believe in omens the three tables sign works for me if it works for you. I'm sorry I can be such a meltdown mess now and then; everything seems to be going great and I guess it unnerves me a bit that my life is all different now than it was a few months ago. It isn't just the money, although it is a good feeling to be able to pay ones bills on time and have food money left. I think we need to renegotiate the lot rental since I will be using as much or more of the house than you will be using once I get all spread out. Can we do that?"

"We can do that right after we roast some dogs maybe? Haven't had a cook-out in a little while but I think I have some Texas sauce left somewhere in the refrigerator. We also haven't heard from Sol in quite a while although I would guess the sound of money arriving in the till makes him happy. I do agree with Ari that Sol can be ferocious defending his clients. I have no idea how much the kids will end up with but I'm guessing most of this will be over when the holidays are behind us. So, stop by the deli to make things easier on us old folks?"

They did stop by the local deli and Lynn ran in to get some items for a basic cook-out; the four kids remained asleep, starting to wake up when they were in the driveway of their own home. Fire started in the fire ring, food stuffs brought outside, and dinner was served within a few minutes. Later that evening after the kids has retired for the evening, complaining a bit but going anyway, Lynn and Alan once again stood in each other's arms before they turned in.

"Alan, thank you for today and for a lot of days past and those to come. I've been thinking things over, not just your van speech I needed so much to hear, but how this has come to pass for me. I do not believe for a second I would be looking at the opportunity of a lifetime without a foundation beneath me, a foundation that holds me up, stands me up when I falter, points the way when I stray, all those things. I am sure Jill had a lot to do with today but I am equally sure if I had arrived there without Alan Behr beside me things would have come out differently. I owe you, of that much I am sure, and we still haven't talked about the lot rental fee alteration."

"Neighbor Lynn, you being you and here with me is all I ask. I don't care about the lot rent; I do care we remain together. Remember when you asked if I could speed up the process we seem to be going through? I think it just got wings. I can't explain it very well at the moment but I do think I see an end goal just over the horizon and drawing closer all the time. It's going to take some time, but will you give me say a couple of months at the most? I know you're tired of waiting for that next step whatever it may be; so am I, but I want to know the moment is right for both of us. Okay?"

It was okay with her, and with a resolved mind she went to bed knowing she had that foundation to stand on and that he would be right there with her.

Chapter Twenty

The Finish Line

Alan was first up Sunday morning, rolling out and running through the usual morning processes, but dressing a little better than the jeans and worn pullovers he usually wore. He had decided this was to be a day off from everything, something the family did need upon occasion to remind them of what is important and what is not important in their lives. Coffee on to brew, he found the package of sausage links and put the whole package on to slow cook; he was right in thinking the aroma itself would awaken people in the house, partly because the kids were always hungry. With the newspaper retrieved there was time for him to just sit on a stool and relax; his decisions for the day were all made, no more were needed, at least none of any major importance.

Elsewhere in the house someone was stirring about but very slowly as thoughts already loose in her head promised to crowd all else out. She had awakened with the enormity of the project she had been handed looming over her in spite of what Alan had done to cut it down to size. Morning routine completed to an acceptable level, she followed the enticing coffee scent, and what was that other smell that had her attention, frying sausage, that was it, frying sausage. She was usually first up and in the kitchen; today was a pleasant change even if she did enjoy feeding people. Alan was there and pouring the fresh brew into her favorite cup as she entered the room; he greeted her with the usual "Good morning neighbor Lynn". She responded.

"Good morning to you also; my apologies for being so neglectful of my duties here and getting up late. What can I do to atone for my neglect?"

"You can sit and have a cup with me; that should be punishment enough. Really though, I should let you know what I'm thinking for today, how to expend this whole new day we have before us. Anything in particular on your mind we need to talk about before I launch into my stump speech, neighbor Lynn?"

"Mostly I woke up with the realization I probably need to use every minute of my days from here on in to see this assignment to a fruitful completion for all. I'm thinking I need to get started as soon as I can, not waste time. I'm not saying I won't get my other normal living things done, like laundry, stuff like that but I have a feeling this whole thing is gonna burn a lot of minutes. So there I am, ready to burn minutes." She was unprepared for what she heard next, his voice clear and assured as he spoke, looking right at her.

"Not gonna happen, not today. Tomorrow you can dive in as deep as you want, probably need to dive in deep, but not today. The kids will be up soon and need fed, so there goes another hour or so. I plan to walk down the street to go to church today, partly because it may do me some good and partly because we have much to be thankful for at this point. After that it's back here for lunch, then off to that rehabbed city park so the kids can ride everything again at least once if not twice. When they tire of that, if they ever do, we will launch the big canoe that will be on top of the van and paddle about on the river. Returning here we may need naps at that point, but if not or subsequent thereto, we will have dinner if you would be so kind as to put this roast and fixin's in the slow cooker; I would do that but defer to your skills in that area. After dinner we can elect to do nothing, sit out in the glider rocking, or maybe talk about the upcoming holiday season soon to be upon us; at no time will the new project or any other work be mentioned, not ever, never. How does that sound to you, neighbor Lynn?"

He was right, she knew he was right, and she wanted to go right along with him; there was also that sound in his voice that the decisions had already been made; somehow the fact he had made decisions affecting her and her family felt good, the right thing to have happened and she wondered to herself how the things this man did could seem so right and what her ex husband did along the same line of thought seem so wrong. Her assent to the plan was barely made known to Alan when the kids started to arrive in the kitchen, ravenous as usual, and fell on the plate of sausage as though they were truly starving. They finished off a large stack of pancakes in the process and made it to church on time, but just barely.

The rest of the day was a joy to her as she came to the realization of what Alan was doing for her, breaking the tension and letting her rest before starting the arduous climb through the mountainous project. She slept well that night with the memory of her lips on his at the close of day, his arms enclosing her in a warm cocoon; there was one lingering thought she could not make go away as she lay down, the thought she wanted to invite him into her bed but didn't know how to do so without maybe scaring him off a bit. She was a grown woman with two children; surely she could find a way to be even closer to him in her growing belief she was in love with him, totally and crazy in love with him, yet had no idea how he truly felt about anything. Yes, he took her hand when she needed his strength and he kissed her and held her close, but was that enough? Had she been able to read his mind she would have known the answers she sought were on their way and would be pleasing to her.

The next few weeks for Lynn were filled dawn to dusk as the piles of "road maps" on the three tables grew. She found a strong partner at Citizens Bank in the form of VP Vance Simmons and an equally strong partner in Lindsey at Wilson Cartage. The Tri-Norse Industries people sent in a representative to work with her in data capture from the work cell production, while Ed Long at PMS knew the coding for the original work cell belonging to PMS; Ron Weston fed her all he could find on the software the various government agencies used. The heretofore unseen other PMS customer sent in a staffer who knew that work cell nomenclature and worked through Ed Long to make sense of it all in a short time. Jill would stop by upon occasion but seemingly only to chat idly, maybe to have a cup of hot tea and not apparently to bore into the situation. The unseen reality was that Jill was checking more on the mental health of Lynn Albert than the status of the project. Each night and each morning as she sat on a stool in the kitchen of the Behr house, Alan Behr massaged her shoulders almost like one would prepare a fighter for the ring; in a way that was exactly what he was doing, letting her know he was there and would be there in the future. They had not indulged in any additional definitive discussion about their relationship but Lynn had a confidence he would not disappoint her. He said the end of the wait was near and she believed him. There was that one incident when she regretted having a filled schedule days ahead, but even then Alan took care of things and she knew it was all right.

About two weeks after Lynn became immersed in the project. Sol Kaplan had called asking for one or the other parent. Alan took the call on speaker just as Lynn came in on a short eye resting break from her research routine. It was a new offer; Sol explained.

"I think you know that Big Flags commercial was shot locally and used local people; even the car is around here in town somewhere, close to your location I think. In fact, my sources tell me the kids even met the girls one time. So, anyway, here's the deal on the table at the moment. The Big Flags corporate guys connected the Construction Kids and expanding operations a bit at the Big Flags theme parks; they have always featured attractions suited for teenagers and up but not so much for sub-teens. They realized if they could somehow connect a park area designed for younger kids to the current Construction Kids craze, they could generate a whole new set of park patrons as the kids age a bit. They are also quite well aware of the success of their current commercials with the three Franz girls, well, one Banning girl now that Andrea got married. Realistically speaking we have maybe one more year with that series of ads, then will reshoot an updated version keeping in mind as the girls age out, and I don't mean that in the slightest negative connotation, not at all, it's just the reality of the situation, they will be past the teen agers Big Flags wants to entice. Now, if we can make this connection via the company that handles marketing for Big Flags, Inc., we can get in line for this upcoming year, probably two years after that a reshoot, and maybe three or four years after that for a full replay. I have already talked to the rep from the marketing group; he is well versed in what the kids can deliver and really wants this under contract before anyone else gets the same idea. The mechanics of the situation look like this: the park near here has the new equipment installed in an expanded area; we would draw up a process showing your kids using the new area, having a good time on the equipment, that sort of thing. I think we all know if the Construction Kids are in an ad, it will sell whatever is being sold. As a precaution, I hooked up again with the guy who put together the original ad with the kids, Gill Lanham; he still says he's a sales rep for the company but I get the feeling he is a lot more than that these days. Anyway, I talked to him about featuring the kids in this new venue, about how that might affect their ad campaign. He got back to me within the hour saying he had cleared it with their legal and his VP, that they felt our campaign could only boost theirs. So, here we are, again. How do the two of you feel about all this, local shoot, all that?"

Lynn spoke first. "Alan, I really want to see this happen but I can't afford to spend a whole day at the park. Even if it isn't a whole day I have been booking meetings and interviews virtually back-to-back, there are so many people involved in this project, so many loose ends I need to wrap up so there is nothing left to chance. I'm sorry; I don't want to see the kids miss this opportunity, but what can I do?" Alan had the answer.

"Mom Lynn, you can trust me to make this all good, take care of the kids, all that. I have nothing really pressing at the moment. Since it's local we won't have to face the hotel and airlines dealing with four rowdy kids and their overprotective parents, so that's a plus. Sol, what kind of time frame are we looking at?"

Sol Kaplan was a happy man; he knew the project was going to fly just by hearing the parents respond. "The Big Flags guys are ready to go, the rebuilt park area is ready to go, the marketing company rep is ready to put a film crew in place, and if I read the local school calendar right, the kids have a school day off next week, Wednesday I think. The new area is still blocked off from general use so we can access it any time. What else do I need to put in place to make this happen next week?"

Alan thought about it for just a moment before responding, finally voicing his concern. "Sol, I don't want to seem negative here but we need to consider the kids a bit more. I can deal with the boys, but who can help with the girls? You and I both know girls are different and I think I need someone along who can answer their needs should something arise us mere men aren't really prepared to deal with. I'll need someone Lynn and I are both happy with and from your standpoint probably someone who understands the filming process. Can you make that happen, and if you can then I think we're good to go."

Sol already had an answer in mind but needed to verify availability and so on. "I will get back to you very shortly. Other than that, can I book next Wednesday, say 9 AM at the park?"

Lynn and Alan agreed provided Sol could find an acceptable female companion for the girls. Lynn went on back to work as did Alan. Sol had an answer in less than half an hour, called Alan to verify, and the project was booked. They talked to the kids that evening, telling them the basics of the process, that it would be done at the local Big Flags park, and that while mom Lynn couldn't go along, there would be a female companion for the girls. Wednesday morning saw the Behr bus depart the Behr driveway at or about 8 AM, then make one stop to pick up another passenger, the promised female companion; the girls were lit up when they realized their new associate was Andrea Franz Banning. For her part, Andrea was taking a day off work and really looked forward to the experience; she well remembered her own experience at the park with her two sisters. This shoot was a bit different from what Andrea had experienced in that these kids would stay in costume; there was no need to change clothes as the Franz sisters had done, but this shoot wouldn't take all day either; the plan was to film a trailer, a short addition to run at the end of a truncated Big Flags commercial. Each piece of equipment was exercised as the cameras ran, showing the four Construction Kids having the time of their lives in the new area.

By late morning the shoot was in the can ready for editing back at the A/V lab. The rep from the marketing company, Darrell Wallen, was again salivating at the prospects he saw for this new series; he had already gained an office with a door and two windows to the outside for his last great adventure at this park, the original ad that was still running; today would maybe bring a reserved parking spot close to the building he worked in. He well remembered working with Andrea Banning, and the clear threat he had received from her now husband, Jeff Banning, to protect the girls at all costs. Today was no different with the presence of Alan Behr. The other clear memory Darrell had was that of working with Sol Kaplan to arrive at what Sol believed was barely adequate pay for his clients; the residuals Sol demanded were still causing money to be deposited in the Franz girl's accounts. The work today would be less expensive because of the shorter length and less complicated shoot process, but Sol still demanded, and got, residuals for the four kids. By voice vote, the group opted to return to Mama Leoni's for lunch, then on home. Their paychecks for a half days work would arrive two weeks later.

Four weeks later a short piece of the new trailer was tagged onto the end of a shortened Big Flags commercial for their test area; Darrell Wallen was given an assigned parking spot next to the building, a raise, and an extra week of paid vacation as management at Big Flags scrambled to get the new parks constructed at all the other Big Flags venues.

Alan took a call from Syd Long, North American marketing guru for TallRight domestic products. She had talked to him that day at Windmere, meeting him in person for the first time and finding out a bit more about what he actually did for a living; in doing so she reconfirmed her discovery of a source for remediating issues that popped up in her realm from time to time. TallRight's designs sometimes were slightly out of line with what the USA consumer would expect. Maybe it was a minor difference that made little impact; other times it was a minor difference that irritated the end user and upon occasion prompted a call to TallRight about their products. She could now circumvent those calls, having found a source that could answer the need: Alan Behr.

As week number eight drew closer, Lynn started to reassemble what she had compiled. What she had perceived as multi-tentacled was even more widespread than that. The original three companies with a simple connect to Wilson Cartage in place had morphed into over a half dozen companies, all involved one way or another with the three originals, some as suppliers of parts, some as consumers of assemblies, some like PMS as assemblers/machinists in the middle of the path, and Wilson Cartage somewhere along the way. The long tables held the documentation, sometimes solely in the form of a zip drive or data disc, sometimes as a stack of paper where no data collection system had previously existed; she had compiled a list of equipment that would be needed, and on a really large chart Alan had hung on the wall for her to draw on was the tree of interconnections. She knew the consumer products' company was always on the edge of calamity in operating their supply chain; she also knew PMS couldn't do the work cell assembly for those consumer products if their supply of parts was somehow curtailed; she knew Wilson Cartage's load tracking system could answer questions all by its self if connected to users properly. Along the way Lindsey at Wilson had told her about the early morning call her husband had received from a semi-trailer sitting in a loading dock. The trailer didn't know anyone was stealing fuel but it did know when the fuel level went low and the refrigeration unit would soon run out, so it made the call for help. It was an interesting piece of information to have. Lynn was on a first name basis with a lot of new people.

Looking at the color coded wall chart it was becoming obvious which connecting link would serve various purposes; she ordered out all the equipment that needed to be installed by others, then would build those connections first, saving the simpler connections for an easier day. The equipment list itself was well into six figures but she didn't flinch when she placed the order. Because she did the basic design as she went along, Lynn had met one of the Windmere goals: figure out what was relevant and what was not before reassembling; keep it as simple as possible. Once the trunk grade lines were in place, the rest was easy. She did take time to test each new link as it went live, sending test data to watch the response. In week eight, on that Wednesday, Lynn keyed in the final software connection, sat back and watched as data flew in multiple directions, arriving wherever it might be needed just in time. She saw the order fly past to Wilson Cartage that a priority load would be ready for pickup at two PM Thursday and that the return trip would be past another supplier of parts. There were a few minor snags, as often as not being nomenclature or perhaps unit sizing, but the system ran on anyway. Thursday morning when she turned on the monitor the system was still running, flashing a warning PMS was about to run out of parts to assemble to the parts supplier. A call was made to Ron Weston to see if he had heard anything at all from his customers; yes, he had received a call asking if he could arrange for a weekly data dump into a Pentagon server; Ron asked Lynn how soon she could comply with the request and got his answer within the hour; they would learn later, much later, that no one at the Pentagon knew what to do with the data, concurrently saying it was a national security issue and had to continue when the suggestion was made the feed could be lopped off as an unnecessary expense. On another hunch, she took a quick glimpse into the "call log", a record of what user had opened a system portal and taken a look at something or other related to their operations; the total was near a hundred calls in the first full day of operation, sometimes multiples from the same nervous customer, sometimes one that apparently satisfied their curiosity for the moment. She realized the system was not exactly a friend to all users in that the suppliers could no longer hide their situation behind dropped phone calls, errant shipments, and other assorted excuses for not having their toes on the line.

On Friday, sitting with Alan in the old shop, she made the call to Windmere with a conference connection to Jill, speaking to Laura directly. "Hi, this is Lynn. I just wanted to let you know firsthand that the Octopus is waving all eight arms at the same time. I finished up data entry Wednesday and except for a couple of minor glitches it has been running on-line since then. I know as we get farther down the road I may need to go back in and resize some registers but for the moment nothing is running over. I truly believe I have a completed project, I do."

Laura was equally excited: "Lynn, day one we knew you could do this, we were sure of it and here we are. I don't know what to say but congratulations; you have slain the dragon and apparently not used up all your ammunition. I wasn't going to say anything just yet, but knowing what I know now I can tell you General Noffsinger at the Pentagon is lit up big time. Just among the four of us here, I'm not sure he knows what the data means but as often as not it is more about one-upmanship than anything else with those guys. So, I know this has been a hard slog for you and it shall not go unrewarded. Next week is yours to do with as you please; we think you deserve that much and more but at least the time will let you reconnect with the world; I'm rather sure there will be something In your paycheck as well so plan on buying something pretty for yourself. And one more thing: our kids caught that change in the Big Flags commercial, the deal where your kids are in the park designed for the younger set. They look so photogenic, they do. Now, I think Alan should at least take you to dinner in celebration, so get off the phone, power down, and enjoy, Thank you for a job well done, truly well done." and Laura was gone.

Alan had heard the suggestion and readily accepted the hint; it fit right in with his own plans for the moment. A few words of discussion and the two headed off into the house to make sitter arrangements, get cleaned up a bit, and head out for an evening of enjoying life. He had long thought about this moment and how he wanted things to go. Her first important clue this evening would be different, very different, was that he walked into the room in a suit jacket, no tie but a suit jacket over a shirt with real buttons down the front; she felt justified in having put on one of her finest dresses for the evening. They would dine at a restaurant one town over, a restaurant that met his needs of the moment. SUV doors opened by staff as soon as they rolled to a stop in the restaurant driveway, they stepped out and followed behind a liveried *maître d'* into the club. Shown into a private room, the two were seated opposite each other at the small table, thick carpet deadening itinerate sounds, lit tapers on the table, subdued lighting, soft music piped in from the trio playing in the large general dining room, table set with real silver, real china, and real linens; Lynn jumped slightly when the waiter on her end picked up her dinner napkin and placed it on her lap using a single hand and a snap of the wrist to fan it open. The two waiters left to be replaced by the sommelier wearing the large gold key on a gold chain around his neck. First approaching Alan, he was waved off as Alan pointed to Lynn. She had no clue what to do as the bottle was presented for her approval, held in front of her so she could see the label, but by watching Alan's hand signals figured out what was to happen. Asked to approve, she nodded in the positive, gave permission when asked "May I have the honor" then watched as he carefully applied the cork screw and extracted the stopper then poured maybe a shot of the wine into her glass. She had truly watched enough television drama to know the rest of the routine, swirled the glass, sniffed, sipped and said only: "Yes, please". Her glass was never below half full the remainder of night.

Alan suggested an entrée, which she found to be wonderfully prepared, served, and consumed, then went for the high calorie dessert. By the end of the meal Lynn was totally taken in by the surroundings, by the actions he had clearly taken to please her, and by his quiet demeanor. What she could not see was that the end he had said weeks ago was just over the horizon was now in the room with them and ready to be seen. He would explain so all would be clear but she had a question first.

"Alan, I've never been in a restaurant like this in my life, yet somehow I don't feel out of place, maybe a little confused when something happens I don't know anything about, like the routine with the wine. The meal you chose for me was out of this world good, my wine glass is never less than half full, dessert was to die for, ambience more that I could ever hope for, and while I know Laura suggested you take me to dinner this is way past that idea. I'm not complaining, far from it, but I feel assured us being here is not exactly spur of the moment; it may be that time wise but I believe being here with you was something you had in mind all along. Am I right, or is the wine better than I think it is? Please, talk to me, tell me things about us, please."

He could do that; in fact that was the entire plan; all he had needed for this day to arrive and give him the backstop he needed was for her project to come in right side up, and it had. Now it was time to let her know where they stood with everything.

"Lynn, you're right; this is no off the cuff decision. I've know about this restaurant for a long time and how much it is worth the few miles to get here. I'll admit I like being spoiled a bit now and then and they do such a good job of it. That, however, is not the reason we are here; what Laura said also is not the reason we are here, although we are in compliance with her directive. We are here because I want to be alone with you, undisturbed as we find our way along the path. My cell is off at the moment; may I ask you to do the same with yours?" She complied somewhere around light speed. "I want to know where you are with life, what you want for yourself and your boys, and I want to know how you plan to get there. I can tell you I want the best of everything for my girls; we may never get to that point but they won't go hungry or uneducated or anything like that. Is that what you want for your own family?"

It was nearly two uninterrupted hours later before they had worked their way through things neither had planned on discussing but which just seemed to arise, things like how permissive should they be with their children, and what about additional children in their respective futures should that happen? They were much alike in so many ways, yet so complimentary where they differed. Alan knew it was time for him to step up but there was one more thing he wanted to know that would tell him exactly where she was in her life.

"Lynn, I know this may sound a little crazy but what if something happened and I couldn't for some reason remain in your life? I want to, but what would happen if I couldn't. Would you and the boys get along, be okay, survive well?"

"Sure, we could make that happen but I don't want it to happen that way. I have a job I truly love, all the physical things we need to get along, money in the bank, but those things aren't what I want to define my life and my character. There was a time when those things were all out of reach for me as I scrambled in a somewhat desperate effort to just stay afloat in the world, but then you came along, tapped on my door one evening, and changed everything. I wanted help, needed help, but was a bit ashamed of our condition and afraid to ask for fear of driving you away with my outstretched hand; yet there you were providing for me anyway, taking me by the hand and somehow making it all seem as the natural progression of things for us. I guess the answer is that we could survive but it would be only that, just survival without you and the girls. Have I asked too much of you? Is that what's wrong? I didn't mean to do that but sometimes I get afraid, like this moment when I'm thinking..." He needed to stop that line of her thinking...and did so.

"No, you have not asked too much of me, not at all, in fact probably not enough. I have had a difficult time heeding my own advice now and then; you are a beautiful smart woman, desirable to a fault, and I will admit to times when I wanted to follow you into your bedroom. I didn't because it would not be the right thing to do; it had every possibility of your giving in because you needed a hand up; I just could not see that happen, not to you, not if I loved you and I do love you. I won't lie; I still have those thoughts, stronger each day. I need to know if that came to pass that you would make your choice not because of any outside need but because you are free to do so, because Lynn wants that to happen, not because some other need had to be met and you saw that as a way to protect your family. Does any of this make sense to you or am I just off the deep end here?"

Lynn knew this moment was way past where they had ever been, but she knew the answer. "It does make sense to me and now I better understand things. Alan, many a night I wondered what I would do if I heard the latch click and knew you were coming in to me. I can't say for sure that is what I wanted to happen but I won't deny my own feelings, lie about my own desires. You are everything I've never had; I would do whatever you want whenever you want to make sure you know how deep this runs in my heart."

It was time, as he reached into his pocket to extract the little box, opening the lid and presenting it for her to see the brilliant diamonds: "Then please meet me halfway and we will discover all the answers together. Please marry me, Lynn, but only of your own free will and because you want to marry me."

She felt the sweet sting in her eyes heralding the arrival of a flood of tears. She would admit to herself later that night he could have proposed almost anything and she would have agreed to it, and while she had what she believed were hopes for her future with him, he had just handed it to her, wide screen and full color. Answer, had to answer, even if her voice was choked by emotion down to a whisper,

"Yes; oh god, yes. I wanted this to happen so very much and now it has and I'm such a mess, I am, and I don't know what to say or do or anything..." Her voice was cut off by his lips on hers as she stood so she could get both arms around this man and hold on forever, pulling herself against him with all her strength.

It would be nearly another hour before they left for home, their home. Later on thoughts raced though her mind as they walked hand in hand the few feet toward their respective beds. She had to tell him, she just did, so he would know and be able to make his own decision. Her decision was to marry him; she wanted to know what his decision would be as they stood outside her bedroom door, arms about each other, good night kiss that could start a fire.

"Alan...I want you to know...I don't know how to say this...my bedroom door isn't locked, not ever for you, I want you to know that. What you do with that information at this moment is up to you; I will accept your decision tonight or any other night. I do love you so very much."

He heard her offer, knew he had to steel himself against thoughts he was having, and didn't turn her down but let her know he believed her. "Lynn, thank you. I do love you, and as soon as we can manage to do so I want us to be married; keep that thought until then, okay?"

It was okay with her, feeling loved rather than rejected. In a few days she would expend all the love she had been saving up for him.

On Monday, Lynn conference called Laura and Jill. She did want that week off, but not today. This day and for the next two weeks she would codify the entire project system for the record, make a few small changes here and there, correct a register that did report an overflow, and wrap up the project to a level anyone could come in and find all relevant data at their fingertips. The week of vacation she saved was also explained: she would be with her new husband, Alan Behr, on their honeymoon. That information alone started any number of wheels turning, putting things in place perhaps sight unseen at the moment but all toward making her wedding a memorable day.

At his work station early, Alan called the minister at the church they attended. Did he do weddings and could he work them into his schedule? The Reverend Jack Hodge was just sure he sensed something special about these people and sure enough, two days later he was called by his primary customer for wedding services: Marti Roberts, wedding planner. Lynn had not planned on things happening that way, maybe a few minutes in front of a judge was all they really needed, but she neglected to consider her Windmere family connection and the fact she had informed the woman who was essentially the Windmere Mother Superior of her want and need to wed this man. Lynn called Laura who called Marti who called the Reverend Jack Hodge who called his list of staff for weddings. Yes, it would be a bit hectic to host this wedding right after an earlier wedding that day but this was Marti Roberts calling, the same Marti Roberts who had virtually saved his church from foundering under debt and closing down, a church that was now seen on the Internet as a destination place to get married. Lynn thought her best dress would be finery enough for the occasion; Marti Roberts picked her up two days later and took her to a bridal dress shop for a custom fitting. When Lynn protested the significant expense for a custom fitted wedding dress, Marti dismissed the protest, telling Lynn it was all covered. The Reverend Jack Hodge, now with a new meeting building on the church campus courtesy of a donating parishioner, booked the hall for the reception; Lynn thought it was too much. Reverend Hodge explained how much fuel they would save by the building being near the church and how that savings would be applied to the event. None of it made any real sense until Lynn protested to Marti that while Lynn had some bank she also didn't want to bankrupt Alan Behr; Marti gave in, sensing her "customer" was really starting to question what was taking place, ready or not.

"Lynn, I need to tell you something about all this before you run off screaming. Right after you called Laura Williams with your project completion news she called me. I don't know all the details but you do know Windmere staff runs with the big dogs, the really big dogs, right?" Seeing Lynn nod, Marti continued. "Laura had a bet on with someone about how the project would come out in the end; Lynn, she bet on you. When you called in the project completion, she called in her marker; I don't know the amount, don't want to know the amount, but that is the funding for your wedding. Put another way, you earned it. Laura asked me to make it happen big time, church, flowers, music, reception, catering, all that; believe me even though she asks so politely, she gets her way, no question. In a day or so Ryan will call Alan to talk about the honeymoon destination, flight there, hotel, all that. So, enjoy, revel in this event, the attention, everything. Your wedding day will be a memorable one; trust me on that. Besides, all things considered, you know and I know it would not be wise to irritate Mother Superior Laura, it just wouldn't. I know her and love her as a friend, an amigo, a sister in many ways, but I also know she has a will of steel, seldom displayed but always ready. I can assure you she will enjoy every minute of this escapade."

With her mind eased from the financial worry, Lynn did remember to tell Alan that Ryan Williams would be calling him soon about the honeymoon destination. Sure enough Ryan did call, saying he was delayed in making the call by the need to put things in place, and confirming that the honeymooning couple really did want to be joined by their assorted kids on day four.

The wedding was a blur for both of them in some ways, although Marti had assured them full documentation was being recorded in the process. Three hours later, reception and a ton of best wishes behind them, they stepped down from the private plane and into the waiting limo to be whisked to a medium sized resort owned by Windmere, Inc. Head chef and part owner Jorge met them in the lobby, telling them a light meal was prepared for them in a private dining room, that he had been directed by Ryan and Laura Williams to treat them as honored guests of the hotel; if they desired the slightest thing, found any amenity missing, anything less than perfect, they were to let him know and he would make it right.

An hour later, after a light but thoroughly delicious meal, the two were taken to the honeymoon suite on the roof garden of the hotel, the only suite on the roof level. Because it was a staffed elevator their privacy was ensured. Entering their domain, each said they needed a minute to "freshen up" in their respective bath rooms. Alan was still reeling a bit from his first sight of her in the church in that beautiful and form fitting wedding gown. Had he not previously been totally smitten with her, it would have happened then. For her part, she was remembering something far different, something interrupted, but which she so very much wanted to play out to the very end. He walked out clad only in one of the luxurious robes the resort provided, thick and warm; she walked out, to his amazement, in a baggy worn gray sweat suit; she could explain.

"That night camping when you came to my rescue, saved my boys and then saved me and made room for me, I remember so well my reactions; I felt you slide into the bag behind me, then wrap me up in your arms as I felt the heat start to pour into my shivering being. I was frightened at first, not knowing how far that was going to go, but you reassured me, calmed me, and I believed you. Warm and safe with you holding me I started to feel things I had not felt in a long time. And then, you were gone, out making the morning coffee and my question went unanswered. I have often replayed that question in my mind, wondering what it would have felt like, what would have happened if you were still in there with me. I know with the kids present at the time and knowing your person being what it is not much could happen, but I do have this continuing question: what if? I need to tell you I did eliminate the part about the wet underwear but I dragged these sweats out of the Behr bus for this moment. Alan, husband, that night my fear was all of a sudden gone, replaced by an urgent need to roll over and face you, to pull myself against you and hold on. If I had done that, can you show me what would have happened, could have happened in the dark of night?"

Alan had an answer as his own memory of that night re-played in his mind. "I remember how you felt next to me; I also remember knowing I could not take advantage of you in your distress. That doesn't mean I haven't played that scenario in my mind a thousand times since then, as I also wonder what could really have happened. Now that the time is right I want to answer that question but have to ask you one more thing first."

"Ask away husband, just don't try to escape!"

Alan had a sort of lopsided grin and she knew this was going someplace crazy; it was one of those things about him she loved so dearly, his way of doing something unpredictable yet fun and safe at the same time. Looking directly into her eyes he continued: "I just need to know if you have ever worried about being attacked by a Behr, a wild Behr that adores your body. Does that thought frighten you, wife Lynn?"

She realized the double meaning of his words. "Never, not one time; I look forward to being attacked by a Behr" and in so saying tugged him toward the California king sized bed in the middle of their first afternoon as a wedded couple. "I know these sweats belong to you and I am ready to hand them over if you want them back; would you like that, taking them off me?" Yes, he would like that, reaching for her as they tumbled into the bed

Lynn had no idea of what time it was, nor did she care. She wasn't even quite sure where she was at the moment, but didn't care about that either. There were two things she did caré about at the moment, this man in a full body press against her with their arms and legs sort of tangled together, and she wanted to know where she had been with him, where he had taken her without leaving the room or her side. She had just enough energy left to whisper to him, ask her question. "Alan?"

"Mmmmm?" She felt his reply as much as heard it as his lips nuzzled her neck.

"What happened to me, what did you do to me? I don't know where I was but I know for sure I have never been there before this moment. I think I want to go back there but I need you to show me the way, tell me what happened to me, please?"

Alan Behr knew exactly where she had been but was puzzled in her words as she told him she had never been there before; could he explain? "Lynn, beloved wife, I took you nowhere you weren't prepared to go; you wanted to go there with me, told me so and rather loudly I might add. I think I might have to add some sound proofing to our bedroom walls when we get home."

"I did tell you but without really knowing what was happening to me; I still want to know what happened. Alan, I'm not a kid; I even have two kidlets, so I can't plead ignorance; I was married before but today, right now, is all new to me. You turned the clock face down so I couldn't see, but I know what things were like before, a few minutes and then nothing; here now is something I have never experienced, never, and mostly I know you held my hand, held me, and we went slowly so I could learn. Every nerve in my body was on fire and I know you made that happen; tell me, please."

"It's the difference between just sleeping with someone and making love with them, caring for their needs before your own. I should probably feel bad it took this long for you to find that magic point, but I am ever so happy I got to take you there for the first time. We can revisit but at the moment I am totally disabled, having done your bidding, your very vocal bidding. Replay in a little bit?"

"Replay in a little bit. I think I want to help you get ready for the replay." That also was not in her playbook but Lynn Behr learned really quickly, aided by a loving husband.

Their conversation fell quiet as both dozed off, warm, contented for the moment, ready to learn more. At the end of the third day four kids arrived full of energy, ready to explore, oblivious that their individual parents were now sleeping in one bed.

Chapter Twenty-One

Everafter

After the combined honeymoon and kid's playtime, all returned home and slowly settled down into more of a routine life. Ari Schoenroth was called to start processing adoption paperwork for the reconstituted Behr family, her boys to Alan with the subsequent last name change, and his girls to Lynn; she would become their mother in every sense of the word. It was true that Lynn wanted to learn more about what had happened to her on their honeymoon; with the kids off at school and otherwise undisturbed time available to them, Alan and Lynn used their time wisely, always making sure they had adequate time for the full process; Lynn learned how to quiet her voice when feelings overtook her and some things about the reactions she was having and why. Alan Behr was a most excellent teacher and appreciated having a most willing student to teach.

The new house was left divided, the front half for her purposes and the back half for his processes. She added some furniture to make it into a functioning office to meet her needs as he added some equipment to get his own services updated and more refined. There was an intervening partitioning wall constructed so the bathrooms could be accessed from either occupancy while ensuring privacy was maintained if needed. Both occupancies were busy, Lynn with added clients now that the big project was completed, a diverse set of client needs to be answered and continuing education at night school. His end of the building welcomed the TallRight group and their own set of different issues between Norse and USA norms for appliance use.

Sol Kaplan called now and then just to check in; TV commercials were seasonal dependent and the holidays were soon behind them. In late December the kids were asked to refresh their play house assembly video using some new products. In the meantime residuals continued to pour into their college savings accounts, swelling them in appreciable amounts. In January Gill Lanham called Sol who called Alan and Lynn: could they schedule in a shoot for some new wireless remote control battery powered sand box toys, some rather expensive toys but which Gill believed would sell well if shown in use by the Construction Kids. They would need to go back to LA for the shoot in an actual sand pile but by now those involved knew and observed the rules for dealing with the Construction Kids and parents, this trip with both parents in attendance. Among other things their now joined parents always kept in front of the kids was that the role playing was a fun thing to do but it was not who they were in reality; they were the kids of Lynn and Alan Behr. The other thing Gill mentioned was that the company was finally catching up in the production of the Construction Kids quad runners; there was still demand but like all items that have a limited audience, the demand was starting to fall off just a bit. The company had some new products in that line in the design process and would need some testing in the near future, Construction Kid testing. Sometime after the Behr family kid count had virtually doubled in size, Sol hit on a new idea; his connection with the Behr family would continue for some time.

Within the next year the Franz girls would shoot their last Big Flags commercial, an ad very carefully concealing Andreas' bulging midsection second pregnancy; the Construction Kids played a somewhat larger part than in the original tagalong piece. The next revision for Big Flags would feature the Construction Kids; by then they would not be eight year old kids but bordering on being teens. They would also find some work demonstrating TallRight domestic products for USA use. Sol kept a tight rein on what he would accept for the kids, even as they aged a bit; anything they were associated with had to be wholesome, had to deliver what they said the product would deliver, or he would hit the reject button. In time the kids would go off in other directions but with an armload of happy memories and fat bank accounts.

Jennette Houser was convicted of kidnapping and attempted extortion; because she was one of the adults involved when the kids blew up the detention house, she was held responsible for the damages inflicted. She had lost everything in her greed; worse was that she had been involved in a prison pecking order fight once incarcerated, a result of which was a miscarriage. Her assailant got an additional five years; Jenn got a lifetime bad memory; her pregnancy had been unplanned but she had bonded with her unborn child and all else didn't matter. She didn't bother to tell Bruce Albert as her bad news would be good news to him. Nearly five years later there came a day when she was released from prison and walked out the gate to find Lynnette Behr waiting for her. Jenn was family; after much discussion with her husband Lynn agreed to give her sister one more chance to be in her life. It was the last lifeline Jenn expected to find. She grasped the line and held tight as she learned how to be a sister, a daughter, an aunt, and a person worthy of love from others.

Bruce Albert served his time but never did pay off what he owed on the house damage by refraining from working beyond subsistence means. Once in a while he wondered about the child he had created with Jennette Houser, thinking maybe he could put the squeeze on her for money; he had no idea there was no child, The one time he did track her down and suggest she pay him to not claim joint parental rights with her raising of their child, she threatened to call police and tell them he had assaulted her. He left the scene in a hurry and never again contacted her.

A short time into her marriage to Alan Behr, Lynn knew their honeymoon playtime had been a lot more than that. She was pregnant, sure she was pregnant, and was overjoyed to tell her husband. She didn't know exactly when it happened but didn't think about it much. She told him that afternoon when she came back from making a call for Windmere; he was lit up, thoroughly lit up with the news. She did tell him there remained a very remote possibility that because of both their backgrounds it could be a multiple birth; it was too soon to confirm or deny that possibility; anyway, she had no real clue as to the situation.

In later years Alan and Lynn would fondly remember the day after they learned the news of her pregnancy, the early morning embrace and conversation in the kitchen before the kids arose. Alan knew he had to tell her what he had dreamed, hoping she could accept that he had seen Maddie in his dream.

"Lynn, I really need to tell you about a dream I had this morning, sort of in that time when a person knows they aren't awake yet but are aware of a dream so real it can be believed as real. I know it was a dream because Maddie was there with the two of us. There weren't any spoken words but I knew what she was telling us, and I knew she understood about us. She just smiled and nodded when I thought about how much I love you but the crazy thing is when I thought about the baby we're having I heard her laugh, I know I heard her laugh out loud, I'd recognize it anywhere, and then she was gone and I was awake. I don't pretend to understand those things but I had to tell you what happened. What do you think it meant?"

Lynn was quiet for a moment while he waited for her response, feeling her seem to tremble just a bit in his arms. "Alan, you weren't alone this morning; you saw me because I was there in the dream with you, I know I was, and I know that was Maddie even though I never met her in life. I agree with you; I don't know if it really was a dream or not, but I do believe she came to bless this marriage. I also heard the laughter and knew it was her laughing; I think it was her way of telling us all is fine with her, let the good times roll, and enjoy the chaos a baby brings. We are making something happen she wanted to happen for you, and here we are. Accept her blessing; I have."

At her next scheduled office call with Dr. Carmen Ruis, OB/GYN, she asked Alan to go along with her. He patiently waited as the exam took place, finally being asked to join them in the doctor's personal office, along with another of the practice doctors. Dr. Ruis opened the conversation.

"Mr. Behr, thank you for coming in. I think today that might be really important for both you and your wife." Alan felt an uneasiness stir within him; this might not be a good thing and they were about to be warned. Dr. Ruis continued. "I did the exam today and found everything to be just ideal at the end of the first trimester. Dr. Ahmed is here with us today because I asked him to confirm my ultrasound interpretation. Sometimes things can be a bit difficult to determine for sure and I certainly do not want to tell you two something that isn't true or perhaps a bit misleading, anything like that. He has years of experience at reading sonograms so I defer to him at this time."

Dr. Ahmed responded. "As Dr. Ruis has informed you, I was called in to substantiate her findings; she read the sonogram correctly and I confirm her finding that you two will be the parents of identical fraternal children in about six months. I will recommend a c-section delivery depending on the development pattern, position in the womb, that sort of consideration, but that is something you will have to discuss with Dr. Ruis when the time comes. Is there anything more I can tell you at this time?"

Neither Lynn or Alan could quite absorb what Dr. Ahmed had just told them. Alan found his voice first. "Dr, Ahmed, I don't understand what you just said. Both of us have twin children, identical twins, but you said identical fraternal; how can that happen? I thought it was one way or the other; what did I miss?"

Dr. Ahmed laughed softly. "You missed nothing at all; I should have made myself much clearer on our findings. This is a rare and unusual case so I think you can plan on going into some record book somewhere. To be specific, there are four babies hiding out in there; that's why the consult was needed, to decide who is who. There is one set of identical twin boys and one set of identical twin girls; we have determined they are not quadruplets from a single egg but from two eggs, thus making them fraternal, identical fraternal. Is that a bit clearer for you?"

Lynn had recovered just enough to ask her question: "Are you sure Dr. Ahmed? This is no time to be playing games; I'll admit to being both surprised and nervous about this already."

"No games; please do not overly concern yourself at this time. Dr. Ruis is right when she tells you everything is fine. You have time to make preparations; the babies will arrive when they arrive. Please, enjoy this rare experience. Quads are one thing, often brought on by the use of fertility drugs; this is truly a rarity. I will be available should you need another consult later on."

A half hour or so later as Lynn and Alan sat on the kitchen bar stools the reaction to what they had just learned started to sink in. All of a sudden, when he looked at her and she looked back at him with widening eyes, both understood the reality and said so at the same time: "Maddie; Maddie knew." Lynn continued: "No wonder she laughed at us; she knew the joke. It wasn't a dream; it was Maddie." While Lynn was the carrier already starting to swell, Alan was the provider and was pondering the situation. The old shop area had remained untouched, having gained some storage items but little else now that he had moved to the new shop area. Alan had already given thought to the idea of a child between them, thinking about where he could create another bedroom as the family expanded; he had not planned on doubling the child count all at one time. What he had told Lynn about lot size and the maximum allowable first floor area let him know the house as it currently existed was already in violation; it had been grandfathered into the zoning codes and he knew if he changed anything, he would be required to conform to current code. Worse was that the back garage was something else that was a violation of sorts, but again had been grand-fathered; it also was subject to compliance if he changed anything. Slowly it dawned on him the statutes addressed only the first floor square footage, never mentioning any upper floor; on a hunch the stars might be aligning for them based on recent events with the demolished house, he called city planning and asked for the plan review section. His thoughts were reluctantly confirmed: there was no code addressing second stories over limited first floor square footage limits. As things began to take shape he wanted to talk to the kids first, then make the final decision on the issue. For her part Lynn was still struggling a bit with her condition. She also had thought she wanted very much to have a child with Alan; that was coming true at the moment but then there were three more babies involved. Her mind finally just accepted the reality and she started to feel the joy of what was happening for them, coming to the realization this was not something put upon them but something they may have created during one of those most interesting afternoon sessions. She would join Maddie in the joy of the moment.

He did explain to Lynn what he had in mind before talking to the kids, sitting them down after dinner and explaining what he had in mind. Lynn had broken the birth news right after the meal, to find four kids anxious for it to happen. Now, he would tell them what they needed to get done in the remaining six months or so, probably five at the most so they would have time to move things around in preparation.

"We have a problem here in that the building codes for this area will only allow a house of a certain size depending on the size of the actual lot itself. That's why the new house couldn't be more than two bedroom. The house we are in existed at the time the zoning laws were enacted so they did something called grand-fathering, letting an existing building remain as is when the codes are enacted, provided the building is never changed in any way. If it is changed, it then has to comply with the current statutes. On a suspicion that only applied to single story buildings I called the city and talked to the people who approve things like that. I can't add bedrooms because this house already exceeds the first floor limits, but I can go up where the statutes don't apply; here's what I want to do but each of you has a say in this because it will become your home, okay? We will add on top of the old shop area two second floor bedrooms with plenty of room for two occupants in each; we will build on the ground floor a full bath, a half bath, and a separate shower room. To get to the second floor I have in storage a circular iron ladder I salvaged out of a theater being demolished some years ago; it is a bit steep but quite useable for young people, and more importantly, it takes up very little floor space. Does this sound like a plan to the four of you since you are about to be evicted by your new brothers and sisters?"

Agreement was universal with the caveat they wanted to do their own room decorating when the time came. The city plan reviewer was reluctant but gave in when Alan pointed out the other house with a similar arrangement next street over. Construction started in two weeks.

The six months flew by although there were a lot of times Lynn could hardly wait to be relieved of her burden, a burden that got bigger and bigger each day it seemed. As soon as she learned about the situation, Laura at Windmere withdrew all field work from Lynn to get her off her feet; Jill would handle it for a while as Laura truly believed Lynn had higher responsibilities. Dr. Ahmed reconfirmed his original findings of fraternal identical.

Nine months to the day or there about time wise, Lynn was already in the hospital for a day of observation when the contractions started. Dr. Ahmed was right about the need to do a c-section; with Dr. Ruis, three other doctors, and an overly populated staff present, all of whom wanted in on this rare action, it was over in less than a half hour start to finish, babies delivered and wrapped up for the in-room nursery warmers. Alan had held her hand throughout so she would know he was there; that simple connection told her all she needed to know and gave her the strength she needed. Hours later, having reawakened after she had rested from the birth, Lynn's hand was still in his, still held tight. Very quietly she let him know she was awake and wanted to tell him something as he leaned in close.

Almost in a whisper, Lynn asked her question: "Did you hear her Alan, did you? It was Maddie, laughing at us, I just know it was her."

"I did hear her; I just didn't want to say anything about it in case I'm getting a bit balmy in my old age. She knew day one I'd guess. I do believe all the days of their lives our children will be watched over by Angel Maddie."

On day two, Lynn heard a tap on her hospital room door. "Come in, whoever it is. I'm awake." She was please to see two of the women she knew from their neighborhood as the two walked in, maybe not bosom buddies but certainly aware of which kid belonged to whom, that sort of thing. She even remembered one of the women residing in a lawn chair at the house demolition event. It was nice of them to visit her. Neighbor Susan opened the conversation.

"Wow, what else can I say but wow. You, woman, make the rest of us look like slackers; four at one time. You have every right to be pleased with yourself. Are you doing well we hope?"

"I am doing well, thank you. C-section gets past some of the other problems with multiple delivery situations. Babies are all doing fine even if I can't really feed all of them; I want to and I do think that is best but reality is reality. I plan to rotate so they won't be on formula all the time. And just so you know, I didn't plan this to happen, no fertility drugs, none of that stuff; it just happened. My job mentor did tell me before we were married that the particular resort we stayed with has a reputation for child birth nine months after honeymoons; guess we're just average after all."

Neither of the visitors were buying that story but had more to discuss. Dee picked up the conversation. "We really came here for a couple of reasons. Obviously, congratulations are in order, sympathy if you need it, understanding of how this can affect your life, all that. I need to confess something here, then we'll tell you how we plan to atone for our transgression. When we knew you had moved into your old house some of us recalled all that to-do with your ex-husband; I have to admit we were a little nervous, knowing you had been married to a guy like that and not knowing you as a person. And then it was obvious Alan Behr had an interest in you and we didn't know how that would work out. I have to say he has been an asset to the neighborhood ever since he and Maddie moved in; we were devastated when she died, yet he managed to carry on and raise those two great girls. He has never once mentioned his loss as any sort of excuse for anything. We were wrong about you, about a lot of things, and we need to make up for that. We need to make up for the fact if one of our kidlets tells us they are going to your yard for a visit we have a comfort level we would not otherwise have. Alan fixes things for us our husbands can't or maybe don't want to figure out. We see the two of you with that hand holding, a simple thing that says so much without a word being spoken; I'll admit to maybe being a tiny bit jealous. Now, to the atonement part. Susan is sort of our defacto leader so I leave that up to her; I just wanted you to know we love having you as a neighbor and not just because of all the free playhouses and quad runners either. Susan?"

"Lynn, you just told us what we need to do. Obviously one woman can't feed four babies, yet we agree with you that is what should happen. We have a sort of loose knit organization in the neighborhood that can help with the problem. It seems at any given time some of us are pregnant or recently delivered and lactating. We have an arrangement with this hospital: they have provided a room for us to use and will store the bottles we fill until needed. With your permission, we will store milk for your babies here and when you go home we will be there for you and keep the process going. Will you let us do that for you, allow us to make up for the error of our ways, please?"

Tears cascaded down the cheeks of Lynn Behr; she was being brought into an inner circle of women who were offering a precious commodity for her babies. "You don't know how down and out I was when Alan tapped on our door that first day. Every day since then has been a bit of a miracle for me, for my boys. Please, I want this to happen for my babies but I want it only if freely given, not because there is some mythical privation. I have never felt any ill will from anyone in the neighborhood and most certainly neither of you. Free will is important to me, at least in my understanding of it now. Alan wouldn't even propose to me until he knew I could stand on my own two feet, didn't need him to carry me; this new job, what can I say, and that's when he asked me. I'm saying that because it is so important things like this be given of one's free will; I will gladly accept it under those terms from friends like I've never had before."

Dee responded. "We accept those terms gladly. Get some

rest girl; you're gonna need it!"

Just getting four babies from the hospital to the Behr residence was a challenge, requiring two vans to hold the car seats along with a brother or sister or two plus a parent plus a driver, all of that. Early on in the process, Lynn's shopworn SUV was traded for a new extended van that with any sort of luck at all would hold all ten of the Behr tribe. It was true the new van was sold at a steep discount related to a picture of the van with the four quad runners and costumed riders in front of it. The Construction Kids had traction in a lot of places.

Routine settled in over the Behr residence, at least some semblance of a routine punctuated now and then by a crying baby. The four older kids relocated to their new digs, decorated to their own tastes, enjoyed the additional room for their "things", and appreciated having an extra bathroom; they would come to appreciate the extra bathroom even more as teenagers. They also enjoyed a bit of envy displayed now and then by visitors over the unique spiral loft ladder.

There was a continuing parade of neighborhood women into the kitchen area as bottles were cleaned and refilled for the growing and always hungry babies. It was a pretty routine process for the most part, sometimes done directly breast to hungry mouth, but quite frequently done in the kitchen often amid laughter and a general good time; coached by his loving wife, Alan Behr learned to make iced Cinnamon rolls to come out of the oven just as the ladies started to arrive. There was also that one moment when a distracted Alan Behr left his shop to find his wife for a discussion about some random subject; she was back at work in her half of the new house but this day had stayed a few minutes longer with the babies and their day nurse. Alan walked through his old shop area and into the kitchen, was stunned at what he saw, and backed out as soon as he could generate a coherent thought. The image of four women sitting at the kitchen table with shirts open or blouses pulled up out of the way, nursing bra's unhooked and pumps in action as bottles were refilled, was cause to stun any man and it certainly stunned Alan Behr. For their part, it all happened so fast none of the four had the presence of mind to cover up or do much of anything but continue the process. Alan stumbled backwards out of the kitchen doorway, recovering his wits a bit as he moved, but with a full color snapshot of the room and the ladies forever burned in his mind. The four looked at each other, burst out laughing, and decided to just continue on with the process; it was over so fast there was no harm done, at least not much, and none of them really felt as though she had been scanned. On the other hand, Alan Behr would never forget the picture, never. He also would never mention the event to his beloved wife nor would any of the ladies. It did puzzle him just a bit in the vast diversity of what he had seen, from the overabundant Susan to the less than abundant Lela, yet each with an equal number of bottles in front of her. It was a puzzle he would never solve.

Not one to miss an opportunity, exactly one year after the multiple births Sol Kaplan called Alan and Lynn for a brief sit down, presented his case, and received their approval. Three weeks later a video featuring a new design baby stroller being brought to market was shot on the Behr premises on behalf of the manufacturer. The association with the Construction Kids still had drawing power. There were no fancy broad slides, nothing like that, but the power of twins and twins and twins and twins was unquestionably worth the effort. The old refrain was updated as the strollers were rolled to be side by side: "I'm Ally; this is my brother Dane." "I'm Brad; this is my sister Chloe." "I'm Ben; this is my sister Clair." "I'm Anna; this is my brother Dan." And the final chorus of "We're all the Construction Kids!

Of all the things that happened during their years together, starting with the day Alan and daughters paid that first visit to the Albert home, really only two entities associated with the Behr team ended up being unhappy. When Bruce Albert saw the stroller commercial with all eight Construction Kids he finally came to realize he was his own worst enemy and had missed out on the income ride of a lifetime; the other unhappy entity was the former employer of Lynnette Albert/Behr when they realized two things: they had erred greatly in treating her so poorly when they had no reason to do so, and one by one she was absorbing their former clients into her portfolio. For the most part everyone else lived happily ever after, maybe a few bumps along the way but nothing they couldn't handle. There was one consumer product tested for which no report was ever written: Alan and Lynn, very very quietly, proved there was room for two very active people in the double sleeping bag.

The End

About the Author

Michelle Tschantré has accrued years of "people" lore, mostly listening and encouraging, letting them find their own way past whatever issue prompted the conversation. The WINDMERE Series of fictional events uses some of those experiences, a little science here and there, some reality now and then, a belief that there may be powers greater than we know, and an everlasting belief in good outcomes for good hearted people. It is what the author has come to believe over the years: plan for the worst, hope for the best, and deal with the reality. In *"Laura's Big Win"*, the foundation is built for the books that have followed, with some of the same people, some new faces and problems, and Windmere in there somewhere keeping it all going.

CPSIA information can be obtained
at www.ICGtesting.com
Printed in the USA
LVHW082354170619
621548LV00030B/524/P